HOW NOT TO COMMIT MURDER

ROBIN STOREY

ISBN:978-0-9875366-0-0

DEDICATION

For Emma, Cassie and Tim

1

Reuben awoke to find himself staring at a large brown nipple. At first he didn't recognise it – it was just a dark blob, blurred because it was almost poking him in the eye, surrounded by a curving expanse of paleness.

He moved his head back a fraction for a clearer view. Some men were turned on by large, dark nipples, although he himself preferred small, pert pink nipples. Of course he didn't let on to the owner of the dark nipples, his wife of six weeks and three days.

Had the nipple been placed there deliberately? Even though he and Carlene had been at it like rabbits since the wedding, he wasn't a morning person, and wasn't sure if he was up to it today. Besides, he had an appointment with his parole officer; and just the thought was enough to put a damper on his libido.

But neither did he want to offend Carlene by ignoring her nipple. She was proud of her generous breasts, and even at thirty-one, hers were as firm and upright as a teenager's. He gave it a tentative lick.

It moved away instantly as Carlene raised herself on her side. Both nipples were now aimed straight at him – like two weapons ready to shoot. She gave him a playful shove.

'Rubie! We haven't got time; it's already past seven.'

'You'll keep, young lady!' he said, with a lecherous wink. He fancied himself as a sex machine – always on idle, ready to rev up at any moment. And after three years inside, he had a lot of catching up to do.

Carlene giggled, planted a kiss on his forehead and sprang out of bed. He watched her as she sashayed to the ensuite – dark curls brushing her back, the pale orbs of her buttocks jiggling. In the past he'd preferred compact, petite women, so he was still getting used to her Marilyn Monroe figure. Her voluptuousness engulfed him – at night she sprawled out in bed, often leaving him balanced precariously on the edge, and when she hugged him she almost suffocated him. During sex she often wrapped herself around him so tightly that his senses were stifled and all he was aware of was the weight of her body on his.

He propped himself up and watched her through the open door as she soaped herself in the shower. There was something so erotic about watching a woman wash herself … though after his long period of deprivation, watching a woman doing anything was erotic. He felt himself get hard. When Carlene entered the bedroom wrapped in a towel he said, 'Hey honey, want to go camping?'

She looked puzzled. He pointed to the sheet, which he had draped over his erect penis. 'I've got the tent.'

She gave a perfunctory smile and rolled her eyes. 'Come on, Mum'll be here soon. She's got some shopping to do in Chermside, so she can give you a lift to the parole office.'

He groaned inwardly. He usually caught the bus to his parole appointments, as Carlene needed the car for work. It would be good not to strap hang with his nose in someone's sweaty armpit, but the downside was a road trip with his mother-in-law. Only a twenty-minute drive, admittedly, but it would seem twice as long. On balance, the sweaty armpit won, but it would be impolite to knock back Nancy's offer of a ride.

He hauled himself out of bed and surveyed himself in the ensuite mirror. Should he bother shaving? His three-day growth gave him a rugged appearance, as if he were about to mount a horse, rope in a few hundred head of cattle and a couple of bosomy cowgirls as well. A lot of women didn't share his opinion on stubble, but it wasn't as if he was out to impress his parole officer, the ugly old bag. Still, he had to go to the employment office afterwards.

He appraised himself again when he'd finished shaving. Now he looked more the smooth, business type who'd hang out in a wine bar after work, and talk about synergies and operational efficiency.

Women had often told him he resembled Brad Pitt, but he suspected it was for the same reason he told them they reminded him of Cameron Diaz. Warren, his cellmate, had told him he looked like Baby Face Nelson. Reuben wasn't into the gangster scene – the violence and lack of morality repulsed him – although he didn't dare say so, and pretended to be flattered by the comparison.

He struck a Mr Universe pose, noting with pride the ripple of muscle in his chest and the bulge of his biceps; and ignoring the soft roll he'd already developed on his belly since his release from prison two months ago. His build was naturally slim, but this time round he'd taken advantage of the facilities in jail and had beefed up. One of the inmates, a brawny, tattooed heavy who was in for armed robbery, had offered him steroids, assuring him they wouldn't show up in a urine test. Reuben had politely declined. He was satisfied with his body – enough muscle to fill out a t-shirt without being bulky. Women didn't like too much muscle. He wondered, not for the first time, if that was what had initially attracted Carlene – along with his charm. Of course there were plenty of good-looking, charming men on the outside, but he held the trump card: he was, in her eyes, a lost sheep who needed to be rescued.

Carlene and Nancy were sitting at the kitchen table yabbering – at least, Carlene was yabbering and Nancy was listening. Carlene had long conversations with her mother every day, either in person or on the phone. He wondered what she found to talk about. He himself had the gift of the gab, essential in the business of fraud; but when it came to himself, he could sum up his day's activities in a couple of sentences.

'Good morning, Nancy,' he said, flashing her as brilliant a smile as he could muster at seven-forty in the morning.

'Morning,' she barked. He felt her watching him as he helped himself to bacon and eggs from the frying pan. From behind her spectacles, her sharp eyes roved constantly like a metal detector.

He sat down at the table and began to eat. Both women had fallen silent. He looked up. 'Don't let me interrupt you.'

He put his head down again quickly, smothering a smile. Nancy reminded him of his Year Three teacher, Mrs Frost. Grey-haired and thin-lipped, she could make you quiver with just a look. One day, on playground duty, she bent over to help a first-grader with her shoelaces. A sudden gust of wind blew up her sensible tartan skirt to reveal voluminous, pink satin bloomers trimmed with lace – the kind that women might have worn in the Victorian era. Mrs Frost quickly smoothed her skirt down and whipped around, eyes flashing, defying anyone to laugh. Only Kenny Morrison dared to whistle and he got a week's afternoon detention. But the damage was done – after that she didn't seem quite as scary. Not that Nancy would wear pink bloomers, though he wouldn't be surprised if she wore boxer shorts – there was something mannish about her. In fact, it wouldn't surprise him at all if Nancy turned out to be a man in drag.

'Mum and Dad were thinking of buying you a car,' Carlene said.

Reuben paused, fork halfway to his mouth. 'Really?'

I take that back about the boxers.

He noticed Carlene's look of expectancy. 'Wow, that's very good of them.'

'I mean, you,' he said to Nancy.

'You have to get a job first,' she said.

The spectre of his botched attempts at employment loomed before him. Two days was his record for longevity so far. Reuben swallowed a mouthful of eggs. 'That shouldn't be too hard. I'm going to the job agency today. There are a couple of prospects in the wind.'

'It's a sort of incentive,' Carlene added.

'And you have to stay in the job for more than two days,' Nancy said.

Reuben nodded thoughtfully, as if considering a business proposition. 'That's fair enough. It's obvious I'm not cut out to be a waiter or a bricklayer. It's just a matter of finding my niche.'

'Considering your experience,' Nancy said, 'maybe you should try running for parliament.'

She pursed her lips into a faux smile; a special smile she kept just for him.

Carlene put her hand on her mother's arm. 'Come on, Mum, you know he's got a good heart.'

'And the rest of me's in excellent working order too,' Reuben said. He realised the connotations as soon as he'd said it. Carlene blushed and giggled. Nancy got up and took the dishes to the sink. 'I'll be going in ten minutes,' she snapped at Reuben over her shoulder.

As Carlene kissed him goodbye at the front door, she whispered, 'Don't mind Mum. You know her bark's worse than her bite.'

'I still hope she doesn't fucking well bite me,' he whispered back.

'Come here, baby,' said Carlene. She drew him into her arms and pressed her body against his. She was warm and soft. The aroma of bacon mingled with her perfume. 'Don't worry, I'll look after you. I love you, Rubie.'

'I love you too.'

The words still sounded awkward, even though he'd said them many times over the last few weeks.

Carlene released him and gave him a lingering kiss on the lips. 'Now go out there and slay some dragons.'

I can think of a couple of dragons I'd love to slay.

***

He buckled his seat belt and sat back in the leather seat of Nancy's old Mercedes. She and Alec owned one each: 1980s vintage, both cream and in immaculate condition. They could afford new ones, his and hers style, but they liked to pretend they didn't have money. What was the term for that? Nouveau poor? They wore their lack of pretension like a badge – a pretension in itself.

'Give me an old Merc any day over a brand-new Jag,' Alec was fond of saying.

How could anyone prefer a boxy, cumbersome Mercedes to a sleek, smooth-throated Jaguar? As Nancy pulled out onto the road, he hoped that she and Alec weren't thinking of buying him a similar car. Beggars couldn't be choosers, but he'd much prefer something smaller and sportier. He saw himself zipping around town in a sleek Corvette, drawing admiring glances at the traffic lights, gliding into a car park at the shopping centre (spaces always magically appeared when you were in a Corvette), springing jauntily out of the car, all eyes following him. And on Sundays, he and Carlene would take off into the hills of Samford, a rug and picnic basket in the boot, the wind ruffling their hair...

He realised Nancy had said something.

'Pardon?'

'I said, "I suppose you're feeling pretty pleased with yourself."'

Reuben blinked. It so happened he *was* feeling pleased with himself, imagining the purr of the Corvette's engine – as responsive as a lover to his foot on the accelerator – as it ate up the winding road to Samford. But of course, that wasn't what she meant.

'What do you mean?'

'You've just got out of jail for the nth time, you've got a nice home and a beautiful wife who loves you and is willing to do everything she can to help you.'

God knows why. Her unspoken words hung in the air. And 'nth time' was unfair. It was only the fourth time, not too bad for thirty-five. There were guys inside who'd spent more of their life in prison than out. And it would be the last time for him.

'I know I'm lucky to have Carlene, if that's what you mean.'

'I hope so, young man, because if you hurt her or do anything to make her unhappy, you'll have me to answer to.'

'I can assure you that's the last thing I'd want.'

He sensed her sharp glance, but he gazed straight ahead at the battered ute rumbling along in front of them An overwrought mongrel dashed from side to side in the vehicle's tray.

Nancy had made it plain from the start he wasn't her first choice as a son-in-law, probably not even her hundredth. She and Alec had tried to talk Carlene out of marrying him, even tried to bribe her with a round-the-world trip; but she wouldn't be swayed. In the end, they capitulated and organised a civil ceremony for the couple in their backyard, followed by a honeymoon in their four-bedroom 'shack' on Stradbroke Island. Their generosity was purely for Carlene's sake, and he didn't doubt the intent of Nancy's warning. Having her to answer to was a vague threat which left room for a lot of possibilities.

They turned into the chaos of morning traffic on Gympie Road. He was still getting used to the speed and noise of the city. The first few times he'd crossed a road after coming out of prison, his heart hammered and he broke out in a sweat, even though the cars had stopped at the pedestrian lights. Brisbane had become much busier in the last three years.

The winter sunshine had dissolved the early morning cloud and bathed the world in a clear, pure light. His spirits soared. It was good to be back in the real world.

'It's a beautiful day,' he said.

'Humph,' replied Nancy. She was still concentrating on the road ahead, hands clasped on the steering wheel. No point wasting his breath on her.

The used car yards, aflutter with balloons and flags like a giant birthday party, gave way to office blocks and shops that sold everything from wedding attire to garden supplies. He knew he could talk his way into a sales job in any of them, but his parole order had stipulated that he was not to have any job in which he handled money.

They stopped at yet another red light. He took in the two blonde, long-legged women in short skirts and knee-high boots, sauntering out of a take-away, coffees in hand. Everywhere he looked, there were women more beautiful and confident than he remembered. He loved to watch them as they strutted past in their high heels, chatting and laughing with the self-assurance of those who knew the world was theirs to devour like ripe fruit. They were clearly savouring every mouthful of the fruit's soft, juicy flesh.

An indignant horn and the screech of brakes jolted Reuben from his reverie of licking fruit juice from their smooth, sun-warmed arms. Nancy darted into the left lane. Reuben looked behind him. A man in a shiny black Range Rover glared at them and gave them the finger. A chill gripped him and he turned around again quickly. Nancy pulled over into the loading zone outside the parole office. The Range Rover sped past, beeping its horn again. A woman with a tight blonde perm and large, dangly earrings glared at them from the passenger's window.

'Bloody four-wheel drives,' Nancy growled, 'terrorising innocent people. They think they own the roads.'

Reuben wasn't about to argue with her. He scrambled out of the car. 'Thanks for the lift.' She nodded curtly.

Reuben watched her as she zipped out into the traffic again, narrowly avoiding a group of school children crossing the road. He was weak with relief that the driver of the Range Rover hadn't stopped to vent his anger. Because he'd recognised him: Frank Cornell, businessman, self-nominated playboy and drug trafficker. Trust Nancy to cut off one of the heaviest crims in the business. That was the last time he was driving with her.

It was only eight-thirty and his appointment wasn't until nine. Rather than sit in the waiting room of the parole office flicking through torn copies of *Woman's Day*, he went into Joe's Cafe next door and joined the queue at the counter. He smiled at the dark-haired, young woman whose name badge said Nina. 'Hi Nina. A short black, please.'

She looked at him coolly, unimpressed by his familiarity in using her name. He mentally shrugged and took a seat at a corner table. The café was half-full with late breakfasters. He watched Nina as she took the orders. Her aloofness, while not rude, was brisk and efficient. At first glance she wasn't attractive at all – her nose was too prominent and her mouth too wide – although Reuben didn't mind a generous mouth on a woman when he considered where it could end up. But there was something exotic about her, with her caramel eyes and her hair, smooth and dark as licorice, tied in a single plait down her back. He imagined her in a long, flouncy dress and high heels, a rose between her teeth as she swirled in a flamenco dance, her haughty gaze sweeping the audience.

She looked in his direction and the haughty gaze became real. He smiled again, but her eyes were already on the next customer. She certainly wasn't savouring the ripe fruit of life. She'd gotten a sour one and was spitting out the pips.

Another waitress brought his coffee. It coursed through his body like an electrical charge. He wasn't used to real coffee yet; the stuff they gave you inside was like pencil shavings. He was ready for anything now – might even be able to outstare the battle-axe. As he left, he shot another smile in Nina's direction, but she ignored him. It was rare for a woman not to return his smile.

On the ground floor of the old, shabby building next door was the office of Delahunty & Brown, Chartered Accountants. A sign announced that the Brisbane North Probation and Parole office was on the first floor, along with Willet & Associates Financial Planners. Ironic, as his latest scam had been as a financial planner.

The wooden steps creaked as Reuben walked up. The air was stale and musty, as if the walls were infused with the sweat and body odour of the thousands of lawbreakers who'd been there before him. The girl at the reception desk behind the glass panel looked far too world-weary for her young age.

'Can I help you?' she asked, in a tone of voice that insinuated he was beyond her help.

'Reuben Littlejohn. I have an appointment with Merle at nine o'clock.'

'Have a seat.'

He took a seat at the end of a row of plastic chairs, next to a drooping plant. At the other end slumped a scrawny, lank-haired girl in a short skirt and jumper. Her gaze flickered over him, then resumed its contemplation of the floor. She took no notice of the grubby toddler scrabbling in the toy box beside her. From her vacant look, she was probably a dope smoker or pill popper. The toddler picked up a small furry rabbit from the toy box and rubbed it all over his snot-encrusted face. Reuben looked away. He had a weak stomach for bodily secretions.

Across from him a young guy in jeans, singlet and beanie was showing something on his mobile phone to his friend. They both snickered. They had a 'fuck-you' air about them, the sort that got their kicks from stealing cars and joyriding. A few seats away, a balding man with a ponytail flicked through a magazine. Drug dealer probably. And/or a bikie. He'd be much more at home in his leathers. They all had one thing in common – they didn't want to be here. The air was thick with it. Even the plant looked as if it were dreaming of greener pastures.

A door to his right opened. A saggy face under a helmet of grey hair peered into the waiting room. 'Come in Reuben,' it commanded.

He took a seat in the interview room. Merle settled herself behind her desk, her shapeless dress streaming over her like a floral waterfall. The flab on her upper arms (bingo wings, his mother had called them) jiggled as she arranged her pens and notebook and fired up the computer.

'How are you?' she asked, without taking her eyes off the screen.

'Fine, thank you. How are you?'

Not that he cared less, but politeness was second nature to him. She had to be seventy, not out. Did they bring her out of retirement because they were short-staffed? Or was she one of those people who worked until they dropped because they had no other life? Perhaps one day, when she was in the middle of firing questions at some poor victim, she'd suddenly gasp, clutch her ample bosom and slump on to the desk; dead before you could shout, 'I didn't do it!' Reuben hoped he wouldn't be the unfortunate witness. Didn't people often vomit or froth at the mouth when they were dying?

Merle was talking. 'I said, have you anything new to report since you were last here?'

'Er ... no. Everything's much the same.'

She stared at him as if trying to bore a hole into his brain with her eyes. *You can't fool me,* her expression said, *I know you've been sweet-talking little old ladies out of their nest eggs.*

To fill the silence, Reuben said, 'I've been looking for a job. There are a few prospects, so it shouldn't be too long.'

'Hmmph, your track record so far isn't impressive.'

'No.'

'Anyway, this is my last interview with you. I've finished your assessment and now I'm going to introduce you to your new parole officer.'

She heaved herself out of her chair, opened the door behind her and called out, 'Lucy!'

Reuben's heart lifted. His new officer had to be nicer than this one. And younger.

Merle stepped aside and a woman entered the room holding a mug of coffee.

'Reuben, this is Lucy. She'll be supervising you from now on.'

Lucy smiled. 'Hi, Reuben.'

Reuben stood up and opened his mouth. Nothing came out. He gazed at the vision before him. Petite and fine-boned, full-cream milk complexion, auburn curls that fell around her face and slanted emerald eyes that lent her a feline air. While his fellow inmates had entertained trite fantasies of long-legged blondes with bountiful breasts, Reuben had dreamed of a redhead with a delicate figure; small, neat breasts and the face of a Botticelli angel. It was a fantasy he'd had since he was old enough to have fantasies – from Grade Six in primary school, when he'd talked Jocelyn Freshwater into kissing him behind the boys' toilets. But Jocelyn had dyed her hair, put on weight and had a tribe of kids by the time she was twenty-one. Since then, no woman he'd met had come close to his fantasy. Until now.

'I'll leave you to it,' said Merle.

Lucy slid into her chair and placed her mug on the desk. 'How are you, Reuben?'

'Fine, thanks.' His voice came out as a croak.

'Just excuse me while I log in.'

He watched her hands as they flew over the keyboard. Small and slim-fingered. A gold band on her left hand. Of course she was married. So was he.

She looked up and smiled again. 'You can sit down.'

His legs had become light as air and he sat down abruptly. He smiled back at her to hide his embarrassment but it felt fake. As if every time he'd ever smiled in his life, it had been fake, and he'd have to invent a new smile worthy of its recipient.

'Now then,' Lucy said. Her eyes reminded him of the ocean, and he imagined diving into them. What would you find at the bottom of someone's eyes? Just a lot of corneal tissue, probably. But Lucy would have the most beautiful corneal tissue imaginable.

'I've read Merle's assessment, so I know a fair bit about you already.'

I can do better. Honestly, I can.

'How are you going with finding a job?'

He put on his let's-be-frank-no-bullshit expression. That felt fake, too.

'To tell you the truth, not very well at the moment. But I have an appointment at the employment agency this morning, so I'm hopeful something will turn up.'

'I like your positive attitude,' Lucy said. When she smiled, faint lines fanned out on the translucent skin around her eyes. Early thirties, he decided. He hoped she wouldn't ask him about his attempts at employment. No doubt Merle had already recorded them, but it would be embarrassing to re-live them.

He was trying hard to forget his first and last night as a waiter in an Italian restaurant, tripping over the leg of a chair with his arms full of plates of pasta. An elderly customer found her lap full of tortellini and her husband garnished with slivers of Parmesan cheese. The boss sacked him on the spot, threatening to deduct their dry-cleaning bills from his non-existent wages.

The next job was an improvement – he lasted two days as a brickie's labourer. On the first day he left the cement in the cement mixer while he went to lunch. When he turned it on afterwards the mixer jumped into the air and crashed to the ground, still grinding, like a huge, ungainly insect stranded on its back. The cement inside it was rock hard. His fate was sealed on the second day when, as he trudged through the site with a plank of wood on his shoulder, someone called, 'Look out, Littledick!' As he turned around, the plank of wood gave the foreman, passing by at that moment, a resounding whack on the side of the head. That afternoon he was given two days' pay and fired. He never found out who'd called out the warning.

'I'm trying to be positive,' Reuben said. His heart swelled as he gazed at her flawlessly sculpted neck, the curve of her jaw and her pale chest, lightly dusted with freckles. She wore a jade blouse that matched her eyes. He felt another part of his body swelling and he wrenched his eyes away from her breasts. *Get a grip! This is your parole officer, for fuck's sake.*

'But it's difficult when selling is the only thing I'm good at, and I'm not allowed to do it.'

This was only partly true. Fraud was the only thing he was good at, the only business he'd ever been in. And that involved selling yourself – if you could do that, you could sell anything.

'I realise this, Reuben,' Lucy said. Not for the first time he wished his mother had not been so given to flights of fancy. A solid name like Jake or Michael would have made his life so much easier. As Jake, he would have been a different person – solid, reliable, law-abiding. As Jake, he could have married Lucy. Or at least slept with her.

'But you have to accept this as a consequence of your offending. I'm sure if you talked to all those people you defrauded of their life savings, they'd have a different slant on it.'

He didn't defraud anyone of their life savings. Not intentionally. Not only were his customers all filthy rich, the funds they invested were undeclared income they wanted to hide from the tax office. He and Derek were strict on those two criteria. Three, if you counted the rule of no drug money. It was too dangerous associating with thugs and there was always the risk of the drug runners being under police surveillance. It was surprising how many ordinary people with normal lives and careers had money they had come by illegally, or 'cash in hand' they didn't want to declare. Conning the conmen – when they lost their money they didn't dare go to the police. It was beautiful. And foolproof, until Derek became greedy and started reeling in people with legitimate money. It was all his fault.

But he didn't say it because he knew Lucy wouldn't be impressed. He'd done the Making Choices Program in jail and passed Victim Empathy with flying colours. But it was hard to change your thinking. When you'd witnessed your mother struggling to pay the bills despite slaving her guts out, and heard her sobbing in her bedroom when she thought you were asleep, it was natural to grow up resentful of the rich.

He looked Lucy in the eye and flashed a smile. 'I know.'

'You're well-presented and you seem intelligent. I'm sure you'll find something.'

She paused, reading something on her computer. He'd give his eye teeth to see what the old bat had written about him.

'I see you got married recently. That must present some challenges, coping with life on the outside and a new marriage at the same time.'

'It has its moments,' Reuben admitted. Moments made up of Nancy and Alec, Carlene's sister Jolene; her husband Wayne and their bratty kids. 'But so far, so good, we're still in our honeymoon phase.'

He was gratified to see a faint colour rise in her cheeks. A little demureness in a woman was a great turn-on. He felt a stirring in his jeans again. Steady on, he'd have to walk out of there very demurely himself if he wasn't careful.

'No doubt Merle talked to you about your management plan,' Lucy said, briskly changing the subject. 'Can you remember what was in it?'

Reuben looked at her blankly. He couldn't remember Merle mentioning a management plan – it made him sound like a natural disaster. But his mind had wandered during the interviews and for all he knew, she could have recommended cold showers and a ten kilometre run every day. She should have been a screw instead of a parole officer.

'Sorry, I don't.'

Lucy gave him a faint look of disapproval. 'It's not too onerous. In fact, you should consider yourself lucky. For some reason, the Parole Board didn't make a condition on your order to attend psychological counselling, which they usually do for people convicted of fraud. So Merle, as your assessment officer, had to decide whether or not to make it part of your management plan. She noted you'd done a lot of counselling in prison and passed all your programs with glowing reports, so she decided not to include it.'

So the old bag wasn't so bad after all. He could almost kiss her fat, smelly, bunioned feet.

'But I still have the option of sending you to a psychologist if I think you aren't coping,' Lucy added.

Reuben nodded. *I'll cope, no worries.*

'So, as you've stated that financial need was the reason for your offending, the only intervention on your plan is to obtain employment. I see you're registered with Employment Initiatives, so I'll be making sure you attend that and are doing everything in your power to get a job.'

She paused. 'How are you managing financially?'

He shifted in his chair. 'Okay. Carlene has a job as an admin officer for an overseas aid charity, and her parents are helping out with the bills until I get a job.'

'That's good of them. You've really fallen on your feet, haven't you?'

She looked hard at him. It suddenly occurred to him that maybe she thought he'd conned Carlene into marrying him because of her wealthy family, so he could have an easy ride. He couldn't blame her, given his history. But in reality, it had been Carlene who'd forced the issue.

Reuben had avoided marriage until meeting her and wasn't keen on the idea, particularly after such a whirlwind courtship – if you could call meeting once a week in the prison visiting room and indulging in a chaste hug at the end of it, a courtship. Carlene was a friend of Warren's girlfriend, Liz, who visited him regularly. Warren had told Liz about his cellmate – 'a good-looking dude, smart, the sort women wet their knickers over', and Liz had suggested to Carlene that she write to Reuben. As an act of compassion, to help ease his loneliness.

After receiving a long, rambling letter from Carlene describing in extravagant detail the saga of her life so far, Reuben wrote back, inviting her to visit. Carlene got permission from the prison authorities and accompanied Liz one Saturday afternoon. Reuben was fascinated by her, despite, or perhaps because she was nothing like his ideal woman. He watched frizzy tendrils of hair escaping from her ponytail as she spoke in her low, slightly breathless tone; and the way she hunched her shoulders when she giggled and played tantalisingly with the top button of her blouse when she was thinking. The two of them, along with Warren and Liz, became a regular double date on Saturday afternoons. When Carlene brought up the subject of marriage, two months before his release, his first instinct was to run, figuratively speaking; and he laughed it off.

But Carlene was persistent in a ruthlessly seductive way. When you're behind bars, a raised eyebrow and wiggle of the backside from a female visitor can be very persuasive, and he'd finally surrendered. He'd already made up his mind that once out this time, he was never going back. He was thirty-five and it was time he settled down. With Carlene's support, he could make a new life for himself. Would he have married her if her family wasn't wealthy? Probably not. But it was turning out to be not as much of a bonus as he'd thought.

'It's not as cushy as it sounds,' he said. 'Carlene's parents are very suspicious of me, and they don't cut me any slack.'

And please don't say it's a consequence of my offending again. Mercifully, she didn't – she was busy writing out his next appointment slip. She handed it to him and he signed it below her name. Lucy Prentice. A perfect name. Compact, with a lyrical beauty – like its owner.

She handed him back his copy of the appointment slip. 'I'll see you in a fortnight, Reuben.'

She stood up. He wasn't going to let her go that easily. He

stood up and put out his hand. 'Nice to meet you, Lucy.'

After a moment's hesitation, she placed her hand in his. It was warm and soft, like a fragile bird, but her handshake was firm. Reuben fought an urge to tighten his grasp and trap her hand in his, the two of them locked in a handshake over the desk. As he left the room, his hand tingled where it had touched hers.

2

His interview at Employment Initiatives was even less stimulating. For a start, his case manager Dave was not the type to inspire confidence. Reuben thought of him as 'Droopy Dave' because he resembled a basset hound with his long face and mournful eyes. Even his ears were droopy – large and elongated, with fleshy earlobes.

Droopy Dave looked at Reuben's file on the desk in front of him and clicked his teeth. 'You're making it very difficult.'

Reuben burned with indignation. It wasn't his fault he'd been sacked from two jobs. Okay, it was, but he didn't do it on purpose.

'There must be something I can do.'

Dave shook his head. 'Nothing that doesn't involve handling money. You've really narrowed your options.'

His face rumpled in concentration. 'Perhaps I can get you assigned to a course. Can you think of any you'd like to do?'

'What about photography?'

Dave looked up, a glimmer of hope in his eyes.

'Are you interested in that?'

'As long as I can do nude models.'

The corners of Dave's mouth sagged. 'I suggest you go home and have a long, hard think. Brainstorm. Write a list of every occupation that interests you. I'll give you a hint – think about what you liked doing as a child, what your talents were. That's your homework for next time.'

***

Reuben stared unseeingly out the bus window. Bloody homework. He didn't have to brainstorm or make a list. He knew what the outcome would be. Zilch. As for what he liked doing as a child – watching TV while waiting for Mum to come home from her cleaning job, daydreaming and thinking up schemes to make money from the kids at school. Nothing you could make a career out of, or at least, a law-abiding career.

And as for things he was good at – the same. He'd excelled at Swindling for the Under-Sixes, from the time in Year One when he stole a packet of his mother's digestive biscuits, re-wrapped them singly, and sold them to his classmates as Apollo Space Cookies. Not only did he make a four-dollar profit, he became the coolest kid in the class.

As he grew older and more experienced, he progressed to more daring schemes, such as running a bookie's tote. Albert, the old man in the apartment next door who smelled of mothballs and rum, had shown him the principles of being a bookie. In sixth grade, he ran a book on whether he could get Poppy Andronicus, the hottest girl in the class, to take her knickers off during school. The odds were 10 to 1 against.

While the class was tending the vegetable plot they'd started as part of their science studies, Reuben, who was on watering duties, lost control of the hose. The result was that Poppy and a couple of her friends were drenched and had to go up to the principal's office to change into clean clothes from the spare clothes box. When those who had bet 'no' demanded their money back, Reuben put his hands in his pockets bulging with coins, and smirked. 'I won fair and square, I didn't say she had to take them off when we were watching. Read the fine print.'

There was no fine print, of course, the premise of the bet having been nutted out in the boys' change room after swimming. But the scheme backfired when Billy 'Boofhead' Barker bailed him up behind the toilets, put him in a headlock and refused to let him go until he'd promised to refund everyone their money. It taught him a valuable lesson – you can't afford to be too smart.

In high school, he ran totes on anything his classmates were prepared to bet on, from who was going to win the cross country to who would be the first to make Peabrain (Mr Peabody the maths teacher), swear in class. He targeted the students from well-off families who had wads of disposable cash and threw large amounts of money on the tote to impress their friends. Sometimes the tote lost to keep his customers coming back, but as he usually had insider knowledge of the likely outcome, the overall result was a healthy profit for Reuben. In between his bookie's activities, he sold false swap cards and fake IDs for buying alcohol. He had a fair idea these credentials would not impress Droopy Dave; might cause him to become even droopier.

He considered Dave's idea of doing a course, but could think of nothing he wanted to study. Besides, he didn't have the dedication or perseverance. After school, at his mother's insistence, he'd started a Bachelor of Business degree at the University of Queensland, having just scraped in on the second intake. He found he was more taken with the idea of being a student than actually being one. He hung around the library chatting up the girls, was a regular fixture in the university bar and lounged around on the lawn with a thick tome open on his lap, smoking roll-your-own cigarettes. For authenticity, he even attended a few rallies – save the green tree frog, violence against women, whatever was the topic of the moment.

But by the end of his first year at university, he knew it wasn't for him and left before the final exams. It wasn't that he couldn't do the work – his school reports had all said the same thing. 'Reuben is an intelligent boy who is not living up to his full potential.' In other words, bone-lazy.

He glanced around at the other passengers on the bus. Mostly shoppers, as it was too early in the afternoon for office commuters. Two men were sitting across the aisle. Overalls, work boots, duffle bag at their feet; staring vacantly ahead, fatigue etched on their faces. Factory workers, probably. Took this same route every day, there and back, to earn barely the basic wage; only enough left after paying the bills for a couple of beers. Nights spent watching the telly, anything for an escape from the here and now, weekends mowing the lawn and cleaning the barbecue.

If that's straight life, shoot me now. Scamming was hard work and you needed brainpower, creativity and nerves of steel. But the rewards were high – the adrenalin rush when it all came together and the money flowed and the satisfaction of seeing a well-planned scheme come to fruition – as long as he didn't think about the people whose trust in him had afforded him that success.

Of course, as in all careers, you started out on the bottom rung. After leaving uni, he started up a mail-order company selling bogus products. As a sideline, he did door-to-door touting for non-existent charities, and started up a variety of internet-based scams. Brisbane soon became too small for him and as he was beginning to be recognised, he moved to Sydney. He kept on the hop from state to state – when the police started showing interest, he'd move on. Even so, he was arrested and charged on a few occasions and did a couple of short stints in prison.

After a while, he became bored with low-level scams and applied himself to studying finance and investment. His university lecturers would have been amazed if they'd seen him hunched over his scratched laminex kitchen table, cracked lampshade glowing, his head buried in a pile of books, and writing pad full of scribbled notes.

Once he'd acquired a working knowledge of the world of finance, he created more complex scams. By now, he'd returned to Brisbane because of his mother's illness. He found a partner, Derek McMaster, an Oxford graduate in economics, from a wealthy family who'd squandered his inheritance on wild living and was searching for a way to recoup his losses. Derek knew finance as if he'd been born with a fistful of dollar notes, and together he and Reuben set up investment schemes to embezzle money from tax-dodging clients. Reuben was the front man, who, with his charm and enough financial knowledge to sound plausible, got the customers in the front door. Derek did the rest - persuaded them to sign on the dotted line, transferred the money into his and Reuben's offshore accounts and did some creative accounting to cover their tracks. They had an office in the city, a secretary and a website. Their business, All Purpose Financial Consultants – deliberately named to sound ordinary – had every appearance of being a legitimate business.

Reuben bought himself a modern apartment in trendy Paddington and a new Audi. He could afford much more, but was careful not to be too extravagant because it would cause suspicion. Derek, on the other hand, couldn't help but indulge himself in a Mercedes sports car, catamaran and a penthouse apartment on the river. A suspicious and embittered ex-girlfriend alerted the Tax Office, the police became involved, and after five years, their dream crashed down around them. Their bank accounts were closed and their homes and possessions confiscated. Derek received a longer sentence as the executor of the fraudulent transactions and was still in prison, not due for parole for another two years.

The bus jerked to a halt and a woman boarded. In her forties, well made-up, hair gelled into submission. Simply dressed but she had money – you could smell it on her. She took the seat beside him. He glanced at her and she caught his eye then looked away. Five years ago, he'd been readily accepted into the social circle of such women and their husbands, flirted with them at cocktail parties and restaurants and was invited into their homes. Now they looked right through him as if he was of no more importance than the street cleaner. Was that contempt he had seen in her eyes? Sometimes he felt as if he had 'jailbird' tattooed on his forehead.

One thing was for sure. He wasn't going back there. The last three years, his longest time in prison, had crawled. Three years lost forever. Besides, he'd promised his mother. He'd visited her in the palliative care hospital six months before he and Derek were arrested. She had lung cancer, was only fifty-five, but looked like an old woman. Her mottled hand rested as light as a leaf in his, her eyes, shrunk within her parchment yellow face, pleading with him.

'Please tell me this business you're in with Derek is legal,' she whispered. She spoke slowly, her breathing laboured. The oxygen machine was next to her bed.

Reuben stroked her hand. It was icy cold. 'Of course it is, Mum, I promise.'

His deception was a dead weight in the pit of his stomach. He could make up the most convincing lies to tell strangers and not blink an eye, but he hated lying to his mother. But what else could he say when she was dying?

Her face lightened and for a moment he saw the mother he'd known as a child. She moved her mouth into a semblance of a smile. He didn't know whether she believed him, but she could pretend as well as he.

Her hand gripped his with surprising strength. 'I want you to promise me something else.'

'Anything you want, Mum.'

'Give up the cigarettes.'

'Okay.'

'I mean it, Reuben. I'll come back and haunt you if you don't.'

All those years he'd pleaded with her to give up smoking and now she was doing the same to him. But he wasn't addicted; he only smoked on social occasions.

He squeezed her hand gently and grinned. 'That's an incentive if ever I heard one. All right, I promise.'

A spasm of coughing wracked her body, bony and fragile with its paper-thin skin. The nurse hurried over and fixed the oxygen mask to her face. Violet Littlejohn picked up the pad and pen she used for communicating when talking became too hard. Her hand moved laboriously across the page. She held it up. On it were written three words. The letters were wobbly, but there was force behind them: 'AND STAY STRAIGHT'.

She died two days later. True to his word, Reuben gave up smoking. If only the second part were as easy.

The bus pulled up at his stop in Kedron, and he got out. He walked the two blocks to home – a worker's cottage Carlene had found for rent before he was released from prison. She had fallen in love with it at first sight, while Reuben thought it rather ugly. Squat and plain with the typical gable-shaped roof, it looked like a Lego house. But he couldn't complain about the inside – fully renovated with polished floors and all the mod cons. It was in keeping with its surroundings, Kedron being an established suburb of older homes – modest low-set timber or high-set gabled Queenslanders. With most people at work, the streets had an air of desertion about them. The afternoon sun was warm on the back of his neck. Winter had been much colder and bleaker in prison, and seemed to last forever.

As he neared the cottage, memories of his mother overwhelmed him. He was a child again, listening for the creak of the rusty front gate, then bounding downstairs and diving into her arms, his cheek against her uniform that smelled of disinfectant, because that made the world right again. Though in reality, he'd got a hiding as often as a hug.

You can't give me an ultimatum like 'Stay Straight' and then die. What the hell am I supposed to do? Give me a sign, a bolt of lightning, a whack on the head – anything!

3

'Don't turn the sausages any more, they'll go all leathery.'

Wayne hovered beside Alec, as he stood at the barbecue presiding over a sizzling array of chicken wings, steak and the unfortunate sausages. The aroma filled the chilly evening air.

Alec poked Wayne's beer gut with his tongs. 'Listen mate, I won't tell you how to tile roofs if you don't tell me how to cook.'

His tone was good-natured and Reuben admired his forbearance. In the short time he'd known his brother-in-law, he'd discovered Wayne was like a jalapeño chilli – to be taken only in small doses. He had opinions on every conceivable topic and ignorance was no hindrance to his expressing them.

Reuben took a cracker from the crystal dish on the table, and piled it with hummus and goat's cheese. Carlene was in the kitchen helping Nancy with the salads. A child's shriek floated out through the open French doors.

'Brayden, come here this minute or I'll slap your bum!' Carlene's sister Jolene yelled. How could she be close enough to slap his bum unless he did what he was told? In which case he wouldn't need to have his bum slapped. It was a no-win situation for Brayden, who at eighteen months was too young to argue the toss, unlike his older sister Indya, who always came out on top and was far too precocious for her four years.

Reuben got up from the table and wandered over to the pool. Large and kidney-shaped, it shimmered in the blazing lights of the patio – as Nancy called it. She made it sound like a quaint little courtyard when, in reality, you could fit his and Carlene's cottage into it and have space left over. In the corner of the lush expanse of lawn, the Balinese rotunda where they had married hulked in the shadows.

The house was in Hamilton, only ten minutes drive from Kedron, but a world away in lifestyle. Perched at the top end of a short, hilly street shaded by jacarandas, it was a sprawling Federation-style Queenslander, immaculately kept, with a double front staircase, a fountain gracing well-behaved gardens and a security intercom on the front gate. From the front verandah, you could glimpse through the trees the shiny ribbon of the Brisbane River and the jumble of boat masts at Portside Wharf.

The original name plaque of the house was still attached to the front gate. Karrawa. According to Nancy, it was aboriginal for 'that will do' – a modest name, suitably nouveau poor.

'There's a lot of old money in Hamilton,' Alec had told Reuben, with a note of pride. Who cared about the age of the money? It was just another way of being a snob. Reuben gazed down at the pool and saw himself spring off the edge, a poised torpedo of rippling muscle, scarcely making a splash as he dived into its aqua-cold depths. Lucy had been constantly on his mind and here she was again, waiting for him in the pool in an emerald bikini that matched her eyes, her hair floating on the water like seaweed. Soft, clean-smelling seaweed. He bobbed up beside her and their eyes met. He held her tightly to him and slowly kissed her tender mouth, his hand tracing the curve of her cleavage and on to her nipple...

A heavy hand clapped him on the shoulder and he jumped. 'How's the job hunting going, mate?'

Wayne was grinning at him, his meaty hand clasped around his stubby of beer. In his wedding photos he had the athletic, fresh-faced looks of the surf lifesaver he had once been, but over the years his features had coarsened and his body had gone soft. Reuben noted with satisfaction that although Wayne was the same age as him, he looked much older.

'Great! I've had six job offers this week. I just have to decide which one I want.'

Wayne narrowed his eyes. 'You're joking, aren't you?'

'Yes.'

He leaned closer to Reuben. 'I've got one for you.'

'A job?'

'Yep. I've just had one of my boys resign, so the job's yours if you want it.'

'Roof tiling?'

He looked at Reuben incredulously, as if he had just offered to perform brain surgery. 'No mate, that's a specialist's job. You'd be unloading the truck, carrying tiles, cleaning up – basic labour. You're okay with heights, aren't you?'

Reuben blotted out of his mind memories of plane flights pretending to be asleep so he couldn't see out the windows, and during his wealthy phase (new money of course), holidaying in a penthouse apartment at the Gold Coast and downing a stiff bourbon, before he could admire the view from the balcony. It would be different at work – he'd be too busy to worry about heights.

'No worries. When do you want me to start?'

'Monday. I'll pick you up, six o'clock.'

'Thanks, that'd be great.' He tried to muster a tone of enthusiasm. His body was not built to function before eight o'clock in the morning; even three years in prison of getting up at six o'clock hadn't altered his body clock. He'd blamed his disastrous performance at the building site on his early morning start, but at least that was on solid ground. He poured himself another glass of red wine to drown the niggle of apprehension in his gut.

As they sat down to eat, Reuben found himself wedged in between Jolene and Brayden in his highchair. Brayden was naked from the waist down, drumming his chubby legs against the highchair as he pulled apart a bread roll and threw pieces on the ground. He didn't seem to feel the cold, and in any case, two large gas burners at opposite ends of the table emanated a cosy warmth.

'Hey, young fella, where are your duds?' Alec said, as he placed a tray of glistening, aromatic meat on the table.

'He won't let me put his nappy on,' Jolene said. 'He screams every time I come near him, so I've given up.'

Two years younger than her sister, Jolene was a thinner, angular version of Carlene, with the same unruly dark hair. Her face had the tired, defeated expression often seen on the mothers of small children.

Nancy cast a pretend-disapproving glance at her grandson, as she coordinated the passing of serving dishes along the table. 'Grandma will have to smack your bare bottom.'

Brayden squealed with excitement at the prospect and threw another piece of bread on the ground. Indya, perched opposite Reuben, wore a pink, sparkly dress and a tiara. With her blonde hair and dainty features, she was an angelic-looking child, but it was obvious that the wheels of her mind were in constant motion. She chewed half-heartedly on a sausage, gazing at Reuben with large, solemn eyes.

'Are you a fairy, Indya?' he asked.

Indya's expression turned to disdain and she drew herself up in her chair. 'I'm Princess Marvella. Don't you know anything?'

'Indya, that's very rude,' Jolene said. 'Say sorry to Uncle Reuben.'

'No,' Indya said. 'He's dumb.'

Nancy pursed her lips. 'It doesn't matter how dumb he is, young lady, you apologise to him this instant!'

Indya cast her eyes downward and muttered, 'Sorry.' Then she threw her sausage on to her plate. 'I can't eat this, it's too tough!'

Wayne cast a sideways glance at Alec. 'I'm sure you can, sweetheart.'

'I can't! I'm going to watch TV.' She slid off her chair and ran inside.

Wayne shook his head with a resigned grin. 'Four, going on twenty-four.'

Reuben grimaced inwardly at the thought of Indya after twenty more years of perfecting her haughty look and condescending tone. She was certainly the most disagreeable child he'd ever met. Not that he'd had a lot to do with children, but those he had met warmed to him instantly, perhaps sensing a kindred spirit. He'd been accused by more than one girlfriend of not having grown up.

An awkward silence followed. Alec cleared his throat. 'So, Reuben, any luck on the job front?'

It was through Alec's contacts that Reuben had scored the jobs as waiter and bricklayer. Since then, he hadn't offered any more help, much to Reuben's relief. He was sure Alec disapproved of him as much as Nancy, but he overcompensated by playing the role of the matey-you-can-confide-in-me-father in-law, that didn't quite come off.

'Up until a few minutes ago, not much,' Reuben said. 'But Wayne has just offered me a job.'

Carlene, sitting opposite him, glanced at her sister then reached across and grasped his hand. 'Oh, honey, that's great!'

'I'll be cracking the whip though,' Wayne said. 'No special treatment because he's family.'

'Of course not,' Carlene said. 'It's so good of you to offer him the job.'

'Cause for celebration,' Alec said. 'Let's crack another bottle.' He fetched another bottle of red from the bar, uncorked it and filled all the glasses. He raised his glass. 'Let's drink a toast to Reuben's new job.'

The others clinked their glasses. 'To Reuben's new job,' they chorused. Except Nancy, who chose that moment to get up and start clearing away the plates. The wine was like liquid velvet sliding down Reuben's throat. There was something to be said for old money after all.

'What do you reckon, Reuben?' Alex said, nodding at the bottle. 'Hardy's Merlot 1980 vintage?'

Reuben shrugged. 'You've got me there. All I know is it's a good drop.'

Alex picked up the bottle and pointed to its plain label. 'Three dollars – from the bargain bin at Liquorland. Would you believe it?'

He looked around the table, daring anyone to challenge him.

'I'd believe it,' Wayne said. 'There's a lot of bullshit about wine. Bouquets and palates and the rest. I read somewhere about a wine-tasting – they blindfolded a panel of so-called connoisseurs who couldn't tell the difference between the el cheapo wines and the top of the range! I say if a wine tastes good, it *is* good. I don't want to write it a poem or make love to it.'

As he took another sip, Reuben felt something warm and wet on his foot. He looked down. A yellow liquid arc was streaming onto his shoe from the direction of Brayden's highchair.

'Fuck!' he yelled and sprang out of his chair. His glass toppled over and a river of red seeped into the white lace tablecloth. Indya appeared in the doorway and surveyed the scene. She looked at Jolene, who was ineffectually dabbing at Reuben's shoe with a linen napkin.

'Mummy,' she said in a loud, high-pitched voice, 'Uncle Reuben said fuck.'

***

As Carlene pulled out onto Junction Road, Reuben turned the car air conditioning to warm and pointed the vent on his side towards his bare feet. His socks and favourite shoes, blue Lacoste plimsolls he'd bought with his prison release welfare payment, were bundled in a plastic bag on the back seat. Even though they'd been washed in hot soapy water in Nancy's laundry, Reuben fancied he could still detect a whiff of urine.

A steady stream of traffic whizzed past; it was still early for a Saturday night. He'd only had one drink, not bothering to refill his glass after the accident, but Carlene had insisted on driving home.

He glanced at her. The line of her jaw was taut; her hands tight on the steering wheel. In that moment she was her mother, the Nancy of thirty years ago. An image flashed into Reuben's mind, of him and Carlene in their advancing years, reincarnations of Nancy and Alec: Carlene, her effusiveness moulded by age into disapproval; and Reuben trying to jolly her out of it, to smooth the waters and avoid conflict at any cost. The premonition was so strong, it gave him goosebumps.

He shook himself back to the present. 'I'm sorry about your mother's tablecloth. And the swearing. But it wasn't totally my fault. How could I know the little brat was going to pee on me? I'm the one who should be mad, it's my shoes that are ruined.'

Carlene's mouth softened a fraction. 'I know, honey. Your shoes will be as good as new after I put them through the washing machine. He's only a baby, he didn't do it on purpose.'

Reuben was sure he'd detected an evil gleam in Brayden's eye as Wayne had hoisted him out of the highchair to clean him up. Was his unerring aim an accident too? The kid had a bladder the size of an elephant.

'By the way, you put Wayne up to offering me the job, didn't you?'

'I asked Jo about it and she asked Wayne.'

'You should have asked me first.'

'I thought you'd be happy. Wayne's one of the best roof tilers in the business, it's a good steady job until something better comes up.'

'That may be, but I'd still like to be consulted first.'

'Fine. I thought it would be a nice surprise for you, but obviously I was wrong.'

Carlene pulled up at the traffic lights leading into Kedron Park Road. Still staring straight ahead, she said, 'Have we just had our first fight?'

'I'd say it was more of a disagreement,' Reuben said.

'What's the difference?'

'A disagreement is when you have different points of view on something, a fight is when you yell at each other.'

The lights changed. Carlene planted her foot and the Corolla shot ahead like a racehorse out of the barriers. On their left, trucks and cranes huddled silently together, dwarfed by the concrete ramps of the Northern Bus route still under construction.

'That's such a man thing to say. You don't have to yell to have a fight, you can be very civilised about it. That was more than just a difference of opinion, it was a fight.'

'So we're disagreeing about whether we're having a disagreement or a fight.'

'I suppose so.'

Reuben stole a glance at Carlene and caught her doing the same. He reached over and squeezed her leg.

'It had to happen, sooner or later. Your first argument's always nerve-racking. I think every couple should have an argument on their first date, then it's over and done with.'

'You're crazy, you know that?'

She was smiling. Reuben slid his hand up her thigh. 'And you know the best part about arguing...'

***

Inside the front door they lunged at each other, undoing buttons and zips and leaving a trail of clothes all the way to the bedroom. They collapsed onto the bed in a tangle of hot breath and naked limbs. As Reuben kissed the soft, sweet meat of Carlene's thighs, he closed his eyes and they became Lucy's – pale and firm, yet malleable, like vanilla ice-cream. When he opened his eyes, all he saw was the creamy curve of Lucy's shoulder, the perfect shape of her breasts, the plateau of her stomach dipping into the neat thatch of silky auburn hair.

Afterwards Carlene murmured, 'Wow, Rubie, you were on fire tonight.'

He ran his fingers through her hair. 'I told you it was the best part about arguing. I think we should have another one very soon.'

She giggled and nuzzled into him. Reuben's insides prickled. He didn't often allow himself to feel guilt, but this time it took him unawares. There was nothing wrong with making love to one woman while fantasising about another, he'd done it plenty of times, but Lucy wasn't some Playboy bimbo you conjured up to get your rocks off. She was a goddess. And his parole officer. It was ludicrous to put goddess and parole officer together in the same sentence.

He drifted off to sleep and in his dream Lucy was doing a photo shoot for Playboy. She was wearing a white robe, sprawled on a lush lawn with her legs apart, her hair fanned out behind her, lips pouted in a suggestive smile.

'Action!' yelled the photographer. She began to unbutton her robe.

'Don't worry, Lucy, I'll save you!' Reuben called out.

He raced over, pulled the robe around her, scooped her up in his arms and carried her back to the parole office.

'You were whimpering in your sleep again,' Carlene said. She was in the ensuite, lips stretched, applying her lipstick in smooth, precise strokes.

He'd remembered his dream as soon as he woke up. He'd had Lucy in his arms, a couple of buttons away from naked, and he'd taken her back to the parole office. Even in his dreams he couldn't win.

'It was a moany sort of whimper, the sort dogs make when they're dreaming about chasing rabbits.'

Not a bad analogy. He yawned. 'No wonder I'm so tired.'

He stretched out and pulled the blankets up under his chin. Through the half open blinds he could see patches of blue sky draped with bits of wispy cloud, like a child's collage. Outside, in the eucalypt tree, a wily wagtail chirped its cheerful soprano.

'Are you sure you don't want to come to church?'

Carlene sat on the edge of the bed and ran her fingers through the hair on his chest. She leant forward and brushed his lips with hers, her hair soft on his cheek.

'I'd enjoy it a whole lot more if you were with me.'

'I'll come on one condition.'

Her eyes lit up. 'What?'

'You let me ravish you in the back pew.'

'Rubie!' She gave him a playful punch on the arm. 'How do you know you won't like it if you don't go at least once? It's not like your usual church service, we clap and sing and everyone's really happy and friendly. Pastor Bryan doesn't believe religion should be about suffering and guilt, it's about peace and joy and living in the moment.'

'It's still religion, however you package it. And as far as I'm concerned, living in the moment means lying in bed waiting for you to come home.'

She sighed, got up and flung her handbag over her shoulder. 'Okay, I'm off.'

She stuck her head around the door. 'Don't forget the lawn needs mowing.'

The front door slammed, the Corolla roared into action and sped away. Silence settled around the house. Reuben huddled under the doona and tried to drift off to sleep again, to recapture the dream about Lucy so he could give it a more satisfactory ending. A chainsaw started up, its whine tearing apart the lazy morning ambience. What was it with these suburban weekend warriors and their chainsaws, whipper snippers and leaf blowers? Were these the new symbols of masculinity?

Reuben dragged himself out of bed and pulled on a pair of old jeans and a jumper. He went out to the garden shed, fought his way through the cobwebs and hauled out the lawn mower. As he started it up, he tried not to think of the factory workers on the bus.

4

The darkness was just beginning to lighten as Reuben stood bleary-eyed on the footpath outside the house. The rest of the street was still steeped in slumber. Snuggled up under their doonas. He was the only person awake on the whole planet.

A stiff breeze whipped around him and he huddled into his jacket. Underneath his tracksuit he wore the singlet and King Gee shorts he'd bought for the labouring job, and his steel-capped boots. On the ground beside him, his cap perched on a small cooler bag in which Carlene had packed sandwiches, fruit and water.

Who was he kidding? Wayne, hopefully. Certainly not himself. He was an impostor – nothing new, he'd been one all his life – but it was a hell of a lot easier persuading people to part with their cash than hauling tiles and clambering around on a roof several metres from the ground (gulp), with the sun beating down on you.

The roar of an engine shattered the stillness. A ute came into view and pulled up with a screech of brakes. In the dawn light Reuben could make out the words 'Wayne's World of Tiles. Best quality, best prices. Experienced tiler, no job too big or too small'.

Wayne's lip curled as Reuben got into the passenger seat. 'Geez mate, are you going to the North Pole?'

He was wearing only shorts and a t-shirt that strained over his gut. He did a U-turn in a spray of gravel and headed towards Gympie Road.

'It'll be warm later on, so I hope you brought plenty of water.'

Reuben nodded. 'Where's the job?'

'Cashmere, out the back of Aspley. Brand new home, would you believe the woman's husband bought it for her as a surprise when she was overseas? A whole fucking house! And she had the nerve to say she didn't like the colour of the roof tiles and wants them replaced. Ungrateful bitch! If I were her old man, I'd tell her to get up there and rip them up herself.'

'Sounds like a big job,' Reuben said.

'It is, and expensive too. But money's no object to them, not like you and me, eh mate? Battling to pay the bills and put food on the table.'

Wayne owned a huge tile warehouse as well as his tiling business, and he and Jolene owned a modern two-storey home in North Lakes, one of the newer estates. Reuben hadn't seen any evidence of financial struggle and wondered whether Wayne, too, was a member of the nouveau poor. Or maybe he'd just been spending too much time around his parents-in-law.

Cashmere was a new suburb, with the flat, desolate air of half-developed estates before trees, parks and people imbue them with life and energy. There wasn't much activity, except for workers on a couple of building sites, at whom Wayne waved and blew his horn as they passed. The house was at the end of a cul-de-sac, a sprawling Mediterranean-style home surrounded by a tidy lawn and palm trees, a tropical oasis in the desert of vacant allotments, their 'For Sale' signs poking above the brown winter grass. The roof tiles were of burnished orange-brown.

'What's wrong with the colour?' Reuben said.

'Too brown, apparently. She wants more orange.'

A cobblestone path led from the iron filigree gate to the front door. On a patch of lawn to their right sprawled a large untidy heap of tiles, glowing intense orange in the pale morning light.

'The "orangest" tiles we've got,' Wayne said.

Beyond the tiles was a large fenced swimming pool surrounded by deck chairs. The water was pristine and looked ice cold, with the deserted air of an unused pool in the middle of winter.

A plump middle-aged woman wearing a terry towelling robe and slippers opened the front door. She had bleached blonde hair and the sort of heavy make-up that's supposed to hide lines and sags, but only emphasises them.

'Hullo, Mrs Landers, I'm Wayne from Wayne's World of Tiles and this is my offsider, Reuben.'

'Thank goodness you're here. Those men made a terrible mess of my lawn when they delivered those tiles. Just dumped them all over the place. The sooner you get rid of them, the better.'

'Right you are, we're on the job.'

'Stupid cow,' Wayne muttered as they returned to the ute to fetch the equipment. 'What did she expect the boys to do? Wrap them in a parcel with a bow?'

Wayne assembled the tile elevator and showed Reuben how to operate it. All he had to do was load it up with tiles, which would move along the conveyor belt to the roof where Wayne would off-load them. A lot simpler than mixing cement. Or waiting tables.

'Load 'er up, mate,' Wayne said. 'There's only the two of us at the moment. The other boys are finishing off another job and they'll be here in a couple of hours.'

'And don't drop any - they're expensive and the old girl will bitch about the mess.'

He shinned up the ladder with the grace of a mountain goat, belying his build. Reuben picked up a stack of tiles, placed them in position on the conveyor belt and watched them climb slowly up to the roof. This was easy, he could handle doing this all day.

No such luck, of course. After he'd sent several loads of tiles to the roof, Wayne held up his hand and inclined his head for Reuben to join him.

Reuben turned off the machine and walked over to the ladder. He put his foot on the bottom rung and took a deep breath. 'Don't look down,' the mantra echoed in his head as he climbed up the ladder. He stepped cautiously on to the roof and immediately looked down.

His head spun. The tile elevator swam into view, an alien mechanical being with its long tentacle, and beyond it the path and the lawn wavered. He looked away and trod gingerly over to Wayne, who was squatting on his haunches as if he pried a tile loose. Beyond him were roofs and trees and acres of sky – it was as if he were walking on top of the world. There was something solid and comforting about the ground – you knew when you stepped on it that it wouldn't suddenly move away from you. No wonder the Pope always kissed it when he got off an aircraft.

Wayne peered up at him. 'You all right, mate?'

Reuben nodded. 'Just getting my roof legs.'

Wayne had stacked the new tiles in heaps around him. 'As I rip up the old tiles, I replace them with the new ones. Take half this lot and stack them on the other side.'

'Right, boss.'

Reuben picked up a couple of tiles. As he turned to move off he heard, 'Hey, mate.'

Wayne sat back on his heels, eyes mocking.

'You'll be getting nowhere pretty fast with two at a time. Not scared of scraping your delicate little hands, are you?'

'Just being ecological, saving energy.'

'Save your ecology for lesbian, disabled tree frogs.'

Reuben stacked four more tiles on top of his load and started off. The tiles were heavy and the dust on the roof made it slippery. Staring down at his feet and trying to think of anything but how far he was from the ground, he made it to the other side of the roof. He put his load down and went to collect another. By the time he'd made ten return trips, the sweat was trickling down his face.

'You can help me here when you've finished,' Wayne said.

As Reuben started across the roof with the last heap of tiles, he looked down again. He felt dizzy and his legs wobbled. As he bent over to put the tiles down, his foot slipped. He looked down and saw his foot sliding down the steep angle of the roof, the other following behind. He tried to scramble back up using the weight of the tiles to brace him, but the surface was too slippery. He looked down again. The pool shimmered, rising up towards him then receding again. *For God's sake don't let go of the tiles*! He held on with all his strength but the tiles were rough against his fingers and he was losing his grip. He managed to hold on to two of them, clutching them to him as he made his inexorable journey down the roof. The edge of the roof came up to meet him and he caught a glimpse of deckchairs, pot plants and a timber deck as he sailed past them into the pool.

As he hit the water he heard an almighty crash. He knew instantly what it was. The coldness of the water took his breath away and instantly numbed him all over. As he rose to the surface, coughing and spluttering, he looked towards the deck. In his fear and panic, he'd lost his grip on the two tiles. The deck was splattered with a myriad of tiny pieces of orange terracotta.

'Holy fucking Jesus!'

Wayne stared down at him from the roof, open-mouthed. The French doors onto the deck flung open and Mrs Landers was about to step out when she saw the mess.

'Oh no!' She put her hands to her head. Then she looked over and saw Reuben hoisting himself out of the pool – a laborious task with boots full of water – and shrieked, 'Oh, my God!'

Wayne scrambled down the ladder and surveyed the damage. He looked at Reuben, cap in hand, clothes plastered to him and water pooling around him. He opened his mouth as if to give him a roasting, then clamped it shut and shook his head.

'What's the water like, mate?'

Guffaws followed. Reuben looked over to see a line of faces

grinning at him over the fence. The rest of the work crew had arrived.

***

'Oh, Rubie!'

Carlene stopped in mid-chop of a shallot, knife poised. 'Tell me you're joking!'

'I could tell you I'm joking, but it wouldn't be a joke.'

'You fell into the pool? And broke all the tiles? On the first day?'

'I didn't break all the tiles, only two. And thanks for your concern, but if the pool hadn't been there, I would have probably smashed myself to bits as well.'

Carlene threw the chopped shallots into the pasta sauce. 'What is it with you and jobs? You're jinxed, I'm sure of it.'

'It was an accident, it could have happened to anyone.'

She sighed. 'But it never does happen to anyone, it always happens to you.'

She sat down at the table with her head in her hands. 'So I suppose Wayne fired you.'

Reuben uncorked the bottle of shiraz he'd bought on the way home to help soothe the troubled waters. He poured out two glasses.

'No, he didn't.'

He handed Carlene a glass. 'But I resigned anyway.'

She looked aghast. 'Why?'

'Because it's a shit way to earn a buck and there's got to be something out there that's better.'

There was no way he would admit to her that just the thought of getting back up on the roof made him dizzy.

'Jesus, I just don't get you. You're offered a job with good pay, the boss is prepared to keep you on even when you stuff up and you just chuck it in! So much for gratitude!'

'Gratitude's got nothing to do with it. It was good of Wayne to offer me the job but it just isn't my thing. Give me a chance, I'll find something, I promise.'

Carlene narrowed her eyes. 'You're not doing this on purpose, are you?'

'What do you mean?'

'Maybe you're deliberately sabotaging these jobs because they're not your thing. Or maybe deep down you think you're not good enough for them. Self-sabotage, it's called. It's in the book I'm reading, *The Psychology of Manifestation.*'

'It's got nothing to do with self-sabotage. I'm just not good at those practical, hands-on jobs.'

After a glass of shiraz, Carlene relaxed and her cheeks took on a rosy sheen. 'I'll have another word to Dad,' she said as they sat down to dinner.

Reuben refilled her glass and took her hand in his. 'I think I've done my dash as far as your father's generosity goes. Leave it to me, honey. Dave at the job agency is confident he can find me something really soon.'

5

'No good news, I'm afraid.'

Droopy Dave shuffled through some papers. Reuben was sure that if Dave scored him a million-dollar job, he'd break the news with the same hangdog demeanour.

'Have you thought about what I suggested last time?'

'About what I liked doing as a kid? I spent most of my childhood working out how to get the maximum amount of money for the least amount of effort. And that's still my ambition.'

Droopy Dave looked sadly at Reuben and shook his head.

'The same could be said for us all. Unfortunately those sorts of jobs don't exist – not for the likes of us, anyway.'

It was obvious he meant 'not for the likes of you.'

'We've just had funding cutbacks, which means we've had to downsize our service delivery and re-prioritise our programs. So at the moment I can't offer you anything specific, but moving forward I'm hoping for some positive outcomes.'

'So I'm supposed to come in every fortnight, for you to tell me there's nothing you can do for me?'

Dave permitted himself a slight turning up of his mouth.

'I know it's a part of your parole plan, and I hope that despite the current circumstances we can work together to achieve your goals.'

The only goal I have is to not have to come here and look at your ugly mug. How did people like that get these jobs? Perhaps he should put in an application for Droopy Dave's job. As he walked the three blocks to the parole office, he entertained a vision of himself sitting at Droopy Dave's desk with Dave on the other side, body sagging and melancholic eyes brimming with tears.

'It's unfortunate that the company has to let you go,' Reuben said, 'but when you don't meet performance objectives...' He shook his head and clicked his teeth. 'But moving forward I'm sure we can employ some initiatives with a view to a positive outcome. I'll get back to you in a few months.'

He was still replaying this satisfying scene in his head in the waiting room of the parole office, when a door opened and Lucy said, 'Come in, Reuben.'

She wore tailored slacks, shirt and jacket, a corporate look that accentuated her femininity. A subtle musky scent wafted in Reuben's direction. It made him want to bury his face in her bare skin and drink it in, slowly, from head to toe.

He stretched his legs out and clasped his hands in his lap.

'How are you today?' Lucy said.

She sounded genuinely interested. And it was on the tip of his tongue to tell her he was pissed off at Droopy Dave and the world in general. But his tongue was in knots. Just being in her presence mesmerised him. She radiated the glow of good health and contentment; her husband undoubtedly gave her a regular rogering. Who wouldn't, if you were married to her? *Think about something else, for fuck's sake.*

'Reuben?' Lucy prompted.

'Oh ... fine, thanks. How are you?'

'Pretty good, thanks. Any luck with employment?'

Employment. His brain came to a dead halt. Of course, jobs. Should he tell her about his latest failure? At least it would prove he'd been trying.

Lucy leaned forward with an encouraging expression, a triangle of chest showing above the top button of her blouse.

He gave her an account of his exploits on and off the roof. By the end of it she was laughing, tiny laugh lines fanning around her eyes. Reuben laughed too, ecstatic that he had made her laugh.

'So what's next in the adventures of Reuben Littlejohn?' she asked. 'Sounds like it should be a movie.'

'Great idea, but unfortunately movie star doesn't pop up too often in the "Situations Vacant".'

She asked him a few more questions. Any financial troubles? No. How's your wife? Fine. How are things at home? (subtext, how's your relationship?) Fine. (subtext, every time we make love I think of you).

All too soon she was writing out his next appointment. He racked his brain to think of something to prolong the interview.

'So what's next?' he said as he signed the appointment slip.

'What do you mean?'

'I'm on parole for three years. What's the plan for the long term?'

'That depends on a lot of factors.'

She tore off the appointment slip and handed him his copy. He longed to brush his hand against hers, but that was overstepping the mark. The last thing he wanted was for Lucy to think him creepy.

'Once you get a job, if you're financially secure and everything else is okay, I can extend your visits to once monthly, perhaps less often further on.'

That was a major incentive not to find work.

'But there's no set time frame, so let's just see what happens.'

She stood up. 'Good luck. I hope you don't have any more disasters to tell me about next time.'

Reuben returned her smile, drinking in the sight and smell of her to file away in his memory, before opening the door.

***

Not feeling in the mood to go home, he went into Joe's Cafe and ordered a coffee. Nina, who was taking orders, was unmoved by his cheery greeting. Reuben picked up a copy of *The Courier Mail* from the counter and took it to his table. He flipped through to the 'Situations Vacant'. Disability care workers, sales assistants, labourers, you had to have qualifications and/or experience for every job. Perhaps he should do a traffic controllers course, it was only two days according to the ad. Standing in the sun for endless hours, swatting flies and being abused by motorists – there had to be an easier way...

Nina appeared with his coffee.

'Thanks, Nina. You make the best coffee.'

'Thank you.'

Her manner was as crisp as her white blouse and apron. As she turned to leave, Reuben said on impulse, 'You don't have any jobs going here, do you?'

She looked hard at him, as if trying to gauge his seriousness. 'No.' She hesitated. 'What sort of job?'

'Making coffee, cleaning, kitchen hand, anything. Oh, except taking orders and money. I, er ... prefer not to have customer contact.'

'Not that I have anything against customers,' he rushed on, 'but I'm more a behind the scenes man.'

'I see.' She looked sceptical. 'There's nothing going at the moment. You can leave your resume if you want.'

'I haven't got one with me. I'll drop it in.'

He watched her walk away. She wore a short black skirt, stockings and flat shoes. Her build was wiry - her legs, though thin, were well shaped and she moved with an easy grace. Even though he wasn't in the least bit attracted to her, the image of her in bed with him popped up in his mind - all bones and angles, not enough rounded flesh to grasp, although the swelling under her blouse suggested that what flesh she had was concentrated in one area.

One of the effects of being deprived of female company while in jail was that since his release, he'd fantasised about every woman he saw who was remotely passable and even some who weren't. Once he even had a vision of himself fucking Merle – why, he had no idea, but it was an image so horrifying he expunged it immediately from his mind. What would Carlene's psychology book make of it? He decided it was a perverse part of his mind testing his limits of revulsion.

He turned his attention back to the 'Situations Vacant'. 'Pizzazz Promotions wants you right now – jobs available for people of all ages, shapes and sizes. Film and TV work our specialty.'

Then the magic words. 'No experience necessary.'

It wouldn't be as simple as it sounded, there'd be provisos. But it was worth a go. He'd enjoyed drama classes at school and didn't mind making a fool of himself in front of the others, particularly if he could raise a laugh. At university he joined the amateur theatrical society, mainly as a way of meeting girls. Who was that gorgeous babe they'd all lusted after, with a body so perfect their stage fright had turned to dumbstruck admiration? When, as Juliet, she dropped to her death on the stage, every male in the audience wanted to get up there and die with her. What *was* her name?

Veronica, that was it. She changed the spelling to Veronika; she thought it more exotic and she was determined to make it big in the movies. He hadn't seen or heard of her since then so maybe she was still waiting for her big break. Film and TV work always sounded more glamorous than it was in reality. A friend at uni had got some holiday work as an extra on a film at the Gold Coast, and spent most of his time standing around in the hot sun drinking bad coffee and waiting to be called on the set. But he was paid hundreds of dollars for it, so it had to be worth it. And easier than standing on a roof for eight hours a day. Or juggling plates of pasta. Or making concrete. Or practically anything else.

Reuben whipped out his mobile phone, dialled the number and made an appointment for Monday at ten o'clock. As he left the cafe, he smiled and waved to Nina behind the counter. She acknowledged him with a half nod before looking away. *You can stuff your non-existent job.*

6

The Edinburgh Arms Hotel was a misnomer – there was nothing the least bit Scottish about its red brick, mould-stained edifice. A faded coat of arms on the sign paid token homage to its name.

Inside it was much the same as any other suburban pub on a Saturday afternoon. Cool and dim, infused with the odour of beer and stale carpet, evoking a sense of refuge, that in here you could forget your problems and temporarily suspend your other life.

Reuben ordered a beer and perched on a stool in the Sportsman's Lounge. After Carlene had left for her refugee support group meeting, he went for a walk and found his footsteps leading him to the Edinburgh Arms. He only intended to have a lemon squash to quench his thirst, but once inside he succumbed to its lure.

He looked around at the three large screen TVs. Horse racing, rugby and motor racing, catering for all tastes. The clientele were mostly male, solitary figures like himself or huddled in small groups, someone occasionally letting forth a yell as his horse or team came home.

It had taken him some time after his release from prison to become used to humanity en masse. Everywhere he went people rushed towards him, pushed past him and encroached on his personal space, barely aware of his existence. Sometimes when it became too much, he'd retreat to the bedroom after arriving home and bury himself in a Mandrake comic with the Boston Stranglers, his favourite band, on his iPod.

Mandrake the Magician had been his comfort and his escape since he was eight, when 'Old Albert' next door had given him his stash of old Mandrake comics. As someone who enjoyed, as one teacher put it, 'a rich inner life', Mandrake's method of outwitting his enemies by hypnotising them and making them see illusions appealed to Reuben. He'd often fantasised about doing the same to Boofhead

Barker and his gang, and as he grew older, to anyone who made his life difficult. Carlene thought his obsession with Mandrake childish, but she couldn't help sticking her head through the door periodically and asking, 'Are you all right, honey?' with the worried expression of a mother who suspects her teenage son of plotting suicide in his bedroom.

But here in the Edinburgh Arms, the atmosphere was just right. He could revel in his solitude, yet still feel a part of the human race. He took a long, appreciative sip of his beer. How many times, while he was inside, had he imagined this, conjured up the bittersweet malty taste of it on his tongue so vividly that he could almost swear he was having a beer, sitting there in his cell. His ability to transport himself to another world was one of the few things that had kept him sane.

He was just debating whether to have another beer when he felt a thump on his shoulder.

'If it isn't Littledick – the people you run into when you don't have a gun!'

A body slid itself onto the stool opposite Reuben and set a beer on the table. Shaved head, protuberant milky-blue eyes, wide, thin-lipped mouth. The face bore a remarkable resemblance to a bullfrog, right down to the folds of loose skin under his jaw. No one dared joke about it to Frank Cornell's face. The open top buttons of his shirt revealed gold chains nestled in a forest of tight, sandy-coloured curls. The last time Reuben had seen Frank this close-up he was wearing the same brown uniform as everyone else, but he had no doubt that the shirt Frank was wearing now was worth more than Reuben's entire wardrobe.

'Likewise,' Reuben said. 'What are you doing in this neck of the woods?'

He forced a jovial tone. He and Frank had scarcely exchanged a few words during his entire time in prison – they mixed in different circles and Reuben kept well away from him – and he wondered why he was singling him out now. *Don't be paranoid, you're not inside now.*

'Minding my own business, as always,' Frank said. 'I was supposed to meet a client here, but he stood me up. First and last time for him.'

He drummed his fingers on the table. Broad and freckled, they were adorned with the kind of showy rings that shouted, 'Rich wanker!'

'Anyway, Littledick, I might ask the same about you.'

'Just having a quiet drink. I only live a few streets away.'

'Yeah, I remember now. Your old girl almost wiped me out the other day, pulling out in front of me.'

'That was my mother-in-law,' Reuben said. 'I'm sorry, she's a maniac on the road.'

'Mother-in-laws are maniacs, full stop,' Frank said. 'I've had three of 'em myself.'

He took a swig of his drink, leaned back and studied the TV screen. His shirt strained against the beginnings of a paunch. He looked for all the world as if he'd settled in for a cosy drink with a good mate.

He downed the rest of his beer in one gulp and nodded at Reuben's empty glass. 'Same again?'

Reuben hesitated. If he allowed Frank to shout him this beer, he'd have to buy another round to return the shout and by that time, his body, unused to large quantities of alcohol...

Frank was already at the bar. He came back with two schooners. Reuben nodded his thanks. That'd teach him to be indecisive, although he had a feeling that when Frank shouted, you drank schooners, no argument.

'So, Littledick, what have you been doing with yourself? Staying out of trouble?'

'Looking for work, mostly.'

Frank took this as a cue to launch into an account of his latest business dealings – buying, selling and developing property. His speech was peppered with million-dollar contracts, weekends on yachts brokering deals and the names of well-respected businessmen about town. Reuben had no idea how much of what he said was fact and how much was self-aggrandisement; considering that Frank was only released from prison a couple of weeks earlier than he, he'd achieved a lot in a short time, even if half of his story was true. He made no mention of his time in jail or his crimes. Not that he was likely to confide in Reuben – there'd been rumours in jail that he'd proclaimed his innocence of all drug-related activities until the day of his trial, when he'd changed his plea to guilty on the advice of his lawyer. The trafficking charges had been downgraded to supplying, for which there was a much lighter penalty.

When Frank stopped to draw breath and realised his glass was empty, Reuben went up to the bar and ordered a schooner for Frank and a lemon squash for himself. He was already feeling light-headed and he wanted to keep his wits about him, especially in Frank's company.

'Piking out, Littledick?' Frank said, nodding at Reuben's drink.

'I'm going out tonight,' he lied. 'Don't want to be over the limit.'

Frank nodded. 'Very wise. We don't want any more contact with the constabulary.'

He said the last sentence in a faux-posh voice, stumbling over 'constabulary'. He leaned forward and lowered his voice. 'You on parole?'

Reuben nodded.

'It's a total crock of shit, isn't it? I'm not allowed to go overseas, not even interstate. I do business all over the world – how the fuck am I supposed to make a living? A bloke may as well be back inside. And my parole officer, that sleazy little jerk, every time I see him I want to punch that smug smile off his face.'

'Which parole office do you go to?' asked Reuben, hoping it wasn't his.

'Spring Hill, I live in Newstead.'

That figured. Newstead was one of the trendy inner-city areas, where you paid half a million dollars for a box-sized apartment in a converted woolshed.

'I suppose I'm lucky,' Reuben said. 'I don't have any complaints about my parole officer. Lucy's a nice lady.'

Frank stopped mid-sip.

'Lucy who?'

'Lucy Prentice.'

Frank banged his glass down on the table. 'So this is where the bitch is hanging out now.'

'What do you mean?'

Frank leaned forward again. His eyes almost bulged out of his head. Reuben had a vision of them popping out into his beer.

'Let me enlighten you, mate,' he said, his voice low and measured, 'Lucy Prentice is not a nice lady; she is a first class bitch. She got me put back inside, for no good reason.'

Reuben flinched inwardly. In his mind the words 'Lucy' and 'bitch' were mutually exclusive. 'How?'

'She was my parole officer when I was living at the Gold Coast and got arrested for possession. Trumped-up charge, of course. But because of that she suspended my parole. You do know that they can suspend your parole if you're charged with an offence, even before you're found guilty, don't you?'

'Yes, I'm aware of that,' Reuben said. To his mind, it was an extra incentive to stay away from anything or anyone that hinted at illegality.

'I got put in the slammer but when the charges were dropped, they wouldn't let me out. The parole board cancelled my parole – said I was a danger to the community or some such crap. Two years I spent inside, before they let me out again – two years!'

A bubble of spittle pooled on his bottom lip. He was so close Reuben could smell his sour breath.

'My multi-million property deal that I was just about to close went down the toilet, then my missus decided she'd had enough of me being in the slammer and pissed off with my brother. Then to top it all off, my fifteen-year-old daughter got herself knocked up by some no-hoper, ran away from home and shacked up with him. A parking officer, for fuck's sake! If I'd been there, I'd have shoved his parking tickets up his arse and wrapped him round the nearest parking meter!'

He slammed his fist on the table. 'And none of that would have happened except for Lucy Fucking Prentice!'

'But surely it wasn't her fault the parole board cancelled your parole,' Reuben said.

Frank looked at him with disbelief then shook his head. 'Mate, have you got the hots for her or something? Of course it was her fucking fault! The parole officers and the parole board are in cahoots with each other – she told them to cancel it! So be warned - she might look all sweet and innocent and you might think you'd like to throw her over the desk and give her one, but she's about as sweet as a death adder!'

He threw back a gulp of beer. 'Anyway, I reckon she'd have a porcupine instead of a pussy. Scar you for life.'

'Well,' Reuben said. 'Thanks for the warning.'

'And I'll tell you something else, Lucy Fucking Prentice better watch her back.'

'What do you mean?'

'Exactly what I said! Karma is about to happen. If you dish it up, you gotta be able to take it.'

Reuben's throat went dry. He swallowed. 'What are you going to do?'

Frank shook his head. 'Three monkeys, mate.'

'What?'

'See no evil, hear no evil, speak no evil. If I tell you, I'll have to kill you.'

He surveyed Reuben, eyes impassive. 'Or recruit you.'

'Recruit me for what?'

'Don't act dumb, Littledick.' He lowered his voice. 'You're in the front line, you're seeing her – what? Every fortnight? You're in a position to find out lots of useful information.'

Reuben took a long sip of his drink to give Frank's words time to sink in. He could hardly believe what he'd just heard. Frank had asked for his help to get revenge on Lucy. What did that mean? Kill her? Or maim her for life? Reuben didn't dare ask. Not that it mattered; either scenario was unthinkable.

'I'll make it worth your while. It's an easy way to make some dough.' Frank grinned. 'Cash in hand.'

Reuben cleared his throat. 'Thanks for the offer, but no thanks.'

'A man of honour, Littledick! I'm impressed! No worries, there's more than one way to skin a cat.'

He downed his beer, stood up and held out his hand. 'Good to catch up.'

Reuben stood up and shook his hand. 'Likewise.'

Frank leaned forward and his face swooped in close to Reuben's. For one weird moment, Reuben thought Frank was going to kiss him.

'Just for the record,' he said in a low voice, 'this conversation didn't happen, so it would be pointless reporting it to the bitch or the cops ... and very dangerous. Life-threatening, in fact. Get my drift?'

Reuben nodded.

'And don't think I won't know if you do. Some of my best friends are cops.'

He pulled away and grinned broadly at Reuben, as if they'd just shared a dirty joke. Then he strode out, waving and calling a hearty goodbye to the bartender and the row of barrel-bellied old codgers perched at the bar. Reuben finished his squash. He'd had enough and should go home. But he went to the bar and ordered another beer. A schooner.

7

Lucy was in a bikini, gagged and trussed. Frank was about to throw her into the shark pool. Even in the midst of his horror, Reuben couldn't help his arousal at the sight of her exposed body as she struggled against her ties – the smooth curve of her shoulders as they wriggled, her bouncing buttocks and jiggling thighs. Frank stepped forward to pick her up. Reuben tried to run over to save her, but his feet were stuck in quicksand. Carlene was shaking his shoulder urgently. 'Come on, Rubie, you have to save her!'

Hang on, why did Carlene care whether or not he saved Lucy? If she knew about Reuben's feelings for her, she'd be on Frank's side, cheering him on.

'Come on, Rubie!' Rueben swam up through layers of consciousness and opened his eyes. Carlene was standing over him, eyes sparking with impatience. 'We're going to the cent auction, remember?'

Reuben sat up. He was on the living room couch. His mouth was dry and his head full of cotton wool. He groaned. 'I'd forgotten about that.'

He'd agreed to go with Carlene to a cent auction at the New Light Mission Church, a fundraiser for one of Pastor Bryan's missions. There was nothing he felt less like doing. He got up, stumbled into the kitchen and poured a glass of cold water. The three World Vision children Carlene sponsored gazed out at him from their photos stuck on the fridge - Kiet from Thailand with his gap-toothed grin, Sahra from Somalia peeping shyly from under her fringe and Ali from Eritrea with his solemn eyes. Their childish innocence was accusing.

'You're drunk!' Carlene said. 'And you were whimpering in your sleep again!'

'I'm not drunk. I've had a couple of drinks, that's all.'

'By yourself?' Carlene looked around as if she suspected Reuben of hiding his drinking companion behind the curtains.

'I went to the pub. Just felt like having a drink. I didn't mean to stay as long as I did.'

She sighed. 'I was hoping you'd have dinner cooked; we've got to be there by seven. I'll do some toasted sandwiches.'

She busied herself in the kitchen. 'You go and have a cold shower to sober up.'

'That's an old wives' tale, it doesn't make the slightest difference.'

'Have one anyway,' said Carlene. 'And I'll make you a strong black coffee.'

***

Reuben felt no better after a cold shower and a black coffee. He remembered now, that was the worst part about drinking in the afternoon, having a hangover at night. It was unnatural, like having bacon and eggs for dinner. His conversation with Frank was forefront in his mind. Were his words just an empty threat, an angry venting from someone nursing a grudge? What if he was serious about maiming or killing Lucy – what was Reuben supposed to do? He couldn't stand by and let it happen to anyone – but especially not to Lucy. He'd never forgive himself. It was too hard to think about it now, his head was throbbing too much.

The New Light Mission was in Coorparoo, on the other side of the Brisbane River through the Clem Jones tunnel. Known as the Clem 7, it was touted as Brisbane's biggest white elephant, due to the low traffic flow and its operator's massive financial loss. But it certainly made the trip quicker and easier, and they arrived at the church in a suburban street, in twenty minutes.

A small figurine of Jesus on the cross, beside the words 'New Light Mission' at the front were the only things that distinguished it from neighbouring houses. Behind it was the church hall where the auction was being held – a long wooden building strung with fairy lights. The scent of newly mown grass filled the air.

'It doesn't look like a church,' Reuben said. He carried a Glad-wrapped plate of buttered pikelets - everyone had been asked to bring a plate to contribute to supper.

'Pastor Bryan purposely had it built like that,' Carlene said. 'He wanted it to blend in with the surroundings because that's how he thinks religion should be – a part of your everyday life, not something expensive and showy.'

In that case, why build a church at all? Why not divert the cost of building it to charity and use someone's garden shed? Reuben kept his thoughts to himself – to Carlene and her family, Pastor Bryan was an angel in disguise.

The hall was a riot of chatter and activity. The cent auction had been billed as a 'fun family night for all ages', a signal for everyone to bring as many children as they could find. Kids ran and shouted on the lawn, and ducked and wove amongst the throng inside. Pastor Bryan stood at the front door greeting the guests as they entered. He was a stout, ruddy-faced man with a thatch of white hair.

'I'm so pleased to meet you, Reuben,' he said with a toothy smile. His trousers and jacket were ill-fitting and he seemed uncomfortable in them. Reuben wondered if he was more at home in his dog-collar. Then he remembered Carlene had said Pastor Bryan didn't believe in elevating himself above his flock by wearing priestly garments. They shook hands – his hand was warm and damp. Despite the chill in the air, his mottled complexion glowed with a sheen of perspiration.

'Carlene has told me so much about you. Perhaps I'll see you one day at church.'

Reuben mustered his warmest smile. 'I'm afraid that won't be happening, Pastor,' he said with deep sincerity. He caught a flash of the Pastor's disconcerted expression as he entered the hall.

A middle-aged woman in a floral pinafore bustled over,

enveloped Carlene in her arms and pressed her to her bosom. 'Hullo, darling, how are you? And this must be Reuben. No wonder you've been hiding him, he's too handsome to let on the loose.'

She released Carlene and lunged towards Reuben. He thrust the pikelets in front of him and held out his hand. 'Pleased to meet you.'

The woman looked disappointed, then smiled and shook his hand.

'I'm Irene. I'll take those, honey.' She whipped the plate from him, crying 'God bless!' as she disappeared through the crowd.

A succession of women emerged from the crowd to greet them. Reuben, defenceless without his pikelet-protection, succumbed to the lavish hugs and 'God Blesses'. A plump young woman with a freshly scrubbed complexion introduced herself as Ruth, clasped him to her pillowy breasts, then held up a sheet of tickets.

'Would you like to buy some?'

'They're all the same number,' Reuben said.

Carlene giggled. Ruth smiled. 'They're meant to be. You buy a sheet of tickets, decide which prizes you want to bid for, and put as many tickets as you want in the corresponding boxes. Then the auctioneer draws out the winning ticket.'

'Sounds fun,' Reuben said heartily. 'Give us ten sheets.'

He gave her a twenty-dollar note and she handed him ten sheets of tickets, from the numbers fifty-five to sixty-four.

'Good luck,' she said, simpering, and scuttled off.

'That's very generous of you, honey,' Carlene said.

'May as well make it worth our while,' Reuben said. 'I don't want to walk out of here without at least one prize. Are there any worth winning?'

Carlene pointed to a stand near the rear wall. On it perched a hot pink motor scooter, shone to brilliance under the lights, draped with pink ribbon and adorned with a large bow on the handlebars. A gaggle of admiring women and girls stood around it.

'That's the main prize – you'd look adorable on that, Rubie.' She squeezed his arm.

'I think I'd look even more adorable,' a voice said behind them. Jolene appeared with Brayden wedged on her hip and Indya beside her clutching a sheet of tickets. With her hair in a bun and wearing a pinafore, tights and boots, Indya looked like a celebrity child from the pages of *WHO* magazine.

'Don't you think Mummy would look better than Uncle Reuben on that motor scooter?' Jolene appealed to her daughter.

Indya gave Reuben a scornful look. 'Uncle Reuben would look silly, pink's a girl's colour.'

'Not necessarily,' said Reuben. 'I happen to like pink.'

'Only homosexuals like pink,' Indya pronounced.

'Indya, that's not very nice!' Jolene gave an embarrassed giggle and rolled her eyes. 'The things they learn in kindy! Say sorry to Uncle Reuben.'

'No.'

'What's my angel done this time?'

Wayne ambled into view and patted Indya's head.

'Uncle Reuben's a homosexual,' Indya said, 'because he likes pink and he wants to win that scooter.'

'Is that so?' Wayne raised his eyebrows and grinned at Reuben. He'd held no grudges against Reuben for his roof escapade and waved away his offer to pay for the broken tiles. Reuben suspected that the amusement factor of the incident, undoubtedly recounted numerous times at the pub after work, far outweighed an angry Mrs Landers and the loss of two tiles; and a worker who'd proved to be not much of a loss at all.

'He's not going to win it, sweetheart, because we are.' Wayne held up two ticket sheets with just the stubs left. 'I put all those tickets in the box.'

'Come on honey, we'll go and put ours in,' Reuben said. 'That scooter would look great with my pink shirt and pink sneakers.'

He took Carlene's hand and led her through the crowd to the large box decorated in floral pink paper, in front of the scooter.

'If that kid makes it to adulthood without someone throttling her, it'll be a miracle,' he said through gritted teeth.

'She can't help it,' Carlene said. 'She's precocious because she's so intelligent.'

'If that's intelligence, give me a dumb blonde any day.' He tore off a sheet of tickets and posted them through the slit of the box. 'Let's see what else we can win.'

The prizes were set up on trestle tables along the rear wall. Each was numbered with a box in which contenders placed their tickets. Reuben put in tickets for a massage, a facial for Carlene and a carry case of handyman's tools. What he'd do with it he had no idea, but it seemed the sort of thing men acquired once they were tamed into domesticity.

Alec stood behind the tables overseeing the process, smiling and nodding, with a look on his face that said he'd rather be anywhere else. Nancy strode in and out of the kitchen at the rear of the hall, a tea towel draped over her shoulder, eyes searching for someone to boss around. A roving MC, a round, jolly-faced man with a treble chin, kept up a running commentary.

'Come on, folks – get your tickets in! We have some tremendous prizes here tonight and the profits will be helping to send some of our disadvantaged youth group members on an aid mission to Cambodia. These are the leaders of tomorrow, ladies and gentlemen, so this is a fantastically worthy cause, and I urge you to spend up big!'

The lone beat in Reuben's head became a pulsating symphony.

Lots one to twenty were drawn. Reuben was relieved when a middle-aged woman won the handyman's tools – she'd get more use from them than he. Jolene won the massage and an elderly mauve-haired woman, the facial.

Then it was suppertime. Aproned women bustled out from the kitchen and placed paper plates of food on a trestle table. Children thronged to the table, arms reaching and grasping, parents following with admonishments. Reuben, realizing he was ravenous, took a handful of sandwiches. He felt something press against his leg. Brayden was on tiptoe, reaching up to the table, his hand dipped in a bowl of cream. His face was smeared with butter and in his other hand he clutched a mashed pikelet. Behind Reuben, a familiar voice whined.

'Mummy, it's not fair, we haven't won anything.'

'We've won the massage,' Jolene said.

'That's a stupid prize,' Indya grumbled.

'There are still plenty more draws to go, sweetheart,' Jolene cooed.

Indya and Brayden were a great advertisement for contraception. Reuben pictured a roadside billboard, a gigantic, sulky Indya scowling down at commuters and a grubby, butter-smeared Brayden, mouth open in a wail – or better still, nappy round his ankles, peeing on a pair of expensive shoes. The caption read, 'One careless night could lead to a lifetime of anguish'.

He moved away from the crowd around the table. From the corner of his eye, he spied Pastor Bryan striding towards him.

Could he pretend not to have seen him? He calculated the distance to the toilets. Could he make it in the next five seconds without breaking into a run? Could he trust the pastor not to follow him into the Gents?

Too late. 'Reuben, my boy! Are you enjoying the night?'

'Fantastic, Pastor.'

'Call me Bryan. Bryan with a "y".' He almost swallowed Reuben in his smile. 'I thought you might be interested in joining my little project.'

'What little project?'

'Youth Aid – that's the purpose of tonight's fundraiser. The idea behind it is to give at-risk youths the opportunity to help someone else in need, to see that there are others worse off than they are. Unfortunately, a lot of them have already come into contact with the law, and I think they could benefit from being involved with someone of your experience – you know, who's been there and done that.'

His face glowed with expectancy, as if thinking there was no way anyone could refuse such an invitation.

'I'm pretty busy at the moment, Pastor.'

'Bryan.' He flashed another smile. 'Your lovely wife tells me you're not working at the moment and you'd be willing to come along, even if it's just to chat to the boys.'

'Did she indeed?'

'They need someone they can relate to, Reuben, and who better than you – you can warn them first hand about the dangers of being on the wrong side of the law.' He paused. 'And it would be a good opportunity to give something back to the community.'

Reuben looked the pastor in the eye. 'At the moment, my main concern is finding a job, so the community will have to do without my input. If you'll excuse me, Pastor.'

After visiting the Gents he wandered through the crowd and

found Carlene talking to Jo.

'I don't know when I'm going to have time to have this massage,' Jo was saying. 'Brayden has playgym and swimming on the days Indya has kindy, and on Thursdays and Fridays, Indya has ballet and piano; and on Saturdays she has Little Athletics.'

'Excuse me Jo,' Reuben said. 'Honey, can I have a word with you?'

He drew Carlene aside. 'Why did you tell Pastor Bryan I'd help him with his project?'

'I didn't say you would, I said you might. And I was going to tell you about it, but he beat me to it.'

'There's no "might" about it, you could have saved your breath and his.'

'Ladies and gentlemen!' The MC's voice boomed around them. Reuben winced. 'It's time to draw the rest of these fabulous prizes!'

The trestle tables became barer as the winners collected their prizes. Wayne and Jo won a gift basket of champagne and exotic foods, which Indya decreed as stupid because there were no lollies in it. Brayden, not so picky, broke into it and began to gnaw on a tin of smoked oysters. Then it was time to draw the main prize. The children who'd been running around outside under the cover of darkness were called in and an expectant hush fell over the crowd. Even the clinking of washing up in the kitchen stopped.

'And now, ladies and gentlemen, boys and girls, the highlight of the evening.' The MC's chin wobbled with excitement. 'I'm about to draw the prize we've all been gazing enviously at all night. Or at least, the ladies have. I don't know about you men, but I'm not sure that riding around town on a hot pink motor scooter would do a lot for my reputation!'

'It might improve it, mate!' yelled a male voice, causing a round of titters.

'You could be right,' the MC agreed cheerfully. 'Because it's such an important prize, I'm going to let one of the little ones draw it. Who wants to be the lucky one?'

A sea of small hands shot up, accompanied by choruses of 'Me! Me!' The MC's eyes roved the room; then he pointed into the middle of the crowd.

'That little girl, the one so beautifully dressed with her hair up.'

The appointed child made her way through the crowd. She stepped up to the small makeshift stage and turned to face the audience with the aplomb of a seasoned actress about to make her Oscar acceptance speech.

'What's your name, darling?'

The MC bent down and put the microphone to her mouth.

'Indya.' Her voice rang with self-assurance.

'That's an unusual name for a little girl. Do you like curry?'

The MC beamed around the crowd, eliciting a couple of chuckles.

Indya looked at him uncertainly and shook her head, obviously not understanding the joke.

'Never mind, we'll see if we can curry some favour here tonight with the winning ticket. Could we have the box please?'

One of the kitchen ladies picked up the box and handed it to him. The MC shook it vigorously and took the lid off.

'Now Indya, close your eyes, put in your hand and pick out a ticket.'

He bent down and held the box in front of her. Indya closed her eyes, put her hand into the box and shuffled around in it for a good few seconds, making the most of her time in the spotlight. She picked out a ticket and handed it to the MC.

'And the winning ticket is number fifty-nine!'

A round of murmurs and rustles ensued as people checked their ticket numbers and heads craned to catch the winner in his or her moment of discovery. The only thought running through Reuben's mind was of a couple of Panadol and sinking into a warm bed.

Carlene nudged him. 'Rubie, isn't that one of your numbers?'

Reuben pulled the sheets of ticket stubs from his pocket and leafed through them. There it was, large and clear, jumping off the page. Fifty-nine.

Smoke billowed from the old Holden in front of him and he could smell the acrid fumes even through his full-face helmet. He held his breath. The traffic lights were taking forever. A horn beeped in his ear and he looked up. A truck idled in the lane beside him and on the passenger's open window rested a beefy, hairy arm. Its owner grinned.

'Hullo darling!' He shouted down in falsetto.

'Hullo gorgeous,' Reuben mouthed back and pursed his lips into a kiss. Surprise and confusion flitted over the other's face. The lights changed, Reuben planted his foot on the accelerator and shot ahead. You had to give this little baby its due – though it was only 50cc, it was nifty in traffic. Even if it did sound like a swarm of enraged mosquitoes. And in one respect, the only respect, its colour was an advantage – he was less likely to be mown down, even if it meant being laughed at by bogans driving in vehicles in inverse proportion to the size of their brains.

It was an act of God, according to Carlene. 'Think about it, Rubie,' she'd said yesterday as they both looked at it basking in all its shining glory in the driveway, after the delivery. It was so hot pink it almost sizzled. 'You need a vehicle and what happens? You win one! By saying you wanted it, God heard you and you manifested it.' She gave a shiver. 'It makes me go all goose-bumpy just thinking about it.'

'If it was an act of God, he's got a strange sense of humour. Why couldn't he have picked another colour? It's not as if I can argue that it's salmon or apricot or crimson – even Blind Freddie can see it's a hot, lurid pink!'

'Don't be so sensitive, baby. I think you look really sexy on it. Women love a guy who's man enough not to care what others think.'

'It's not women I'm concerned about,' Reuben said. 'Seeing

you love it so much, why don't you have it and I'll drive the car?'

'You're forgetting, I have to go out and visit sponsors for our fundraising. I can't turn up there wearing riding boots and helmet hair. And what if it rains?'

Reuben tried not to think about that possibility as he puttered along Lutwyche Rd to the office of Pizzazz Promotions in Spring Hill. He already felt exposed and vulnerable, with almost every other vehicle on the road towering over him - sometimes they roared past so close to him that his heart jumped and the hair on his forearms stood up.

Even though he'd owned it for less than twenty-four hours, he'd decided to get rid of it as soon as possible. When Wayne and Jo and the kids called around to inspect the scooter at close quarters, Jo was so rapturous in her admiration that Reuben offered to give it to her once he had his own car. Her sallow face lit up.

'Thanks heaps. Indya, won't it be fun riding around on the back of the scooter with Mummy?'

Indya surveyed the scooter. Brayden was crouched beside the front wheel, testing the durability of the tyres with his teeth. 'Where's your pink shirt and shoes?'

'Pardon?' said Reuben.

'You said you had a pink shirt and shoes to match it.'

'Um ... I must have thrown them out. I'll paint it red to match this shirt.' He pointed to the red pullover he was wearing.

'You're not going to paint it, are you?' said Jolene, looking stricken. 'Pink's our favourite colour, isn't it, Indya?'

Indya nodded. 'You said you like pink!' Her face glowed with indignation.

'All right, I'll leave it pink,' Reuben said.

'Good decision, ducky,' Wayne said with a lisp and an

effeminate curl of his wrist.

'What's its name?' Indya said.

'It doesn't have a name.'

'We can give it a name if you like, sweetheart,' Jolene said. 'What should we call it?'

'The Barbiemobile,' Indya said promptly.

***

If it wasn't for the small brass plate inscribed 'Pizzazz Promotions' on the front door of the refurbished terrace house, you could be forgiven for thinking the office was someone's home. It was the latest craze in the trendier suburbs – to make offices appear cosy and intimate, so that when you opened the front door you half expected to be greeted by a dumpling-cheeked old lady in an apron and ushered into the living room for a cup of tea.

It was apparent as soon as Reuben entered, that gentle old ladies and cups of tea were in short supply. His immediate impression was of being in an art gallery. The walls exhibited an array of abstract paintings of brilliantly coloured misshapen objects, like a psychedelic acid trip. Framed photos covered the ochre feature wall behind the reception desk – some appeared to be of movie scenes, in others a tall man with bouffant fair hair and golden complexion posed beside vaguely familiar figures.

The receptionist, flawlessly groomed right down to her impossibly long fingernails, looked up from her computer. 'Take a seat, Mr Littlejohn,' she said, with no change of expression. Only her mouth had moved, the rest of her face frightened into botoxed submission. She picked up the phone and whispered into it.

Reuben sank into a plush leather chair and stretched out his legs. The rhythmic tap of the receptionist's fingernails on the keyboard lulled him into a trance. His eyes were heavy. The last couple of nights, sleep had been fitful and full of disturbed dreams of Lucy – always the same theme. She was naked, about to seduce him when Frank sprang out of nowhere and started hacksawing off her limbs; or tied her to a tree Robin Hood style and shot an arrow right through her heart, or a dozen other creative means of disposal. Carlene had complained of him keeping her awake with his tossing and turning.

A hand shook his shoulder. He jerked his eyes open. A woman stood in front of him, hand extended.

'Hullo, Reuben.'

Reuben sprang out of his chair. 'God, I'm so sorry, I didn't mean to fall asleep.'

'I certainly hope not,' the woman said, smiling. Her voice had a musical lilt. 'My name's Posie.'

She was tall and thin, her body barely filling out her tailored suit. Straight, snow- blonde hair sprung up in a curl from her shoulders. Her eyes were a startling blue, fringed with luscious eyelashes like fat spider legs. Her skin had the even burnish of a fake tan and her pneumatically enhanced breasts almost bounced out of their corporate confines. She could have been anywhere from thirty-five to fifty-five.

Reuben shook her hand. It was soft and slightly greasy, as if she'd just moisturised them. Long orange talons jutted out flame-like from her elegant fingers. It seemed they were *de rigueur* in the promotions industry. Reuben gave an inward shudder – he found long fingernails a complete turn-off. Too painful having your skin raked to pieces in the throes of passion.

'Would you like coffee?' The spider's legs fluttered at him. 'I think you need one.'

'Thanks, that would be great.'

Posie waved her talons towards the reception desk. 'Coffee please, Sam.'

Reuben followed her as she minced down a short hallway to her office. She couldn't help but mince, as her heels were so high he got vertigo imagining walking in them. Without them she would barely be of average height.

Her office had a calming ambience of feminine elegance, with its pastel colours, pale timber desk and matching swivel chairs. In the corner, a leather settee and coffee table displayed a carelessly artful arrangement of glossy magazines. They sat down and Posie inclined her head in the direction of his motorcycle helmet, which he'd placed on the floor beside him.

'You have a motorbike, Reuben?'

'Yes.'

Posie clasped her hands together and parted her Angelina Jolie lips in a smile of delight. 'That's fabulous! Every now and then we get a request for someone with a motorbike licence and it's so hard to come up with someone at short notice.'

Reuben cleared his throat. 'It's more a scooter than a bike. I don't have a motorbike licence.'

'Oh.' She looked downcast then leaned forward, her breasts perched on the desk. 'So, you're interested in film and TV?'

Her gaze was intense, as if encouraging him to divulge his deepest, most secret desires to be on the screen.

'I don't know – can you tell me what's involved?'

Posie launched into an overview of the company. Pizzazz Promotions covered a variety of fields from modelling to casting for advertisements, TV and movies. It cost $295 to join the company, which included an internet profile – much cheaper than many of its competitors. Reuben would also need to supply a photo portfolio, although the company could do that for him at a very reasonable cost.

He was so fascinated by her that he found it hard to concentrate on what she was saying. In the space of a few minutes of introductory spiel, Posie expressed the full gamut of emotion from hopelessness to exhilaration – as if she were in a drama class and had been instructed to give an example of every emotion. If indeed she were acting, she threw herself so fully into it that it appeared to be her natural way of speaking; in contrast to her body, most of which seemed to be false, coloured or plastic, down to her brilliant sapphire contact lenses.

'So what do you think, Reuben?'

Posie leaned forward, pencilled eyebrows raised.

'Er ... I'll have to think about it.'

Two hundred and ninety-five dollars was a lot out of his meagre savings for something unproven and he really should talk it over with Carlene first. She'd been unenthusiastic about his going to the interview in the first place, being of the opinion that promotions work was not high on the list of respectable occupations.

'Of course you do.' Posie nodded. She leaned forward and said with a conspiratorial air, 'But I'll do a special deal, just for you. If you sign up and pay today, we'll do your photos for you – free of charge!'

She watched him as he thought about her offer. He felt like a moth being drawn in by the powerful radiance of a bright light. A photo portfolio would be expensive and to have it done free of charge sounded like a good deal. Surely Carlene couldn't argue with that.

'Okay,' he heard himself say.

'Excellent.' She gave a vigorous nod of approval. 'It just so happens that the owner of the agency, Simon Broadbent, is here today. He does our photography, so he can do your photo shoot and your audition as well.'

'Audition?' His voice came out as a squeak and he cleared his throat. 'I didn't come prepared...'

'It's nothing.' Posie waved her talons dismissively. 'I'll give you a few lines to memorise while you're having your coffee. Now, just fill out this form. Credit card or savings?'

He paid the $295, then filled out the form requiring the usual personal details and attached his resume to it, as requested. His resume had required at least as much creativity as any of his schemes. But he was proud of the end result – the Reuben

Littlejohn of his CV was versatile and enterprising, experienced at a range of occupations from sales assistant to manager, displaying a steady pattern of progression in his career. He'd also included a couple of overseas holidays of a few months' duration, in between jobs, to demonstrate his sense of adventure, and to show his compassionate side; one of them had been a trip to Uganda to help build an orphanage.

He'd done enough research to be able to answer standard questions about his occupations and overseas trips, although, he had of course supplied false names and phone numbers for his referees. In the event of a potential employer phoning both those numbers and finding that both businesses must have folded and the owners moved on ... he'd have to put that down to bad luck. He didn't have a plan for that, indeed he'd hoped to score a job on face value alone – up until now his whole life had been based on making favourable personal impressions. He'd only done the resume because Droopy Dave had insisted he have one.

When Dave had read it, he fixed Reuben with his basset hound gaze. 'How much of it is true?'

'None.'

He sighed and shook his head, earlobes flapping.

Reuben lost patience. 'Look, if I put in only legitimate jobs, the resume would be blank, except for a couple of telemarketing jobs during the uni holidays. Is that likely to get me anywhere?'

Droopy Dave drew in a deep breath. 'If you wish to use that resume, it is entirely your decision. I just want it put on record that I do not condone it and I have, in no way, been associated with its creation.'

'I should hope not,' Reuben said. 'There's no way I'm sharing the credit.'

And today was the first occasion he'd been asked to produce it. He handed it to Posie with his completed application form, but she gave it only a cursory glance. Reuben was disappointed but at the same time relieved.

'Now, can you take your shirt off, please?'

'Pardon?'

'Your shirt – can you take it off?'

Was this a joke? Posie tapped away on her computer as if it were a perfectly normal request. She stopped and looked up.

'Come on, honey, there's no room for shyness in showbiz. Unless...' She gave a knowing smile, 'you're just pretending to be shy.'

'I'm not shy, I didn't expect this.'

He stood up, undid the buttons on his shirt and draped it over the arm of the couch. At that moment there was a knock on the door and Sam entered with a tray of plunger coffee and two mugs. If she were surprised to see a half-naked man in her boss's office trying desperately to maintain his cool, she hid it well. She poured the coffee with deadpan efficiency and left, with just a telltale flicker of her eyes in Reuben's direction.

Posie came around from her desk and stood in front of him. She surveyed him from all angles with a thoughtful expression, as if he were a painting she was thinking of buying and she was considering whether he would go with the rest of her decor.

'You need to lose a little bit of this.' She patted her own non-existent stomach. 'Then I could possibly get you some modelling work.'

Reuben looked down at the slight roundness of his belly and sucked it in. She was right about that. But modelling! Never in his wildest dreams had he imagined himself as a model – casually strolling through the pages of *Vogue* magazine, with granite jaw and faraway eyes, holding the hand of a haughty-faced child-woman with endless legs and the smallest of skirts. Too pretentious. He'd knock back the *Vogue* offers and stick to jeans and t-shirt, with an air of devil-may-care ruggedness, advertising protein supplements for *Men's Health* magazine.

'Thanks,' Reuben said. 'I'll work on the stomach.'

Posie retrieved a sheet of paper from her desk and handed it to him.

'These won't take you long to learn. I'll go and give Simon the heads-up.'

'Oh,' she added, with a playful smile, 'you can put your shirt back on.'

Fully clothed again, he read the short paragraph headed 'Wheat Flakes Ad'. He was to pretend to take a box of Wheat Flakes from the pantry and pour some into a bowl, at the same time looking at the camera saying, 'A bowl of Wheat Flakes lasts me all morning – it gives me protein for muscle-building, energy to burn, and vitamins and minerals for good health. I can't start the day without my Wheat Flakes.'

By the time Posie reappeared, Reuben had committed the lines to memory. She escorted him into the room next door – a large, bare room with drapes over the windows and a white backdrop covering one wall. A man was bent over fiddling with a camera on a tripod.

'Simon, this is Reuben Littlejohn,' Posie said, as if announcing his presence at the Oscars.

The man stood up and held out his hand. Reuben instantly recognised him as the tall, fair-haired man in the photos in the reception area, shaking hands with the almost rich and famous. He was tall, broad-shouldered and square-jawed. Everything about him was smooth and shiny, from his carefully coiffured hair to his shiny leather shoes – even his trousers and shirt seemed to have a lustre about them. He looked as if he himself belonged in one of those TV ads featuring the perfect family – sitting on the couch with two angelic children on his knee, gazing adoringly at his wife in the pristine kitchen whipping up a gourmet dinner in her skirt and heels.

'Nice to meet you, Reuben,' he said with an arm-wrenching handshake. 'I'm always glad to welcome a new face to our books. We'll do the audition first.'

He explained the process to Reuben. In a nutshell, he was to be as over-the-top as he could. 'We can always tone down a performance if we need to, but it's much harder to ramp it up if it's dull and lifeless.'

He positioned Reuben in front of the backdrop, placed a small table behind him and an empty packet of Wheat Flakes on it.

'The table is the pantry. There's an imaginary table in front of you. You take the packet from the pantry, then pretend to pour Wheat Flakes into a bowl on the table while you're talking. And don't forget to smile.'

Simon adjusted his video camera, counted back from three and yelled, 'Shoot!' Reuben concentrated so hard on pouring, talking and smiling simultaneously that he forgot to put any feeling into his lines.

'We'll do another take,' Simon said. 'And this time with feeling!'

'Take two' was more lively, but Reuben was so engrossed in the feeling that he forgot to smile. Simon sighed and put down the video camera.

'Wheat Flakes are not only good for you, they make you happy! Imagine that box is a hot bird you're chatting up at the pub and she's just agreed to go home with you.'

Ping! A light bulb of enlightenment appeared before Reuben. 'Take three' saw him pouring and beaming, and declaring his admiration for Wheat Flakes with the ardour of a Renaissance poet. It wasn't the box being a hot bird that did it, but the hot bird on the box. How could he not be inspired by Lucy's angelic face smiling up at him from under a brimming bowl of Wheat Flakes and strawberries, and a jug of milk?

Posie, who'd been watching from the corner of the room, clapped her hands. 'Fabulous, Reuben! It makes me want to run out this very minute and buy some Wheat Flakes!'

'You'll have to restrain yourself,' Simon said. 'I need you to book an appointment for me with Hugh.'

'That's Hugh Jackman,' Posie told Reuben, then took her cue to exit with a cheerful wave. Simon changed the backdrop to pale blue and took a number of head and shoulder, and full-length shots. By the end of it, Reuben's eyelid had developed a twitch, his face was aching from smiling and the only angle Simon hadn't photographed him from was hanging from the drapes.

'Done.' Simon shook his hand. 'We'll be in touch.'

When? Is that next week or next month? When do I start work? Simon was packing his gear and his manner didn't invite questions. Reuben left the room. Posie's office door was open and she called him in. She was nibbling at her lunch – sliced hard-boiled egg on a bed of lettuce and tomato.

'No Wheat Flakes?' Reuben said.

'Good heavens no, full of carbohydrate.' She pointed to her plate. 'This is from Dr De Jong's high protein, high energy diet. I can lend you the book if you like.'

'I'm fine, thanks. I just need to get more exercise. What happens next?'

'We'll post the photos to you in about a week. We also have a number of courses available that would really benefit you. There's introductory modelling – we've just started a men's course – and also Basic Drama and Screen Presentation, which would be fantastic to get you on the right path for TV and film work.'

'They sound interesting,' Reuben said, 'but I'm afraid I'm not in a financial position to do any courses at the moment.'

'Oh? I got the impression from your resume that you'd done quite well for yourself.'

'Bad investments.' He made a gesture of helplessness. 'Lost all my savings.'

'That's a pity.' She wiped her hands on a napkin and picked up a kiwi fruit. Her fingernails pierced the skin and peeled it back. Reuben cringed.

'I'm only allowed one piece of fruit a day, so I make the most of it. I can make a kiwi fruit last half an hour.'

She took a paring knife and sliced the kiwi fruit into delicate slivers. 'We do tend to give preference to people who've done the courses when we're hiring, but there's always the chance that you'll have just the right look that someone wants. I'll be straight with you, though – and most agencies won't tell you this because they just want your money.'

She leaned forward and pointed the knife at him. 'Don't expect to get rich quick in this business. In fact, if you get rich at all, it will be a fluke. It's a matter of taking whatever work you can get, no matter how mundane, and getting yourself known. *And being professional* – turning up on time, being courteous. Then you might just have a chance.'

'I appreciate your advice,' Reuben said. *After I've paid my money.* But still, it wasn't as if he had any hopes of becoming the next Brad Pitt. Any work would be good, even doing a Wheat Flakes Ad. Or modelling. As he walked out to the street where he'd parked the Barbiemobile, he sucked in his stomach. Tomorrow he'd start jogging. Today, he had to solve the problem of Lucy.

9

Reuben stretched out on the living room couch, his most productive thinking position, reliving for the thousandth time his meeting with Frank in the Edinburgh Arms. He still couldn't decide if Frank's threat to take revenge on Lucy was genuine. If half the stories he'd heard in prison about him were true, Frank was more than capable of carrying it out.

Frank considered himself a big-time criminal, part of Brisbane's underbelly, although general opinion in prison was that he was a wannabe, trying to muscle in on established territory. It was rumoured that a small-time drug dealer, Edward Theodore, known as Eddie Teddy, who was working for Frank, had had a one-night stand with his ex-wife. As Eddie loitered one night outside a Narcotics Anonymous meeting waiting to do a drug deal, a car mounted the footpath, ran him down and killed him. It was general knowledge that Frank had organised it, although no-one knew why – why seek revenge on account of an ex-wife? Maybe he was still in love with her. Or perhaps he was trying to prove a point – mess with me and you'll pay the price. The apparent irrationality of his motive made him all the more dangerous.

It would be foolish not to take the threat seriously. But what to do? He couldn't stand by and allow Lucy to be maimed or killed, knowing he could have stopped it. Not Lucy, of all the women in the world. If he warned her, she'd undoubtedly report it to her superiors and the police would become involved. Even if he asked her not to report it to the police because it would put his life in danger, he couldn't be sure she'd take his request seriously. Was it true that Frank had friends in the police or was that just a bluff? There'd been rumours in jail that he had a well-known high-ranking police officer in his pocket, but you couldn't put much credence on those – Frank may well have started the rumours himself. Even if it was a bluff and

Reuben went to the police, they'd start digging around and set up surveillance on Frank and he'd find out, one way or another. Reuben didn't have a lot of confidence in the ability of police to be discreet in their investigations – he'd witnessed and heard of too many bungles. He had to assume the worst-case scenario – that if he told the police and Frank found out, he would meet the same fate as Eddie Teddy.

In any case, all he had to take to the police was a verbal threat. He had no idea how Frank planned to carry it out, if he had a plan at all, and no evidence of his intention. Chances were the police would just laugh at him.

The more he thought about it, the more helpless he felt. There was no solution. What illusion would Mandrake conjure up to scare Frank? A sabre-toothed tiger or white pointer shark about to attack, baring its menacing display of teeth? Or even better, Lucy herself as a vampire: red eyes flashing, blood dripping from her fangs, a 'return to prison' warrant sticking out of her pale cleavage. God, even as a vampire she was irresistible.

***

Someone was tugging at his arm. They were trying to save him from the vampire.

'But I want her to bite me!' Reuben protested. 'I want to be a vampire too, so we can live happily ever after!'

'Rubie, wake up!'

He opened his eyes. Carlene's face swam into focus. She was leaning over him.

'You're drooling.'

Reuben sat up and wiped his mouth. 'Must have been dreaming about you, baby.'

'You're a smooth-talker, Reuben Littlejohn.'

She got up, went into the kitchen and turned on the kettle. She was still in her work clothes. It was five-thirty. He'd slept for over three hours.

'That seems to be your default position lately,' Carlene said.

'I've only fallen asleep on the couch twice, I'd hardly call that default. And anyway I've been busy preparing myself for stardom.'

'Oh yes, the promotions agency. How did you go?'

As he predicted, she wasn't impressed.

'Jesus, Rubie, you've just gone and thrown the best part of three hundred dollars down the drain!'

'You don't know that at all.'

'Yes, I do. A friend of mine registered with one of those agencies, it cost her a small fortune, and they didn't call her once.'

'Maybe she didn't stick at it for long enough, or maybe she needed to be more proactive. I'll be ringing them constantly so they won't forget me.'

'If you're lucky, you might get in a crowd scene in an ad for five seconds. That's hardly a regular, secure income.'

'I'm not looking at it as regular income. I'm just going to see what comes out of it. Meanwhile, I'm still looking for other work.'

'All I can say is, it's a hell of a lot of money to pay for the possibility that you might get some work.'

She stalked off to the bedroom.

As they were getting ready for bed, Carlene said, 'I wish you'd let Mum and Dad help you. They know a woman who's a life coach and she does vocational training. She's pretty expensive, but it would be worth it.'

'Honey, there's nothing a life coach could tell me that I don't already know.'

She was in the ensuite removing her make-up, her eyes two

reproachful islands in a sea of cleansing foam.

'How do you know if you've never been to one?'

'I know enough about them to know what they talk about.'

'It's not the same as actually going to one. And I know that if you were willing to go, I could talk Mum and Dad into footing the bill.'

'That's very generous of them. But I really don't need one. I'm sure if I keep slogging away things will fall into place.'

She splashed water on her face and towelled it dry. 'But that's the point – things don't just fall into place. You have to get out there and make them happen.'

'That's what I'm doing.' He came up behind her and put his arms around her waist. The thin silk of her nightdress was soft against his skin, hinting of the more alluring softness underneath. 'And if you tell me to put it out to the universe, I'll have to deal with you as I see fit.'

His cock grew hard as he hugged her body against his. She struggled out of his grip. 'Don't, I'm not in the mood.'

He dropped his arms. 'So you're angry at me because I won't go to a life coach.'

'It's not just that, you're so stubborn, you won't listen to anybody. You think you know it all.'

'That's not true, I – '

'I'm tired, I'm not in the mood for an argument.' She got into bed and burrowed down under the sheets.

Reuben gave an exaggerated sigh. 'Not in the mood for sex, not in the mood for an argument, you used to be such a fun person.'

She didn't reply and in a couple of minutes she was asleep, hunched in a ball with her back to him. Reuben lay awake staring into the darkness. It was the first time she'd rejected his advances. Was it a significant milestone? Did it happen in all marriages? Surely not after two-and-a-half months.

But at the moment he had a more pressing problem. He wished he'd never set foot in the Edinburgh Arms and that he'd never run into Frank Cornell. Could he pretend he hadn't, that it was all just a bad dream?

He saw Lucy lying on the floor of her home, eyes frozen in horror, neck sliced by a deep gash and rivers of blood streaming onto her chest. Or dumped in a dingy alley amongst the industrial bins, as lifeless as an abandoned doll, a gunshot wound to her head. No, damn it, he couldn't pretend ignorance.

***

When he awoke, he felt as if he'd been churning round all night in a giant washing machine. But at least he'd come to a decision.

'What are you doing today, honey?' Carlene asked. She was back to her normal self, rifling through her wardrobe for the hundredth time as she tried to decide what to wear to work.

'Just the usual – slay a few dragons, ravish a few maidens, then after breakfast I'll do the really exciting stuff.'

'Like vacuuming?'

'I was thinking more along the lines of the usual job searching, but vacuuming sounds more fun.'

Carlene stepped into a black skirt, wiggled it over her hips and zipped it up. Then she turned back to the wardrobe and peered into it again, as if expecting some item of clothing she hadn't seen before to suddenly manifest itself.

'I'm sure a man of your capabilities could do both in one day,' she said, slipping on the first blouse she'd taken out of the wardrobe and buttoning it up.

'Oh shit!' Reuben remembered he'd decided to start jogging today. He bounded out of bed, pulled on shorts and a t-shirt, laced up his joggers, picked up his keys and gave his startled wife a smacking kiss on the lips.

'Going for a run. See you tonight.'

'Can you pick up some steak for dinner?' she called after him.

The morning was overcast and a bitter August wind whipped around him. He picked up his pace to stop himself from freezing solid. As he took a circuitous route around the suburban streets, faces peered at him from front yards or from the windows of passing cars. His aching legs and burning lungs diverted his attention from his woolly head. He was now a bona fide member of the panting, red-faced, masochistic fraternity he had disparaged until yesterday when he'd decided to join them. Joggers, he'd always maintained, were ruining their bodies and would end up in middle age with dicky knees and shin splints. And if it were so enjoyable, why did they always look as if someone was shoving a hot poker up their backside?

As he burst in through his front door and collapsed in a sweaty heap on the bed, he realised both those points were irrelevant. At this rate he'd die of agony before middle age and having a hot poker shoved up his backside would at this moment be a welcome respite.

He forced himself off the bed, showered and dressed. Over coffee and toast he considered his decision – if 'decision' was the right word. It was a wimpy imitation of a decision, borne not from courage but desperation and cowardice. He had to let Lucy know her life was in danger. But not by telling her outright – which would put his life in danger – and not by giving her enough information to justify her going to the police. He had to let her know in a subtle way that she should be careful.

He didn't have a clue how he was going to do it. He was tempted to take the easy way out and send Lucy an anonymous warning letter. But that would attract attention and undoubtedly police involvement. He'd have to do it in person. His next appointment with her wasn't until next Tuesday, so he had a week to figure it out. And hope to God Frank didn't do anything before then.

10

'How are you today, Reuben?'

'Fine, thanks.'

Lucy gave him a quick glance as she fired up the computer. 'You look tired. Are things okay with you?'

He couldn't argue with her first comment. Thinking about his appointment today and what he was going to say had kept him awake – that and Carlene's snoring, which according to her, was a figment of his overactive imagination. In the end, he reminded himself of one of the maxims of his previous career: success depended on knowing when to plan and when to wing it. And this was a time to wing it.

Lucy, on the other hand, was looking delicious in a fresh white blouse and rose pink, hip-hugging skirt. Crisp yet soft at the same time, like a strawberry donut topped with cream. But whereas overindulging in donuts could make you sick, with Lucy, you'd just keep wanting more....

'I'm okay. I guess the strain of looking for work is catching up with me.'

Jesus, cut the self-pity crap.

'But there's some good news. I enrolled with a promotions agency and did an audition. The manager thinks she can get me some modelling work.'

Lucy raised an eyebrow. 'Really? That's something ... different.'

Why the hesitation? Did she think he wouldn't make it as a model? For one of the few times in his life he felt self-conscious. He shifted in his chair.

'I suppose it is. It's a starting point, though.'

'Of course it is. Don't get me wrong, I think it's great, you never know what it will lead to. It's certainly not something I can see any of my other offenders doing.'

Was that a compliment or not? Then she smiled at him, warmth shining from her eyes like the sun glancing off the ocean. His heart almost burst out of his chest. *I'll take it as a compliment.*

She asked him a few more routine questions then reached for her appointment pad. 'You seem to be going fine, I'll make an appointment for another two weeks.'

He watched her print the date on the appointment slip. *Say something now. It's your only chance.*

'You know, in another life, I'd like to have been a parole officer.'

She looked up. 'Really?'

'I think it'd be interesting – all the different types of people you meet.'

'That's certainly true.'

'And some of them must be dangerous – not the sort you'd want to meet in a dark alley.'

Lucy handed him the appointment slip. 'Dark alleys aren't promising places to meet anybody.'

As he signed the slip, he said with studied casualness, 'So I suppose you have to be really careful not to expose yourself.'

Whoops, Freudian slip.

'I mean, you'd have to avoid situations where you could run into those dangerous types.'

She looked at him as he handed her back the appointment slip.

'Is there a point to this conversation?'

There was a cool edge to her tone. *You've blown it. She thinks you're an idiot.*

But I've got to keep going. I'd rather her think me an idiot than be dead.

Reuben mustered up his most charming smile. 'Not as such. Not really a point. It's just that I know a lot of offenders hate the so-called "system" - not me, of course - and that includes parole officers, and I assume you have to be extra careful in case one of them decides to ... er ... get really nasty.'

She tore out his copy of the appointment slip and handed it to him. 'I really don't think there's any need...'

'The reason I brought it up,' he interrupted, an idea suddenly flashing into his mind, 'was that I read the other day about this case in the U.S. where a guy had a grudge against his parole officer and he hired a hit man to run her down. Did you hear about that?'

'No, I didn't.'

'That made me wonder if the same thing could happen here.'

Jesus, you're making it sound like a threat. She'll report you now.

'That's why I was concerned,' he finished and smiled again to reassure her that hiring a hit man was the last thing on his mind.

'I appreciate your concern,' Lucy said, 'but I don't think you should lose any sleep over it.'

She gave him a curious look. 'Unless you have some specific information.'

Reuben shook his head. 'No. Just thought you'd be interested in the case.'

She stood up and he did likewise. 'See you in a fortnight,' he said.

He was out the door and about to close it when Lucy said, 'Reuben!'

He turned back, heart racing. She suspected something, was going to demand he give her the information.

'Where did you read about it?'

Reuben looked thoughtful. 'I think it was on the internet, maybe one of the online newspapers. Was it in California? Or maybe it was Alabama.' He shrugged. 'I forget which state.'

'Thanks,' Lucy said. 'See you next time.'

***

When he arrived home, a large brown packet was sticking out of the letterbox. He pulled it out, unlocked the front door, went inside and flopped onto the couch. The packet was from Pizzazz Promotions; presumably it contained his photographs. He sat staring at it, reliving his interview with Lucy.

It had been pointless, had achieved nothing, apart from making her think he was weird. When it came to the crunch and she'd asked him if he had any specific information, he couldn't tell her. Anyway, if he had no idea how Frank planned to do the deed, how could he warn her? *Just to be on the safe side don't go anywhere after dark, avoid sidewalks, city streets, crowds, uninhabited places – in fact, just lock yourself in the house and don't answer the door.*

What now? He opened the packet and slid out the photos. Apart from the inevitably contrived look of studio photos, they were good, enhancing the boy-next-door demeanour that had been the backbone of his success, the type a woman could take home to her mother – except Nancy, who would remain unmoved if George Clooney appeared before her and started grovelling at her feet. Reuben automatically sucked in his stomach as he looked at the photos taken of him shirtless. He'd started doing sit-ups as well to tighten his stomach muscles – one hundred every afternoon. Just as boring and painful as his morning jogs, but mercifully, much shorter. The things you had to do when you wanted to be in showbiz.

He hadn't heard from Posie in the week since he'd registered. There was no way he was going to be ripped off, like Carlene's friend, and become just another name in the database. He'd ring Posie every week until she got so sick of him, she'd give him a job to shut him up.

He got up and went to the phone on the kitchen bench. The orange message light was flashing. He pressed the play button.

'This is Kurt from the employment agency. Ring me on...' A mobile number followed.

The voice was vaguely familiar but he didn't know anyone called Kurt. Maybe he was new, a replacement for Droopy Dave. Maybe Reuben had caused Droopy Dave to go on stress leave, a 'positive outcome' indeed.

He dialled the number. 'Littledick. You're prompt. An admirable quality.'

Reuben's skin prickled. How the hell did Frank Cornell get his phone number? It was listed under Carlene's maiden name of Rutherford, as she'd organised the phone connection before he was released from prison. And he had an inkling that Frank wasn't phoning to invite him out for a friendly drink.

'I have a business proposition for you.'

'I'm not in the market for a business proposition at the moment,' Reuben said. 'But thanks for the offer.'

'I guarantee you'll be interested in this one.'

'Why is that?'

'It's not something I can discuss on the phone. Meet me on Sunday, at 2pm, at The Grosvenor in the city. Public bar.'

11

The radio alarm blared into the morning silence. Reuben reached out and fumbled for the 'off' switch. What day was it? Saturday. Thank God. He'd forgotten to switch the alarm off last night.

'Are you going for your jog?' Carlene mumbled into his shoulder.

'No, I'm giving myself the weekend off.'

'Good.'

She pressed her warm body into his back, slipped her arm under his and began to circle her fingers in his chest hair. 'So what are your plans for this morning?'

'I don't have any.' Her fingers moved down to his belly with feather-light strokes. 'But I do now.'

He turned over onto his back, pulled her down to him and they kissed – a slow, lazy kiss, that got his nerve endings pinging and his cock springing to attention.

'I thought,' Carlene murmured when they came up for air, 'we could go shopping later.'

'Keep talking dirty to me, baby. I love it.'

She was stroking his pubic hair now, her fingers almost on his cock. He caressed her breasts and circled her nipples, watching them grow hard.

'What are we shopping for?'

She giggled and gave his cock a playful tug. 'You should know better than to ask a woman that. I have a couple of birthday presents to buy. And a few things for the barbecue tomorrow.'

'What barbecue?'

'The family's coming over for lunch. I'm sure I told you.'

'You might have, but I don't remember.'

Her fingers stopped. 'Why, what's the matter?'

'Nothing.'

'Yes, there is.'

'Honestly, there isn't.'

She removed her hand from his cock and propped herself on her elbow, looking down at him. 'Something's up, I can tell. Don't you want them to come?'

He sighed inwardly. 'It's not that at all – it's just that I have to meet a friend in the city at two o'clock.'

'What friend?'

Reuben resented the implication that it wasn't possible for him to have a friend that Carlene didn't know about. Never mind that it was true. Before he went to jail he'd had lots of acquaintances, but few he could call friends. Those he had known who weren't on the wrong side of the law had dwindled away after he was charged.

'A friend I went to school with. His name's ... Finn.'

'Oh. You've never mentioned him before.'

'I hadn't heard from him for years then he rang me yesterday out of the blue. He lives in Sydney, he's in town on business and we organised to meet for a drink tomorrow afternoon. I didn't know about the barbecue.'

'Invite him along then we can all meet him.'

Reuben racked his brains. 'The thing is, he's not feeling very sociable at the moment. He's just gone through a horrible divorce and he's very depressed. If he came to the barbecue, he'd probably cry all the time and make everyone else depressed.'

'It sounds like he needs some counselling.'

'I'll suggest that to him. Now, where were we?'

He reached out to take her hand. She drew it away, looking pointedly at his deflating cock.

'I think the mood's gone. For both of us.'

She jumped out of bed, went into the ensuite and turned on the shower.

Reuben laid back on his pillow watching the steam fog the shower door. *Fuck you, Finn. Or Frank. Whoever!*

***

Despite her assertion that the barbecue was to be 'nothing fancy,' Carlene spent the morning cleaning the kitchen and preparing salads and dips while Reuben hosed the patio and degreased the barbecue.

He'd lied when he said he didn't mind her family coming. Not a week went by when he and Carlene didn't visit her family or were visited by them, usually for dinner or a barbecue. At first, he thought it a quaint, cosy custom – as a child, there were just him and his mother. According to his mother, Reuben's father, an occasional lover with itchy feet and a shady past, had vanished into thin air after she broke the news of her pregnancy and she'd never heard from him again. Reuben had yearned to be part of a big, close-knit family like *The Brady Bunch* or *The Waltons*.

As he grew up, he'd come to realise that families were nothing like those on TV, and the bigger they were, the more likely there was to be bickering, fights and even estrangement. But still he held on to his romantic notion of family and after jail, the prospect of any family life at all was inviting. But the appeal had worn thin, even after only a few weeks. There were times he felt suffocated; other times he felt the burden of obligation.

At least this time he'd have an excuse to escape early. Disturbing as the excuse was – a brick of apprehension had been lurking in the pit of his stomach since his phone conversation with Frank. What business could he and Frank possibly have in common? Unless Frank wanted Reuben to set up some sort of scam for him, there was only one other thing – or rather, person – they had in common. He tried to put the thought out of his mind, scrubbing the barbecue so hard that he put a hole in the scourer and took a layer of skin off his middle finger.

The family arrived all at once, filling the house with noise and bodies and clatter. Nancy immediately took over the kitchen. Jo tried to convince a sceptical Indya that Uncle Reuben didn't have cable TV so she couldn't watch 'The Wonder Years', while dabbing at a glue-like substance leaking from Brayden's nose. Alec and Wayne hovered near the barbecue, Wayne regaling Reuben with barbecue horror stories about exploding gas bottles and singed eyebrows.

When the food was ready, they served themselves in the kitchen and sat outside squashed around two small outdoor tables. Reuben and Carlene's patio, in keeping with the rest of their home, was tiny – just a narrow rectangle of pavers under an awning, with a built-in brick barbecue at one end. The backyard, in comparison, was quite large – Reuben didn't understand why the renovators couldn't have made the patio much bigger, also resulting in less lawn to mow.

As they ate, Carlene brought up the subject of Finn, his unfortunate circumstances and why Reuben had to rush off soon to meet him.

'Poor guy, how terrible!' Jo said. 'He should join a men's group.'

'Lot of namby-pamby stuff if you ask me,' Alec said.

'Would you prefer that he spent all his time at the pub instead?' Nancy asked.

Alec gave an elaborate wink around the rest of the table. 'Is that what you think I'd do if you left me, dear?'

The look she gave him was clear. Don't think for one moment I'd give you the pleasure.

'I'm with Alec on that one,' Wayne said. 'I knew a guy who went to one of those groups. He said all they did was sit around, eat pizza and complain about what bitches women are!'

'Just like the pub,' Alec said.

'Finn's an unusual name,' Jo said. 'Why did they break up?'

'I don't know, he was too upset to tell me.'

'Maybe his wife was having an affair,' Jo said.

'Or maybe he was having an affair,' Carlene said, 'and she threw him out.'

There were more questions and speculation, especially from Carlene and Jo, to which Reuben either professed ignorance or made things up. He was soon feeling sorry for abandoned Finn, whose life was being dissected by a bunch of people he'd never met. He looked at his watch. One-thirty.

He jumped up. 'I'm running late, can I take your car, honey? It'll be quicker than the scooter.'

'It needs to be filled up, it's almost empty,' Carlene reminded him.

No time for a petrol detour. He'd take the Barbiemobile and hope for an opportune parking space. He was almost at the front door when Indya called out, 'Uncle Reuben, you said you'd take me for a ride on the Barbiemobile!'

'Some other time, Indya.'

'That's what adults always say,' Indya whined, 'and some other time never comes.'

'I'll take you for a ride very soon,' Reuben said, knowing he'd regret that promise.

He rode as quickly as he dared into the city. The Sunday afternoon traffic was steady but flowing freely. The Grosvenor was near the City Botanic Gardens, and of course the few on-street parks were full. In desperation, he slid into a loading zone outside a dingy Thai restaurant.

A stiff wind whipped papers and leaves around his feet as he strode the block to The Grosvenor. Despite the stream of people ambling along the streets, the city had a desolate, Sunday afternoon air about it. He entered the public bar with a minute to spare.

Frank was sitting at a corner table talking to a beefy, tattooed man with a rat's tail. Rat's Tail gave Reuben the once-over as he approached the table, then heaved himself up and ambled off.

Reuben sat down. Frank downed his schooner and placed the empty glass in front of him. 'I want you to help me get rid of the bitch.'

Reuben swallowed. 'What do you mean - get rid of?'

'Don't act dumb, Littledick, I'm not sending her on an all-expenses-paid holiday. I'm talking permanently.'

'Right. So you want me to help you kill her.'

It was even more horrifying now he'd said it out loud. Frank grinned. 'You got it!'

'But why?'

'I've already told you why.'

'I mean, why me?'

What Reuben really wanted to say was, 'Why don't you hire one of your thugs, like the one who killed Eddy Teddy?' But he thought it prudent not to divulge what he knew of Frank's past.

Frank made a noise of exasperation. 'Do I have to spell it out? You have to report to her, you can turn on your pretty-boy smile and your charm, and get information from her and find out her movements. You're the perfect man for the job.'

Reuben took a deep breath. 'And I've already told you I'm not interested.'

Frank reached into his inside jacket pocket, took out an A4-sized envelope and tossed it on the table. 'Tell me again after you've seen these.'

He got up and went to the bar. Reuben opened the envelope and emptied out the contents. Four colour photos, ten by eight. A familiar figure in each. Carlene standing outside the front door of her office building, below the sign announcing 'Moondream Foundation – Not For Profit Fundraising.' She was facing the camera, handbag slung over her shoulder, obviously about to go out on an errand or leaving for the day. In the next photo she was in a department store beside a rack of dresses, holding one out on a hanger. Then in their front carport getting out of the car, her skirt rucked halfway up her thigh. And finally, unlocking the front door of the house, a bag of groceries in one hand, her hair escaping from its ponytail.

Reuben laid the photos on the table and stared dumbly at them. Frank returned with two schooners and placed one in front of Reuben.

'So, what do you think?'

'Who took these?'

Frank looked at him levelly, his eyes giving away nothing. 'I have friends everywhere, not just in the police force. Good quality, aren't they? He usually does weddings and christenings – not much of a thrill factor, though.'

'So you've hired someone to follow my wife and take photos of her. Why?'

Frank leaned forward. Reuben caught a whiff of cologne and stale beer. 'It's obvious you need a little persuasion to see the light. So here's the deal. You help me get rid of the bitch, or you'll come home one day and find your beautiful wife has disappeared. God knows what will happen to her – there are some really nasty people out there. Such a pity, she's a hot little number.'

Reuben looked away. He couldn't bear to look at Frank's smug expression. For one crazy moment he wanted to call Frank's bluff – he pictured himself standing up, saying calmly, 'Sorry, Frank, no go' and walking out.

But his backside was stuck firmly to the chair. Would Frank really carry out his threat? It was menacingly non-specific, just that Carlene would disappear and something nasty would happen to her. Kidnapped? Tortured? Killed? Or all three? Frank was set on killing Lucy, so what was one more woman in the scheme of things?

It all boiled down to a choice – who would Reuben rather see dead? Lucy or Carlene? Any normal person would choose his wife over his parole officer. But if that normal person had a parole officer like Lucy ... Why couldn't it be Merle who'd cancelled Frank's parole?

Reuben stared at the untouched schooner Frank had bought him. He was damned if he was going to accept a drink from a low-life who was coercing him to take part in a murder. He had principles.

Frank drummed his fingers on the table.

'You haven't left me much choice,' Reuben said.

'Excellent, Littledick, I admire your decisiveness.'

He grinned, revealing stained teeth with a glaring gap at the bottom. Nothing shouted 'criminal' more than bad teeth. With all the money he was supposedly earning from property deals, the least he could do was shout himself a new set of choppers.

'This is what I want you to do. Follow her for a week – find out where she lives, when she leaves for work and when she gets home. I want to know what sort of car she drives and where she goes after work and on weekends.'

'How can I do that without her seeing me?'

'That's your problem. You're a smart bloke, you can work it out! And I want photos. Her house, her car, everywhere she goes.' He nodded towards the photos. 'Like those.'

'That's a pretty tall order. What if she catches me taking photos of her?'

Frank shrugged. 'That's easy. Don't get caught. Because if you do, you're on your own. I'll deny any contact with you. It's one crim's word against another's.'

He tapped his watch, a clunky, busy-faced Rolex.

'You're wasting valuable time sitting here when you could be out there right now, perving on her.'

For a start I don't know her address. But Reuben thought it better not to argue the finer details.

Frank took out his wallet, pulled out a card and threw it across the table at him. 'Phone me when you're done, Wednesday week at the latest. And when you call, no names. Just Operation Luce End.'

He grinned again. 'Neat name, eh?'

Reuben didn't answer. Frank pushed his chair back and stood up.

'Just a minute,' Reuben said, 'have you thought of looking up her address on the electoral roll?'

Frank gave him a look that would have felled a death adder about to strike. 'Do you think I'm a complete idiot?'

There was no satisfactory answer to that question.

'She's not in the phone directory or the electoral roll.'

That figured. She wouldn't want unsavoury types tracking her down.

'I'll look forward to your call, Littledick.'

He strode out, Rat's Tail joining him at the door. Reuben picked up the shiny, gold-embossed business card. 'Frank Cornell, Mercantile Imports. Property developer and business consultant.' A mobile number but no business address.

Reuben sat for a few moments, replaying the conversation in his head. He looked down at the table. The photos were still there. So was the schooner. He touched the glass; it was still cold. He picked it up and took a large gulp. Fuck his principles. He finished the drink, but it did nothing to ease the overwhelming feeling of having fallen into a dark, murky hole, trapped like a wild animal, from which there was no escape.

And when he got back to his parking spot, a council officer was standing next to the Barbiemobile scribbling out a ticket.

12

Talk about your life changing in an instant. It was a cliché; something from a book cover blurb or movie trailer. When he woke up this morning, he was a trying-to-go-straight conman whose greatest challenge was finding a job. Now he was a would-be killer, about to stalk and take photos of his victim; an innocent woman who was trying to help him.

Carlene was hunched into a ball under the covers, snoring. He rolled over on his stomach and buried his head in his pillow, but one question pinged around his mind like a ball in a pinball machine.

He'd told Frank that he'd given him no choice, but was that true? Any sensible law-abiding person would go straight to the police. But he couldn't trust the police not to stuff things up, and he couldn't expect them to protect him and Carlene from Frank. There was no way he wanted to call Frank's bluff when it came to Carlene's life, let alone his own safety – even the thought of being beaten up filled him with terror. He was taking the coward's way out.

Then it occurred to him. There was another option. Go along with Frank's plan, but somehow make sure it didn't succeed. How, he had no idea. But it would buy him some time to figure out what to do – how to save Lucy's life and his own as well. It was risky. Foolhardy. Full of holes. But it was all he had.

He woke up with a dull headache and the doona twisted and knotted around his legs. Carlene was already up, dressed for work and brushing her hair in front of the mirror. She glanced over at him.

'You had a restless night, tossing and turning. And you were moaning again.'

Her tone was accusing, as if he'd deliberately had a bad night just to annoy her.

'Sorry, honey. I had a nightmare about being in prison again.'

It was a cheap trick to get some sympathy, but it worked. She came and sat on the edge of the bed, and stroked his forehead.

'You poor thing,' she said softly. Her perfume was delicious and her hand was soothing. 'You haven't been yourself lately.'

'Haven't I? Who have I been?'

She gave him a playful slap. 'You know what I mean. You've been distracted these last few days as if your mind is on another planet.'

She bent over and pressed her cheek against his. 'You know what I think, baby? I think you're suffering from post-traumatic stress disorder, from coming out of prison. I've been reading about it and you have the symptoms – being detached from others, easily distracted, lack of ambition.'

'So that makes it a diagnosis? There were guys inside who had PTSD and compared to them, I'm as together as the Pope. Anyway, I don't lack ambition, I just haven't found anything I want to be ambitious for.'

'There's no need to be defensive, it's quite normal under the circumstances. I think you need to see a psychologist.'

'I don't need a psychologist. Even my parole officer says so.'

She took her hand off his forehead and stood up. 'All right, but just listen to yourself and you'll realise what I'm talking about.'

She stomped out. Even her ponytail was stiff.

***

How the hell could he follow Lucy for a whole week on a pink motor scooter without her noticing? It was impossible – even following her for a day would be stretching it. Could he hire a private detective to do it for him? It would be the ideal solution, but they didn't come cheap and he didn't have that sort of money to splash around.

He was on the homeward part of his morning jog, digging deep for a burst of last-minute speed, when the germ of an idea appeared in his mind. By the time he stumbled in through the front door it had grown into a fully-fledged plan. He showered and dressed, made coffee and toast, and sat down at the dining table with pen and paper.

- Follow Lucy home one afternoon after work to find out where she lives.

- Take photos of her and her home.

- Invent a weekly schedule for her.

- Take photos of the places she supposedly frequents.

- Superimpose images of her arriving at and leaving these places.

Thank God for Photoshop. With a bit of knowledge and experience, it was easy to manipulate photos to your exact requirements; and with such a smooth, professional result that the average person would never guess they weren't authentic.

It was a stroke of good fortune that Reuben happened to be experienced in the art of photoshopping due to a travel scam he'd operated some years ago – an online travel company that sold bogus guided tours. He'd obtained photos of a number of popular holiday destinations and superimposed images of tour members beside the company tour coach: smiling and waving, sipping cocktails on a palm-fringed beach, feasting on a seafood banquet and relaxing on a yacht on a dazzling blue ocean. Of necessity, it was a short-lived scam – once the customers turned up on day one to meet the tour coach and found it didn't exist, the game was up. By then the travel company had, overnight, ceased to exist, and Reuben decamped with a handsome profit.

As he mulled over the finer details of his plan, a bolt of energy surged through him. It was a familiar feeling from what seemed forever ago – the excitement of knowing you were breaking the rules, tinged with apprehension or even dread, knowing you could be caught. But that only added to the challenge and the thrill of it. Only this time, if Frank found out he was being scammed, there was a lot more at stake than a stint in prison.

***

Reuben entered Joe's Café with helmet in hand and backpack slung over his shoulder. A man was behind the counter wiping the coffee machine – short and paunchy, with grey wispy hair arranged untidily over his shiny head.

'Yes, mate?'

'A double-strength espresso, please.'

A stiff Bourbon would be preferable, but hopefully the extra caffeine would give him the jump-start he needed, as his adrenalin had deserted him. He sat at a corner table and ran over the plan in his mind. He'd phoned Lucy before he left home on the pretext of checking his next appointment time, to make sure she was at work, then parked the Barbiemobile in the small car park behind the café. It presented a clear view of the parole office car park next door. For the hundredth time, he mentally listed the contents in his backpack – had he remembered the lipstick? He unzipped the side pocket of his backpack and stuck his hand in. His fingers curled around a cylindrical shape. Thank God.

His coffee appeared in front of him. 'Double-strength, knock your shoes off,' the man said, nodding and smiling.

Didn't he mean socks? He had a heavy Mediterranean lilt, so maybe it was a foreign saying. He was right anyway, it was strong enough to knock your shoes off. Reuben put in four sugars to counteract the bitter taste.

Nina appeared at the counter from the rear of the shop.

He waved. 'Hi, Nina!'

'Hullo.' She stopped then came out from behind the counter.

'Were you having an afternoon tea break?' he asked.

'No, I was cleaning the kitchen.'

'Oh. Doesn't sound like much fun.'

Dumb thing to say. His normal conversational brilliance had deserted him.

'No,' Nina said. She hesitated. 'Are you still looking for a job?'

'I sure am.'

'There's one going here as a kitchen hand. Ours walked off the job yesterday.'

Reuben had tried a stint as a kitchen hand in prison, but after he cut his finger, bled into the mashed potato and had to be rushed to hospital for stitches, he'd been taken off kitchen duty. On the outside, it would be different though. Being paid, for a start.

'Great. When do I start?'

'Not so fast. I need to ask you a couple of questions.'

'Ask away.' He pulled out a chair for her and she sat down, clasping her hands on the table. She had a serious intensity about her, as if she were weighing up everybody and everything around her. He wondered what it would take to make her laugh.

'Have you done kitchen work before?'

'No. But I'm a fast learner.'

'The work isn't difficult, but Uncle Joe's very particular that everything is done just right.'

She nodded towards the counter. 'That's him. He owns the place.'

The short man was in voluble conversation with a customer at the counter while preparing the coffee.

'And I have to warn you, he's got a bit of a temper.'

Reuben smiled at her. 'Are you trying to put me off?'

'No, just giving you fair warning. There's something else I need to know.'

She studied her hands then looked up. 'I've seen you go into the building next door.'

Her face gave nothing away but her eyes were watchful.

'So you've been spying on me? I don't know whether to be flattered or not.'

She shrugged. 'I just happened to notice, that's all.'

'And you assumed I wasn't visiting the accountant?'

'I didn't assume anything. I'm asking you because a lot of those people come in here and some of them are off their faces. If you're doing drugs, I'm not interested.'

'Tell me, Nina, do I look like I do drugs?'

She hesitated. Reuben glimpsed the thick, satiny plait that snaked down her back. Undoubtedly it was part of the job regulations to have her hair tied back, but it didn't flatter her – it made every feature of her face appear larger and sharper, from her heavy eyebrows down to her elfin chin. He imagined her hair let loose, thick and lustrous, tumbling over her bare shoulders...

'No,' Nina said. 'But appearances can be deceptive.'

'In this case, they're not.' He could think up a convincing lie, but he lacked the will to do it. 'I'm on parole for fraud. I'm not allowed to have a job where I'm handling money. But apart from that, I'm a fine, upstanding citizen.'

He was gratified to see the hint of a smile. Aim for a smile first, then a laugh.

'Save your breath for Uncle Joe. He's the one you have to convince.'

She got up, went to the counter and said a few words to her uncle. He nodded, finished serving the customer and approached Reuben. He held out his hand. 'Joe Scarparo.'

Reuben stood up and shook his hand. 'Reuben Littlejohn.'

Joe's handshake was powerful and despite his corpulence, he emanated raw strength. He wrenched out a chair and sat down.

'Reuben,' he said, stretching the name out and rolling it round his tongue. 'That is a strange name.'

'Yes. Do you know how hard it is to buy a coffee mug with my name on it?'

'My heart bleeds for you. So you are looking for a job.'

'Yes.'

'And you have no experience as a kitchen hand.'

'That's right.'

'So why should I hire you?'

His eyes were the same shiny caramel as Nina's, nestled in shadowy pouches that made him look as if he never slept. But they radiated a vitality that belied his worn-down appearance.

'Perhaps you need a challenge.'

Joe threw back his head and laughed. It rumbled from deep down and erupted like a volcano.

'I tell you, boy, that's the last thing I need. But Nina said you are okay and you make me laugh, so I give you a go.'

'Thanks very much Joe, I appreciate it.'

'Don't thank me. You'll be working your arse into the floor. None of this disappearing outside every hour for a coffee or cigarette.'

'Nina warned me you were a slave driver.'

'Did she indeed?' His face softened and he looked over at Nina, who was taking an order at the counter. She glanced at Joe and he smiled at her.

'She is too serious, my little Nina. I don't blame her, she's had a tough life but she needs to laugh more.'

'I'll see what I can do,' Reuben said.

Joe's eyes flickered over Reuben's wedding ring. 'Stay away from my niece, you hear? You have a wife?'

'Yes.'

'Show me her photo.'

'I don't have one with me.'

Joe looked at him with raised eyebrows.

'You don't carry a photo in your wallet?'

'No.'

He produced a battered wallet from his back pocket and snapped it open at a portrait photo. A young couple beamed out – a dark-haired young man resembling a young Sylvester Stallone and a blonde, pixie-faced woman with gentle eyes.

'My wife passed away ten years ago. But this photo never leaves me.'

He closed his wallet and slid it back into his pocket. 'Do you have children?'

'No.'

'We weren't blessed with children. Don't leave it too late, that's my advice.'

'Thanks.' Reuben checked his watch. 'I have to go. When do you want me to start?'

'Tomorrow morning, seven-sharp. You'll be working seven to three, Monday to Friday. And I insist on punctuality.'

'Of course.' Reuben gave an inward sigh. It seemed that early morning starts were unavoidable in a regular job.

'We will sign the papers tomorrow. Ciao.'

On his way out, Reuben leaned over the counter and said to Nina, 'Thanks for recommending me. I got the job.'

'I didn't recommend you.'

'Even better, I got the job on my own merits. See you tomorrow!'

Slinging his backpack over his shoulder, he walked out and down the street to a group of shops in the next block. A sign pointed to the restrooms down an alleyway between a DVD rental store and a Chinese restaurant. He paused outside the Ladies, listening. Silence. He opened the door and peered in. The three cubicles were empty. He went into the nearest cubicle and closed the door.

He opened his backpack and pulled out a pile of clothes and a blonde curly wig. He did a nervous pee, undressed to his jocks and slipped on a long, floral skirt. He'd had to guess his size, as trying it on in the dressing room of the pre-loved clothing shop was not an option. Even so, pretending he was buying the clothes for his wife earned him a suspicious look from the sales attendant. The skirt was a bit tight around the waist, but bearable if he pulled his stomach in. The blouse, in a green and black swirl design, just fitted. A hearty laugh might burst some buttons, but that wasn't a likely event. Over the blouse he pulled on a pink and yellow spotted jacket, which he'd chosen for its deep pockets, and slipped his camera into one of them.

Then he took the blonde wig and fitted it carefully over his head, fluffing out the curls. It was hot and heavy, and looked as much like natural hair as a wig bought from Crazy Tony's Warehouse. Which it was. He surveyed his face in the small hand mirror he'd taken from Carlene's make-up bag, along with the lipstick. He'd shaved just before leaving home – not that he expected anyone to get close enough to notice his complexion under his helmet. But it was important to get right into the role.

He stretched his lips out the way he'd seen women do, and applied the lipstick. After testing all the lipsticks in Carlene's considerable collection, he'd decided that Ruby Rose was the most flattering for his colouring. Shit, his lips appeared lopsided, he looked as if he'd had a stroke. He tore off a piece of toilet roll, wiped off the lipstick and started again. It was vital to get it right – nothing shouted 'drag queen' more than crooked lipstick. And he didn't want to be a drag queen, he wanted to be a real woman. He'd figured it was the only way he could follow Lucy home – if, despite his best efforts, she noticed a pink motor scooter trailing her, she wouldn't recognise him in his disguise and a woman would be less likely to arouse her suspicion.

A door screeched, footsteps clacked in and the cubicle door beside him opened and closed with a bang. He heard the rustle of clothing then the rush of urine into the toilet bowl. Reuben held his breath, feeling like a toilet voyeur. The stream of urine trickled to a stop and his neighbour tore off some toilet paper. Why was he holding his breath? It would be obvious to her there was someone in the next-door cubicle. Reuben ripped off several more bits of toilet paper, rattling the holder loudly, so she'd know he wasn't doing anything untoward.

He finally achieved a reasonable job with the lipstick and checked his face again. His complexion looked sallow; maybe he should have packed blusher. He wouldn't say he was the most attractive woman he'd seen, but he certainly wasn't the ugliest. He stuffed his jeans and shirt into his backpack and waited for his neighbour to leave. When he heard the restroom door bang shut, he donned a huge pair of sunglasses, also from the op shop, opened the cubicle door and ventured out.

He gave himself a final once-over in the mirror. Talk about an op shop fashion tragic. But there was something missing from the woman staring back at him. She had no breasts. How could he, tit lover and connoisseur extraordinaire, have forgotten his own? Too late now.

The restroom door swung open and a large woman swept in, almost bowling him over. 'Sorry,' he squeaked in his best soprano and hurried out. He tried to take small feminine steps, but it was difficult in boots and he was aware that they looked incongruous with the rest of his outfit. But wearing high heels or any feminine footwear while riding a motor scooter was courting disaster.

He reached the carpark behind Joe's Café without incident, walking with his shoulders hunched forward to hide his pitiable lack of bosom. He looked at his watch. Four-thirty. He hoped Lucy hadn't left early. How was he going to hang around inconspicuously for the next thirty minutes? He leaned against the Barbiemobile, opened his backpack and rummaged around in it, as if he were looking for something. He wished he hadn't given up smoking – at least it would give him something to do.

He heard footsteps and glanced behind him. A man in a business suit was approaching. He shot Reuben a curious look and his top lip curled as he opened the door of the Audi parked nearby. The Audi purred into action, backed out and passed him on its way to the exit. The man was staring at him in the rear-view mirror. Reuben's mind flashed back to the time at university when the theatre company had put on a spoof of Hamlet called Spamlet. Reuben had played the part of Ophelia Balls. He had the audience in tears of laughter just by being himself; albeit a larger and more outrageous self. It was scary, yet exhilarating, to discover that his real self was a woman with a penchant for drama and drowning herself.

Think Ophelia Balls. As the driver reached the exit, Reuben gave him the finger and watched with satisfaction as he braked suddenly, almost mowing down a man on a pushbike, who yelled at the driver and gave him a double whammy of the finger.

Noise in the next-door car park diverted Reuben's attention. Three women were strolling through, chattering and laughing. The woman on the far side was Lucy. Reuben's heart raced. The group split up, with cries of 'Bye! See you tomorrow!' as they went to their cars. Lucy's auburn hair glinted in the pale sun. Watching women as they walked, he often became aware of the individual parts of their body – buttocks swinging, breasts bouncing, arms pumping. But Lucy moved with precision and grace, all parts of her body in tune with each other. He wondered if she'd been a dancer, could see her in a tutu, arms curved above her head, slim muscled thighs tensing under the stiff frills...

He whipped out his camera and using his zoom, took a couple of shots of her from the back, side-on and getting into her car, a silver Mazda 2. He pocketed the camera, put on his helmet, slung his backpack onto his back and started up the motor. Lucy had already pulled out onto the road, so he exited the car park and out into the traffic directly behind her. He made a mental note of the number plate. As they turned into Gympie Road, he pulled back and allowed another car to go in front, so he could still keep an eye on her without being too conspicuous – or as inconspicuous as a blonde in a skirt and boots riding a pink motor scooter could be.

Despite the bite of afternoon coolness in the air, it was hot under his wig and helmet, and sweat soon dampened his face and neck. Thank God there was no wind – he'd had visions of his skirt billowing out and getting caught in the wheels, exposure being the least of his problems.

Progress was slow in the peak hour traffic. Children's faces slid by plastered against car windows and bus passengers smirked down on him from their lofty superiority. He ignored them – he was used to being stared at on the Barbiemobile.

By the time they got to Aspley, he was two cars behind. He couldn't see her indicate and suddenly she was in the left hand lane to turn down Webster Road. Reuben slid into the lane in front of a shiny green ute, smiling and waving at the driver, who just looked bemused and shook his head. He was now three cars behind and had to crane his head to keep her car in sight. The wig was making his head itch and it was murder not being able to scratch it.

He followed Lucy through a succession of streets in suburban Aspley. Boys played football on a sports field, parents watching from the sidelines in director's chairs, people walked their dogs and a couple of teenage boys on skateboards played chicken with the traffic. The car in front of him turned off and he suddenly found himself directly behind her. That wasn't supposed to happen - what was Plan B? He didn't have one, wasn't even sure he had a Plan A.

He slowed down and dropped back a few yards. Lucy's indicator flickered and she turned right. He puttered up to the street. The sign said Elm Street, No Thru Road. He couldn't follow her now; it would look too obvious. He continued straight ahead, glancing down Elm Street as he passed it. It was a short U-shaped street with three parking bays in the middle. He saw Lucy's car turn into the driveway of the fourth house on the left. He'd give her a few minutes to get out of her car and into the house, then take a quick drive down the street.

He continued down the road for a couple of blocks and stopped in front of the Henry Mitchell Park. It was a patch of brown-tinged grass the size of a large backyard, boasting two faded picnic tables under a group of scraggly gums. If he were Henry Mitchell, he'd be insulted to have this piece of ground named after him.

After ten minutes, he headed back. He imagined by now she'd be in her house, cooking dinner or perhaps having a shower. *Don't think about her having a shower.* He turned into Elm Street. An old man watering the front garden of the house on the corner stared at him. A child's muffled shouts and a dog's yap floated towards him from the other side of the street. The fourth house on the left, number eight, was an unpretentious brick home with a double lock-up garage set in a small square of lawn. Much like all the other houses on the street. Obviously parole officers didn't earn as much money as he'd thought. How disappointing that Lucy didn't own a house that matched her loveliness. He felt a rush of tenderness – that was part of her allure, that she was so normal and down-to-earth.

One of the garage doors was open and Lucy's car was parked in it. Reuben looked around quickly. The street was quiet and no one appeared to be watching him. He paused in front of the house and took a couple of quick shots of it and her car. Then he took off to the end of the cul-de-sac and made a U-turn. As he zoomed up the street, a small furry bundle rushed out onto the road in front of him. He braked and swerved to his left, hit the kerb and bounced off the seat.

As he sailed over the handlebars, his only thought was, 'for fuck's sake hold on to your skirt.' He hit the ground headfirst, arms flailing as he tried in vain to keep his skirt from flying up. He lay on the footpath, winded, pillowed by his backpack. A chilly breeze tickled his bare thighs and he tugged his skirt down over them.

'Muttley, come here! Naughty dog!' a woman's voice said, followed by a child saying, 'Mummy, the lady fell off.'

Reuben sat up. A dumpy woman in a tracksuit and ugg boots was hurrying towards him, a grubby-faced urchin trotting behind her. Muttley stopped and looked back, tongue lolling, as if laughing at the devastation he'd caused, then continued sedately down the street.

'I'm so sorry,' the woman said. 'Are you all right?'

Reuben nodded. It hurt when he breathed and his left arm was sore where he'd fallen on it. He wiggled his toes within his boots and tensed his calf muscles. All good, he wasn't paralysed. He hauled himself to his feet. The woman stepped forward and put out her hand to help him. He batted it away.

'I'm fine, thanks,' he said, but it came out as a muffled squeak through his helmet. The woman looked uneasy and stepped back.

'I really am sorry; it's all Cooper's fault. I've told him before not to chase the dog on the street.'

Cooper peered at Reuben from behind his mother's legs. She swung around. 'And you get on home, boy!' she shouted. 'Or I'll give you the biggest walloping you've ever had!'

Cooper took off, little legs pummelling the pavement. Reuben brushed himself down, smoothing the skirt over his legs, and hoisted his backpack into position. The woman was staring at his chest. He looked down. A button had popped off his blouse and a tangle of hair peeped out through the gap. Fuck. He pulled his blouse together, although there hardly seemed much point now, and stepped over to where the Barbiemobile lay on the side of the road.

He picked it up and inspected it. Apart from a dent and some scratches on the front mudguard and a bent mirror, it looked okay. A gate clicked. A ruddy-faced old man stood in front of them holding a can of beer, resting it on his protruding belly like a shelf. Reuben's hand went to the gap in his blouse.

'You all right?' the man growled.

'Yeah, *she's* fine,' the woman said, looking him up and down.

Reuben nodded and smiled at the man. As he mounted the Barbiemobile, his skirt rucked up, revealing an expanse of hairy leg.

'Holy Jesus,' the man said.

Reuben rearranged his skirt and turned the ignition. *Please let the engine start.*

The man shook his head and clicked his teeth. 'Never thought I'd see one of them in me own street.'

'Now you've seen everything, hey, Ralph?' the woman said. She looked across the road and waved. As the engine spluttered into life, Reuben looked over. Lucy was standing at her front gate. In her arms was a curly-haired toddler in a jumper and pink overalls, and they were both staring across the across the road straight at him.

Reuben revved up the Barbiemobile and took off in a spray of gravel. Muttley sat at the end of the street, his furry face slit in a self-satisfied grin as he continued to ignore the entreaties of his owner. Reuben kept an eye on him as he rounded the corner, then put his foot down and sped off.

All the way home his mind oscillated between two thoughts. *Surely Lucy didn't recognise me, not in this get-up,* and *She has a child! I didn't expect her to have a child. Maybe she was minding it for someone else.* But he knew it was hers from the way she held it and it clung to her; as if they belonged to each other.

As he neared home, he realised he needed to find another public toilet. Arriving home in drag would do little to convince Carlene he was not suffering from post-traumatic stress. Scanning his surrounds, he concluded there was a notable lack of secluded public toilets where a person could change sex without fear of scrutiny. He pulled into a Hungry Jack's two blocks from home. It was buzzing with families and groups of teenagers. He found the rest rooms, squared his shoulders then opened the door of the

Mens. He almost collided with a lanky youth coming out, who did a double take and said, 'Hey, Mrs, the Ladies is next door.'

Head down, Reuben made a beeline for the nearest cubicle and slammed the door. His body sighed with relief as he peeled off his wig and clothes, and stepped back into the familiar comfort of his jeans and shirt. He wiped off his lipstick with toilet paper and stuffed everything back into his backpack.

He left the cubicle and took a quick look at himself in the mirror. The corner of his mouth was still smudged with lipstick. He wiped it off with his hand. In the mirror, his eyes met those of a burly, bushy-haired man standing at the urinal. He looked as if he wrestled bulls for a living. The man pursed his lips and made a smacking kiss in Reuben's direction.

'Hey, sweetie, I got something you could put those gorgeous lips around.'

He rubbed his hand back and forth across his crotch. Reuben was tempted to retaliate with a scathing remark. *Not a good idea to upset him – especially if he sees you make a getaway on a pink motor scooter.*

Reuben buttoned his lip and made a quick exit.

13

He stashed the backpack in a corner of the garage behind a pile of empty boxes, making a mental note to collect it at the first opportunity and consign the contents to the nearest Lifeline bin.

The aroma of frying onions greeted him as he entered the house. Carlene was in the kitchen stirring something in the electric frypan. Reuben put his arms around her waist and kissed her cheek.

'That smells fantastic.'

She pulled away from him and swung around. Her mouth was tight. It jolted him back to the look on his mother's face when she'd arrive home from a double cleaning shift at the hotel, to find that Reuben hadn't done his homework or cleaned his room.

'I don't know what you were brought up to believe, but these days it's supposed to be an equal sharing of the housework. And when one partner isn't working, it's not unreasonable for the other to expect them to cook dinner occasionally.'

'I'm sorry, I went for a ride, I had to get out of the house. And don't bring my mother into this.'

'I didn't even mention your mother.'

'You mentioned my upbringing and as there were only me and my mother, by association you did.'

Carlene waved the spatula in the air. 'Jesus, Rubie, get a grip, I'm not criticising your mother! Anyway, you told me you brought yourself up – "yanked myself up with fast talking and fast women" were your exact words.'

It was true – if you counted Joanne, the silicone-planted, peroxide blonde from Elite Escorts as a fast woman. She'd relieved him of his virginity at the age of fourteen in exchange for a couple of tickets to the Bon Jovi concert at the Entertainment Centre, which of course, turned out to be fake. And if you counted all the girls he'd had in high school – if they weren't fast women then, they were rapidly heading towards that goal.

'Anyway, you'll be glad to hear I've got a job.'

She paused in between throwing slices of beef into the pan. 'I'm scared to ask what it is.'

'I'll save you the trouble. It's a kitchen hand at Joe's Café, next door to the parole office, so I can call in for appointments after work.'

Over dinner Carlene thawed out in the heat of Reuben's enthusiasm for his new career, a supreme test of his acting prowess.

'I guess it's a start. It's just that I keep imagining you coming home with a finger missing.'

'What's a finger or two between friends?'

He leaned forward and planted a lingering kiss on her lips. 'Come to bed and I'll ravish you while I'm still able-bodied.'

As they lay in each other's arms in post-coital somnolence, the image of Lucy standing at her front gate popped up before Reuben. Not only did he have to share her with a husband, whom he pictured as a nerdy, boring intellectual, but also a child. Changing nappies, wiping sticky hands and cleaning up vomit were not congruent with being a goddess. But the more he thought about it, the more he convinced himself that motherhood added to her appeal. It gave her a warm, earthy depth; another dimension to her sensuality. He knew from conversations with women and his own observations, that motherhood changed them in a profound way – brought their emotions closer to the surface, made them more vulnerable. And vulnerability was a great turn-on.

Carlene was snoring. She tightened her arm around him and flung her leg over his body. He moved away a little and managed to loosen her grip without waking her. If Operation Luce End was successful, Frank would be depriving a child of its mother. He was also depriving a husband of his wife, but whereas a man could find another wife, a child could never find another mother. There was always Lucy's husband, of course, but a father, no matter how devoted, was a poor substitute for a mother's love.

Now there was another life for which he was responsible. When he eventually drifted off to sleep, he dreamt that Lucy was riding topless on a ferris wheel, pert breasts pointing skywards. As she swung down to the ground, he tried to run to meet her. But his backpack was full of rocks and he couldn't move, and he watched helplessly as she was lifted up into the air again.

***

He'd just parked in the car park behind Joe's Café when a battered Volkswagen pulled up beside him and Nina got out. She watched him take off his helmet.

'Nice scooter.'

'Thanks,' Reuben said. 'It's only temporary until I can afford to buy myself a car.'

'Oh? I'm disappointed.'

'Why?'

'I thought you'd be a bit of a rebel and deliberately buy a pink motor scooter to make a point.'

'What point?'

She shrugged. 'Whatever point you like.'

'What if I told you I bought it as a promotion for breast cancer research?'

'I wouldn't believe you.'

'What if I told you I won it in a church raffle?'

She laughed. 'Now I know you're bullshitting me.'

Her laugh transformed her face in an instant – it was warm and exotic, like the Mediterranean he imagined was her heritage. He saw her in a long, flouncy dress, her hair fanned out down her back, laughing, dancing, whirling round and round, absorbed in the joy of the moment.

She took a couple of hairpins from her pocket, wound her ponytail into a makeshift bun and pinned it onto her head. Reuben realized he was staring and looked away.

'Come on,' she said, 'Uncle Joe will be getting antsy.'

He followed her in through the back door. *Wait till I tell Joe I've already made her laugh.*

There was no chance of that. Joe was in a full-length white apron grating carrots at the workbench. He tapped his watch. 'You are late. It's one minute past seven.'

'Sorry.'

'Sorry's not good enough.'

Nina shot Reuben an 'I told you so' expression before disappearing into the front of the café.

Joe pointed a half-grated carrot at Reuben. 'I saw you talking to Nina. I warn you again, stay away from her.'

'We were just having a conversation. I'm not out to seduce her, I'm happily married.'

'That may well be so, but sometimes things happen if you don't watch out. My good mate Charlie, he came out from Malta the same year I did, he had a chain of storage warehouses, very successful business and a beautiful home in Ascot. He had an affair' – he grimaced as he emphasised the word – 'with his office manager and ran away with her. His wife was furious and took him to the dry cleaners.'

Reuben had a vision of the hapless Charlie being sponged, steam-pressed and hung on a rack wrapped in plastic.

'Then his mistress left him for another man and now he's living alone in a one-bedroom unit and working for the same company he used to own! Charlie, I say to him, you shit in your own bed, now you have to lie in it!'

Joe slammed the last bit of carrot against the grater as if imagining it was Charlie's head he was mashing into pieces. 'Don't just stand there, boy! There's a pile of lettuce over there to be washed and chopped!'

After Reuben had washed the lettuce, he separated the leaves and dried them in the salad spinner. It made a satisfying whirr as he turned the handle, and reminded him of the octopus ride at the Royal Show. Was it true that plants had feelings? He imagined the lettuce leaves huddled together in terror inside the spinner as he turned the handle faster and faster.

'What are you doing?' Joe yelled above the noise. 'Trying to take off?'

Reuben placed the lettuce leaves in a heap beside the chopping board, picked up the terrifyingly large, shiny knife and began to shred the lettuce. Joe stood beside him, shaking his head.

'Mother of Jesus, where did you learn to chop like that?'

He pushed Reuben aside and took the knife from him. It flew over the chopping board in a blur of silver, in its wake a pile of neatly shredded lettuce.

'I finish this,' he said. 'You unpack those boxes in the corner. Later I teach you how to chop like an expert. It's all in the movement of the wrist.'

He made a limp gesture with his thick hairy wrist. 'It should be easy for you young fellows – what do you call yourselves? Met, metero....'

'Metrosexuals?'

'That's it!'

'I don't consider myself metrosexual,' Reuben said. 'And anyway, they're not limp-wristed.'

'What are they, then?'

'They're guys who have some feminine qualities but they're not gay. Some wear eye make-up, for example...'

A look of disgust flitted across Joe's face.

'And their wrists are probably more supple than limp.'

'Whatever they are, it's not right. Men should be men and women should be women. If Nina brought home one of those fairies, I'd shove his lipstick up his arse.'

Lipstick. It was still in his backpack, stashed in the garage. He must remember to bring the backpack with him tomorrow and get rid of the clothes on the way to work. And return Carlene's lipstick to her make-up case.

'Don't stand there in a daze, boy! Get back to work!'

By the end of the day, Reuben had learned that in Joe's parlance, the term 'kitchen hand' was a synonym for general dogsbody. He did everything from unpacking supplies to washing dishes and mopping the floors. The cafe catered only for the breakfast and lunch crowds and shut at four pm. The menu was basic – a choice of half a dozen dishes for breakfast and lunch, as well as the usual sandwiches, rolls and hot takeaway foods. As the dining area only consisted of about a dozen tables, most of the orders were for takeaways.

In between his other tasks, Reuben made sandwiches, warmed up pies and quiches in the oven, and presided over the deep fryer. In his first attempt at French fries he forgot to set the timer, resulting in a pile of charred remains beneath a cloud of smoke.

'Holy smoke!' Joe yelled at him, seemingly unaware of his pun. 'Are you trying to burn the place down on your first day?'

After that, Reuben became obsessive about checking the timer to make sure it was on and peering into the deep fryer every few seconds, as if it were likely to trick him and burn the fries again if he left it alone.

As he placed the last dish on the drying rack he looked at his watch. Five to three. Damp with perspiration, he sighed with relief. When was the last time he'd looked forward so much to knock-off time? This was how it was going to be. One day after another, longing for knock-off time as soon as he arrived. He splashed cold water on his face and sank down on an upturned milk crate in the corner.

Joe burst in from the shop. 'Move your arse and bring me those onions. I teach you now how to chop.'

'But I thought three o'clock was my knock-off time.'

'You thought wrong, boy. The only way you're going to learn is to practise. You will chop till you drop.'

Reuben was about to protest again then thought better of it. He fetched a bag of onions and placed it on the bench. Joe took one and peeled the skin off. With a flourish of the knife he cut it in half, then in half again.

'Now watch. The point of the knife stays resting on the board and you just move the blade along, while your other hand controls the food.'

In a series of swift movements, he'd reduced the onion to a pile of tiny pieces. Then he moved aside and held the knife out to Reuben.

Reuben took the knife and an onion, peeled it and began to chop the way Joe had shown him. But he couldn't keep his onion together and it collapsed into a pile of uneven pieces.

Joe shook his head and clicked his teeth. 'Hold the onion firmly, it won't bite you! And go a bit slower to start with until you get it right. Here, try another one.'

Reuben didn't fare much better with the second one. Joe shook his head as Reuben scrabbled around on the floor picking up the onion pieces.

'You need lots of practice.' He nodded towards the onion bag. 'You can do the rest before you go home.'

He disappeared back into the shop. The onion bag held at least another two dozen onions. What could Joe possibly want with so many chopped onions? Reuben gritted his teeth and dumped the bag next to the chopping board.

Nina came in, handbag slung over her shoulder.

'Still at it?'

'Not through choice, I assure you.'

'I warned you he was a slave driver.'

'You did, and about his temper too.'

'He's got a good heart, you know. He's all smoke and no fire.'

'That's not exactly a tactful analogy right now.'

'Sorry.' She didn't look at all sorry. 'See you tomorrow.'

***

Carlene was huddled on the living room couch with the phone to her ear. Her conversation petered out as he came in. Her eyes were red-rimmed. Had her boss been giving her a hard time? He was one of those employers who took out his stress on everyone around him. Reuben leaned over and kissed her forehead.

'I'll call you back, Jo,' she said and pressed the 'off' button. 'You stink of onions.'

'Sorry, I chopped so many onions today I feel like I really know them now.'

She looked at him as if he were an ugly and dangerous species of insect.

'What's the matter?'

She burst into loud sobs. He went to put his arms around her, but she sprang up from the couch and pushed him away.

'Leave me alone, you pervert!'

She flounced out of the room. What was going on? He'd been called plenty of unflattering things over the years, but never a pervert. His stomach gripped as he thought of Lucy. Had he talked in his sleep, called out her name? But surely Carlene would have said something this morning.

She returned to the living room, holding an object in front of her at a distance, as if it were infectious. His backpack. Oh, fuck. Why hadn't he got rid of its contents straight away?

Carlene dropped it on the floor in front of him.

'Well?'

She had her hands on her hips, tears running down her cheeks. Whatever you say, I won't believe it, her expression said.

'How did you find it?' Reuben asked, stalling for time. As soon as the words were out of his mouth he realised they incriminated him even more.

'Why does it matter how I found it?' Her voice verged on hysteria. She took a deep breath. 'If you must know, I was getting some boxes from the garage to lend to a girl at work who's moving house, and it was there. Not hard to find at all, almost as if you wanted me to find it.'

What the hell did that mean? Of course he didn't want her to find it. Obviously he couldn't tell her the truth – a dozen possible explanations flashed through his mind, but none that was remotely feasible.

He sank onto the couch. 'What can I say?'

'The truth would be a start.'

He shook his head. 'You wouldn't believe it if I told you.'

'Try me.'

Her eyes were hard with suspicion, as if she expected him to throw off his clothes then and there to reveal frilly underwear and stockings. He shrugged and looked down at his hands.

The couch sagged and Carlene was beside him. Her arms engulfed him and she pressed her cheek against his.

'Baby, you can tell me, I promise I won't laugh. I know you've been under a lot of pressure, trying to find work and adjust to life on the outside. We can work through it together.'

Her eyes were pleading, but in their depths lurked something else. Was it panic? Or fear?

'It's ... difficult to talk about.'

'I know, honey.' She hesitated. 'How long have you been doing it?'

'Doing what?'

'Don't play dumb. Dressing up in women's clothes.'

'Not long.'

She gripped his shoulders. 'I'm going to ask you something and I want you to be completely honest with me.'

'I'll try.' As long as she didn't ask him if he was taking part in a plan to kill his parole officer. Or if he fantasised about other women, or was associating with unsavoury characters....

'Do you .... are you ... you know ... attracted to men?'

Reuben was so relieved he burst out in a loud guffaw. 'Christ, no! I'm as red-blooded hetero as they come. You of all people should know that.'

She permitted herself a tight smile. 'I know, but you hear all those stories about what happens in jail, and when I found the clothes, I naturally thought there's a whole side of you I know nothing about.'

Reuben took Carlene's hand. 'Look, it isn't anything to get upset about. I didn't harm anyone. To tell you the truth, I got the urge to dress up but when I actually did, it wasn't that exciting. In fact, I can tell you for certain I'll never do it again.'

'How do you know for sure? I've looked it up on the internet, and the men who do it say they can't help themselves, it's part of who they are and if they deny it they feel miserable.'

'I'm not one of those men. When I took those clothes off and stuffed them in that backpack, all I felt was a huge relief.'

'You didn't go out in them, did you?'

'Of course I didn't! What do you take me for? An exhibitionist? I just wandered around the house and went out into the yard and scared the magpies.'

From her expression it was clear that doubt and the desire to believe him were waging war in Carlene's mind. Reuben drew her to him and planted soft kisses on her cheek.

'Promise you'll tell me if you get that urge again,' she whispered.

'I already said I won't but, okay, I promise I'll tell you the minute I even think about trying on your underwear.'

'That's not funny.'

Reuben continued to kiss her, moving down to her neck.

'And that was my favourite lipstick you took. I wondered where it had gone – never would I have dreamed that my own husband had stolen it.'

'I'm sorry, honey.'

His mouth moved back up again to hers and she responded. He could always win her over with his kisses – women had complimented him on his kissing technique. He picked her up and carried her into the bedroom.

***

Reuben's second day at work consisted of hours of unrelenting labour in a cramped kitchen with little ventilation, and an overriding odour of stale cooking oil and boiled cabbage. An exact replica of the first day. The boiled cabbage odour was a mystery, considering no cabbage was cooked there. Perhaps the smell was ingrained in the walls from a previous era. Not surprisingly, there were no onions to be chopped. When Joe wasn't around, Reuben opened the back door to take in a lungful of fresh air.

At three o'clock, he washed his hands and got ready to knock off. Joe appeared at his elbow.

'Not so fast, boy, I want that bag of carrots and celery chopped before you go. Practice makes perfect.'

'But I have an appointment at three-fifteen.'

He had an appointment with Lucy, but he wasn't about to disclose that to Joe, not being sure whether Nina had told him about his being on parole.

'You'd better get started then.' He winked at Nina, who had just appeared in the doorway.

'I'm going, Uncle Joe.'

'All right, my sweet. Do you have college tonight?'

'Yes.'

'I'll keep you some meatballs.'

'Don't go to any bother, I'm going to the library after lectures. I'll fix myself a sandwich when I get home.'

Joe wagged his finger at her. 'You're burning the candle too fast, young lady. It's not good for you, and you can't live on sandwiches.'

'Okay, save me some meatballs,' Nina said.

Reuben rolled his eyes at her. Joe whipped around. 'What are you looking at?' he thundered. 'Get to work!'

It was three-twenty when Reuben finished chopping enough carrot and celery to feed an army of vegetarians. Joe tapped his watch. 'Three minutes, that should have taken. I think you're a lost cause, boy.'

He made a quick exit before Joe could conjure up another chore, and apologised to the receptionist at the parole office for his lateness.

'That's okay,' she said airily, 'Lucy's running late with her appointments anyway.'

It was a different receptionist today – young, with a fluffy mass of blonde curls. She looked too innocent and untarnished to be in her job. 'Five minutes late is nothing, we're happy if you actually turn up on the right day.'

She leaned forward with a conspiratorial air. 'Don't say I said that.'

'My lips are sealed.'

The waiting room was standing room only. Reuben found a spare bit of wall to stand against; next to a young guy in dreadlocks and board shorts who was sitting on a chair with his girlfriend sprawled across his lap. Slim and tanned, she wore the most micro of miniskirts. He ran his hands constantly over her body, making her giggle, and every few seconds their lips locked.

The other occupants of the waiting room looked away but kept an eye on the couple's antics in their peripheral vision. Except for a greasy-haired, pimply-faced youth sitting across from them, who was staring right up the girl's skirt.

'Hey mate,' Dreadlocks said. 'Keep your eyes to yourself.'

'It's a free country, mate. I can look wherever I like.'

'Really? Where'd you get that idea?'

'Tell your missus to stop flashin' it then.'

Dreadlocks tensed, his veins rope-like on his arms. His eyes glinted. 'Get off,' he said to his girlfriend. She jumped off, smoothing down her tiny skirt in a pointless gesture. Dreadlocks advanced towards Pimples and stood over him.

'Get up and say that again.'

Pimples scrambled to his feet, hands out in front of him. 'Steady on, mate, it was a joke.'

'Some fuckin' joke...'

'Ben, calm down!' The receptionist glared at him through the glass. There was nothing innocent or untarnished about her now. 'If you start anything, the police will be here in two minutes.'

Ben clenched and unclenched his fists. His arm muscles twitched with the supreme effort of not knocking Pimples out. He gave Pimples a malevolent look and turned away. 'Come on,' he said to his girlfriend.

'We're going out to have a smoke,' he told the receptionist.

'Good idea,' Pimples said.

'Don't push your luck, Josh,' the receptionist said.

'Jesus fucking Christ,' Josh said as he sat down again. 'The guy's a maniac.'

'What do you expect at the parole office, mate?' said a skinny, greasy-haired man. 'It's worse than the loony bin.' He wore a t-shirt with the words 'Trainee gynaecologist. Volunteers wanted for oral exam.'

There was a wave of sniggers. Reuben had watched the episode with a feeling of deja vu. He'd encountered many like Ben in prison, their stance and their swagger containing a simmering anger that boiled over to rage at the slightest provocation. On the one hand he empathised with them, knew that the anger had come, in many instances, from being beaten, neglected and abused; and that they knew no other way of dealing with it except to inflict the same punishment on others.

Conversely, he was also contemptuous of them, of their inability to rise above their upbringing and their circumstances. It was a contempt born of fear, fear of being hurt. A fear he'd lived with every day in prison, that he'd risen above because he could act as if he didn't give a shit and make them laugh in the process.

It was a fear he'd succeeded in forgetting about since his release, except when he encountered guys like Ben. And Frank Cornell. They brought it all back with a chilling vividness.

The door of the far interview room opened. 'Reuben, come in.'

Lucy flashed him a quick smile as he sat down. Her face was paler than usual and there were shadows under her eyes. Had her child been ill? Or perhaps she and her husband were having marriage problems. He felt buoyant at the thought. He saw himself envelop her in his arms and bury his face in her soft hair smelling of apples and sunshine. He'd soothe her and tell her it was all okay because he would look after her. And he'd kiss her perfect shell of an ear, and it would taste so divine he would have to keep going, down her neck, into the hollow of her collarbone; she had the sexiest collarbone he'd ever seen...

He was aware she'd said something. She was looking at him half-reprovingly, like a teacher who'd caught her favourite pupil daydreaming.

'Sorry,' he said, 'I'm tired, it's my new job.'

He held out his hands. 'Look at them, almost worn to the bone.'

'Welcome to the world of earning an honest living.'

Her smile took the sting out of her words, but before he could stop himself, he said,' If that's earning an honest living, no wonder there are so many criminals around.'

Shit. In the list of Worst Things to Say to Your Parole Officer, that would have to be number one.

'But I'm not about to go out and commit more offences,' he added hastily.

Only if it means saving your life, of course.

She clasped her hands together on the desk. Her gold wedding band glinted under the fluorescent light.

'I know that what you're doing now doesn't afford a lot of job satisfaction, but it's a step in the right direction. Perhaps you should look at doing a course of some sort.'

'Droop - I mean, Dave at the employment agency, was looking into that for me. I've never been much into study though.'

'What you did or didn't do in the past doesn't have to dictate your future. If you're going to succeed, you have to be able to break your old behaviour patterns and try new things.'

She sounded like Carlene. He had a vision of the two of them with their heads together, plotting and planning his future. But it was easier to forgive Lucy; it was her job after all.

As she wrote out his appointment slip, he had a premonition of what it would be like reporting to the parole office if Lucy were dead. Being questioned and lectured at by someone else, his life dissected by a complete stranger. Of course, Lucy was a stranger when he met her but only in theory – in his mind she'd always existed. Perhaps he'd have to report to Merle again. Yet another incentive, if he needed any more, to stop Frank from killing Lucy.

As he stood up to go, Lucy said, 'By the way, I couldn't find a report anywhere about that parolee hiring a hit man to kill his parole officer.'

'Really? That's strange.'

'Not recently anyhow. There was a guy in Arizona who made threatening phone calls to the parole office, said he was going to skin his parole officer's cat and hang it from a tree in the main street. But that was five years ago.'

'Maybe that was it,' Reuben said. 'I might have got the story a bit mixed up.'

'But the funny thing was,' Lucy said, 'his parole officer didn't own a cat.'

Reuben smiled and shook his head. 'There're some crazy people around, aren't there?'

14

'Where have you been?'

Carlene watched him with her hands on her hips as he brought the groceries in from the car and placed them on the kitchen bench.

'You know where I've been. At the supermarket.'

'You took two hours to get three bags of groceries?'

'I like to check all the prices, make sure I get the best value.' He busied himself putting away the groceries. 'And I had a coffee while I was there too.'

It was half true. He'd had a coffee while shopping, but had done it all in fast forward mode in the last half hour, battling the Saturday morning crowds. He spent the first one-and-a-half hours driving to various locations, taking photographs of Lucy's imagined haunts from the list he'd painstakingly created.

Carlene didn't answer but her silence was accusing. She'd been acting strangely during the few days since the backpack incident. He'd caught her on a few occasions staring at him while twirling her fingers through her hair, and once he'd come upon her in the bedroom with his mobile phone, scrolling through phone numbers.

She flushed. 'Just looking for the number of Pedro's Pizzas.'

'You haven't got it,' she added unnecessarily, placing the phone back on the bedside table.

She'd also resisted all sexual contact, pretending to be asleep when he came to bed, curled up with her back to him. She lay perfectly still as he kissed her goodnight, her body tense with the effort of not moving a muscle. Last night he'd caressed her neck and chest and slid his hand down to her nipples. They betrayed her by hardening under his touch and she removed his hand. Admitting defeat, he turned over and went to sleep.

There was a knock at the front door. It opened, followed by a 'Hullooo!' Reuben recognised the voice. Why did Jo even bother to knock?

'We're on the way home from ballet. I brought some bun loaf.'

She barrelled in but stopped when she saw Reuben in the kitchen. She had Brayden on her hip chewing on a ratty blanket, and Indya beside her in a pink tutu and satin ballet slippers, looking too angelic to be true.

'Hi Jo.' Reuben greeted her with a kiss. She stiffened and turned her head away. Carlene made coffee and they sat on the patio to have morning tea. Jo avoided eye contact as she passed him the plate of bun loaf. He was about to ask her what the problem was, when Indya, fixing Reuben with her most melting gaze said, 'Uncle Reuben, will you take me for a ride on the Barbiemobile?'

Before Reuben could reply, Jolene said, 'I don't think so, sweetheart, Uncle Reuben's very busy.'

Indya looked at Reuben sitting back on his chair with his feet up on another, stuffing bun loaf into his mouth.

'No he's not. Are you, Uncle Reuben?'

'You haven't got a helmet,' Jolene said.

'I have, Mummy, I put it in the car!' Indya said triumphantly.

An undecipherable look passed between the two women.

'I'm sure she'll be fine,' Carlene said. 'Rubie's a very careful rider.'

'We have to go now anyway.' Jolene sprang out of her chair and picked up Brayden, who was dribbling half-masticated bread onto the table leg. 'Come on, Indya.'

'I'll never get to ride on the Barbiemobile,' Indya wailed.

'How about we call into McDonalds on the way home and get a chocolate sundae?' Jo said.

'I don't want a chocolate sundae, I want to go for a ride with Uncle Reuben!'

Jo bundled Brayden and a still-protesting Indya into the car, kissed Carlene goodbye and shot Reuben a cold look. Indya's stormy face was framed in the car window as Jo drove off.

'What's eating Jo?' Reuben said.

'What do you mean?'

'Surely you noticed it. She treated me as if I were a piece of dog shit she'd just stood in.'

'I'm sorry she was so rude, I'll have a talk to her.'

'What have I done to deserve that treatment?'

Carlene shut the door of the dishwasher. She picked up the sponge from the sink and dabbed at a coffee mug ring on the bench.

'I told her about finding your backpack.'

'Jesus ... why?'

'I was out of my mind with shock and worry, I had to talk to someone.'

'Are you telling me that's why she's pissed off at me?'

'It mightn't be such a big deal to you, Rubie...'

'I don't see why it has to be a big deal for Jolene. It's got nothing to do with her.'

'She's my sister and she's concerned about me.'

'That's very touching but it still doesn't explain her attitude. And what was with her not wanting to let Indya come for a ride with me? Have I suddenly turned into a child molester?'

Carlene looked down at the bench again, rubbing at the coffee stain that was no longer there.

'Jo thinks that any man who dresses up as a woman is a pervert and capable of anything. I've tried to explain to her...'

She faltered. A cold wave of shock hit Reuben with such force, it took his breath away. Child molester. The words he'd tossed out rashly in anger echoed in his head.

'Well, that's just fucking great, isn't it? My wife thinks I'm a transvestite and my sister-in-law thinks I'm a paedophile. Why don't you call the cops right now and put me back inside?'

'Rubie, don't be like that.' Carlene put her hand on his arm and stroked it. 'I don't think you're a transvestite. I know I've been a bit distant lately, but you've got to understand it was a big shock. But I've been thinking a lot about it and I've decided it's just the stress you're under at the moment, starting a new job. People cope with stress in different ways. I met this lady once, at a fundraiser for Friends of the Mentally Ill. She told me that every time she gets stressed she goes into a supermarket and shoplifts. And you know what she takes? Condoms! And she doesn't even use them – she's in her seventies and hasn't had sex for years!'

She ran her hand lightly up and down the inside of his forearm. It set his teeth on edge.

'And I promise I'll talk to Jo – there was no excuse for her being so rude to you.'

He took her hand off his arm. 'Don't feel you have to do it on my account. I'd hate her to think she has to be civil to me when it's so fucking obvious to her that I want to molest her daughter.'

Ten minutes later, he was in the bath, the water so hot his skin was stinging, absorbed in Mandrake's battle to smash the mysterious Octopus Spy Ring. As the glamorous but dangerous Sonya confronted Mandrake, he stared hypnotically at her. In her eyes, he transformed into a skeleton and she promptly fainted. Reuben pictured himself hypnotising Jo – a skeleton was too good for her. She hated spiders and screamed even when she saw a daddy-long-legs. He'd appear as a giant hairy tarantula and she'd be out cold for days. The vision only went a little way towards displacing his anger.

The strains of the Boston Stranglers' first album, Stranglehold, blared out from his iPod speakers. They were a seventies folk/punk rock/blues band who'd had a couple of hits and sunk into oblivion. General opinion was that they'd tried to encompass too broad a range of music, but Reuben liked their discordant harmonies and underdog status.

'Poor little ole me,' rasped lead singer Kenny Wrangler. 'No one understands me, not even my dog, poor little ole me.'

**

Now that he had all the photos ready, the problem now was that he could only do the photoshopping when Carlene wasn't around. Fortunately, he was able to get a head start on it when she went to church. She was usually away for about two hours as Pastor Bryan always held a morning tea after the service.

The day was windy, grey and miserable; one of only a handful of truly cold days in a Brisbane winter. A perfect day for sleeping in.

'You're up early,' Carlene said as she kissed him goodbye. 'Seeing as you're dressed, why don't you come with me?'

Reuben shook his head. 'You can't trick me that easily. Be gone with you, devil woman!'

She gave him a pretend-reproving look. 'Seeing as you're going to be lolling around doing nothing, you can have a hot chocolate waiting for me when I get home.'

She seemed to be thawing out. He gave her a smacking kiss on the lips. 'Your wish is my command.'

As soon as he heard the car's throaty grumble, he went into the study and turned on the computer. It was really Carlene's computer, as his personal computer had been confiscated by police along with the company computers and never returned. He downloaded the photos from his camera and saved them in a WinZip file called 'Mandrake Stuff'. Carlene wouldn't bother to open the file if she came upon it. He hoped.

As the computer didn't have Photoshop, he downloaded Gimp – a similar free program – and after a quick refresher online tutorial, began work.

During the week, he'd hung around the shops near Joe's Cafe, killing time after work, until close to five o'clock when Lucy knocked off. From the car park outside the cafe, he took a few more shots of her walking to her car. It was important to get as many photos of her as possible in different outfits, to 'prove' to Frank that he'd been trailing her.

He was just putting the finishing touches to a photo of Lucy entering a building inscribed with the sign 'St Mary's Aged Care', when he heard the car pull up. He quickly saved the photo into his 'Mandrake Stuff' file, dashed out to the kitchen and turned on the electric jug. He was spooning chocolate powder into two mugs as she burst into the kitchen. Her cheeks were flushed and her eyes shone.

'You should have come, honey, it was brilliant. Pastor Bryan talked about forgiving ourselves and each other for being human because we all have flaws. And then it all clicked into place and I decided to forgive you, and I felt as if God had reached down and taken a huge load off my shoulders!'

'What exactly are you forgiving me for?' Reuben poured the boiling water onto the chocolate.

'For dressing up in women's clothes and causing me so much anguish! And I forgave myself too for not forgiving you earlier. I feel fantastic!'

'That's great,' Reuben said, handing her a mug of hot chocolate. 'And I forgive you for not forgiving me earlier. And for not forgiving yourself as well.'

'It's not up to you to forgive me for not forgiving myself,' she said pointedly. That's something only I can work out for myself.'

'Oh I see,' Reuben said. 'Well, I s'pose I should forgive myself for being so ignorant about forgiveness.'

She gave him one of her looks as she cupped her hands around her mug.

***

As he'd only done one photo and his deadline to call Frank was in three days, he decided to stay up late that night after Carlene had gone to sleep, to get a few more hours in. After they'd watched the Sunday movie cuddled up on the couch, Carlene yawned and stretched.

'Coming to bed now?'

'I'll be there soon; I'll just watch some of the late news.'

She slipped her hand under his t-shirt and stroked his chest. 'Don't be long then,' she breathed into his ear. Her breath was warm and so was her hand. She jumped up, gave a seductive pout and sashayed out.

He sat staring at the TV, hoping that Carlene would fall asleep waiting for him. This was a first – he was actually hoping not to be seduced. *This is all for you, Lucy, I'm actually knocking back sex to save your life – in a roundabout way.*

He jerked his head up with a start. Gunshots rang out and cowboys on horseback galloped across the TV screen. He looked at the clock. Five to midnight. He'd fallen asleep waiting for Carlene to fall asleep.

He got up and peered into the bedroom. A gentle rhythmic snore emanated from the hump under the doona. He went into the study, turned on the computer, opened 'Mandrake Stuff' and started working on another photo.

'What are you doing?'

He jumped and instinctively went for the minimise button. Carlene was standing at his shoulder in her dressing gown and slippers, tousled hair falling over her face. How did he not hear her come in?

'Who's that?' she demanded.

140

'I'm just practising using this new software I've downloaded.'

'But who's that woman? And why did you hide it?'

You idiot, why did you do that?

In one swift movement, she reached over, clicked the mouse and brought the photo back to life on the screen. It was of Lucy getting into her car, whom he'd transposed, with the help of some Gimp magic, from her office car park to a large shopping centre car park. Thank God Carlene hadn't met her.

'It's no one in particular, just a random photo I got off the net. I'm just having a bit of a play around.'

'But why? And why do you have to do it at two o'clock in the morning?'

'Is that really the time?' His amazement was genuine. 'I didn't mean to stay up so late. You go back to bed, honey, I'm coming right away.'

She gave him a hard look and stomped out. He saved the photo into his 'Mandrake Stuff' file, turned off the computer, undressed and got into bed. Carlene was lying with her back to him. He reached out and drew her warm, naked body closer to his. She turned over onto her back.

'What were you doing exactly with that photo?'

'I was experimenting with colour and retouching, seeing what I can do with Gimp. It's just for fun, nothing sinister, I promise.'

'I find it weird that you're doing it when I'm asleep, as if you're trying to hide it from me.'

'That's not true. You never know, if I get good at it, it could lead to a job.'

'Doing what? Airbrushing models? Making fifty-year-old women look as if they're thirty? It's dishonest, just another way of conning people.'

She turned away from him, lying on her side. Reuben reached out and ran his hand over her hip. There was something so irresistible about that part of a woman's body, the smooth undulation of her hip sloping gently into the length of her thighs. 'I wouldn't have to airbrush you, you're perfect as you are.'

His hand moved back up to her shoulder, making its way over it in the direction of her breast. She wriggled away from his grasp. 'I've got a big day at work tomorrow.'

Reuben turned over and huddled into himself to get warm. *So much for forgiveness.*

15

Over the next couple of days, he managed to finish the photos in the two-hour window he had in the afternoon, between when he got home from work and when Carlene arrived. He didn't want to risk her catching him at it again in the middle of the night. Anyone would think from her attitude that she'd caught him looking at porn.

On Wednesday afternoon after work, he rang the number on Frank's business card. It rang several times before a voice snapped 'Yes!'

'Operation Luce End.'

He felt ridiculous as he said it, as if he should be wearing a false nose and talking into his shoe phone.

'And?'

'I've got what you wanted.'

'Good. Meet me tomorrow, five-thirty pm. La Cantina Restaurant in the city.'

As Reuben lay in bed that night trying to think of an excuse for his meeting with Frank, there was a stirring beside him. Carlene leaned over him, her hair tickling his chest. 'Are you okay, honey?'

She was naked and holding up a bottle of massage oil. 'I thought a massage might help you to unwind.'

'Great. Do I get extras?'

She giggled. 'Only if you're a good boy and do as I say. Now lie on your stomach.'

She rubbed oil into his back and shoulders, her strong, assured hands kneading the knots and tension out of his muscles. It was blissful – he hadn't realised how stressed he'd been. Of course stress was all relative. Doing scams was stressful – always needing to have your wits about you, keeping one step ahead of the police, often down to your last dollar before the money started coming in, constantly moving and thinking up new ideas. But it was stress he understood and could cope with, and the rewards were worth it.

This stress was different, uncomfortable, as if he were wearing ill-fitting clothes. Finding a job, being a husband, trying to live up to expectations when he wasn't sure of his own.

As it turned out, there were extras. As Carlene kneaded her way up his thighs and added an oral component to the massage, a thought flashed through his mind. Was this forgiveness sex? Or maybe guilt sex, because she was embarrassed about Jo's treatment of him? Followed by another thought. Who cares?

***

Carlene was still asleep as he dragged himself out of bed, showered and dressed. With his early starts at Joe's Cafe he'd had to change his jogging routine to the afternoons after work, although he hadn't had time to go at all this week. And the sit-ups had gone completely out the window. He lifted his shirt and looked in the mirror – the soft roll of stomach was still there, perched on top of his jeans belt. Maybe he should just buy bigger jeans. Or only model flannelette pyjamas.

He slipped on his shoes then bent over Carlene to say goodbye. She was lying on her side, sprawled over the entire bed. The covers had slipped down to reveal her breasts, squashed in between her arms. She was so still, she could have been dead except for the faint rise and fall of her chest.

What would he feel if she were really dead? He'd be upset, of course, but it would be nothing like the pain of his mother's death, all the more potent because he hadn't realised how much he loved her until she was gone. He'd known when he married Carlene that he didn't love her, but she was sexy, well connected and crazy about him. Who could resist that combination? And in his subconscious he'd hoped that sooner or later the love would come. Only it hadn't yet.

Carlene's eyes fluttered open. 'Morning.'

She opened them wider. 'What are you staring at?'

'Just thinking how beautiful you are.'

That's so corny, you're losing your touch. But Carlene didn't seem to think so. She smiled and stretched out under the sheet, languorous as a cat. He could almost hear her purring. He bent over and kissed her on the cheek.

'I'm meeting Finn at the pub at five-thirty tonight for a drink, so I'll be home late. Don't keep dinner.'

'He's in town again?'

Carlene sat up, wide-awake.

'Just for tonight.'

'Why don't you invite him home for dinner?'

'He's already arranged to go out for dinner with some other friends.'

Carlene sprang out of bed and pulled on a robe.

'Which pub are you going to?'

'Don't know yet. He's going to ring me later today.'

She followed him out to the front door and gave him a long, lingering kiss on the lips. 'Bye, honey. Don't be too late tonight.'

He turned around to wave to her. She was standing in the doorway, a provocative smile on her face. Her robe had fallen open to reveal her naked body.

***

Joe bawled him out for his slowness, popping into the kitchen every few minutes to make sure he wasn't taking a break to breathe.

'You wouldn't have survived a day back in Malta, boy. I was up at five in the morning preparing food for my parents' restaurant before I went to school and then all afternoon washing dishes and cleaning up when I got home! And I had to do my homework as well! I was top of the class too.'

Then why the fuck are you running a cafe? Reuben wiped the sweat from his face and plunged his hands into the hot washing-up water.

Joe pointed to the rubber gloves on the shelf above the sink. 'Didn't I already tell you to put those on?'

'I can't wear them, they give me a rash.'

He'd discovered it in prison, wearing rubber gloves on dishwashing duty. His hands had broken out in itchy, red blotches that turned into sores when he scratched them. He'd been taken off dishwashing duty and put on toilet-cleaning duty, unfortunately not being allergic to toilet cleaner.

'You metrosexuals, you'll get dishpan hands, you know.'

Joe chuckled to himself as he went into the storeroom and reappeared with an industrial-sized bottle of tomato sauce. 'And, of course, you haven't filled the sauce bottles. That would be expecting too much of your delicate little hands.'

He picked up a squeeze bottle of tomato sauce from the workbench, unscrewed the top and began to fill it from the larger bottle. In his Mandrake alter-ego, Reuben conjured up a metrosexual vision of himself with kohl-smudged eyes, black fingernail polish and man purse slung over his shoulder. Slipping on a pair of fluorescent pink rubber gloves, he picked up the large bottle of tomato sauce and upended it over Joe's head. So satisfying was the fantasy that he replayed it several times and hardly felt the heat of the water on his hands.

At three o'clock, Reuben took the last tray of clean cups and mugs out to the cafe before knocking off. Joe had gone to the bank, only a couple of the tables were occupied and Nina was wiping down the others. He watched her as she sprayed cleaner on them from the bottle hooked in her belt and moved the cloth over the formica tops in ever-widening circles. Her long, smooth strokes mesmerised him.

She looked up. 'Do you want something?'

'Just admiring your graceful style. I'm a cleaning voyeur, I get my kicks watching other people do it.'

She didn't answer, moving to the next table.

'What course are you studying?'

'Film and Television.'

'Really? You want to be an actress?'

She gave him a withering look. 'The correct term is actor, for males and females. And no, I don't want to be one. I'm studying screenwriting, directing and editing.'

She looked at the clock. 'Isn't it your knock-off time?'

'So it is.' He reached into his pocket, drew out some coins and handed them to her. 'May I have a double-strength espresso?'

She gave him another look, pocketed his money and finished her cleaning. Reuben sat at a corner table. When she brought the coffee he said, 'Now you have to talk to me, I'm a customer.'

She shrugged. 'I'll give you a minute. Your time starts now.'

He pulled out a chair. 'Have a seat.'

She sat down.

'What are you hoping to do when you finish your course?' Reuben asked.

'I'd like to do it all, but so far I've enjoyed screenwriting the most.'

'Interesting,' Reuben said. 'I've just joined a promotions agency, hoping to get some ad work, or maybe as a movie extra.' He grinned. 'We could join forces, you write the movies, I'll star in them.'

'I thought you said you were a behind-the-scenes person. Although at the time I thought that was a load of crap.'

A straight talker. That was refreshing in a woman.

147

'Obviously I'm not as good an actor as I thought I was.'

'On the contrary, I think you're a very good actor. You do the sincere, charming persona very well.'

'It's not a persona, that's how I really am.'

She raised an eyebrow. 'Okay.'

'What do you mean, "okay?"'

'Nothing.' She glanced at the clock. 'Your time's up.'

She got up just as Joe was walking back into the cafe. When he spied the two of them at the table, his face instantly turned to thunder.

Reuben got up as well. 'Must be off, I've got lots to do.'

He waved a cheery goodbye to Nina and Joe and made a hasty exit. He could feel Joe's eyes burning into his back. What the hell did Nina mean by 'persona?' And the way she looked at him, as if she didn't believe that he really was sincere and charming. What did she think he was? A latent serial killer? Women! Always trying to psychoanalyse you.

***

He arrived at La Cantina right on five-thirty, satchel over his shoulder. Although its advertised opening time was 6pm, the front sliding door was open a few centimetres. Reuben stepped inside. Frank and another man sat at a corner table. The interior was as dingy as the outside and smelt of stale alcohol and cheese. Mexican parrots wearing sombreros dangled from the ceiling.

'Littledick!' Frank clicked his fingers. 'Another beer please, Gunther!' He nodded to his companion. 'Meet Bomber.'

The other man stood up and held out his hand. 'Pleased to meet 'cha.'

He was tall and rangy with a goatee beard and long grey hair tied back in a greasy ponytail. He wore white wrap-around 'happy pants', woven sandals and a tie-dyed shirt. A relic from hippydom, right down to the glaze in his eyes that suggested a fondness for cannabis. It was hard to imagine anyone who looked less like his name – although you had to admit that any man who wore 'happy pants' in public displayed a certain sort of courage.

'Likewise,' Reuben said, shaking his hand. As he sat down, a slight, dark-haired man darted over to the table and delivered Reuben's beer with a bow and a wide grin.

'Service here is next to nothing,' Frank said. He raised his glass. 'Here's to Operation Luce End.'

Bomber and Reuben raised their glasses. 'Operation Luce End.'

I don't mean it Lucy, I've got my fingers crossed.

'Now Littledick, what have you got for me?'

Reuben opened his satchel, took out a document wallet and handed it to Frank. Frank opened it, and took out a bundle of photos and a sheet of typed A4 paper, on which Reuben had neatly tabled Lucy's weekly schedule. He affected a casual air as he watched Frank perusing the paper, in contrast to his stomach, which was churning into overdrive.

Inventing Lucy's weekly schedule, imagining how a parole officer would spend her spare time, had tested his powers of creativity; and he'd done extensive research on the internet. He hoped he hadn't gone overboard with the pole dancing classes. According to his research, pole dancing was the new pilates. Women from all walks of life were signing up and they were doing it for fitness, not because they wanted to slither up and down a pole in a nightclub, in a G-string.

Pity, because Reuben preferred the latter fantasy. The night before he'd dreamt of Lucy dangling upside down from a pole in a sparkling bikini. Stuffed in her cleavage was a note, which she whipped out and handed to him with an inviting smile. He tingled with anticipation as he opened it. Was it her phone number? He studied her neat, precise handwriting: 'Your next parole appointment is at 3.30 on Thursday.'

'Pole dancing?' Frank said.

'Classy,' Bomber said, with a smack of his lips.

'It's all the rage,' Reuben said. 'All the women are doing it. Even accountants and lawyers.'

Frank smirked. 'I know where I'd like to stick that pole.'

He looked down at the list again. 'Jesus, is she ever fucking home? Monday night, yoga; Tuesday, gym class; Wednesday, pole dancing; Thursday, shopping; Friday, out for dinner; Saturday, gym class then the nursing home; Saturday night, barbecue; Sunday, picnicking at Samford; Sunday night ... where did she go Sunday night?'

'She stayed home Sunday night,' Reuben said. He'd thought it safer for her to have an active social life; to make it harder for Frank to get to her while she was at home. Her husband, whom Reuben had named Nigel, had one good point – he looked after their child in the evenings so Lucy could attend her classes. But poor Lucy, exhausted by her weekly schedule, needed to spend at least one night at home to wind down.

Frank flipped through the photos. The classes were real, their venues researched to make sure they were all within a reasonable distance of Lucy's home. Reuben had taken a photo of each venue and superimposed a photo of Lucy either entering or leaving the premises – with the surrounds suitably altered to reflect the time of day or evening. For her shopping on Thursday night, he'd created a photo of her at the front entrance of the Westfield Shopping Centre at Chermside and for extra effect, another of her browsing in one of the jewellery shops. Nigel would be too wrapped up in his own nerdy world to think about buying her jewellery or any of those other luxuries women liked.

Frank pointed to a photo of Lucy walking down the front steps of the St Mary's Aged Care Residence, a few blocks from her home. 'What's she doing there?'

Reuben shrugged. 'Maybe she has a relative in there. Or perhaps she does voluntary work there.' In his mind it was the latter – he'd included the visit to the nursing home to demonstrate her compassionate, community-minded spirit.

Not that it would impress Frank or make him change his mind.

Frank's lip curled. 'Real little do-gooder, isn't she?'

Lucy's weekend social life proved to be more of a challenge as in real life it would be unlikely she'd go out without her husband and child. Reuben found an image on an internet photo site of a man who looked similar to how he imagined Nigel – tall, skinny and bookish with glasses. There was little chance Frank had seen Lucy's husband or knew what he looked like. For their Friday dinner outing, Reuben created a photo of Lucy and Nigel arriving at Mama Spaghetti's Restaurant in Aspley; Lucy's mother having offered to babysit. Nigel would probably have droned on all night about the All-Ordinaries or economic rationalism.

Saturday night was a barbecue at a friend's house – a large brick home Reuben had randomly chosen a few streets away from Lucy's. As her poor child had not had much of a social life during the week, certainly nothing to match her mother's, Reuben had decided she'd better accompany her parents to the barbecue. He found a photo of a curly-haired toddler and inserted her in the photo, holding Lucy's hand as they stood at the front gate of their friend's home. As an extra touch, Reuben had also included the friends – a clean-cut young couple who looked as if they'd popped straight out of a TV bank ad, greeting them at the front gate with wide, pearly-toothed smiles.

The last photo was of the picnic in Samford, a popular spot in the west of Brisbane. That had been easier, as Reuben and Carlene had visited it a few Sundays ago. Reuben had taken a photo of Carlene sprawled on the picnic rug in a secluded spot they'd found – a stretch of lush grass bordered by a tangle of rainforest, a stream tinkling away behind them. He deftly removed Carlene from the picnic rug and replaced her with Lucy, sitting demurely with her legs tucked under her, hair glinting in the sun as she watched Nigel throw a ball to their daughter. The perfect 'happy family' picture.

Frank tossed the photo on the table. 'So she's got a husband and kid.'

'Yes.'

His expression hadn't changed one iota. The fact that his plan would leave a young child motherless made no impact on him.

'How did you do all this without her spotting you?'

'Disguises and different vehicles. I assure you, I was very discreet.'

Frank looked hard at Reuben. 'I hope so for your sake.'

Gunther materialised with another round of drinks then scurried away and returned with a steaming mountain of nachos, on a plate the size of a sombrero. They shuffled things around the table to make room for it.

'Dig in,' Frank said. 'If this isn't the best nachos you've ever had, I'll eat my Mexican hat.' He jerked his thumb in the direction of the kitchen. 'On the house. Gunther's an illegal immigrant. Not his real name, of course.'

He scooped a mound of meat onto a corn chip and waved it around in the air to dislodge the strands of melted cheese dangling from it. Bomber picked up his napkin and tucked it into his shirt, so it billowed out like a large white bib. The last time Reuben had seen anyone do that was Pa Kettle in the old movie *Ma and Pa Kettle Go To Town*.

'Thanks, but I'm not hungry,' he said. Nachos was usually one of his favourite meals but the spicy, cheesy aroma was making him nauseous. Or maybe it was the company. What was he, Reuben Littlejohn, doing here, plotting and planning with these cold-blooded killers?

'So, down to business,' Frank said, mopping sauce from his chin. He looked at Bomber. 'She drives a Mazda 2.'

Bomber nodded. 'Mazda's easy.'

'The plan is this,' Frank said. 'Bomber will plant an explosive in her car. When she turns on the ignition...'

He stopped for dramatic effect, undoubtedly relishing the vision of Lucy and her car being blown to smithereens. A spasm shot through Reuben, chilling him to his core.

'Bomber will have to leave the country immediately; that's why the timing is crucial.'

'How's he going to do that without being caught?' Reuben said. 'The minute the police find out, they'll have the airports on alert.'

'Who said anything about airports?' Frank said.

'Right on,' Bomber said. 'I hate flying - stuck-up hosties, screaming babies, and then you get some fat-arsed chick next to you who's always elbowing you. You can't even take a razor on board to have a shave and make yourself nice for the missus.'

He gave a self-mocking grin, exposing nicotine-stained teeth to match his fingers.

'How are you going to leave?' Reuben said. 'Swim?'

'Cruising. Much more relaxing, just miles of ocean, and as much as I can eat and drink.' He grinned again at Reuben's expression. 'I have a mate in the merchant navy. That's all I'm saying.'

'Just one question,' Reuben said. 'Why is all this necessary?'

'What do you mean?' Frank said.

'All this planning and subterfuge ... why don't you just hire someone to shoot her or do a hit and run?'

Frank shot a look at Bomber and let out a guffaw. 'I think you've been watching too many cop shows. What do you think this is, *Underbelly?*'

He glanced over to where Gunther was setting up tables and said in a low voice, 'I'll let you in on a secret. When you're at the top, there are very few people you can trust. There's always someone waiting in the wings to stab you in the back – literally. I've been fucked over before and it's not going to happen again. Bomber and I go back a long way and he wouldn't do the dirty on me because I know too much.' He waved a loaded corn chip at Bomber. 'Isn't that right, mate?'

Bomber waved a bigger one back at him, his corn chip buckling under the weight. 'You bet,' he grinned. 'And vice versa.'

'We keep each other honest,' Frank said. 'As for you, Littledick, you've got your hot little wife to keep you honest – nothing more off-putting than a cold corpse. Not that I'm speaking from experience, though the old girl does a good imitation of one when she's not in the mood.'

'I can always get them in the mood,' Bomber said. 'Amazing what a bit of mull can do.'

'Thanks for that tip, Dr Ruth,' Frank said. He looked at Reuben. 'Plus, the cops will have no reason to suspect you and Bomber will be out of the country before you can say "Lucy Loose Lips."'

He gestured to Gunther to bring more drinks. The restaurant was starting to fill up. 'We need a time and place that's fool-proof. Looks like home's out, unless we can catch her by herself, which doesn't sound likely.'

So he had a heart. He was prepared to spare the husband and child.

Frank picked up the photos and flipped through them again. 'What about the car parks at some of these classes? Any of them in a secluded area where we could fix the car without being seen?'

'Not really,' Reuben said. 'They've all got open-air parking which is pretty exposed.'

Thank God. Maybe that would put him off the car-bombing idea.

'Don't forget it'll be at night,' Bomber said, 'and I only need ten minutes.'

'Too risky,' said Frank. 'A lot can happen in ten minutes.'

'I could do Breakdown Bob,' Bomber said.

'Go on,' Frank said.

'Bob's Breakdown Service – spray painted van, overalls, it will look like it's his car that's broken down,' he nodded at Reuben, 'and I'm fixing it.'

'Wait a minute,' Reuben said, 'Who said anything about me being there?'

'Of course you're going to be there,' Frank said. 'Bomber can't do it on his own.'

Reuben opened his mouth then closed it. There was no point in arguing. He had no choice. Promoted from stalker to accomplice. What was the legal term? Accessory after the fact. The upside was that no matter which night and venue they chose, Lucy wouldn't be there. The downside was explaining it to Frank.

'That's settled then,' Frank said. 'Breakdown Bob it is. When's the ship sail?' he asked Bomber.

'There's one going Thursday next week.'

'Perfect!' Frank said. 'We'll do it the night before when she's at pole dancing. She'll be all wet and slippery, thinking about sliding up and down hubby's pole when she gets home, then kaboom! Lucy in the sky, but no diamonds!'

Reuben's stomach parachuted to his feet. Next week! He wasn't ready for this. Couldn't they put it off a bit longer?

'Can you get Breakdown Bob organised by then?' Frank asked.

Bomber looked doubtful. 'I'll need extra cash. My mate who does the van will charge me double to have it done by next week, same for the tools. Express service surcharge, he calls it. And the old lady's been on at me for ages about getting her hair done.'

Frank took out his wallet, slipped out a bundle of fifties and thrust them at Bomber. 'I don't remember paying for her hairdos being part of the deal.'

'It was in the fine print,' Bomber said, pocketing the cash, 'and you can't expect me to do my best work with her nagging me all the time.'

'Bomber's a good, clean-living bloke,' Frank said. 'Lives with his mum who thinks he works in the mines, and takes him to church every Sunday.'

'Not so clean-living,' said Bomber. 'Those mines are pretty dirty.'

'Not as dirty as those sheilas you hang out with,' Frank said.

Frank looked at Lucy's schedule again. 'The classes start at 6.30. Allowing for latecomers, you should be at the car park at 6.45. The address is corner of Benson and Wyatt Streets, Chermside. Correct, Littledick?'

Reuben nodded. 'Commonwealth Bank Building.'

'I'll find it,' Bomber said.

Frank dug into his jacket pockets, produced two mobile phones and handed them one each.

'Phone me Tuesday night to confirm it's all good to go. From now, all your contact with me will be with these phones. You're to get rid of them as soon it's done. Littledick, I've put your number in Bomber's phone and vice versa. False names, of course. Tom and Jerry.'

Bomber grinned. 'Good one.'

'One other thing – that phone stays with you at all times. You don't want nosy wives or mothers getting hold of them.'

'No chance of that,' Reuben said. 'There's no way I'd want anyone knowing I've only got one friend.'

'Gunther, more beer!' Frank shouted.

'No more for me,' Reuben said. 'I have to go.'

'That's right, better get back to wifey – you don't want to miss out on a bit of pussy.'

Reuben didn't bother to reply.

***

As he opened the front door, the aroma of roast lamb wafted towards him. Domesticity wasn't so bad when you could come home to a beautiful woman and roast lamb. Even if the woman wasn't the girl of your dreams, there was always the lamb – with a glass of red.

Carlene was transferring the lamb from the baking dish to the carving board. Reuben put his arms round her waist and kissed her cheek. 'Here, let me do that.'

'Thanks. How was Finn?'

It was a casual enough question but he sensed undertones. Or was that just his guilty conscience?

'Oh, you know, the usual. He's still depressed but hanging in there.'

'Is he seeing a counsellor?'

'Er ... I don't know.'

'He's lucky to have you to talk to.'

He stole a glance at her as she lit the candle on the dining table, but there was no hint of sarcasm.

'I suppose so. That's what friends are for. I'm sure he'd do the same for me.'

'Not that I'm thinking of getting a divorce,' he added hastily.

'I should hope not.'

They sat down to eat and Reuben poured the wine. 'This is very romantic.'

Carlene gave him a provocative look over the flickering candle. 'It's a full moon tonight. And my stars said my evening would be full of romance.'

He put his hand over hers. 'What a coincidence! Mine said the very same thing.'

Carlene smiled. 'Liar.'

A few minutes later, she put down her knife and fork. 'I've been thinking.'

The three words every man dreaded hearing. It was shorthand for: 'I've come to a decision, which it would be in your best interests to agree with.'

'What about?' Reuben asked. There was no way you could avoid asking the question. You could pretend to take the statement on face value that your loved one was simply keeping you informed of her cognitive processes, and move on to the next subject. He'd tried it a couple of times in past relationships, with a resounding lack of success.

'Children. What do you think about them?'

'They're a rude, sticky-fingered species that should be taken with a grain of salt and served up with plenty of butter.'

'Rubie! You know what I mean. Us having them.'

'I haven't thought about it. I don't think we should rush into it at this stage. Besides,' he nodded in the direction of the photos of Kiet, Sahra and Ali on the fridge, 'we already have three kids.'

'Please be serious!' She took his hand. 'The other night when I was lying in bed, you know what I heard?'

'Me snoring?'

'Besides that.' She began to stroke his fingers. 'I heard the ticking of my biological clock.'

'Honey, you're only thirty-one, I don't think the alarm is going to go off just yet.'

'How do you know? One of us might be infertile. Or both of us. You don't know until you start trying.'

'That's true. But I think we should wait until we're a bit more settled.'

She stopped stroking. 'You mean until you get a proper job.'

'Yes, amongst other things.'

'What other things?'

'Well ... get used to married life, give us a chance to have some time together, just the two of us.'

She studied his face.

'You don't want to have kids, do you? You may as well tell the truth, I can see it in your eyes.'

'It's not the truth at all. I just haven't given it much thought. You have to admit, Indya and Brayden aren't the greatest advertisement for the joys of family life.'

'It doesn't mean our kids would be anything like them. I know Jo spoils them but I've seen a lot worse.'

Reuben sighed inwardly. He sensed Carlene was steering the conversation into deep waters in which he would find himself floundering.

'I'm sorry, honey, could we discuss this another time? I'm too tired to think at the moment.'

Carlene gave him a resigned look. 'All right. But we shouldn't leave it too long. It took Jo two years to fall pregnant with Indya.'

They had another glass of wine and retired to the couch. Carleen became giggly and amorous, and peeled off his shirt and jeans. They made love on the couch, moved to the floor and finished it off in the bedroom. While his body was going through the motions, his mind was filled with visions of Frank's reaction when he learned that Lucy hadn't turned up for her pole dancing class. So she was sick, or had another more important commitment. No reason to be suspicious; just bad luck. Of course Frank would see it that way.

If Carlene noticed that his mind wasn't on the job, she didn't comment. They snuggled up in the afterglow and she was snoring within minutes, her arm and leg flung over him. Reuben lay awake staring into the darkness, the cloud of foreboding still hovering over him.

16

Reuben quickly got into the routine of making sure he finished his work by three o'clock, even if it meant skipping lunch, so he could be out the door right on the dot before Joe could find him extra work. He had no desire to be there for a moment longer than he had to.

As he stood in the car park strapping on his helmet, Joe appeared at the back door of the kitchen with a bag of rubbish. He looked from Reuben back to the Barbiemobile with growing incredulity. He walked over, still holding the rubbish.

'Hey, boy! You borrowed that from your wife?'

'No, it's mine.'

'You're not serious?'

'I'm afraid so.'

He chuckled. The chuckle gained momentum and became a guffaw, which then turned into a belly laugh that echoed around the car park. Two women walking past turned and stared, and a flock of sparrows pecking on the ground nearby took off in startled flight.

'It's not my first choice of vehicle,' Reuben said. 'I won it in a church raffle.'

Joe stopped and looked at him, then threw back his head in another round of laughter. 'That's a good one. Boy, you kill me!'

If only. Reuben started the Barbiemobile and zoomed away, leaving Joe staring after him, holding the rubbish bag with one hand and his quivering belly with the other.

He'd been calling Posie every week as he'd vowed, and this morning she'd trilled, 'Reuben! Lovely to hear from you!' as if it hadn't been just a few days since she'd spoken to him. 'As a matter of fact, I do have a job for you. Come in and see me ASAP.'

When he arrived, the receptionist was tapping out a message on her iPhone while talking on the office phone. She looked up briefly and motioned for him to go through. Posie was also on the phone; a Tupperware container of chopped carrot and celery in front of her. She motioned for Reuben to sit down and held out the container of vegetables. Reuben shook his head.

'Okey-dokey, Simon, will do.' She put the receiver down. 'Simon's in LA talking to Guy Pearce,' she said breathlessly.

'Really?' Reuben said. 'What about?'

She put her finger to her lips. 'Top secret,' she whispered.

She straightened up and put on a business-like demeanour. 'Did you like the photos?'

'They're okay.'

She pointed a disapproving fingernail at him. 'You're too modest. This job I have for you is the chance of a lifetime.'

'What is it?'

'Modelling. Verity McLaughlin, one of Brisbane's top young fashion designers, has put out a new range of swimwear and she's doing a photo shoot tomorrow at Southbank. The guy she originally booked is down with the flu and she needs someone urgently.'

'What sort of swimwear?'

Please don't say Speedos.

'Mini board shorts.'

'What the hell are mini board shorts?'

'Exactly what they sound like. They're a shorter version of the traditional board shorts, for men who like to show off a bit of thigh.'

She arched her eyebrows. 'For those men who have the thighs to show off.'

'I don't think I'm the mini board shorts type.'

'You don't have to be the type; you just have to model them. They're going to be the next big thing in men's fashion – wouldn't it be fabulous to be on the first wave of a fashion revolution?' She clasped her hands together excitedly. 'It'll be great for your career – think of the exposure!'

'Literally,' Reuben said.

She gave a peal of laughter. 'Of course, very funny!'

She leaned forward on the desk, eyes sparkling. 'Do you realise what an opportunity this is for you, Reuben? It's not often I'd recommend someone who's had no modelling experience. But you've got the right look and I think you can carry it off.'

Questions jostled in Reuben's mind. How 'mini' were the board shorts? And how revealing? Wouldn't it be embarrassing doing a photo shoot in a public place? What if he got an erection? And what about work? He'd have to take a day off, ring in sick. As if he needed anything else to lower his worth in Joe's eyes.

Posie was standing beside his chair. 'Take off your shirt, please.'

'Again?'

'I want to see how you're going with your weight-loss program.'

Reuben got up and unbuttoned his shirt. He sucked his stomach in.

'Don't suck it in,' Posie commanded.

He let it go. She stood back and considered his stomach, head on one side.

'On the other hand, I think you'd better suck it in. Just for tomorrow.'

Was she now going to ask him to remove his jeans so she could test his thigh muscles?

She went back to her desk and started rummaging through her bottom drawer. Whew! Reuben buttoned up his shirt.

'I can lend you this if you like.' She held up a large paperback. On the cover was a young couple, toned and airbrushed, in gym gear. The title was *Dr Yang's Thirty-One Day Guide to a Slimmer, Fitter You*. 'It's got some great stomach exercises.'

'I'm doing sit-ups,' Reuben said. 'Or I was, but I stopped because they're so damn boring. All you do is sit up. At least with jogging you get to see a bit of scenery. Takes my mind off the pain.' *Sort of.*

She sighed and shook her head. 'Typical man, won't take advice. Now, let's get this paperwork signed.'

She picked up some papers and flipped through them. Had he accepted the job? He couldn't remember saying yes, but apparently that wasn't a prerequisite to getting it.

***

Carlene paused mid-stab of her steak.

'You mean you accepted the job and you don't know how much you're getting paid?'

'I'm sure it was on the contract somewhere.'

'But you didn't read the fine print?'

'Well ... no, but there must be a standard rate for modelling, and it's got to be better than a kitchen hand's wages.'

Carlene pursed her lips. 'But it's only one day, it's not exactly a new career. And for God's sake, what are mini board shorts?'

He gave her Posie's explanation. 'Apparently they're the next big thing in men's swimwear, so you never know, I could get some more work out of it.'

'But modelling, Rubie, I don't know, it's not very...'

'Not very what? Secure? Masculine? Not something you can boast to your friends about?'

'Don't be ridiculous,' she said sharply. 'Although...' she hesitated, 'I'd appreciate it if you didn't say anything to the rest of the family. They're not as understanding as I am.'

***

He arrived at Southbank Parklands at ten to eight. A pale sun had broken through the cloud, but it wasn't enough to take the chill off the biting wind that whipped around him, bending the tops of the palm trees fringing the small man-made beach. It was two weeks into September, supposedly spring, but winter was hanging on, determined not to go without a fight. Far from the ideal day to be walking around half-naked.

He'd phoned Joe just before seven. 'Sorry I can't come in, I've got a gastro bug.' All he had to do was think of Frank beating him to a pulp when he discovered that Operation Luce End had failed, to conjure up a suitably unwell tone of voice.

As expected, Joe was not pleased. 'You'd better not let me down tomorrow, boy,' he commanded before hanging up on him. The undertone was clear – Reuben had deliberately got sick to inconvenience him.

In summer, the Southbank beach was packed and even had its own lifesavers, though there was no surf. But on a winter's day, in the middle of the week, it was almost deserted except for a group of people at the far end. A man in track pants, pullover and beanie was setting up a camera on a tripod. Two young women – one tall and slender and the other shorter and sturdier – were standing nearby. The tall woman wore a long sleeveless dress and the other was sensibly dressed in jeans and a woolly jumper.

She came forward as Reuben approached and held out her hand. She had ginger hair, freckles and an open, friendly face. 'Hi, I'm Verity. Sorry to drag you down on such a revolting day.'

Reuben shook her hand. 'No problem, I guess it comes with the territory.' His hearty tone didn't even convince himself.

'Unfortunately, we couldn't put it off till another day – it's for a fashion spread in the *City News* and the deadline's tomorrow. Come and meet the others. This is Celia, the other model, and Jed.'

Celia had straw-straight blonde hair and was attractive in a Nordic, ice queen way. Her handshake was limp, her eyes not quite meeting his, as if she were on the lookout for someone more interesting to turn up. She obviously didn't feel the cold, or maybe she was in training. Jed nodded, said 'Hi' and went back to his camera. He was unshaven and his clothes looked as if he'd slept in them. The luxury of being in a creative industry was that you were able, even expected, to show a complete disregard for dress standards – particularly for a fashion shoot.

Verity handed Reuben a plastic bag. 'They're all in here,' she said. 'Just go into the Gents and put the top pair on.' She indicated a block of public toilets behind the beach. 'And you don't need to keep your jocks on.'

'I don't?'

'They have jocks sown into them.'

'Oh ... right.'

She laughed. 'Don't look like that. You'll see what I mean. It's just a little insert sown into the board shorts; like men used to have in their trunks in the old days, only these are more snug, to hold you all together.'

'Sounds ideal,' Reuben said.

'It is. I did a lot of research in this area, and all the guys I asked said they always wear jocks under their board shorts because they chafe. So I thought, why not invent board shorts that already have them in-built? And of course, with the mini shorts, you have to make doubly sure that everything is firmly in place. I know you men are very sensitive about that.'

From her matter-of-fact tone of voice she could have been a salesperson from Bunnings discussing the latest in corking guns rather than a man's most prized body part.

'Yes, I suppose we are.'

'Don't worry, I've had them road tested. Or should I say surf tested. The guys love them – they're going to be all the rage this summer. Oh, and the material is non-chafe, specially imported from Peru.'

'You've got me convinced,' Reuben said. Who would have guessed the Peruvians were experts in non-chafe material? Something to remember for his next conversation with Wayne.

He took the top pair of board shorts from the pile in the bag and made his way to the Gents. After diving into the nearest cubicle, he closed the door and held up the shorts. They were bright purple with hot pink swirls and did look rather mini. He undressed and slipped them on. After adjusting himself into the inner jocks, he had to admit they were quite comfortable, though he would have preferred a little more length, as they stopped just short of halfway down his thigh. The payoff for the material being non-chafe was that it was clingy – if you could call it a payoff.

He gathered up his clothes, bracing himself for the cold. The minute he set foot outside, the wind attacked him with gusto and within a couple of minutes he was shivering uncontrollably. A man heading towards the toilets holding a little boy's hand gave him a strange look.

When he returned, Verity gave him the once-over. 'Not bad – although I was expecting someone with a bit more muscle. But that's okay, we'll work with what we've got.' She patted her waist. 'Just hold your stomach in a bit; that'll accentuate your abs.'

Jed's head popped up from the camera. 'Ready when you are.'

'Excellent,' Verity said. 'First up, I want you two in the water, about knee-deep.'

'You mean *in* the water?' Reuben said. 'As in really *in*?'

'I believe that's what knee-deep means. Come on, don't be a wimp. You don't want Celia showing you up, do you?'

Celia had appeared from nowhere in a tiny iridescent blue bikini adorned with frills. She glided into the water, golden and lithe, and turned to face them with a pout, like a girl from a Bond movie. Reuben took a deep breath and gingerly put one toe in the water. He was already numb. It couldn't get any worse, could it?

It could. By the time he'd waded out to Celia, his body had been taken to a new level of numbness. He was using all his concentration to stop himself from shrieking like a girl. Who needed inner support? His balls had shrivelled up to nothing.

He and Celia had to stand arm in arm, as if they'd been swimming and were coming out of the water. Even the pleasure of having his arm around the waist of an attractive woman did little to mitigate his pain. The fact that this woman treated him with the disdain of a professional for a rank amateur played a large part. There were a few more poses in the water, with both looking ahead and then at each other – Celia gazing at a spot over Reuben's shoulder and Reuben trying not to let her breasts in his peripheral vision distract him.

Finally Verity gave them the nod and they were allowed to come out of the water. The wind turned his wet legs into poles of ice as he padded into the Gents to change into his next pair of board shorts. For the next eternity, he and Celia pretended to be entranced with each other in between costume changes; standing, sitting and lounging under the palm trees; on the hard, cold sand; and even on the nearby children's playground. Jed darted around them, changing cameras, clicking furiously and grunting encouragement.

As Reuben posed behind Celia on the slippery slide, he hoped that Verity wasn't going to demand he do the monkey bars – they were never his strong point at school and it would be just his luck for Celia to be a monkey bar expert.

It was looking as if it might finally be a wrap, when Verity said, 'Okay, guys, just one more water shot and we'll call it a day.'

Reuben couldn't help a small sigh. 'I've just got dry.'

'For God's sake, stop whingeing,' Celia snapped, as she headed back towards the water.

That was unfair – apart from his initial shock at getting into the water, the only whingeing he'd done was to himself. He waded back in after Celia – the water was only bone-chilling this time instead of brain-freezing.

'Reuben, I want you to pick Celia up in your arms, as if you're about to carry her out of the water.'

He looked askance at Verity.

'And don't forget to smile. You're lovers, remember?'

This was testing his acting prowess to the limit.

'Come in, let's get this over with,' Celia said.

Right you are. Reuben bent down and scooped her up in his arms. She was quite heavy considering her slender build; her skin surprisingly soft and warm. They both smiled at the camera until Reuben's arms and face ached, and Verity called out, 'Okay, wrap it up.'

Reuben dropped his arms and Celia plummeted into the water.

***

The photos appeared three days afterwards in the *City News*, Brisbane's weekly lifestyle magazine. It was a double-page spread called 'What's Hot This Summer', featuring Reuben and Celia under the palm trees, on the playground and wading out of the water as if they'd just had an invigorating dip. Jed had obviously photoshopped off Reuben's blue-tinged goosebumps. The photos of him carrying Celia in the water were conspicuously absent.

Despite herself, Carlene was impressed. 'You look pretty sexy in those mini board shorts, babe. All the girls at Women for World Peace thought so too.' She squeezed his thigh. 'But I don't like the way she's draped herself all over you.'

'It's only for the photos, honey. I can assure you, in real life she's not a nice person.'

Celia had lodged a formal complaint with Pizzazz Promotions about Reuben for his 'unprofessional behaviour,' after first informing him that he'd be lucky if he got any more modelling work in Brisbane, or anywhere else, for that matter. Posie had to go into damage control to make sure the agency didn't lose any business as a result and called Reuben in to admonish him.

'Celia is really going places,' she told him. 'She's just been signed by a New York agency, and she'll be a big name one day. So to get on her bad side like that was not a good idea, was it?'

'I'm sorry for the trouble it caused you,' Reuben said. 'But if I never model again, I won't lose any sleep over it. As for Celia, she doesn't have a good side and I'm not in the least bit sorry I dropped her.'

Not wanting to spoil his few moments of glory, he didn't tell Carlene about the incident with Celia. And she certainly had no complaints when he received his payment of five hundred dollars a few days later. It was worth it just to remember the look on Celia's face as she rose to the surface of the water, spluttering and gasping.

17

Wednesday night loomed ahead of him like a shadow of doom – the closer it got, the larger the shadow. On Tuesday night he phoned Frank, as instructed.

'All systems go,' Frank said. 'Meet Bomber in the car park at six forty-five. Park a couple of streets away and walk there. Afterwards, don't contact me, wait for me to call you. Understood?'

'Right.'

On Wednesday morning as he dressed he decided on his plan of action. He'd come home after work, shower and change, leave Carlene a note and go before she arrived home. He racked his brains for a reason to be home late. If only he had some friends he could rely on to provide him with an alibi. But there was only Derek, who, apart from the fact that he was still in jail, was too crazy and unpredictable to be a friend. He'd have to fall back on good old Finn again. It was pathetic – he had one friend in the whole world, and he was imaginary.

At the cafe, he cut himself twice; blood leaking on to the chopping board. He didn't hear the deep fryer alarm go off and a basket of chips burnt to a pile of charred remains. For once, Joe seemed to run out of insults. He made a gesture of tearing out his hair and strode out of the kitchen.

'What's the matter with you today?' Nina said. 'You seem a bit jumpy.'

Reuben shrugged. 'I didn't get much sleep last night.'

She raised an eyebrow. Implicit in the gesture were all the erotic possibilities behind his lack of sleep. Reuben said nothing – let her think he didn't sleep well because he was shagging himself senseless.

At five-thirty, he was at Hungry Jack's having an early dinner to kill time. After two bites of a double beef 'n' bacon burger on top of an already churning stomach, he was close to throwing up. He threw the rest in the bin and forced down half a cup of weak coffee. At six-fifteen, he left the restaurant and arrived at the Commonwealth Bank building in Chermside at six-thirty. It was an easy ride as most of the peak hour traffic had abated. He parked the Barbiemobile a block away in a side street and strolled back to the car park.

He pulled the collar of his jacket up against the crisp night air. Not wanting to be seen loitering in the area, he crossed the side road to a small block of shops and pretended to be browsing in the window of a second-hand bookshop. He arrived back at the car park at six forty-five, just as a ute rumbled in. Under the entrance light, the words 'Breakdown Bob' painted on the side – in large red letters – were visible.

The car park was half full. Reuben approached the ute as it nosed into a space on the far side. Underneath 'Breakdown Bob' were inscribed in smaller letters '24 hour service', and a mobile number after it.

A figure in dark overalls and a peaked cap got out.

'G'day,' Bomber said. 'Where's the car?'

'It doesn't appear to be here.'

A horrible thought struck Reuben. What if, by the wildest of coincidences, she actually did do pole dancing and her car was there after all?

Don't be ridiculous, that wouldn't happen even in the worst movie.

'Doesn't appear to be?' Bomber said, mimicking Reuben. 'What's that supposed to mean?'

He took a brief stroll around the car park and returned. 'No silver Mazda 2. Did you check the side streets?'

'Why would she park further away when there are spare parks here?'

Bomber shrugged. 'Fuck, I dunno. She's a woman. Who knows why they do anything? Where's the action?'

Reuben pointed to a lighted window at the top of the three-storey building, in which the tops of two poles were visible.

'Should have brought me binoculars. How are you at shinning up the sides of buildings?'

'Sorry, I left my Spider-Man costume at home.'

Bomber looked at his watch. His hair was pulled away from his face and tucked under his cap, accentuating his narrow features and receding chin. He reminded Reuben of a ferret. Ferrets looked harmless, but could bite you when you least expected it.

'Maybe she needs to rest her fanny after all that slipping and sliding.'

'Maybe,' Reuben said.

'We'll give her till seven. C'mon.'

He opened the driver's door of the ute and got in then leaned across and unlocked the passenger's door. Reuben climbed in. The stuffing leaked out of the torn vinyl seats and the cabin smelt of stale tobacco and greasy food.

'If anyone asks, I'm logging a job and you're my offsider.'

He pulled a battered packet of tobacco and a packet of papers from his overalls pocket. 'Want one?'

'No, thanks.'

Bomber lit his neatly rolled cigarette and acrid smoke filled the cabin. Reuben coughed and wound the window down a little. The street lamps threw dim light over the car park. The lights of the main road and the whoosh of passing traffic were just a few metres away.

'You're a strange dude,' Bomber said.

'Why do you think that?' Reuben asked, in what he hoped was a casual tone of voice.

'For a start, I never met a crim who didn't smoke.'

There was truth in that remark. In prison, Reuben had been part of a tiny minority of inmates who didn't smoke. It gave him a certain amount of clout, though, as he bought his weekly ration of tobacco along with the rest of them, then sold it to the highest bidder for a handsome profit.

'It's the stress,' Bomber said, 'and all the sitting around and waiting.'

'That's for sure.'

Reuben flexed his fingers. 'I bite my fingernails instead,' he added, to reassure Bomber that he also suffered some occupational stress.

'And you talk posh, like all them people where Frank lives. He thinks he's one of them, but he's kidding himself.'

'You don't like Frank?'

'I'm only doing business with him, I don't have to like him.'

He inhaled deeply, as if he couldn't get enough smoke into his lungs, and exhaled in an explosive burst.

'Don't get me wrong I love the guy. Until this job is finished and he pays me then I'll piss off out of his life forever, without so much as a Christmas card.'

He pointed to the window on the third floor. 'Look.'

A blur of movement was visible in the lighted square; too far away to distinguish any details.

'Fuck, I wish I'd brought me binoculars.'

Reuben scanned the cabin of the ute. 'Where's your gear?'

'Secret compartment. And don't ask where – that's why it's a secret.'

'How many ...'

Reuben was about to ask Bomber how many people he'd blown up in his career, but realised the question sounded nosy and naïve, and if Bomber took it the wrong way, judgmental. He didn't want Bomber to think that he thought there was anything wrong with blowing people up.

'Have you done many of these jobs?'

'Enough to get by.' He looked sideways at Reuben. 'Why?'

Reuben shrugged. 'Just wondered. It's obviously a high-risk occupation. Must take a lot of guts.'

His tone held just the right combination of admiration and respect. Bomber sat up in his seat and all but puffed out his chest.

'Kin oath. This'll be my last one. Set me up nicely for my retirement.'

He rolled another cigarette. 'Anyway, what's your form? Frank told me he met you in the Big House.'

'I was in for fraud.'

Bomber nodded knowingly. 'That explains it then.'

'Explains what?'

'White-collar crime. Pen pushers don't like to get their hands dirty. Think their shit don't stink.'

Reuben opened his mouth to defend himself then stopped. *Don't rock the boat; who cares what he thinks?*

Bomber looked at him and grinned. 'Nearly gotcha, didn't I? No names, no pack drill. I was just talking in a general sense.'

His watch beeped. He looked at it. 'Seven bells. No sign of Loose-Lips Lucy, Frankie-baby won't be happy.'

'It's hardly our fault Lucy didn't turn up for her class,' Reuben said. 'Anything could have happened – she could be sick, or have something else on.'

'Or she could be home showing hubby her moves.'

Bomber turned the key in the ignition. 'I'm off then.' The motor grumbled and rasped then died. After two more attempts, it shuddered into life.

Reuben opened the passenger door and jumped out. 'Sounds like you need a breakdown service.'

Bomber grinned. 'I'll give you the pleasure of breaking the news to Frankie.'

I thought you were the one being paid the danger money. Reuben watched the ute pull out onto the main road and disappear into the traffic. As he walked through the car park, he glanced up at the window. A long, bare leg entwined itself around the top of a pole then slid down out of view. *Thank you Lucy, for not being a pole dancer.*

He was only two blocks down Gympie Road, stopped at the lights, when a police car suddenly appeared behind him. Reuben's throat went dry. In his rear view mirror, he saw the orange light flashing and the driver gesturing for him to pull over. The traffic lights changed and Reuben pulled over on the side of the road. *Keep calm, they've got nothing on you, the worst thing you've done tonight is hang out with a professional killer.* He took a deep breath to slow his racing heart.

The police car pulled up behind him. Two uniformed policemen got out and swaggered over. One was tall and brawny, the other short and pudgy; as if they'd stepped out of a B-grade cop comedy. Did they teach them that swagger at the police academy, make them strut up and down like models learning the catwalk?

Reuben took off his helmet. 'Evening, officers.'

Neither answered. They looked at him then at the Barbiemobile and back at him.

'This your vehicle?' the taller one asked.

'Yes.'

'Impressive,' the shorter officer said. He was chubby-cheeked and olive-skinned. As he was the closer of the two, Reuben could just read his name badge in the street light. Senior Constable Bonazzi. 'Could I see your licence please?'

Reuben dug his wallet out of his jeans pocket, slipped out his driver's licence and handed it over. SC Bonazzi studied it and gave Reuben a long, hard stare.

'Reuben Littlejohn. You're the guy who had the finance company racket.'

'Yes.'

'Done your time already?'

'I'm on parole.'

'Lucky you. Not so lucky for the poor buggers you swindled.'

He handed the licence to his colleague, who walked away with it in the direction of the police car.

'Who did you con that one from?' SC Bonazzi nodded towards the Barbiemobile. 'Some rich old tart?'

'I won it in a church raffle.'

'Of course.' He narrowed his eyes. 'Seems like you didn't learn much in prison.'

'It's the truth. You can check up if you want. Father Bryan from the New Light Mission.'

SC Bonazzi's lip curled. 'So you've found God? If I had a dollar for every time I'd heard that one I wouldn't be standing here listening to your bullshit.' He looked Reuben up and down. 'Where are you off to?'

'I've been visiting a friend, and I'm on my way home. To my wife.'

'So I was right about the rich old tart.'

Reuben itched to punch the supercilious grin off his face. He drew in a deep breath. 'If you're going to stand here and insult me, I've got better things to do.'

'Oh, I'm sure you have.'

The other policeman reappeared and handed Reuben back his licence. Reuben checked his name badge. Constable Andrews. 'All clear,' he said to his colleague.

He looked at Reuben. 'Behaving yourself on parole, Mr Littlejohn?'

'Yes, I am.'

SC Bonazzi whipped out his notebook and pencil. 'This friend you were visiting, what's his name and address?'

'John Robertson, I don't know his address, he just moved house. We met at the Aspley Hotel.'

'What's his date of birth?'

'I don't know.'

SC Bonazzi looked at him suspiciously, pen poised. 'You don't know your friend's date of birth?'

'We're not in the habit of exchanging birthday cards.'

'Where did you meet him?'

Reuben opened his mouth to protest at the questioning then thought better of it. 'At the employment agency.'

SC Bonazzi shook his head in mock sympathy. 'Times are tough. No jobs going for scammers?'

Fortunately Reuben was saved the trouble of replying by Constable Andrews appearing beside him with a breathalyser. 'Have you had anything to drink tonight?'

'No.'

SC Bonazzi looked at him disbelievingly. 'You went to the hotel and didn't drink?'

'I told you, I'm a law-abiding citizen now.'

Reuben blew into the mouthpiece. The reading was zero. Constable Andrews looked grimly disappointed.

SC Bonazzi shook his head, 'You put up a good front, Littlejohn, but you're not kidding anyone.' He took a step closer to Reuben. 'You white-collar crims think you're so much better than all the others,' he said in low, measured tones, 'but you're not. You're just as bad as the junkies and thieves and housebreakers.

And I'll give you fair warning – we're watching you. Not just us, but all the boys. The minute you put a foot over the line, even your little toe, you're gone.'

He turned abruptly and the two of them headed back to the police car. 'You have a good evening too, officers!' Reuben called after them.

***

Two blocks from home, the phone Frank had given him buzzed in his pocket. He pulled over on the side of the road, in front of a house with lights blazing in every window and TV noises blaring out. It sounded like a fight scene, with lots of banging and shooting.

'Hullo!' he said briskly to cover his nerves.

'Well?' Frank said.

'She didn't show.'

Silence. 'Are you sure?'

'Positive. We stayed until after seven. Checked the car park thoroughly.'

'So what do we deduce from that? That she's given it up the night we plan the operation? Or that you're not on the level with me?'

'You know I'm on the level. Anything could have happened – she might be sick. Or her kid might be. Or she might have had a social engagement. Or...'

'Shut the fuck up. Meet me at the Bulimba Soccer Club. Midday Saturday.'

Frank hung up.

18

Carlene was sitting on the bed painting her toenails, feet splayed on a towel and all the accoutrements on the bedside table. She looked up as Reuben entered the bedroom. He braced himself for the inevitable outburst.

'Hi babe,' she said. 'How was your evening?'

She was smiling and there was no hint of sarcasm in her voice. Was this a trap?

'Er ... fine. How was yours?'

She shrugged. 'Same as usual. Watched a bit of telly, called Mum. How's Finn?'

'He's okay. Well he's not, actually. That's why I'm a bit late. He's had another setback and I had to be there for him while he cried into his beer.'

'Oh no!' Carlene stopped, mid-brushstroke. 'What happened?'

'He met this girl and things were going great guns. Then she phoned him and told him she'd met someone else, and it was all off.'

'That's terrible, honey! But hadn't he only just split up with his wife?'

'It was a few weeks ago now.'

She looked at him, aghast. 'A few weeks! He didn't even give himself a decent mourning period! No wonder the relationship didn't work out; he hadn't resolved the issues from his marriage break-up.'

Reuben felt bound to defend Finn. 'How do you know? Anyway, he told me his wife left him for someone else, so it's not his fault the marriage broke up.'

'But she wouldn't have left him if she was happy in their relationship.'

Reuben bit his lip, not wanting to start an argument. He watched the neat, precise strokes of the brush as it glided over her toenails, leaving streaks of vermillion red in their wake.

She surveyed her toes then screwed the lid back on the bottle. She looked up at Reuben from under her eyelashes.

'Anyway, I'm glad you're home. I missed you.'

'I missed you too.'

It was sort of true – he would rather have been at home with her than loitering in a cold car park being an accessory after the fact to a non-existent murder. Or for that matter, listening to the marital woes of a non-existent friend.

'While you were out, I was thinking.'

He felt a sudden weariness – sapped of what little energy he had left. 'Yeah?'

'I was thinking about children again. Why bring another child into the world when there are so many out there who need a good home?'

'You make it sound like getting a dog from the pound.'

Her mouth tightened. 'Be serious, Rubie. We could adopt a child from overseas, from Africa or Asia, an orphan or one of those kids whose parents can't afford to look after them.'

'Shit, Carlene, I've got to get my own life together before I can be responsible for someone else's.'

'But honey, you do have your life together. Once you get a decent job we'll be fine. We've got a great future ahead of us – don't you think it would be nice to share it with a child who doesn't have one?'

'I'm confused. First you say you're being deafened by your biological clock, then you want us to be the Brad and Angelina of

Brisbane.'

'It's just an option, that's all. Something to think about.'

Carlene leaned forward and brushed his lips with hers. 'It's okay, honey, we'll talk about it another time. I know you're tired.'

She gave his neck and shoulders a rub as she waited for her toenails to dry. The touch of her hands reinvigorated him, and overtaken by desire, they made love – fast, but mutually satisfying. Afterwards Carlene snuggled into his side and ran her fingers through his chest hair.

'I'm sorry that I've been so shitty with you about Finn,' she murmured.

'It's okay, he has been rather demanding lately.'

'He's a friend and that's what you do for friends. When I thought about it, I realised what a beautiful quality it is; that you stand by him when he's in trouble.'

Reuben felt a warm glow of pride.

'And then I reminded myself that I need to give you space. When you've been crammed into a prison cell for three years with no privacy, you need psychological as well as physical space.'

Although 'crammed' was an exaggeration, it was true there had been little opportunity for time alone. Even in his bunk after lights out, the presence of the others around him was suffocating. Through the thin walls of his cell he could hear the snores, grunts and moans of the others as they settled to sleep, the night air stale with despair and hopelessness. Sometimes he dreamt that he was still there and when he woke up and found he wasn't, he could almost convince himself the whole three years had just been a bad dream.

Carlene propped herself up on her elbow and traced the outline of his face with her finger. 'Now, when are you going to bring him home for dinner?'

Reuben gave an inward sigh. 'I'll talk to him before his next visit and organise something.'

Except there wouldn't be a next visit. *Sorry, Finn, the time has come for you to stand on your own two feet, there's only so much I can do for you.* Finn would either run into some financial problems so he could no longer afford to fly to Brisbane, or meet another woman who would shag him senseless, thereby rendering him with no energy or inclination to get on a plane. The second option was obviously more preferable for Finn, and Reuben drifted off to sleep thinking of the various scenarios in which Finn could meet a woman so stunning that he'd drop his oldest and closest mate like a hot potato.

***

Why did Frank want to meet at the Bulimba Soccer Club? Surely he wasn't a soccer player. Maybe he had a kid who played soccer. Reuben couldn't imagine Frank as a father at all, let alone a soccer dad. He hoped Frank wasn't going to suggest another attempt in the pole dancing car park. He, Reuben, would have to come up with a better idea.

On the way to work, he racked his brains but alternative scenarios for murder refused to materialise. After parking, he took the phone Frank had given him out of his pocket, slipped out the sim card, and wrapped the phone tightly in a plastic bag he'd brought for that purpose. He disposed of it in the industrial garbage bin near the rear entrance of the cafe.

He tried not to think about his meeting with Frank. He mixed up several orders and sent an opened can of beetroot skidding off the preparation bench onto the floor. Joe was standing nearby at the time, his white apron adorned with splashes of pink.

'Jesus Christ, boy, what is the matter with you? Sometimes you leave me speechless!'

He ranted and raved while Reuben cleaned up the mess, threw his apron off and rifled through the storage shelves to find another.

'In trouble again?' murmured Nina as she dumped an armload of dirty dishes onto the sink.

'He's always in trouble!' Joe shouted. 'Always a hundred miles away, God knows where! I don't know what you saw in him! And me, I don't know why I hired him!'

'You said he makes you laugh,' Nina reminded him.

Joe snorted. 'Laugh! I laugh on the other side of my face!'

After Joe had gone back out into the shop, Nina returned with more dishes. She glanced sideways at him. 'You weren't daydreaming about being at the beach, were you? Lounging around with a gorgeous blonde?'

She busied herself washing her hands with an enigmatic half-smile. It took him a few seconds to realise she was referring to his photo spread in the latest *City News*. Was there anyone in the entire city of Brisbane who hadn't seen it?

'As a matter of fact, no,' Reuben said. 'At least not with that gorgeous blonde, we didn't exactly hit it off.'

'Really? Are you telling me your charm and good looks didn't impress her?'

There was no sarcasm in her tone, just gentle teasing. Her hard edges had softened a little and he'd come to realise that her brusqueness was a cover for shyness. Or maybe a protective mechanism she used for men.

He grinned. 'Once in a blue moon it happens. Sometimes I think there's an inverse relationship between a woman's beauty and her niceness. Present company excepted, of course,' he added.

'Of course.'

She swished past him out the door.

***

Reuben glanced in the Barbiemobile's rear-view mirror numerous times during the trip to the Bulimba Soccer Club. SC Bonazzi's warning echoed in his mind. Surely the cops wouldn't be following him, they had bigger fish to fry. But if they happened to see him with Frank and Bomber, they'd be asking questions – apart from the fact that he was breaching his parole. Frank's maxim was 'invisibility in a crowd'. In other words, meeting in a public place was less likely to draw attention to you than sneaking around undercover. Reuben wasn't so sure, but even so, he wished he'd taken the bus. It was impossible to be invisible in a crowd on a pink motor scooter.

He'd told Carlene he was shopping for her Christmas present and so needed to go out alone. That had impressed her as Christmas was still ten weeks away.

'I've never known a man to be so organised – usually they leave it until five o'clock on Christmas Eve.' She entwined her arms around his neck and pressed herself against him. 'What are you buying me? Give me a clue.'

'You'll have to wait and see,' he whispered into her ear.

His mysteriousness was authentic as he had no idea what he was buying her. And as he would return empty-handed, the decision was so important it would require further excursions.

He arrived at the soccer club with ten minutes to spare. The spring sunshine blazed down on the field swarming with children in their soccer gear. The muddy-coloured Brisbane River lurked in the background. At one end of the field, a coach was taking his teams through some moves. At the other end near the grandstand, a few rows of wooden seats with no shelter, a match was in progress. The players looked about ten to twelve years; one had blonde plaits, another a ponytail. As Reuben stopped to watch, the ponytailed player kicked a goal. Her teammates cheered, slapped her on the back and punched her arm. He was sure that as a kid he would have enjoyed soccer a lot more if girls had been allowed to play.

He hadn't had lunch, so he joined the queue of jostling, chattering children at the canteen. He ordered a hot dog and a coke, and stood in the shade of the clubhouse to eat it. As the sauce dripped down his arm, he realised it was the first hot dog he'd had in almost four years. He'd always found that the amount of sauce dribble was in direct proportion to the palatability of the food. Some things never changed.

The ponytailed girl's team scored another goal and the opposition looked downcast, scuffing their shoes on the grass. Reuben thought of his own short-lived soccer career. He'd tried out for the under-tens – he was small for his age, not naturally sporty; but he ran and tackled and kicked his heart out, and finally made it into the B-side.

When he told his mother, the creases in her face softened. 'That's great, Rube, I'd love to come and watch, but Saturday is my busiest day. I'll organise a lift there for you with Michael's mum.'

When he pleaded, her face grew stony. 'I said no and I meant it. How do you think I'm going to afford the fees and the clobber you wear if I don't work?'

She turned away from him and fumbled with a cigarette. Reuben, close to tears, yelled, 'If you gave up smoking, you'd have enough money!' and ran from the room before she could retaliate.

He played regardless, but after a few lacklustre performances, was dropped from the team. From then on, he avoided sport altogether, throwing his energy into inventing ingenious methods of dodging PE classes and selling his best ideas to his classmates.

Someone slapped him on the back. Bomber stood in front of him, grinning, a roll-your-own cigarette stuck in the corner of his mouth.

'His Highness awaits you,' he said. He inclined his head towards the grandstand. Frank sat in the middle of the back row, sipping on something in a polystyrene cup. The grandstand was about half full, but the seats around him were vacant. He wore cargo shorts, t-shirt and cap, eyes on the game, looking like any other devoted soccer dad. Reuben stuffed the rest of his hotdog into his mouth and followed Bomber. He steeled himself for Frank's greeting, reminding himself that in this public setting, the worst thing Frank could do was throw his coffee at him, and the coffee at these places was always lukewarm anyway.

They climbed up to the back row and sat one each side of Frank. Eyes still straight ahead, Frank said in a low voice, 'I'm pissed off, Littledick.'

'How was I to know she wouldn't turn up for her lesson? She could have been doing anything – maybe she was Christmas shopping.'

'People don't go Christmas shopping in October. And besides, the shops aren't open on Wednesday nights.'

How come Frank was so knowledgeable about shopping?

'And I'm wondering if there was a reason she didn't go – maybe she had a little premonition that something was going to happen.'

Reuben met Frank's steely gaze. 'What are you saying? You think I forewarned her?' At least he didn't have to fake his indignation.

'You've got the hots for the bitch; you could have dropped a hint.'

Reuben swallowed. 'Why would I do that? I'm not going to risk my wife's life for her. She means nothing to me.'

A cheer went up from the crowd. A goal had been scored by the losing team. Bomber jumped up in his seat. 'You beauty!' he yelled, punching the air. 'Gotta play the part,' he muttered out of the side of his mouth as he sat down again.

'Think about it, Frank,' Reuben said. 'I could hardly have warned her not to go to her pole dancing class. How would I have known about it? She'd have me charged with stalking.'

'You could have been more subtle as in "don't go anywhere tonight because you'll be blown to smithereens".'

'And she'd have believed me, of course. The first thing she'd do would be to call the cops.'

Another cheer went up from the crowd and Bomber jumped up again. 'Good onya, kid!'

Reuben looked over. 'That was the other team.'

Bomber shrugged. 'Hey, I don't care who wins. I'm just here for the party.'

A large family, armed with hot chips and coke, straggled up the grandstand and sat down in the row in front of them. Frank scowled, inclined his head and got up. Reuben and Bomber followed him out of the row onto a grassy knoll to the side of the soccer field and out of earshot of passersby. Frank lowered himself onto the grass and sat awkwardly with his legs out in front of him.

'All right, Littledick, I'm giving you another chance to prove yourself. And this time there'll be no room for error. Does she park her car behind the parole office?'

'Yes.'

'Do the windows of the parole office overlook the car park?'

Reuben hesitated. No point in lying – Frank could easily find out the truth.

'No. The parole office is at the front of the building; there are financial planners at the back.'

'Perfect. When's your next appointment?'

'Not next Tuesday, the one after. Three-thirty.'

Frank looked at Bomber.

'I'll check with me travel agent,' Bomber said. 'Should be okay though. I've got somewhere offshore I can hole up until the next ship sails.'

'Good,' Frank said. 'You do the car while Littledick is smooching with Loose-Lips.'

'That's a bit risky, isn't it?' Reuben said. 'An open car park in broad daylight?'

'That's where Plan B comes in,' Bomber said.

'Breakdown Bob, again?'

'You never use the same get-up twice, mate. You should know that.'

'Of course,' Reuben said.

'Different modus operandi,' said Frank. He pronounced it 'operandy.' 'You ring Bomber's phone just before you go into the interview room – two rings, then hang up, that's the signal. Bomber will be in the car park, he'll unlock the car, plant the bomb under the driver's seat and be gone in the space of a few minutes.'

'What excuse are you going to have this time for breaking into her car?' Reuben said.

'Dan's Detailing Service,' Bomber said. 'Leaves your car fresh as a daisy.'

'Make sure you string the interview out for as long as possible,' Frank said, 'because while she's talking to you she's not going to her car for any reason. And if someone from the financial planners happens to look out the window and see Dan's Detailing at her car, there's no reason for them to think it's not legit – they probably won't even know whose car it is.'

The hooter sounded for half-time and the players straggled off the field, panting and red-faced.

'Frank, you're not on orange duty, are you?' Bomber said.

Frank ignored him. 'Are you both clear on your instructions?'

'Yep,' said Bomber. Reuben nodded.

Frank reached into his shorts pocket and pulled out two mobile phones. He handed them one each. 'Not to be used until the day. Same deal – after the job's done, wait for me to call then get rid of them.'

The players huddled in their respective teams, swigging on water as their coaches talked them up for the second half. A tall, lanky boy broke away and sauntered towards them. His restless eyes took in the group.

'You made it, Dad,' he said. 'Were you watching?'

'Of course I was,' Frank said. 'You were great.'

The boy looked down at his feet and kicked at a tuft of grass. 'No I wasn't, I was shit.'

'We all have our off days, mate,' Bomber said, 'even your dad, believe it or not.'

'Shut up,' Frank said. Then, to the boy, 'You did good, kid.'

The boy looked up at Frank from under his eyebrows.

'Did you see the goal I kicked?'

'Sure did, mate, it was a beauty!'

The boy's head jerked up. His eyes blazed.

'I didn't score a goal. You're so full of shit. Why do you even bother coming?'

He turned and strode back to his team, shoulders squared and head high.

'Bloody kids,' Frank muttered. 'You give them the world and they're still not happy.'

'You got kids?' Bomber asked Reuben.

Reuben shook his head.

'I got five,' he said.

'Five!' If it was hard to imagine Frank as a father, it was impossible to imagine Bomber in that role. 'Where are they all?'

Bomber shrugged. 'Dunno. Haven't seen any of them for years. Five different mothers, I've lost track of them.'

Reuben tried not to look incredulous. Was Bomber having him on? It was hard enough believing that one woman had found him attractive enough to sleep with, but five? If he was using marijuana to seduce them, it must be powerful stuff.

Bomber grinned. 'I had a hard time keeping it in my pants when I was a young fella.'

'And you can fucking well keep it in your pants until this job is over,' Frank said. 'I need your mind on the job, not on your next piece of pussy.'

The whistle blew for the game to recommence. The players trailed back to the field. Shouts of encouragement echoed from the grandstand. Frank's son looked pointedly away from the spectators and in a show of bravado, shadow-boxed a teammate back on to the field.

'Gotta go and watch the star player,' Frank said. 'Remember, Littledick, keep her occupied for as long as you can. Have it off with her on the desk, if you have to.'

***

Holy fucking hell. How am I going to get Lucy out of this one alive? A dozen ideas bounced around in his head as he rode home: ring her up and reschedule the appointment to play for time; tell Frank she was sick; had gone on holidays; had resigned even. But it would be easy enough for him to check if Reuben was telling the truth.

He had ten days to come up with something. Even if he could think of a way to foil Frank's plan, he'd be furious at another failure and even more suspicious of Reuben. The only way out was to alert the police so they could set up surveillance and subvert the operation. But in the event they managed to do that without bungling it, there were so many other things that could go wrong. What if they arrested Bomber, being the man on the ground, but not Frank? What if Bomber refused to dob Frank in, and the police couldn't find any evidence to link Frank with the operation? Even Reuben's testimony was just his word against Frank's, and both Frank and Bomber could deny having any contact with him. Frank at large and on the warpath seeking revenge didn't bear thinking about. If it was a choice between his and Lucy's death ... *Much as I adore you, Lucy, I'm not prepared to die for you.* He would never have made it as a medieval knight.

As he walked through the front door, voices floated out to him from the back patio. He recognized Nancy's imperious tones and Alec's quiet acquiescence. That was all he needed to ramp up his stress levels. Why the hell couldn't he and Carlene have just one weekend without a visit from them, or even a whole week without their 'popping round for a cuppa'?

'Hi honey,' Carlene said, jumping up and flinging her arms around his neck. 'How did your shopping go?'

'Oh ... good.'

'Obviously,' Nancy said, staring pointedly at his non-existent parcels.

'I was just looking around to get ideas,' Reuben said.

'Just go to the jewellery store,' said Alec. 'Any woman will tell you it's full of ideas. You've had some of your most creative thoughts there, haven't you, dear?'

'Don't be ridiculous, Alec,' Nancy said.

Reuben looked at her pearl necklace and the diamond rings jostling for prominence on her fingers. Was she going to pronounce them to be fake in keeping with the principles of the nouveau poor?   Maybe it didn't extend to jewellery. If Carlene was expecting something sparkly in a tiny box for Christmas, she'd be sorely disappointed.

'By the way, Posie rang,' Carlene said. 'She asked could you phone her back, something about an audition. She tried your mobile but you didn't answer.'

Nancy pursed her lips. It was obvious she wanted to ask who Posie was, but good manners prevented her. Reuben stepped back into the living room and dialled Posie's number.

'Reuben! I'm so glad you called back! A film company called New Wave Productions is calling for auditions for a beer commercial. I thought you might be interested.'

'What do I have to do?'

'They'll tell you when you get there. All I know is that you have to be the quintessential Aussie male in his thirties who drinks beer. And who has film presence.'

'I fit the first category, anyway,' Reuben said.

'That's false modesty and you know it,' Posie said reprovingly. 'Get out there and show them what you've got. Monday morning, nine am.'

Shit. Another day off work. Joe would kill him. Or fire him. Reuben wrote down the address she gave him. It sounded promising, much more up his alley than modelling. Could he give up jogging now?

'Oh, and keep up the jogging,' Posie said. 'The quintessential Aussie male likes his beer but still likes to keep fit and look good.'

'What was that about an audition?' Carlene said as Reuben returned to the patio.

Reuben told her.

'A beer commercial? For TV?'

'I presume so.'

'An audition, eh? Sounds interesting,' Alec said.

Nancy looked unimpressed.

Reuben could see Carlene weighing up its long-term career prospects and finding it light on.

'From what I've heard, the money's pretty good. You stand around all day, say a few words for your six seconds of fame and get paid a few hundred for your efforts.'

He had no idea if that were true – at least the bit about the pay – but hope imbued his comments with conviction.

'So we might have a TV star in the family,' Alec said. 'Bit of a step-up from swimwear, eh?'

Nancy made a noise between a snort and a grunt, though it was unclear whether it was due to the possibility of Reuben being a TV star or the thought of him modelling swimwear. Contrary to Carlene's wish for the rest of the family not to know about his modelling, she hadn't been able to stop them from reading the *City News*, which was delivered free to homes within a certain inner city radius.

'I suppose we'll have to wait and see how he goes in the audition,' Carlene said. 'Anyone for more coffee?'

Fortunately, Nancy and Alec left shortly afterwards to go home and get ready for a charity cocktail party in aid of homeless orangutans in South Africa. Reuben went into the bedroom and checked himself from all angles in the full-length mirror. He was sure his stomach was flatter, but he'd give it one last-ditch effort. Digging deep into his reserves of motivation, he donned his shorts, t-shirt and joggers.

19

Reuben phoned Joe at six forty-five. 'I'm sorry to let you down again, but this gastric bug's come back.'

He steeled himself for Joe's outburst. It didn't happen – just a noisy sigh like an elephant farting. 'Boy, you're not worth wasting my breath on. Just be here at seven am, sharp, tomorrow.'

Reuben didn't know whether to be relieved or disappointed that he hadn't been fired. It would be just like Joe not to fire him because he knew that was what Reuben was secretly hoping for. Not that he was going out of his way to be fired, but if he was, he wouldn't be beating down the door begging for his job back.

New Wave Productions was also in Spring Hill, a couple of blocks from Pizzazz, on the ground floor of a towering concrete and glass building. The receptionist's generous smile matched her breasts. For once, both were real.

'Mr Littlejohn?' She studied the list. 'Here you are, right at the bottom.'

She pointed down the hallway. 'First door on your left.'

Reuben opened the door and reeled back in surprise. It was five to nine, but already the room was crowded. The chairs lined up against the walls were occupied, and the rest of the hopefuls were standing, some alone with their arms folded, others in pairs or groups. In the centre of the room was a long table on which stood two jugs of water, two towers of plastic cups and a huge platter of cream biscuits. Two youths, tanned and clear-eyed, biceps bulging out of their t-shirts, sat on the edge of the table; chatting, laughing and radiating self-confidence.

'Come and join the party,' said a man standing by himself near the biscuits. He picked up a Monte Carlo, shoved it in his mouth, and held out his hand.

'Tom, but everyone calls me Thommo.' Biscuit crumbs sprayed out from his mouth.

Reuben, dodging the crumbs, shook his hand and introduced himself.

'Your surname's not James, by any chance?' Thommo asked.

Reuben returned his grin as if he hadn't been asked that question a thousand times before. There'd been many occasions when he'd wished it *was* James – anything but Littlejohn.

Thommo took another biscuit, a chocolate cream. He was of solid build, with a thatch of dark hair that flopped over his eyes. His facial features were too coarse for conventional good looks but in his jeans, boots and checked shirt, he exuded an air of beefy ruggedness.

'I haven't had any breakfast,' he confided,' and by the look of it, these will be lunch too.'

Reuben looked around the room. Apparently the quintessential Aussie male was buff and tanned, t-shirt sculpted on to his chest and jeans so tight you could tell his religion. Thommo was one of the few who'd come from a different mould. Reuben had opted for his best black jeans and a polo t-shirt. He wished now that he hadn't – it made him look like a Young Liberal member about to play golf. He sucked in his stomach.

'Looks like there's a lot of competition.'

'Don't worry, most of them are just pretty faces. You have to be able to look like you're having fun, not like you've got your head stuck up your arse.'

He patted his stomach, showing the beginnings of a paunch. 'I thought they might want someone who looked like they actually drank beer and didn't spend all day posing in front of the mirror at the gym.'

'Let's hope so,' Reuben said. 'Have you been to many of these?'

'Thousands. Beer, cat food, toilet rolls, I've even done one for tampons.'

'Not to use them myself,' he added, 'I was to be the husband who wanted to sleep in while she bounded out of bed and went horse riding and water skiing, all because of her super slimline tampons.'

'So, how many ads have you been in?'

'Actually ... none.'

He scooped up another biscuit. 'I'm an expert on auditions because I've been to so many. I'm thinking of writing a book – Auditioning for Dummies.'

Reuben wondered how many of the others were novices. Some stared vacantly into the distance as if this were just another daily chore; others looked expectant or hopeful, then tried to look blasé if they caught someone's eye. A few gazed around with an amused expression, as if they were there just for the fun of it, so they could impress their girlfriends or recount it to their mates at the pub. Three men standing in the corner laughed loudly at something one of them had said, glancing around to see if they were being noticed. They were overdoing it – obviously first-timers.

'It's a good idea,' Reuben said, 'but don't you think you'd have to be successful in at least one audition to write it?'

'That's where you're wrong,' Thommo said, spraying more biscuit crumbs down his shirt front. 'It's experience that matters. The more auditions you go to, the more experience you have. It's as simple as that. For example, I can tell just by looking around the room who's going to get the gig.'

'Who?'

Thommo wiped his mouth with a paper napkin. 'You, for example.'

'You think?'

'Yeah. They don't want good looks.'

'Right.'

'They want someone other guys can relate to, that they can see on the screen and say, "Yeah, that's me." So you have to be a bit better looking than average because the average guy always overestimates how attractive he is, but still be someone he can imagine having a drink with at the pub.'

It was a tough call. Maybe he should walk out the front door right now.

A door opened, revealing a tall, stick insect of a man in faded jeans and a torn-off t-shirt exposing a pale, hairless stomach. He was holding a clipboard.

'Could I have your attention, gentlemen!' he called out in a high voice. The hubbub stopped. 'I'll give you a quick rundown of what we want from you so you'll be prepared when it's your turn to audition. We're doing an ad for a new boutique beer from Germany called Becker's Beer. This is the scenario.'

He looked down at his clipboard. A few took the opportunity to exchange amused glances. 'You're in the pub with your mates drinking Becker's Beer when the most beautiful girl you've ever seen walks in and sits at a table. Your mates egg you on to go and talk to her, so you pluck up the courage to go over and offer to buy her a drink. You go up to the bar and order two Beckers. When you bring them back, she's not too happy but she drinks it anyway, and soon it's obvious that you're becoming increasingly attractive to her. By the time she's finished her drink she's gazing into your eyes and hanging off your every word. When you offer her a lift home, she says, "Let's go back to your place."'

There were a few appreciative whistles and someone yelled, 'Where can I get a carton?' to a round of guffaws.

The stick insect looked around the room like a teacher waiting for a classroom of unruly students to quieten down. 'The slogan is "The World Looks Better with Beckers."' He consulted his clipboard again. 'We have a lot of auditions to get through, so let's get started. First is Mr Adam Johnston.'

A man standing near the doorway, arms folded against his chest, stepped forward. He wore jeans and a singlet, his brawny arms a riot of tattoos. Perhaps too common a touch. The stick insect stood aside and motioned him through with an effeminate wave of his hand.

'The industry's full of them,' Thommo said in a low voice. 'Not that it worries me. I went to the gay Mardi Gras last year.'

'Yeah?' Reuben said. 'Which float were you on?'

He grinned. 'Same one as you, mate.'

Thommo took another biscuit from the platter and held it up to the light as if it were a glass of wine. 'Kingston, my favourite. This is my last, I swear.'

He launched into an account of his career, short on success for all the effort involved. From years of auditions for plays, commercials, films, drama school (he'd applied for the National Institute of Dramatic Art five times), all that had transpired was the odd bit of amateur theatre and a few gigs in crowd scenes as a movie extra.

'The chicks love the whole struggling actor thing, think it's so romantic and noble, but they soon get sick of it when the only dinner date you can afford is a barstool for two at the Greasy Diner. And after a while you get sick of sympathy fucks.'

'I can imagine,' Reuben said, although he couldn't at all. Wasn't a sympathy fuck better than none at all?

The stick insect reappeared at the door, looked down at his clipboard and called another name. Mr Tattoo hadn't been in for very long; not a good sign. A man with burnt-brown skin and dreadlocks came forward.

Thommo shook his head. 'The surfie look is so yesterday.'

An idea had been formulating in Reuben's mind – had started off as an idle thought which he'd ignored at first as it seemed too ridiculous. But it had festered in his subconscious until it suddenly presented itself as a complete plan.

'Feel like going for a beer when we're finished here?' Reuben said. He looked at his watch. Nine-thirty. 'Maybe coffee would be better.'

'Let's stick with the beer,' said Thommo. 'We'll need it. How about The Crown, down the road?'

The stick insect appeared again. 'Thomas Leader!'

'That's me. I'll wait for you in the public bar.'

It was close to midday by the time Reuben was called in. The boardroom had emptied by half and the platter of biscuits was just a pile crumbs.

'Reuben Littlejohn.' The stick insect repeated his name. He looked up at Reuben. His eyes were a milky blue, almost translucent. 'There's a name to remember.' He held out his hand. 'Damian Blackbutt.'

Reuben kept a straight face with a supreme effort of will. This could possibly be the only time in his life he was thankful for his own name. He shook Damian's hand; it was moist and limp.

In the audition room, a desk and swivel chair had been pushed against the far wall, exposing an expanse of plush blue carpet. Against the nearest wall to the door, a man with a bushy beard sat behind a camera on a tripod. A man sitting next to him got up.

'Bruce Berkeley,' he said, shaking Reuben's hand.

He was a taller, thinner version of Simon Broadbent, with the same smooth, polished finish, right down to his knife-edge pressed trousers and shiny shoes.

He handed Reuben a sheet of paper. 'Your lines.'

There were three lines typed on it.

'*Can I buy you a drink?*'

'*Two Beckers, please.*'

'*So, can I give you a lift home?*'

'That's it?' Reuben asked.

'Don't be deceived – you might only have three lines but there's a lot going on between them.'

He gestured in the direction of the bushy-bearded man. 'Mike here is going to film you, so do the best you can, we don't have time to do a lot of takes. So we start off with you over there near the desk, having a drink with your mates. Damian will help you out by being one of your mates.'

Reuben acted out the scene, from Damian egging him on in his high voice to talk to the 'hot chick' in the corner, to downing an imaginary beer while being drooled over by an invisible goddess. He felt awkward and self-conscious, and the whole scene was stilted.

'Okay.' Bruce's expression gave nothing away, but there was no way he could have regarded Reuben's performance as anything but crap. He looked at his watch. 'One more take and that's it. Let me just ask you, who in your opinion, is the most beautiful woman in the world?'

'My parole officer' would undoubtedly be dimly received. Reuben's mind went blank and refused to come up with any women at all, beautiful or otherwise. On Bruce's crisp, pale blue business shirt, the words 'New Wave Productions' were balanced on the crest of a large wave. Underneath was inscribed 'B.B.' in red. What sort of tosser had his initials inscribed on his shirt?

'Brigitte Bardot,' Reuben blurted out. A chortle came from behind the camera. Bruce's face creased momentarily and Damian raised an eyebrow.

'When she was young,' Reuben added.

'Right,' Bruce said. 'Imagine it's Brigitte Bardot, when she was young, of course, sitting at the table. And try to forget the rest of us are here, you're here to sell yourself.'

Sell yourself. The words clicked into place in his mind, like the pieces of a puzzle. He'd been doing it all his life. To sell something to other people, you had to believe in it yourself. Each time he'd collected a bogus charity donation, sold a membership to a non-existent organisation, signed someone up to a fraudulent investment scheme, he'd immersed himself in the scenario beforehand, convinced himself it was real. It was all a matter of balance – to be convincing but not too pushy; warm and friendly but not too familiar; and to act as if it was okay if they weren't interested in the product because you were enjoying their company. Add to that a touch of machismo for male customers and boyish bashfulness for females, and you had them in the palm of your hand. But it was all just a role-play. Like now.

Reuben took his position near the desk next to Damian.

'Take two!' Bruce called.

Reuben drew a deep breath. He was in the pub; he'd just spotted Lucy for the first time sitting alone. He remembered the first time he saw her at the parole office, how the world stopped and was about to tilt off its axis, and he was out of breath and speechless. Then sitting at her table, she was so close to him that he could feel the warmth of her skin. He was heady with the magic of her as she gazed into his eyes and he gazed back and he had to stop himself from reaching out and stroking her hair. And when she said 'Let's go back to your place', her voice, husky with desire, sent a thrill through him right to his backbone and gave him a strange feeling in the back of his throat...

'Cut!' yelled Bruce.

Reuben hurtled back to reality.

'That was better, obviously Brigitte Bardot does it for you.'

'Whatever floats your boat,' Damian smirked.

'We'll be in touch,' Bruce said with a dismissive handshake.

***

By the time Reuben had walked the two blocks to the Crown Hotel, his stomach was growling. The Crown was one of the last old hotels in the city area that hadn't been demolished or revamped. The shabby exterior gave way to an even shabbier, dingy interior with the musty smell peculiar to old buildings, as if the lives of all its past patrons were somehow entombed within its walls.

Thommo was perched on a barstool in the public bar chatting to the barman and shoving peanuts into his mouth. The barman was as old and desiccated as the building itself. Thommo's face shone with beer and good humour.

'G'day mate! How did you go?'

'Crap on the first take, better on the second. How about you?'

Thommo's face fell. 'They let you do two takes?'

'I'm sure that means nothing,' said Reuben. 'I don't expect to hear back.'

Thommo looked like a puppy that'd lost its ball.

'Come on, let's have lunch. My shout.'

Thommo brightened up. They went into the lounge bar and looked at the menu. It was basic, befitting its surroundings. Meals were an optional extra; this was a pub for the serious business of drinking. They ordered pies, chips and peas and sat at a corner table. The only other customers were two whiskery old men in the opposite corner, prodding at their meals with shaky hands.

'I've got a proposition for you,' Reuben said.

Thommo grinned. 'Hey, I take that back about going to the Mardi Gras.'

'A work proposition.'

Thommo straightened up. 'Fire away.'

'Are you free Tuesday next week at about three o'clock?'

'Let me consult my diary.'

He looked down at the table for a few seconds then looked up.

'I believe I am.'

'All you have to do is turn up at a car park in Chermside, and talk to a guy from Dan's Detailing for about ten minutes.'

'Is this for TV or a movie?'

'Neither. I just want his attention diverted for a while.'

'How much?'

Reuben thought quickly. Not too much to arouse suspicion but enough to seal the deal for an unemployed actor. 'Three hundred dollars. Cash.'

Thommo looked incredulous. 'Three hundred dollars for ten minutes? What's the catch? Do I have to dress up as a fairy?'

'No catch, wear whatever you want – preferably not a fairy costume. And there's not a lot of acting needed, you just have to be yourself.'

'You realise that telling an actor to be himself could spin him into a major identity crisis?'

The meals arrived, borne on a tray by a withered old woman with two veiny twigs for legs; she may well have been the barman's wife. The pies floated like large flaky tankers on a sea of glutinous gravy next to an island of chunky chips, with the odd green pea bobbing up to the surface.

'I hope these pies aren't as old as everything else in here,' Thommo said as he tucked in.

He looked up, his chin adorned with pastry crumbs. 'You've got my interest. But I'm curious. What's the purpose of it?'

Reuben chewed slowly as he gathered his thoughts. He couldn't divulge the real purpose of the job, but he was taking a risk even going this far – a risk that Thommo would suspect something underhand and inform the police. But he didn't seem the dobbing-in type, and there was nothing illegal in what he was asking Thommo to do. The main thing was making sure he kept his mouth shut.

'I can't tell you; you'll have to trust me on this. All I can say is that it's vitally important that you keep this guy in conversation for at least ten minutes, so it might be an idea to bone up on cars.'

'Can't you just give me a clue? Does it involve a woman?'

Reuben hesitated. 'It does, but not in the way you think. If I give you a clue, you have to promise not to breathe a word to anyone, not even your girlfriend; *especially not* your girlfriend.'

Thommo held up his hand. 'Scout's honour. I won't say anything to my girlfriend when I get one.'

'I'm trying to prevent a crime from being committed.'

Thommo's eyebrows shot up. He opened his mouth.

'And that's it,' Reuben said. 'Don't even bother asking anything else.'

'So I'm being paid three hundred dollars for ten minutes of being myself, whoever that may be, and having no idea why, apart from the fact that I'm helping keep law and order in our community.'

'You got it.'

'Sounds fair.' Thommo held out his hand. 'It's a deal.'

Three hundred dollars, over half his take-home pay. That was going to hurt. He should have gone for two hundred. Or a carton of beer. A pity he couldn't give Frank an account for expenses rendered.

20

A loud knocking woke him up. He jumped up from the recliner, flinging the weekend newspaper from his lap onto the floor. He looked at his watch. Three o'clock. He'd been asleep for over an hour; couldn't even remember nodding off. Working in a real job took it out of you.

He opened the front door, blinking at the sun. Wayne stood there, grinning at him. 'G'day! Did I wake you up from your grandpa nap?'

'Yes, actually.'

'Sorry,' he said cheerfully. 'Thought you might like to come down to the club for a couple of beers. Seeing as the girls are off doing their charity stuff.'

Carlene and Jo had gone to help out at the Bookfest at the New Life Mission Church, selling second-hand books to raise more money for Pastor Bryan's Youth Works mission. Carlene had tried to persuade him to come, but he'd refused point-blank. Spending hours surrounded by dusty piles of books, dodging effusive hugs from Carlene's church buddies and Pastor Bryan's overtures, was far from his ideal way to spend a Saturday. Almost anything else would be preferable – except going to the club with Wayne.

'Thanks for the offer but I've got a bit to do this afternoon...'

'Like what?'

'Er ... mowing the lawn, for a start.'

Wayne looked around at the tiny strip of straggly front lawn. 'Looks fine to me.' He clapped Reuben on the shoulder. 'Come on, mate it'll do you good. You look like you could do with a drink.'

It was obvious he wasn't going to take 'no' for an answer. Which was odd, as he'd never sought out Reuben's company before and Reuben was sure that like the rest of the family, Wayne only tolerated him for Carlene's sake. He would never have offered Reuben the roof-tiling job if Carlene and Jo hadn't put the pressure on.

'Okay, just give me a minute to change.'

Reuben went inside and changed from his shorts to jeans and a collared shirt. Maybe he could have just one drink and plead a headache. God, that sounded so girly and pathetic, he could imagine Wayne's reaction. Maybe he could sprain his ankle on his way to the Mens – didn't sound a whole lot manlier. If he left before Wayne, he'd have to find his own way home. He checked his wallet; he had enough money for a cab.

Wayne had arrived in his sparkling white Range Rover. Like many city four-wheel drive vehicles, it had never been near a speck of off-road dirt. He bullied his way through the traffic to the local Services Club, conquered a space in the car park and they went inside.

The clientele were mostly older men who looked as if they were leftovers from the night before. 'It's mainly old dudes who hang out here,' Wayne said out of the corner of his mouth as they fronted the public bar, 'but I like it because of the snooker tables. Fancy a game?'

Reuben was about to refuse, snooker not being something he excelled at, then decided it would take the pressure off having to make conversation with Wayne.

'Okay.'

With their beers, they walked up a flight of stairs to the snooker room containing six tables. The only other occupants were two old codgers playing a slow, shuffling game at the far end of the room. Wayne untied the cover from the table closest to them and put a coin in the slot. He set up the balls, picked up a cue from the rack on the wall and chalked it with the air of an expert.

'You've played before? You know the rules?'

'Yes and yes,' Reuben said, 'but it's a while since I've played.'

Years, in fact. The last time he'd played pool was at Paul and Janice Hendry's mansion in Ascot, a suburb full of 'old money.' The Hendrys were clients of All Purpose Financial – Derek had signed them up and they'd invited him and Reuben to a dinner party at their home with several other guests. After dinner they'd played snooker in the huge games room and Derek had flogged them all, boasting he'd majored in it at Oxford University. It wasn't until Reuben was undergoing a marathon of questioning in a stuffy police interview room that he'd realised that the money the Hendrys had invested with them, was legitimate. And that there were at least a dozen more clients in the same boat, all reeled in by Derek. He'd conned Reuben as well.

Before their trial, he and Derek had been lunching at a city restaurant when he felt someone watching him. He looked over and saw Janice at a table with another woman. Their eyes met and he braced himself for a hostile reaction. But she didn't look angry – just small and crumpled, as if someone had let the air out of her.

He pushed the image from his mind, took a cue and chalked it to make it look as if he knew what he was doing.

'Ready?' Wayne said. He did an exaggerated limber up, positioned himself and then executed the first break off shot. It was a powerful shot, yet purposeful; as balls scattered all over the table, one red ball made its steady way towards the pocket and dropped in. Shortly afterwards a pink ball followed suit.

The pressure was on already. Reuben positioned himself and took a careful shot. A couple of red balls rolled aimlessly, stopping far short of the pocket.

'You're crooked,' Wayne said. 'Your arm's not in alignment with the rest of you.' He demonstrated the correct way by a potting a red and a yellow, followed by another red.

Reuben corrected his positioning and managed to pot a red. He missed potting the blue, which stopped just short of the hole, ready for Wayne to shoot it in, which he promptly did after potting the obligatory red. At this rate, it would be a mercifully short game.

Wayne picked up his beer from the shelf behind them and took a sip. 'So, mate,' he said with elaborate casualness, 'how are you settling into married life?'

'Fine, thanks.'

'Carlene's a great chick, isn't she?'

'Yes, she is.'

Wayne took another shot, missing for once, then stood up, leaning against his cue. 'Just between you and me, I think I married the wrong sister. But,' he shrugged, 'that's life. You're the lucky one who won her over.' He nodded towards the table. 'Your shot.'

What makes you think Carlene would have you anyway? Reuben tried not to let his disgust affect his shot, but to no avail. Balls scattered all over the table, everywhere but in the pocket.

'You haven't quite got the hand positioning, mate,' Wayne said, 'the cue's pointing too far down. Look, like this.' He did a slow motion of positioning his hand and the cue, and potted another two balls.

'Thanks,' Reuben said through gritted teeth. He took another shot and potted a red.

'Good shot!' Wayne said with exaggerated heartiness. He looked over at the old guys in the corner and lowered his voice. 'It must be hard being locked away from women for so long. You must be really horny when you get out – like you want to root every chick in sight.'

No way would Reuben admit to Wayne that he was right. He shrugged. 'I'm pretty picky. When you've waited so long, you want the best when it finally happens.'

Wayne winked. 'I get it, mate – why have a hamburger when you can have rump steak?'

If you make any allusions to Carlene being rump steak, I'll ram that cue right up your arse.

'It's your shot.'

Wayne took a shot and sank three balls. The table was looking rather bare. He leaned forward and said in a low voice, 'I s'pose there are guys inside who take what they can get – you know, desperate measures and all that.'

Suddenly it all clicked into place. *On second thoughts, I don't want to go anywhere near your arse. I'll gouge your eyes out instead.*

'No, I don't know,' Reuben said, 'because I was never that desperate. And you can tell your wife I'm not gay, a paedophile or a cross dresser, and just for the record, not that it's any business of hers, I'm not cheating on Carlene, either.'

He picked up his cue and took a wild shot at the last red ball, not caring where it went. It rolled straight into the pocket, and with the same erratic carelessness, he sank the yellow and the green.

'Bravo!' Wayne said and sank the remaining four balls in quick succession. He placed his cue on the snooker table and cleared his throat. 'Look mate, I'm sorry. I know you're okay, but Jo's not convinced. You know what women are like, they get an idea in their head and you can't talk them out of it.'

She's basing that idea on one incident of my dressing up as a woman. A few hours in a blouse and skirt hardly makes me a pervert. He opened his mouth to say as much then thought better of it. He had no desire to talk about dressing up in women's clothing with Wayne. He had no desire to talk to him about anything.

He made a show of looking at his watch. 'I've got to go. I just remembered I promised to go to the shops for Carlene.'

'Are you sure you don't want another game? Or another drink? By the way, it's your shout.'

'I'll buy next time. You stay, I'll make my own way home.'

***

Carlene arrived home from the Bookfest with an armful of books. 'Of course I had to buy some, they were so cheap.'

She put them in a pile on the table. The top one was a shabby paperback called *Meditation and Your Guardian Angels*. She gave him a playful punch at the expression on his face. 'There's a couple of Harlan Coben books you might like.'

'I'm giving up crime, remember?'

She giggled and flopped onto the couch. 'What did you do this afternoon?'

'I went to the Services Club with Wayne.'

She raised her eyebrows. 'Really?'

'He called around and insisted I go. He flogged me at snooker and gave me the third degree about my sexual preferences.'

He'd wondered if she'd known beforehand, if she and Jo between them had persuaded Wayne to talk to him. Though why they would think he'd confide in Wayne he had no idea. But Carlene's surprise seemed genuine.

'What do you mean?'

Reuben recounted the conversation to her. 'He didn't deny that Jo had put him up to it.'

'I'm sorry, honey.' She got up and put her arms around him. 'Jo's just jumped to the wrong conclusion, that's all. I know it's upsetting, it's upset me too.'

That's not a jump, that's a massive leap. But it wasn't worth starting an argument over. And though it made his stomach roil thinking about it, there was nothing he could do to change Jo's mind.

'Wayne also asked me in a roundabout way whether I was having an affair. You know I'm not, don't you?'

She tightened her arms around him and pressed her body into his. 'Of course I do, honey.'

As he pressed his face into her soft, sweet-smelling hair, he wondered if she were as good a liar as he was.

21

Reuben felt in his jeans pocket for the mobile phone Frank had given him, although he'd checked at least fifty times since he'd left home. He flicked through a *Woman's Day* and looked at his watch again. Two fifty-six. One minute after he'd last looked.

He took a deep breath to calm himself. He hadn't alerted the police – his hand had hovered over the phone numerous times but he couldn't make it dial the number. Somehow he would convince Frank that this failed operation was due to a run of bad luck and that it was third time lucky. And meanwhile a brilliant idea would come to him, he was sure of it. It always had before when he was in a tight spot.

A few seats away, a pudgy woman with dyed red hair was having a heated conversation on her mobile phone. 'Well, fuck you, Jason, you can just go and get fucked.' She threw the phone into her handbag, got up and marched over to the receptionist. She wore a singlet top and on her left shoulder was tattooed a heart with an arrow through it and the words 'Jason' inscribed inside. 'I'm going outside to have a smoke.'

The other occupants of the waiting room exchanged furtive smiles.

'Jason's fucked then,' observed one youth.

'I reckon he'd be out celebrating,' said his mate.

The middle-aged woman sitting next to Reuben leaned over. 'Looks like another visit to the tattoo parlour,' she whispered.

Reuben forced himself to smile. 'Unless she meets someone else called Jason.'

Five minutes after three. What was Lucy doing? She was usually on time. Bomber would be waiting for Reuben's signal, and Thommo would be waiting for Dan the Detailer to appear. Reuben hoped Thommo had positioned himself somewhere discreetly as

Reuben had instructed him. He had to walk through the car park at just the right moment, as if he were on his way somewhere else and stop to engage Bomber in conversation. When Reuben had phoned him in the morning to confirm he was still okay to go ahead, Thommo said, 'Mate, I've been up all night on the internet studying cars and their inner workings. Still a mystery to me, but I'm sure I can fudge it.'

A door opened and Lucy poked her head out. 'Come in, Reuben.'

He pulled out his mobile phone and dialled Bomber's number. He waited for it to ring three times, pressed the end button then followed Lucy into the interview room.

Lucy nodded at his phone. 'Was that important? I don't mind if you need to make a call.'

'No, it's fine.'

Reuben shoved the phone back in his pocket. 'It was just to my wife, to let her know I'll be home soon. That's my signal, I ring three times and hang up.'

Stop garbling, for fuck's sake.

Lucy clasped her hands on the desk. 'So what exciting adventures have you had since I last saw you?'

There was that funny feeling again, the tickle he always got in the back of his throat when Lucy looked at him. He diverted his mind from what was happening in the car park and took a deep breath.

'Er...'

The only exciting adventures he'd had, had been with her in his fantasies. Thank God she couldn't read his mind.

'I went for an audition for a beer commercial the other day.'

'Really? Does that mean we'll see you on TV sometime soon?'

'I haven't got the part yet.'

He told her about the audition, including the bit about his supposed fantasies of Brigitte Bardot, which made her laugh - a delicious, full-throated laugh.

'I'll keep my fingers crossed for you, Reuben.'

She reached for her appointment pad. 'We'll keep this short today. I have a meeting to go to in a few minutes.'

Reuben looked at his watch. He'd only been in there five minutes; he had to keep her occupied for at least another five.

'I don't think I told you about my swimwear modelling,' he blurted out.

Lucy's pen poised over the pad. 'No, I don't believe you have.'

Reuben related the saga of his photography session, spinning it out for as long as he could. He was just at the part where he was going blue with cold in the water when Lucy said, 'Wait a minute. Did you say mini board shorts?'

That was the only bit he'd rushed over, hoping she wouldn't notice. Why didn't he say he'd been modelling jeans and turtlenecks? That was the effect she was having on him; he was losing his ability to lie.

'Yes.'

'What on earth are they?'

'They're a cross between Speedos and board shorts, for guys who like to show off their bodies but for obvious reasons don't want to wear Speedos.'

'I'm not one of those guys though,' he added, 'I was just modelling them.'

That was lame – like saying I do skin flicks but don't like sex. Lucy gave a slight smile.

'Of course,' she said.

She's going to think I'm sleazy, forcing her to imagine me in a pair of mini board shorts.

She picked up a pen and tapped it on the desk. 'It's certainly something different to put in your CV,' she said. 'What did your wife think about it?'

'She wasn't impressed. There's not much of a career in mini board shorts, especially as they don't seem to have taken off so far.'

'Still, it's all experience. Something different to put on your CV.'

Was that a compliment? It was hard to tell from the tone of her voice. She resumed writing. 'I'm going on holidays in a couple of days – I'll be away a few weeks, so your next appointment will be with another officer. I'll see you in the new year, in early January.'

Fuck, Frank's not going to like that.

She handed him the appointment slip to sign. He took his time with his signature, adding some twirls and flourishes, and handed it back. He glanced at his watch. One-and-a-half minutes to go.

'Where are you going on your holiday?' he asked.

'Scotland.'

Frank would be doubly angry – he couldn't kill her while she was in Scotland – but at least she'd be safe there. That was presupposing that today's plan had worked and she was still alive to go to Scotland. *Keep it going, say something intelligent about Scotland.*

'I've always wanted to go there. All those green hills and sheep and...'

What else was there in Scotland?

'Haggis,' he finished.

Why would anyone eat haggis? The name was enough to put you off – it sounded like someone gagging. The only way he'd even consider eating haggis was if Lucy was draped in it.

Lucy smiled. 'I won't be sampling the haggis if I can help it.'

She stood up. In a last ditch attempt to extend the interview, Reuben stood up and held out his hand.

'Have a great Christmas and New Year, and I hope Santa brings you everything you want.'

'But no haggis,' he added.

She shook his hand. 'Thanks, Reuben, same to you.'

'There's no danger of Santa bringing me any haggis...'

'See you next year,' she said firmly.

As Reuben opened the door, he heard the tinkling of a mobile phone. He recognised the ring tone as the theme song from the TV show *The Addams Family*. He glanced back and saw Lucy pick up a mobile phone from the desk.

'Hullo,' he heard her say as he closed the door. So she liked *The Addams Family*, the first thing he knew they had in common. As a child, he'd watched every re-run and even at that young age was fascinated by Morticia with her glossy black hair and impossibly tight dresses.

But there was no time to reflect on this important discovery. On the pavement outside the parole office, Reuben dialled Bomber's number and let it ring three times again to signal the end of the interview. Almost immediately the phone rang back. Reuben swallowed hard. 'Yes?'

'Meet me in the Parkside Tavern in ten minutes. Public bar.'

'Okay.'

The Parkside Tavern was two blocks away, modern tiled brick, fronted by a huge sign proclaiming that Monday nights was all-you-can-eat pasta for $8, Tuesday was karaoke night and on Saturday night the Rusty Screwdrivers were playing. Apparently nothing much happened between Wednesday and Saturday.

Bomber was hunched over a beer staring at a surfing clip on the TV. Reuben bought a light beer and sat down across from him.

'This operation is jinxed,' Bomber said.

Thank God. It had worked.

'Why do you say that?'

'Some bloke was hanging around in the car park, reckoned he was waiting for his girlfriend, and chewed my ear off. He wouldn't fuckin' shut up – he was a bit simple, a sandwich short of a picnic.'

'That was bad luck. Why didn't you tell him to fuck off?'

Bomber drummed his fingers on his beer glass and looked away. 'I got a nephew like that. Goes to special school. He's the greatest kid...'

He took a swig of his beer. 'I told him to piss off but he didn't understand.'

He paused. 'Not a friend of yours, is he?'

Reuben met his gaze. 'What do you mean by that?'

The words came out with more force than he intended. Bomber said nothing, just stared at the TV screen. A gigantic wave barrelled a hapless surfer off his board to disappear in a flurry of foam.

'Are you saying I've deliberately sabotaged this operation?'

Bomber shrugged. 'It's funny that something's happened both times to put a spanner in the works.'

'Do you really think I'd be so stupid as to try and deceive Frank?'

'Mate, I hardly know you, I don't know how stupid you are.'

'Not that stupid, I can tell you. I know Frank and I know what he's capable of. He's threatened to kill my wife if I don't do this, so I'm not about to stuff it up.'

Bomber downed his beer and slammed the glass on the table. 'This business is shitting me. I just want the moolah and to fuck off outta here. The old girl's driving me crazy.'

His eyes lit up and he gave a low whistle. Reuben followed his gaze. Two young women in short dresses, tights and boots were standing at the bar. As they headed towards a table, drinks in their hands, Bomber called out, 'There's a seat here, sweetheart!' He dragged a chair from a nearby table, placed it next to him and patted the seat.

The girls looked at each other. 'In your dreams, loser!' one of them called.

'As if !' the other said, and they sauntered off, giggling.

'Stupid little sluts.' Bomber got up. 'Well, it's nice not doing business with you, Littledick. No doubt we'll meet again soon.'

He ambled out the front door. His hair looked as if it hadn't been washed for days, his shirt hung out over his belt and his jeans sagged in the crotch. The two girls, sitting near the door, exchanged glances and burst into giggles again. Reuben finished his beer and resisted the temptation to have another.

***

As he started the engine of the Barbiemobile, his jeans pocket vibrated. There was a text message on the mobile phone Frank had given him. 'City Botanical Gardens 3pm tomorrow. Now dispose.'

Bad news travels fast. Reuben drove through the car park to the rear of the hotel and stopped at the industrial garbage bin. He took the sim card out of the mobile phone and threw the phone in the bin, where it lay glinting amongst the food scraps and papers. He placed an empty pizza box on top of it so it wasn't visible and zoomed off.

The house was in silence when he arrived home. Carlene hadn't arrived home from work yet. He ran the bath, pouring in some of her scented bubbles, and submerged himself in it with a Mandrake comic and the Boston Stranglers, in their punk rock phase, screeching from his iPod speakers.

He was on a yacht with Lucy, the water lapping gently at the hull. Lucy stripped off and dived into the ocean, the firm, pale moons of her buttocks sliding into the glassy water. Reuben dived in after her. The water was freezing and he broke out in goosebumps. When he opened his eyes, Carlene was standing beside the bath with his mobile phone in her hand. She put it on the sink.

'Your phone was ringing.' She was still in her work clothes. 'And you're drooling again.'

He wiped his mouth and glanced down at his nether regions. Thank God he didn't have an erection. The bubbles had disappeared, exposing his cock floating on the cold water like a listless sea slug.

Carlene leaned over and gave it a playful tug. 'Your poor baby. You must have been tired. Did you remember the lamb?'

Shit, the lamb for tonight's curry. Somehow it had slipped his mind, what with saving Lucy's life.

Carlene's shoulders stiffened. 'You're hopeless. I ask you to do just one little thing and you can't even do that.'

She stalked out. Reuben got out of the bath and dried himself. There was a voicemail message on his phone. A voice hummed the first few bars of Mission Impossible, then said in a conspiratorial tone, 'Mission accomplished. Except for the moolah. Ring me.'

Reuben sent a text message. 'Tomorrow 4pm. Coffee Club, Adelaide St, City.'

The reply came back immediately. 'Skinny iced chocolate with cream please.'

***

At ten past three, Reuben arrived at the front gates of the Botanical Gardens. He'd had to leave work half an hour early, pleading a doctor's appointment. Joe glared at him. 'You look as strong as an ox to me. What's wrong with you?'

'Er...' Reuben racked his brains for an affliction that was not too serious or socially unacceptable. 'I've got an ingrown toenail, the doctor said it needs immediate treatment.' He assumed a pained expression. 'It's very painful.'

Joe shook his head. 'When I was in the army in Malta, I marched twenty miles with an ingrown toenail. And a twenty kilopack on my back.' He waved his arm in dismissal. 'You ... you metrosexuals, you have no idea!'

Thank God for that. 'Thanks, I appreciate you giving me the time off.' Reuben limped out as quickly as he dared before Joe changed his mind.

He sped into the city on the Barbiemobile. Each time the speedometer crept up over sixty kilometres, he glanced nervously over his shoulder, half-expecting to see a police car appear and pull him over. SC Bonazzi's warning was still fresh in his mind. What if the police had somehow found out about his association with Franks and Bomber? *Forget it, you're becoming paranoid. That's what a guilty conscience does to you.* In the city, he parked in an underground car park and ran the three blocks to the Botanical Gardens, dodging and weaving through the pedestrians.

Stopping inside the entrance gates, he surveyed the path winding through the rolling expanse of lawn, garden and gigantic Moreton Bay fig trees. Frank hadn't specified a meeting place – how in hell was he supposed to find him? Was this supposed to be some kind of test? Did he leave a trail of breadcrumbs?

Reuben jogged down the path, noting with satisfaction that he was only slightly breathless, whereas not so long ago he would have been ready to collapse by now. The lawn was iridescent in the spring sunshine and looked soft and springy enough to sleep on. The couple entwined in each other's arms under a nearby tree obviously thought so. A toddler on a tricycle pedalled past him, followed by his harassed mother. Ahead of him a group of students with backpacks laughed and jostled each other. Where would Frank go, to blend in with his surroundings? He wasn't exactly a picnic-in-the-park kind of person.

To his far left was a small pond, a family of ducks weaving gracefully through the lily pads. An elderly man and a little girl stood at the edge of the pond watching them. On a nearby seat, with his back to Reuben, sat a man in a pale blue shirt and black cap, a newspaper spread out on his lap. It was obvious he wasn't reading it.

Reuben walked over to the seat and sat beside him. The little girl threw a piece of bread into the pond. 'Look, Grandpa!' she squealed as the drake paddled over and scooped it up in its beak.

Frank wore large wrap-around sunglasses that made him look like a gigantic blowfly. Without acknowledging Reuben's presence he said, 'I love the simple things in life, don't you?'

Expecting a reprimand for being late, Reuben said nothing, surmising the question to be rhetorical.

'Ducks swimming on ponds, a cold beer on a hot afternoon and I especially love it when a plan comes together.'

The little girl shrieked and jumped up and down as the ducks gobbled up the bits of bread as quickly as she threw them in.

'That's why I'm mightily pissed off, Littledick. Not to mention Bomber. And a pissed off Bomber is not someone you'd want to have around.'

What did he mean by that? That Bomber would exact revenge and blow up the Barbiemobile? Was it possible to hide a bomb in a motor scooter? Perhaps a small pink bomb – anything was possible with modern technology. He saw himself turn the ignition and the Barbiemobile explode in a ball of flame; pieces of flesh, bone and pink fibreglass flying through the air. He gulped.

'Believe me, Frank, I'm just as pissed off as you are. I don't want it dragging on either.'

That at least was the truth.

'So you're telling me it was pure coincidence that dickhead just happened to be walking past when Bomber was about to do the deed?'

'Of course it was, do you honestly think I'd sabotage your plans and risk my wife's life?'

'Maybe you don't like your wife; maybe you just married her for the money.'

'That's not true. I love my wife.'

Did he just say that? He'd never said those exact words before, probably because in the normal course of conversation you didn't tell people you loved your wife – they just assumed you did.

Reuben was about to protest further but stopped himself. *Don't say too much, it makes you sound guilty.*

Frank foraged in his pants pocket and pulled out a fat cigar. He unwrapped the cellophane, lit the cigar with a silver and gold lighter, and puffed furiously on it. Clouds of foul-smelling smoke billowed around them.

'Yuk, Grandpa, what's that smell?' the little girl said.

The old man darted a hostile look at Frank. 'Some people are very inconsiderate, sweetheart. Come on, we'll go and get an ice-cream.'

The little girl tucked her hand into her grandfather's and trotted beside him, twisting around to stare at Frank with big, appraising eyes.

'Thank bloody God,' Frank grunted. 'Now I can think without that kid screeching in my ear.'

Reuben's eyes were watering. He leaned back in his seat, away from the smoke stream.

'Okay, Littledick, I'm giving you one last chance. You're so fucking smart, you come up with a plan. And it better be fool-proof or the deal's off, and you can kiss good-bye to wifey-poo.'

'Can I give it some thought and get back to you?'

Frank looked at his watch. 'I'll give you five.'

'Five hours?'

'Five minutes.'

'Right.'

Think. Plan. Kill Lucy. Reuben's brain froze.

'So we're still going with the car bomb?'

Frank gave a heavy, cigar-smoke filled sigh. 'The good thing about a bomb, Littledick, is that it can be planted to go off at a certain time, which means we're out of there when it happens. Unless you have any other brilliant suggestions?'

'No, car bomb is fine.'

Frank looked at his watch again. 'Four minutes.'

That damn well wasn't a minute. Think, for fuck's sake. Reuben glanced at the newspaper folded in Frank's lap. A paragraph caught his eye.

'Hackers Cost Millions.'

'Computer hackers have cost businesses world-wide millions of dollars in fraudulent transactions and damage control...'

An idea appeared like a huge, shining light bulb above him. 'I know a guy,' he blurted out, 'a genius with computers. I'll get him to hack into Lucy's Facebook page and suss out her social life.'

'How do you know she's got a Facebook page?'

'Of course she has, they all do. If it's not Facebook, it's Myspace or something similar. Whatever it is, he'll find it. I'm not kidding, this guy could hack into the World Bank.'

'And then what?'

'If he can find out where she's going to be on a certain night, a party or some other do, then we go and do the deed on the car while she's there, under the cover of darkness.'

Frank leant back and stared at the sky, puffing on his cigar. Reuben could almost hear the cogs turning in his brain.

'This mate – has he got enough sense to keep his mouth shut? And what's in it for him?'

'He wouldn't be doing what he's doing if he was the sort who blabbed. And he owes me a favour, a big one. I got him out of a nasty scrape.'

'What sort of scrape?'

'It's a long story – suffice to say it involved a woman, a very stroppy woman.'

'They always do.' Frank said. He sat up and stubbed out his cigar on the seat. 'It needs more work. Get the Facebook thing happening and we'll go from there.'

'Just one thing - she's going on holidays in a couple of days, won't be back until the New Year.'

'Bloody hell! Where's she going?'

'Scotland.'

'Scotland? Why the fuck is she going there?'

Reuben shrugged. 'I don't know, perhaps she has relatives there. Or maybe she likes men in kilts.'

'Anyway,' he added, 'my mate will need some time. It's not something he can do in a few hours.' He had no idea if that were true, but at least it would buy him some time.

'At this rate she'll die of old age before we get to her. And just tell your mate as much as he needs to know to do the job. I'm warning you, if there's a leak, I'll know exactly where it's coming from. And then...'

He made a gun with his fingers and pointed it towards Reuben's head.

22

Thommo stuffed the fat envelope in his jeans pocket. 'That's the easiest three hundred dollars I've ever made. You got any more jobs like that?'

Reuben shook his head. 'Afraid not. How did it go?'

Thommo shovelled a large dollop of cream into his mouth. 'I decided beforehand to pretend to be a bit simple – some would say, not much pretence. Usually people are more tolerant if you're handicapped. I raved on about cars and how much I loved them, and he was getting impatient so he got his gear out and started cleaning the windscreen, hoping I s'pose that I'd go away. But instead I grabbed a cloth and started helping him.'

He grinned. 'That tested his patience because I made a few smears on the windows and he got really agitated then. He was almost bursting with the effort of not telling me to fuck off. Then a woman who'd parked her car near us came back from her shopping and was listening to me, and that made him even more annoyed. Then when the time was up, I said I was meeting my girlfriend and hoped to bump into him again one day. He just sort of smiled through gritted teeth. But I bet he gave the cat a good hard kick when he got home.'

'That was a good call, doing the simpleton thing.'

'So, mission accomplished?'

Reuben nodded.

Thommo polished off his iced chocolate with a slurp and a belch. He leaned back in his chair and patted his stomach.

'I really must lose some weight. Why does food have to be so fucking delicious?'

The tinkling of a mobile phone sounded nearby. The man at the next table dug into his pocket, and two women on the other side scrabbled around in their handbags. Reuben suddenly recognised the ring tone and dragged his phone out of his pocket just in time.

'Reuben, this is Bruce Berkeley.'

'Who? ... Oh, hullo.'

'I have some good news. You have a part in the Becker beer ad.'

'Really? Wow – I mean, thank you.'

'It's not the part you auditioned for, though. I want you to play the barman.'

'The barman?'

Thommo was looking at him intently.

'It's not a speaking part but it's an important one.'

'So what do I do?'

'Look obliging and pull a few beers.'

'I think I could probably manage that.'

'Fantastic, I'll ring you soon with the details of the shoot. Enjoy the rest of your day.'

'You got a part in the beer ad, didn't you?' Thommo said.

Reuben nodded.

Thommo thumped the table. 'Fuck it, it's so unfair! I've been slaving away for years and the best I can do is an extra in a crowd scene and you score a part at your first audition!'

'Chill out,' Reuben said. 'I got the part of the barman; it's not even a speaking part. All I get to do is pour beer.'

'At least you can't forget your lines. And they might let you drink the beer.'

'I doubt it. And what's so good about not having any lines? It'll be boring as batshit standing there looking – how did he put it? – obliging and not saying a word.'

Thommo considered this. 'I s'pose it doesn't sound that good.'

'Spot-on. And by the end of the day, my face will be aching from all that smiling, and I'll be so sick of pulling beer that it will put me off it for life. Or at least, a few days.'

'So really, it's a crap job, isn't it?'

'Totally.'

Thommo blew out a sigh. 'Thank God for that. For a moment there, I thought you were one up on me.'

He eyed off the chocolate mint beside Reuben's coffee. 'Mind if I have that?'

Reuben's mobile phone rang again. 'Hi, honey, just reminding you about picking up the milk. Where are you?'

'I'm in a coffee shop.'

'By yourself?'

'No ... I'm with Finn.'

'You didn't tell me he was in town again! Why don't you invite him home for dinner tonight?'

'He's busy tonight.' Reuben watched Thommo as he returned to the table after ordering another iced chocolate. An idea flashed into his mind. Two in one day – he hadn't lost his touch after all.

'I tell you what, he's in town for a few days, I'll see if he's free on Saturday night.'

He put his hand over the phone. 'Are you free on Saturday night?' he asked Thommo.

'Let me check my diary.' He stared into space, frowning. 'I could have a hot date.'

Reuben drew a dollar sign on the table with his finger.

'But then again, probably not. What's the occasion?'

'I'll tell you in a minute.'

'He's free on Saturday night,' he said into the phone, 'so I've invited him over. He's looking forward to meeting you. And I won't forget the milk.'

He pressed the 'off' button and looked at Thommo. 'How would you like another job after all?'

***

Reuben went into the study and retrieved his folder of personal documents. Although he'd gone through his effects and thrown out everything pertaining to his old life, it was possible he still had Curly Hansen's number somewhere. It had been a while since Reuben had last spoken to him. Six years ago, Curly had set up his and Derek's computer system for the business, to ensure their financial transactions couldn't be tracked. In the end though, the police cracked it but only because Reuben and Derek confessed all in return for the prospect of a lighter sentence.

A couple of years later, Reuben heard on the grapevine that Curly had married a rich old Chinese woman. It hadn't surprised him as Curly was a notorious gold-digger, but the price he had to pay was making love to an old woman. Reuben shuddered at the thought.

He flipped through his papers. Birth certificate, Year Twelve exam results, the last letter his mother had written him in her spidery handwriting, a dog-eared faded photo of him and his mother at his Year Seven graduation - Reuben chubby-faced and grinning, his mother tall and proud in her best dress and hat. A sharp pain stabbed his chest. Old computer manual, instructions for a TV he no longer owned, a solicitor's account for representation in court – had he paid that? He flipped back to the computer manual. Operating instructions for a Dell, top of the range back then. On the back was scribbled in pencil 'Curly' and a phone number. It was unlikely he still lived at the same address, but it was worth a try.

He dialled the number. A lazy-voiced female said Curly no longer lived there.

'What do you want him for?'

'He's an old friend, I just want to catch up.'

'Honey, Curly has no friends; only creditors and complainants. Which one are you?'

'As a matter of fact, he does owe me money.'

'Join the queue. I'll give you his mobile number, but I'm warning you, you'll get fuck all. That old 'Chink' he's shacked up with is the one with all the dough.'

Reuben wrote down the number and thanked her.

'Good luck, luv, you'll need it.'

He rang the number. A male voice answered. 'Yes?'

The voice was faint against the blaring of a TV.

'Curly? How are you? It's Reuben.'

'Who?'

'Reuben. Reuben Littlejohn.'

'Rubie! How the fuck are you? Hang on, I'll turn the telly down.'

A pause then sudden silence. 'To what do I owe this pleasure? I thought you were still inside.'

'I was a good boy so they let me out. I've got a favour to ask you.'

'What sort of favour?' His tone was instantly wary.

'A computer-type of favour. You're still into that, aren't you?'

'For a select few. I'm in semi-retirement, mate, got myself an old lady who's loaded and as much mull as I want.'

'This is kind of urgent, so I'd like to see you ASAP.'

'I'm pretty busy at the moment.'

His voice was slow and languid; he was probably smoking a joint as he spoke.

'I thought you said you were semi-retired.'

'Doesn't mean I'm sitting on my arse all day waiting for people to call around and ask me favours. Tell you what, I'm free tonight. Why don't you come over? The old lady's doing her specialty; deep-fried pig trotters.'

He and Carlene had been invited to a dinner party at Alec and Nancy's. He was sure the guests would include at least one local industry bigwig who would profess an interest in finding Reuben a job. Weighed up against the pig trotters, the trotters won hands-down. But there was no hope of weaselling out of the dinner party.

'Where do you live?' he asked Curly.

'Highgate Hill, 34 Wesley Street.'

Not too far. Into the city, over the William Jolly Bridge and another couple of kilometres. He could be there in half an hour. He looked at his watch. A quarter to five. They were expected at her parents' place at six-thirty. He made some quick calculations. It was tight, but doable.

'How about I come over now? I'll have to pass on the pig trotters though.'

'Suit yourself.'

He left a note for Carlene. 'Had to go out. Will be home in time to go to the dinner party.' The traffic was heavy and the Barbiemobile weaved its way through the cars like a small pink missile. Thirty-five minutes later, he arrived at Curly's house.

It was a sprawling, well-preserved Queenslander, set on a hill amongst a tangle of lush, untamed vegetation. Below it the Brisbane River gleamed a sullen brown in the afternoon sun. The house was set back from the road and by the time Reuben had climbed the steep path to the front door, brushing away ferns that leapt out at him and ducking overhanging branches, he was out of breath. So much for the jogging.

The house was high-set, the underneath built in as a lower storey. At the top of the front steps, a notice on the front door said

'Xio Changu. Chinese Medicine and Acupuncture. Monday to Friday 9am to 5pm. After-hours by appointment'.

A door opened from beneath him and a head popped out. 'Down here, mate.'

Curly hadn't changed, apart from a few more grey hairs. Contrary to the tradition of Australian nicknames, Curly actually did have curly hair. Along with his cherubic face he'd borne an uncanny resemblance to Leo Sayer in his younger days and he still did so now, if a craggier, wilder Leo. His hair stood up from his head in a halo of frizz, as if he were in a permanent state of electrocution.

'Come into my den of iniquity.'

He ushered Reuben into an expansive living room – dark panelling, polished wooden floor and expensive furniture. A huge flat screen TV dominated the room; the evening newsreader smiling cheesily. The sweet burnt smell of marijuana lingered in the air.

'Want a beer?'

Curly was barefoot, in torn jeans and t-shirt, cigarette dangling from his mouth. Without waiting for an answer, he went behind the small bar in the corner and came out with two stubbies of beer.

Reuben sank into the leather couch and Curly stretched out in the recliner chair opposite. 'So mate, you're looking well. The Big House treat you okay?'

'I survived it. But I'm not going back there.'

'They all say that. And they all end up going back. Even me. But Delores looks after me now, she makes sure I don't get into any trouble.'

'Delores?'

'My old lady. I can't pronounce her Chinese name. You got a girlfriend?'

'A wife, actually. Carlene.'

'Congratulations!' He held up his beer in a toast. 'Didn't think you'd ever tie the knot. She must be some chick, huh?'

'Yeah, she is. We're going to a dinner party tonight and she'll kill me if I'm late home, so I'll have to get down to business.'

He gave Curly a brief outline of what he wanted him to do, with no mention of the plan to kill Lucy, or of Frank and Bomber.

'I thought you said you weren't going back inside?' Curly said.

'I'm not.'

'Whatever you're doing is obviously not legal, and you're asking me to stick my neck out as well.'

'Come on, Curly, cracking a Facebook password is just kindergarten stuff for you. It's not as if you're robbing a bank. The cops have bigger fish to fry.'

'And what's in it for me?'

'You owe me.'

Curly's face was blank. 'I do?'

'Two words. Fiona Watford.'

He stared into his beer. 'Oh ... yeah.'

Fiona Watford was an heiress with a pug-like face and a body to match. Curly had been dating her and convinced her to marry him – the only problem was that Fiona was pathologically quick-tempered and the slightest incident could provoke her into a rage. After she threatened Curly with a knife, he called the wedding off, which made her even more furious and she threatened to set her brother, a hulking ice user who was just as unpredictable, onto Curly. Reuben stepped in, took Fiona out for a drink and convinced her that Curly himself was not only a psychopath but a member of the Hells Angels and she should consider herself very lucky she'd escaped from his clutches. Fiona gave him a prolonged kiss of gratitude and left town the next day.

'You said you were indebted to me for life,' Reuben said. 'Or words to that effect.'

'I don't remember saying nothing like that.' He grinned. 'But fuck, she was a mad bitch and you saved me from a thrashing.' He raised his beer again. 'Okay, it's a deal.'

He got up, went over to the bar and came back with a small clip seal bag and a packet of cigarette papers.

'You gonna join me?'

Reuben shook his head.

'Not even for old time's sake?'

Reuben hesitated. When Curly was setting up the computer system for All Purpose Financial Consultants, and Reuben and Derek were getting the office ready to move into, the three of them would light up a joint in the afternoon and as the furniture had not yet arrived, sprawl on the carpet. As the setting sun glinted on the windows, a spectacular sight after a smoke, they discussed their favourite subjects – money, women and sex. Afterwards they'd reconvene to a smoky downtown bar, then dinner at a seafood restaurant on the river.

Those were heady days – full of hope and the invincibility of youth. The weight of sadness overwhelmed Reuben and he felt a deep longing to be back there. Even as he was tempted to light up a joint to take him back, he knew it was futile. He was stuck in between, wanting to and not wanting to, and either decision was painful. Anyway, he couldn't afford to get stoned – he had a dinner party to go to.

Reuben shook his head again. Curly rolled himself a joint with deft fingers and lit it, settling back in his chair.

'I need some info,' he said. 'Everything you can tell me about her.'

He gave Curly the basic stuff – Lucy's name, address, occupation, an estimate of her age, married with a young child.

'A parole officer? You're in dangerous territory, mate. Are you stalking her?'

'No.'

'It's your funeral. What else do you know about her?'

'That's about it.'

Curly closed his eyes and exhaled a cloud of pungent smoke. Was the furore about passive smoking true? Reuben breathed in deeply; he hoped so.

'You're making it bloody hard,' Curly said.'

'Aren't there programs you can use to crack a password?' Reuben asked.

'There are, they're called dictionary attack and they literally try every word in the English language. You only get so many attempts at one time and then they boot you off, so then I have to log in to another computer with a different IP address and a new identity, so they can't trace me. So it can sometimes take weeks. And I'm assuming you want it sooner than that.'

'The sooner the better. I've got someone breathing down my neck, and it'll be very nasty for me if I don't come up with the goods.'

'Sounds like heavy stuff, mate.' He placed his joint in the ashtray beside him and leaned forward, his large bony hands dangling between his knees. 'See, it's a lot easier to crack a password if you have a psychological profile of the person, like those police guys on telly. You have to know their likes and dislikes, what sort of clothes they wear, favourite food, favourite rock group, all that sort of stuff. It could be the difference between me making a thousand hits and a hundred. You'd be surprised how many people use really obvious things for their passwords, like their kid's name or their favourite food.'

'I don't know any of those things, I really don't know much about her at all.' Except what he'd made up. In his fantasies, Lucy liked long dresses with slits all the way up the leg; skinny-dipping in the middle of the night, her bare skin luminous in the moonlight; anything dipped in chocolate; and music with a primal beat that thrust right into your very core...

'Think, mate. There's got to be something,' Curly said.

'The only thing I know is that she's going to Scotland for the Christmas holidays. And she doesn't like haggis.'

'Fan-fucking-tastic. So we know haggis isn't her password, besides the fact it's not long enough, and that only leaves several million other words.'

A pair of tiny feet appeared on the internal staircase leading up from the den. They trod lightly down the stairs, to reveal a petite woman in a long cherry-red silk dress. Despite the lines criss-crossing her face like a map of the Underground, she resembled a Chinese doll with her shiny black hair cut in a short bob and her dark, slanted eyes.

'Delores, babe, meet a friend of mine, Reuben.'

She glided over to Reuben and held out her hand. 'Pleased to meet you.'

She smiled and instantly you forgot about the wrinkles. Her eyes shone like two black marbles. Reuben stood up and shook her hand.

'You like some green tea?' she said.

'No thanks, I have to go soon.'

Delores waggled her finger at Curly. 'You naughty boy, you smoke too much weed. It makes you forget.'

She spoke in a singsong lilt.

'Babe, you don't have to worry, I'll never forget you.'

Curly leaned forward and pinched her on her almost non-existent backside. She slapped his hand and winked at Reuben. 'It makes him sleepy too. Then he doesn't want to fuck.'

'Okay, Delores, that's enough. Get up there and cook those pigs trotters.'

Delores winked at Reuben again and scampered up the stairs.

'Can't keep up with the old lady?' Reuben couldn't resist it.

'Not at all, mate. You can't give it to them every time they want it; they'll just take it for granted. Keep 'em keen, that's my motto.'

Reuben looked at his watch. 'Gotta go. How long will it take you?'

Curly shrugged. 'Could take hours, could take weeks.'

Weeks? Reuben had met a guy inside – everyone knew him as Harry the Hacker – who'd boasted that he could hack into anyone's password on any site in an hour. Pity he didn't know where to find Harry – he didn't even know his surname. Maybe Harry was exaggerating, but to take weeks seemed excessive. Frank couldn't make a move until Lucy came back from Scotland in the New Year, but he'd be constantly on Reuben's case.

'I'd appreciate it if you could make it top priority,' Reuben said.

'Don't worry mate, I'm onto it,' Curly said, lighting another joint. As Reuben left, he called out, 'If you can find out anything more about her, call me.'

***

Of course Reuben's calculations had not taken into account the three-car pile-up on Petrie Terrace that brought the traffic to a standstill. He wove his way through the line of cars, only to be stopped at the head of the queue by the gloved hand of a policeman. His mobile phone rang in his pocket. He knew it was Carlene, and he was glad of the excuse not to answer it. By the time the traffic had cleared and he arrived home, it was dark.

Carlene whipped open the front door. 'Where the hell have you been?'

'I'll explain later,' he said, rushing past her into the house. He had a shower and dressed in record time. Carlene was sitting on the living room couch with a face like thunder.

'We're already late,' she hissed. 'You'd better have a fucking good excuse.'

Reuben felt a jolt of shock - it was the first time he'd heard her swear. 'Let's go and I'll tell you on the way.'

Neither of them spoke as they got into the car, and he backed out of the driveway.

'Well?' Carlene said.

He'd tried to think of a reasonable excuse all the way home. He didn't want to use Finn again – he was becoming far too demanding and he wouldn't be at all surprised if Carlene accused him and Finn of having an affair. Or dressing up in women's clothing together.

'I needed to get out. I went for a drive and lost track of time.'

'Where did you go?'

'Just around the neighbourhood. I found a park and sat there for a while.'

'What park?'

'I don't know the name of it,' he said irritably. 'Just a park, okay?'

He was driving along Gympie Road as fast as he dared. Luckily, the worst of the peak hour traffic was over. He stole a glance at Carlene. Her expression was a mixture of anger and disbelief.

On impulse he said, 'The usual sort of park, you know, swings and slippery slides. I had a couple of swings and went down the slippery slide a few times. That's probably why I forgot the time.'

He felt her eyes boring into him. 'Reuben' – it was the first time she'd called him by his full name – 'there is something definitely wrong with you. Listen to yourself! A grown man playing on the swings and slippery slides! What's next? Playing in the sandpit?'

'I see nothing wrong with playing in the sandpit; it's a healthy outdoor pastime.'

Carlene took a deep breath and said in slow, measured tones, 'When people are under extreme stress, they sometimes revert to a happier time, like their childhood. That's what you're doing, trying to avoid the present because it's too painful.'

Reuben's hands tightened on the steering wheel. 'I'm not avoiding the present and the only fucking stress I'm under is you telling me I'm under stress.'

Carlene stared out the window, her body as rigid as a steel pole.

'I just don't know what to believe any more,' she said wearily.

'What do you mean?'

'You've been behaving very strangely, going out at odd hours. And you say you've been spending time with Finn, but sometimes I've wondered if he even exists.'

'Of course he exists – you'll meet him on Saturday night. Do you think I've been spending all this time with an imaginary person?'

She ignored his question. 'And then there's the jogging. Men often take it up when they're having an affair.'

'I've told you already, I'm jogging to tone up and improve my chances of getting work with Pizzazz. Believe me, I wouldn't put myself through the agony for any other reason.'

'And what about staying up late at night on the computer? A girl at work's husband was doing that and she found out he was having cybersex with a woman in Romania!'

'For God's sake, that was only one night and I wasn't having cybersex! How do you do that anyway? Sounds very uncomfortable to me.'

A red light loomed in front of them. Reuben braked and glanced at Carlene. A tear spilled out from her eye and rolled down her cheek. He felt a pang of remorse for the joke, and reached out and stroked her knee.

'Honey, I promise you, I'm not having an affair.'

Carlene burst into a fit of loud, gasping sobs. Why did women always pick the worst possible time to turn on the waterworks? The traffic light turned green, Reuben darted into the left lane and pulled over on the side of the road outside the Little Bo-Peep Adult Shop. He took Carlene in his arms and stroked her hair until her sobs had died down to soft little sighs. She sat up and gave him a half-smile. Her hair was rumpled and her eyes red and mascara-smudged. Reuben's good shirt was wet with her tears.

'We'd better go,' she sniffed. 'Mum and Dad will be getting worried.'

23

He didn't have the opportunity to tell Carlene about getting the part in the ad until they were on the way home from the dinner party.

'How much are you they paying you?' she asked.

'I forgot to ask.'

She stared at him in disbelief. 'You forgot to ask? Again?'

'With the excitement of getting the part, I didn't think of it.'

'The excitement of getting the part of a mute bartender who's on screen for probably all of four seconds?'

'He's not mute; he just chooses not to say anything. The strong, silent type. And I think it's actually six seconds.'

'Whatever. What next? Any roles coming up as a non-speaking gorilla? Or maybe more modelling – a centrefold for Cleo?'

'Look, I know it doesn't sound much, but who knows what it could lead to?'

His words rang with false confidence. He didn't have a clue where it could lead to.

'To the employment agency, I expect,' Carlene said.

'You're just shitty because I didn't take up Greasy Gavin's offer.'

'Damn right I am.'

Gavin Topfer had been a guest at the dinner party. A portly man exuding after-shave and self-importance, he owned the biggest chain of used car dealerships in Brisbane. He'd offered to pull some strings and get Reuben a mature-age apprenticeship in car mechanics. Reuben declined, saying he didn't fancy wobbly rear ends and had no desire to know the difference between a monkey wrench and a screwdriver.

'Honestly, honey, can you see me as a grease monkey? It's a job for pimply-faced kids who get high on engine grease, and anyway I don't look good in overalls.'

'How do you know until you've tried it? It's not the most glamorous job in the world but that's how Gavin started out, and look where he is now.'

'Gavin is a pompous prick. Is that what you think I should aspire to?'

'I haven't heard you come up with any brilliant ideas of your own yet. You're so .... so ... frustrating!'

They spent the rest of the trip home in silence. He knew he should try to make amends, but a night at Nancy and Alec's, nodding and smiling and being polite to a bunch of boring snobs had left him exhausted.

***

Carlene scraped the remains of the bacon and eggs into the bin. 'I've invited Wayne and Jo and the kids over tonight. It'll make it more of a party.'

Reuben's chest burned with irritation. 'I don't think Finn is up to partying.'

'Don't be such a spoilsport,' Carlene said. 'I'm sure he'll enjoy himself. Anyway it's only a barbecue, nothing fancy.'

She delegated Reuben to cleaning the barbecue while she went out shopping for pre-dinner savouries, salads, marinated meats, breads, desserts and after-dinner chocolates. As he cleaned the barbecue, he thought about Curly. He was having serious doubts about the decision to enlist his help – doubts not only about his ability to do the job but his commitment to it. Even in his heyday as a technical geek, he'd been easily distracted by illicit substances and pleasures of the flesh. Any day now Frank would be demanding a progress report. Reuben tried desperately to think of something about Lucy that could be a clue to her password, but nothing presented itself.

Wayne and Jo arrived at six o'clock and settled the children in front of the TV with an *Ice Age* DVD and a bowl of popcorn. The doorbell rang at six-fifteen. Reuben opened the front door.

Thommo stood there dressed neatly in jeans, a polo t-shirt and sneakers.

'G'day mate!' He grinned broadly.

'Come in. Don't forget you're supposed to be depressed,' Reuben muttered as Thommo stepped inside.

'Oh, sorry,' he said, assuming a mournful expression. Reuben had given him the bare details of Finn's life so far, and he'd deduced that Reuben had been 'fooling around' and had invented Finn as an alibi for his nocturnal activities. Reuben let him think it because there was no other explanation he could offer.

They went into the kitchen and Reuben got him a stubby of beer out of the fridge. Thommo looked at it.

'You haven't got anything stronger by any chance?'

'What sort of stronger?'

'I'm rather partial to a Jack Daniels if you've got it.'

Reuben was on the verge of saying he didn't have any then decided it would be mean to hold out on him. When he'd told Thommo he couldn't pay him for his Finn gig until payday next week, Thommo said, 'Don't worry about it – we're mates now, aren't we? Buy me a carton of beer.' It had given Reuben a warm feeling in the pit of his stomach.

He opened the pantry, dug deep at the back and produced a bottle. Thommo's eyes lit up and he whistled.

'Whew! Gentleman Jack! The best bourbon in the world!'

Reuben poured it over ice with a splash of soda water. In his previous life, it had been a regular indulgence. He and Derek shared many a bottle, kicking back after work on the days they'd run out of weed, with a couple of Gentleman Jack's on ice to soften the sharp edges of the day. He often wondered what genetic mutation had resulted in his being blessed, despite his humble circumstances, with an innate sense of quality and an aspiration to the good life. He was born with a silver spoon in his mouth but brought up with a plastic one.

Now Gentleman Jack was a special occasion drink only – he'd bought it to celebrate his wedding and it was still three-quarters full. But what the hell – a visit from your imaginary friend, your only friend, was a special occasion. He got another glass, threw in some ice and poured himself a drink. With just a drop of soda.

They joined the others on the patio. After the introductions Jo said, 'You're nothing like I imagined.'

'Why?' Thommo said.

'I thought Finn was a Scandinavian name – I imagined you to be tall and blonde, like a Viking.'

'Sorry to disappoint you,' Thommo said. 'My grandmother had a fling with a Swedish cello player though. Does that count?'

Jo giggled. Wayne tipped his chair back and rested his can of beer on his stomach. 'So what do you do for a crust, mate?'

'Marketing,' Thommo said.

'Computers,' Reuben said at the same time.

'Marketing computers,' Thommo said.

'I see,' Wayne said. 'So you get around a bit in your job?'

'All over the place. One day I'm in Perth, the next I'm in Darwin. Sometimes I have to turn on the TV to know where I am. It's not as glamorous as it's cracked up to be, you know. It's pretty lonely in those hotel rooms at night...'

He hung his head and looked broodingly at his shoes.

'Reuben tells us you're a free man now, mate,' Wayne said. 'You should go out and hit the town, meet some of the local talent.'

'Wayne!' Jo glared at him.' That's so insensitive! You can see poor Finn is still upset about his marriage break-up.'

'As far as I'm concerned, any woman who cheats on her husband isn't worth crying over.' He placed his beer on the table and folded his arms. 'I'm sorry, but I tell it the way I see it and I don't make any apologies for it.'

'None needed,' Thommo said. 'I agree with you. She's chosen her bed, now she can lie on it. There'll be no more tears from me!'

He caught Reuben's eye. 'Not many, anyhow.'

Carlene brought out the tray of meat, and Reuben threw the sausages and steak onto the barbecue.

'Is the barbecue hot enough yet?' Wayne said.

'Yes,' Reuben said.

'It's got to be really hot when you put the meat on to seal in the juices.'

'It's hot.' Reuben indulged himself in a vision of Wayne being roasted over an open fire, like a large, hairy pig on a spit.

'So, Finn, you went to school with Rubie,' Carlene said.

'Yep, I sure did.'

'What was he like as a kid? You're the first person I've met from his childhood.'

'Well,' Thommo said, 'he was very funny.'

'In what way?'

'He was always playing practical jokes – you know, putting frogs in the girls' desks and spiders in their schoolbags.'

'Oh Rubie, that's awful,' Carlene said.

'There were some good ones though – the time he put the whoopee cushion on the headmaster's chair...'

Thommo continued his saga until he'd credited Reuben with just about every hackneyed practical joke known to schoolboy kind.

'I had a kid like that in my class at school,' Wayne said. 'Absolute pain in the arse. I got him out the back of the toilets one afternoon and blew up his bottle of exploding ink. All over him.'

'But that's only one side of him,' Thommo said. 'He was also very heroic.'

'Yeah?' Wayne said.

'Once, we were on a school excursion looking at rock formations and one of the girls fell into a lake. She couldn't swim, so Reuben ... sorry, Rubie,' he smirked, 'dived in, clothes and all, and pulled her out. Of course he had to give her mouth-to-mouth, and she was a hot babe, even dripping wet and blue in the face.'

'Very noble of you,' Carlene said.

'And then there was the time...' Thommo was on a roll, well-lubricated by Jack Daniels. By the time they'd finished their steaks, Reuben's passion for practical jokes had been vindicated by his ability to save his classmates from certain death and recruitment into the school choir.

'Did you actually do any schoolwork?' Jo asked coolly. Lately, she'd deigned to acknowledge Reuben's presence and occasionally speak to him, though her attitude was still distant. Reuben didn't know if Carlene had spoken to her about it, and he didn't want to know. The whole scenario was too distressing to think about – he felt as if he himself had been violated and held a smouldering resentment towards Jo.

'I managed to fit some in,' he said.

'Not one iota,' Thommo said at the same time. 'He was a natural, straight A's for everything, never opened a book.'

'I thought you said you just scraped through with passes,' Carlene said to Reuben.

Reuben gave Thommo a pointed look. 'I think you're confusing me with someone else.'

'Am I?' Thommo looked vague. 'Maybe I am. Or maybe I knew that underneath, you were naturally brilliant and should have got straight A's.'

He eyed the remains of steak and sausage on Jo's plate. 'Mind if I finish that off? Thanks.'

'Unfortunately that brilliance was misdirected,' Carlene said. 'But you've turned over a new leaf now, haven't you, honey?'

'Really?' Thommo said. He stopped shovelling food into his mouth and gave Reuben an appraising stare. 'Glad to hear it, I always said he'd come good.'

He held up his glass. 'How about another Gentleman Jack?'

'I think you've had enough,' Reuben said.

'Bullshit,' said Wayne. 'Let the poor bloke drown his sorrows. And what's this about Gentleman Jack? Have you been holding out on us? I'll have one too, thanks.'

Gritting his teeth Reuben went inside, poured Thommo another bourbon and one for Wayne.

'It looks like Rubie has well and truly turned over a new leaf,' Thommo was saying as he returned with the drinks. 'Now that he's going to be on TV.'

'Yeah?' Wayne said. 'Doing what?'

Reuben told them about his new role.

'So you don't actually say anything?' Wayne said.

'No, just smile and pour beers.'

'That's a useful skill to have,' Jo said in sarcasm-drenched tones.

'Damn right it is,' Thommo said. 'He did bloody well for a first audition. There were hundreds there.'

'Did you audition as well, Finn?' Carlene asked.

'Er ... yes. I happened to be in Brisbane at the time so I thought I'd go along for a bit of a laugh.'

'You didn't tell me that.' Carlene looked at Reuben as accusingly as if he'd neglected to tell her that Finn was a terrorist.

'Must have slipped my mind.' Reuben got up and started gathering up the dishes. 'Anyone for dessert?'

***

He and Carlene stacked the dishwasher then flopped into bed. Carlene, as usual after a couple of drinks, was giggly and amorous.

'Finn wasn't at all what I expected,' she said as she unbuttoned his shirt.

'Why?'

'He didn't seem at all depressed. Quite the opposite. And eat! I've never seen anyone eat as much as he does. And drink.'

'Yeah,' Reuben said gloomily. Between the two of them, Thommo and Wayne had finished off the Gentleman Jack. They'd forged an alliance based solely on that partiality and bolstered by a rousing rendition of football songs. It was at that point Reuben called a taxi for Thommo, poured him into it and helped Jo out to the car with her tired, overwrought children and barely standing husband.

'He's not usually so over-the-top. It was just the alcohol – he's been drinking a lot more since his wife left him.'

'He'll end up with an alcohol problem if he's not careful.' Carlene moved her hand up to his face and she traced the outline of his lips. 'You're lucky you've got me to look after you.'

Irritation niggled him. Again. At the beginning of their relationship, he'd gone along with her self-appointed role as his saviour, with a sense of playful irony. In a strange way it had turned him on. But as it became increasingly obvious that she viewed herself in this role with an enthusiasm bordering on obsessive, he became proportionately more annoyed. He removed her hand from his mouth.

'Yeah, I sure am.'

Carlene made her way slowly down his body with her lips and fingers and he became aroused, despite his irritation. As they made love, visions of Lucy filled his mind and he imagined it was her body lying beneath him, quivering and puckering under his touch. His last interview with her, as Thommo was diverting Bomber from his task, replayed itself. He was just coming to the end, when her mobile phone was ringing, when a brilliant idea flashed before him. Her password! In the same moment he climaxed.

'Ohhhhh ... yeah!' It was a cross between a yell and a moan.

'You went off like a firecracker.' Carlene snuggled into him and draped an arm over his chest.

'You were smoking hot yourself,' he said, stroking the hair off her forehead. It was true. She *was* hot. It just wasn't her he'd been fantasising about. Within minutes she was asleep, emitting her rhythmic little pffts. Reuben wanted to leap out of bed and ring Curly straight away, but he knew he'd get short shrift. Curly was more than likely to be in a deep, cannabis-induced sleep.

***

'Curly! How's it going?'

'What are you referring to when you say "it?" My state of health or this cunt of a job you've got me doing?'

'Both.'

'The first answer is "fucking terrible" and the second is "absolutely nowhere".'

'That's not good, on either count.'

'You realise I've been out of this industry for a while – it's not as easy as it used to be.'

'I thought you said you still did a few select projects.'

'I lied.'

So the one person he'd pinned his hopes on to get him out of this mess was useless. Too much alcohol and weed had killed his brain cells. Or all the useful ones. Reuben cast out his last line of hope.

'I just thought of something that might help. Lucy's ring tone on her mobile phone is the theme song from *The Addams Family*.'

'You think she might have the hots for Lurch? Or fancy herself as Morticia?'

Reuben saw Lucy gliding down a long staircase, an auburn-haired Morticia, her long dress plastered to her like a second skin, accentuating every curve. At the bottom, Reuben, in an imitation of Gomez, kissed her feverishly all the way up her arm to the swell of her breast...

'I'm thinking something to do with *The Addams Family* could be her password.'

'You could be right.'

Curly sounded distracted, as if his mind was on something else. Which it probably was.

'Thanks for the tip,' he said.

'Listen, this is a matter of life and death...'

But Curly had already hung up.

***

When Joe went to the bank, Reuben stood at the back door of the kitchen, breathed in a lungful of steamy air and checked his phone. One text message. 'Got it, ring me.'

He dialled Curly's number.

'You got a pen?'

'No, I'll remember it.'

'Her email address is lucyp33@gmail.com and her password is Addamsfamily. All one word.'

'I knew it!' Reuben said triumphantly.

'Addams has two D's.'

'I know.'

'I wish you'd fuckin' well told me; I nearly gave up.'

'Anyone who was a fan of *The Addams Family* would know that.'

'Well mate, I wasn't. I didn't spend my time watching the box when I was a kid. I was doing wholesome things out in the fresh air, stealing hubcaps and going for joyrides.'

'Thanks Curly, I appreciate it.'

'No worries, consider the debt repaid.'

After work, Reuben went into the city and found an internet cafe on George St. It was too risky using his home computer, too easy for Carlene to find out what internet sites he'd visited. The cafe was grimy and depressing. The pasty guy at the front desk nodded behind him, and Reuben took a seat in a corner cubicle. On one side of him a young Asian man wearing headphones gabbled away on Skype, and on the other side an overweight man stared at the computer screen, puffing laboured breaths through large, moist lips. Reuben glanced at the screen before he sat down and caught a glimpse of bare flesh and pendulous breasts.

He logged into the Facebook site and held his breath as he typed in Lucy's email address and password. On the screen appeared a photo of Lucy in shorts and t-shirt, standing on a beach holding a curly-haired baby. Towering over her with his arm around her shoulders stood a man who, apart from wearing just board shorts and thongs, could have stepped off a fireman's calendar. Shoulders like a front row forward, well-defined chest with ripples in all the right places, ironing board stomach (the bastard) and legs like tree trunks. As far removed from Nerdy Nigel as you could imagine. He and Lucy were both smiling – he looked especially self-satisfied. As well he might. Reuben hastily dismissed the image of them in bed together (did she really go for the brawny types?) and looked at the latest entry on her wall from someone called Lisa.

'Och, aye, you two'll have a grand time. Don't eat too much haggis and we'll see you on New Year's Eve.'

He scrolled down through the other comments on her wall from the past couple of weeks – mainly repartee between Lucy and her friends about her trip to Scotland. He learnt that Lucy's husband, Duncan, was Scottish (of course his name was Duncan - he probably went to a private school and had his own box at the Ballymore Rugby Union Club) and they were going to Edinburgh to spend Christmas with his parents, who would also meet their granddaughter Chloe for the first time.

He scrolled down further. On 29 November, someone called Susie Q had written – 'By the way, Luce I've got two extra tickets for the New Year's Eve Ball at the Grand Plaza Hotel. I booked for Matt and Carlie but they can't come now, so they're yours if you want them. It should be great – black tie, eight-piece band, the whole box and dice, I'm going to wear my new dress and fuck-me shoes. It's a charity do in aid of Amnesty International, so we can be full of warm and fuzzy do-goodedness at the same time.'

'I don't know if we'll be in the mood for a ball,' was Lucy's reply. 'We only get back on 29 December – we'll still be jetlagged. And it's impossible to find a babysitter for New Year's Eve.'

Susie Q had replied, 'Latest scientific research shows that the best way to get rid of jetlag is to drinks heaps and stay up all night! Lisa and Spike are going too, Lisa's Mum will babysit. You have to come – don't you agree, Dunc?'

'Och, aye,' Duncan wrote back.

'OK, OK,' Lucy replied. 'Just don't blame me if I fall asleep in my champagne at nine o'clock.'

Reuben stared unseeingly at the computer screen. A black-tie charity ball at one of the most exclusive hotels in the city. An auspicious start to the New Year. Or maybe not. That would depend entirely on him.

He took out his mobile phone, dialled Call Connect and asked to be put through to the Grand Plaza Hotel. *Please let there still be tickets*. These society functions often sold out quickly, especially for New Year's Eve.

'Good afternoon, this is the Grand Plaza Hotel. My name is Amy, how may I help you?'

'Good afternoon, Amy. Do you by any chance still have tickets available for your New Year's Eve Ball?'

'You're in luck, sir. We had sold out but due to demand, the organisers have just released another fifty tickets. How many would you like?'

Reuben gave himself a mental high-five. 'Two, thanks.'

24

'Cut!' yelled the director.

Reuben froze mid-smile.

'It's Vanessa you're serving, not her tits. Keep your eyes on her face.'

'How many barmen do you know wouldn't check her tits out when she's flashing them right in front of him?'

Vanessa gave a sultry smile and recrossed her legs, exposing a slim, black-stockinged thigh.

'This is an ad; we're not looking for realism. Take four.'

'Do you want me to make another shandy?'

'No, for Christ's sake, just take it from where you're handing it to her. Take four!'

Reuben handed Vanessa the drink, looking straight into her eyes as he put on his most winning smile. In his peripheral vision, her breasts almost bounced out of her low-cut top, creating a cleavage deep enough to fall into. He imagined himself as Tom Thumb, diving straight off the bar into her cleavage, a soft, warm landing...

'Cut!'

Reuben looked across at Scott Henley, a short, ruddy-faced man who paced constantly, leaving his director's chair forlornly empty.

'Your smile's too high wattage, you'll take the attention off Adam. Low beam is fine.'

Adam sat at the bar next to Vanessa. He played the guy who'd just summoned the courage to approach her and offer to buy her a drink. He was tall and gangly, with long hair that flopped over his eyes and thick-rimmed Buddy Holly glasses. After

Vanessa had drunk her Beckers, she was to see a vision of him filled out with muscle, his hair neatly trimmed and his glasses off to reveal his captivating blue eyes. Reuben had consoled himself with the thought that he didn't look wimpy enough to get the part. He gave an inward sigh. How had he ever thought it would be a cinch playing a non-speaking bartender?

'Get it right this time. I'm sure we'd all like to be home for Christmas! Take five!'

The remark was not as facetious as it sounded, given that Christmas was only four weeks away and Becker Beer wanted the advertisement shot, edited and ready for the screen in time for their launch in the New Year.

Reuben handed the shandy to Vanessa again, trying his best for a medium intensity smile while keeping his eyes steadfastly on her face. She took the drink with a 'thank you' and a flutter of her false eyelashes. Reuben paused, waiting for the 'Cut!' but there was none. He looked at Scott. 'Was that okay?'

Scott took a deep breath. 'If I don't yell "cut", you keep going,' he said through gritted teeth. He flung his clipboard onto his chair. 'We have to cut now.'

He hauled a packet of cigarettes and a lighter out of his pants pocket. 'Have a ten-minute break, and I mean ten minutes, not eleven!' He stomped out of the rear entrance of the hotel.

Reuben exchanged glances with Vanessa and Adam.

'Who does he think he is?' Adam said. 'Steven Fucking Spielberg?'

He slid off his bar stool and mooched off.

'Would you like a coffee?' Reuben asked Vanessa.

'Love one,' she said. Reuben followed her pert, mini-skirted backside into the public bar next door where the staff had laid out tea, coffee and sandwiches for the actors and crew. The ad was being filmed on location at a hotel called The Horse and Coach in the far western suburbs, where acreage homes and equestrian clubs abounded. It was a Saturday and although the interior bars were closed to the public during the shooting, the beer garden was overflowing. Security guards stood at the front and rear entrances of the hotel to make sure that no one gatecrashed the proceedings.

Reuben fetched two paper cups of home brand instant coffee with a side serve of cardboard biscuits. He and Vanessa perched on barstools. The decor was rich brown and smelt of leather, watercolour prints of horses adorned the walls and the barstool seats were in the shape of saddles.

'Cute,' said Vanessa. 'I think I'll ride side saddle.'

She flung her legs out to the side and crossed them, flashing plenty of thigh in the process. A group of male extras nearby, young and aggressively exuberant, fell silent. One of them whistled softly through his teeth. Seemingly oblivious to the attention, Vanessa said, 'Sorry if my boobs put you off before.'

'They didn't put me off,' said Reuben.

They jiggled in front of him, taunting his words. 'Maybe they did a bit, but in a nice way.'

'I figured that's why they hired me. These babies cost me three thousand dollars, so I may as well show them off and get my money's worth, don't you agree?'

'Absolutely.'

From the corner of his eye, Reuben saw someone approaching their table.

'Hullo, Reuben.'

'Nina! What are you doing here?'

She was in jeans and t-shirt, her hair loose. It was the first time he'd seen her outside of the coffee shop. She looked different, somehow softer and rounder.

'Marcus, a friend of mine from Uni, is doing some work experience with Scott,' she said. 'I decided to come along to give him some moral support.' She nodded in the direction of a bearded guy in baggy jeans, in earnest conversation with one of the film crew. Reuben had noticed him earlier, getting the bar set up for the scene and acting as a gopher for Scott.

'You can give us all some moral support,' said Vanessa. 'The guy's a total prick.'

'Oh, Nina, this is Vanessa. She's the star of the show.'

'I don't know about star; it's not exactly Hollywood.' But she simpered and leaned back in her chair to give her chest maximum exposure.

'No, it's not,' Nina said.

'How long have you been here?' Reuben said.

'Long enough to see you perform,' Nina said. She looked as if she were trying hard not to smile.

'I never realised how hard it was being a barman. Just as well I didn't have any lines to learn.'

'That's showbiz for you,' Vanessa said. 'You get shouted at all the time, the coffee's crap and the director gets shitty when you won't sleep with him.'

She pulled her skirt down to her mid-thigh and flicked a wisp of blonde hair off her face.

'Well, I'll leave you two to it,' Nina said. 'See you later, Reuben.'

Marcus suddenly spied her and loped over. She gave him a peck on the cheek and they walked away, chatting.

'I don't think she likes me,' Vanessa said.

'What makes you say that?'

'Animal instinct. Contrary to what you guys think, we women have heaps more of it than you. And my instinct tells me you really like her.'

'She's a nice person, but I don't like her in that way.'

Vanessa shrugged. 'Whatever.'

'Besides, my wife won't let me have a girlfriend.'

Vanessa leaned forward and gave him a soft, lingering kiss on the lips. 'Why, kind sir, that's a damn shame,' she said, in a southern belle accent. She slid off her stool and trotted off in the direction of the ladies toilets.

***

The shoot wrapped up at six o'clock with Scott stalking out into the beer garden again for a cigarette after ordering Marcus to tidy up and rearrange the furniture. The cast scattered quickly before Scott could reappear and demand another take.

As Reuben hurried out the front door of the hotel, he almost bowled over Nina standing outside.

'Oops, sorry! Do you need a lift?'

She shook her head. 'I'm waiting for Marcus.'

'Is he your boyfriend?'

She hesitated.

'Sorry, I didn't mean to be personal.'

'We're friends, it hasn't progressed that far yet.'

'He seems nice,' Reuben said, although having only spoken a couple of words to Marcus, he had no idea if this was true.

'Yes, he is.'

Silence. For once in his life Reuben was tongue-tied. It was different in the cafe – their conversation revolved around coffee, hamburgers and dishwashing. She wasn't a small talk person and he felt now that anything he said would sound glib and inane.

Nina inclined her head towards the hotel. 'You weren't too bad in there.'

Reuben felt absurdly pleased at this half-compliment. 'You think so?'

'Marcus says you have a natural screen presence.'

Reuben decided that his original summation of Marcus was correct. 'Thanks. Maybe this means that one day I'll be able to get out from under Joe's feet.'

She smiled. 'He likes you, you know.'

'He's got a funny way of showing it.'

'Maltese men are like that, very fiery, but it's all just bluster. You put up with his shit but you don't let him walk all over you – he respects that. And you make him laugh.'

Laughing at me, not with me, Reuben wanted to say. But he refrained because it was clear Nina adored her uncle.

Marcus appeared by her side. 'Are you ready?' He took her hand in his and squeezed it.

'Bye Reuben,' Nina said. 'See you at work.'

As they walked away, she slipped her hand gently out of Marcus's.

25

Frank threw back his head and downed his Scotch. A pair of breasts leading a skimpily dressed platinum blonde sashayed past. A volley of wolf-whistles followed her. He smacked his lips appreciatively.

'View here is unsurpassed, don't you agree?'

'Not bad,' Reuben said. He glanced around him. At seven pm, The Lido was still half asleep, like a tart waking up, yet to put on her face and costume. A couple of tables near the stage were occupied by businessmen, shirtsleeves rolled up and ties loose, staking an early claim for a bird's eye view of the show. Occasionally, one of the dancers, attributes on show, strolled through to give them a special preview. A menu in a holder graced each table, but no one seemed interested in food. The air was thick with the fumes of alcohol and expectancy.

'There are more holes in this idea than a Swiss cheese,' Frank said. 'How do you know she's going to take her car?'

'An educated guess. It's impossible to get a cab on New Year's Eve, she'll be jetlagged and won't drink much; and if she wants to go home early, she's got the car right there. That's what I'd do if I were her.'

'And what's your role in this?'

'I'll be at the ball, keeping an eye on her and making sure she doesn't disappear before the job's done. It'll probably take Bomber a while – he'll have to hang around until the traffic in the car park dies down.'

Frank motioned to a waiter to bring more drinks. 'So you're going to be fart-arsing around in a penguin suit drinking Moet and hobnobbing with the rich and famous while Bomber is breaking into Lucy's car and risking life and limb in the process. Seems to me an unfair division of labour.'

'What's your idea, then?' said Reuben, heart sinking because he knew already.

Frank pointed a stubby finger at him. 'You follow the bitch into the city, suss out where she parks her car and give Bomber the lowdown. Then, Cinderella, you can go to the ball and keep your beady little eye on her for as long as you like.'

The waiter arrived with the drinks – another Scotch for Frank and a mineral water for Reuben, as he had to drive home. Hopefully, very soon. Frank gave the waiter a twenty-dollar note and waved away the change.

'It's a good plan,' Reuben said, 'but there's one small flaw. My wife is going to be very suspicious if I have to go off somewhere without her on New Year's Eve. Not to mention pissed off because we'll arrive at the ball late. Come on, Frank, you know how women are. Can't Bomber tail her?'

Frank narrowed his eyes.

'You seem to have forgotten, Littledick,' he said, his voice menacing, 'that I'm running this show. And I don't give a rat's arse that you can't keep your missus under control. Bomber can't do the tailing, he's got enough on his hands. Do you have any idea what's involved in his line of work? It's a specialist's job, he has to prepare beforehand, limber up.'

'Like a ballet dancer?'

'Exactly. And I think you're forgetting the other reason you should do what you're told. Five-foot-six, big tits, legs right up to her bum.'

Anyone else might have thought Frank was referring to the voluptuous Mrs Santa trotting past at that moment, bursting out of a red fur-trimmed bra and mini-skirt. He looked at his watch. 'Much as I'd love to sit here shooting the breeze with you, I have a business meeting.'

He produced a mobile phone and handed it to Reuben. 'Call me on the 29th. And for your sake, it had better be all systems go.'

Reuben was halfway to the exit when he called, 'Hey, Littledick!'

He stopped and turned. All eyes were upon him. Someone sniggered.

'Merry Christmas!'

Frank raised his glass in a toast, grinning. Mrs Santa had now taken Reuben's seat, cosying up to Frank, and she smiled and waved. Business meeting? She looked as if she meant business. Reuben deigned to reply and walked out. Operation Luce End, Mark Three was now in motion and he had two weeks to come up with a plan to subvert it.

***

The doorbell rang just as he and Carlene were tucking into the pizza he'd bought on his way home from The Lido.

'It's probably Jo,' Carlene said, getting up from the couch. 'She said they might call in on their way to their Christmas party.'

Jo and Wayne seemed to have an in-built radar for the most inconvenient visiting times. Reuben imagined them with a huge satellite telescope set up on their top balcony, reading signals from his and Carlene's home ten kilometres away. 'Quick,' Wayne would shout, rubbing his hands together gleefully, 'they're having dinner (or an argument, or a nookie). Let's go! And don't forget the kids because they've got runny noses and the whinges!'

Reuben braced himself for the onslaught. A familiar voice floated through the front door. 'Ho ho ho! Merry Christmas, young lady! Have you been a good girl?'

Thommo stepped inside. He was wearing a Santa hat and clutching two bottles of wine. His cheeks shone and he looked like a Santa who'd had one too many rum toddies.

'I hope for Reuben's sake you've been very naughty,' he said, and enveloped Carlene in a bear hug, the wine bottles clanking together behind her.

'Finn! What a nice surprise!' Carlene said, disentangling herself.

Reuben jumped up and wrestled the wine bottles from Thommo's grasp. 'Yes, what a surprise! Considering we were only having drinks together an hour ago.'

A Christmas drink with Finn had been his excuse for his meeting with Frank. Thommo looked at him. 'Oh ... yeah. Well, I just decided I couldn't go back home without bringing you and your beautiful wife a Christmas present.'

'That's so sweet of you,' Carlene said. 'Would you like to stay and have some pizza?'

Reuben opened his mouth. 'I'd love to,' Thommo said quickly. 'Have you got Bacon 'n' Egg? That's my favourite.'

'No, we haven't,' Reuben said. 'I thought you said you had to go home and pack for your early flight tomorrow.'

'I got the times mixed up,' Thommo said. "I don't leave till later.'

He held up the bottles of wine. 'Crack one open and we'll have a Chrissy drink.'

Reuben looked at the labels. Cleanskin chardonnay and bargain basement red. He took them into the kitchen and pulled out some wineglasses from the cupboard. Thommo followed him in. 'You've got some explaining to do, mate,' he said in Reuben's ear.

'What?'

'Gone down the wrong path? Turning over a new leaf? I've got a right to know if you've involved me in some underhand activities.'

'Keep your voice down. And for fuck's sake, remember you're supposed to be depressed.'

'I won't have to pretend if you don't tell me...'

'What are you two whispering about?' Carlene appeared in the kitchen.

'Rubie can't decide which bottle to open,' Thommo said. 'I'm helping him make up his mind.'

Carlene rolled her eyes. 'You men! Open them both if you want.'

Thommo beamed at her. 'A woman after my own heart.'

Reuben uncorked the bottle of red, poured three glasses and they polished off the rest of the pizza. Carlene watched Thommo as he stuffed the last piece in his mouth and licked his fingers.

'It's good to see all your problems haven't affected your appetite,' she said.

Thommo stopped mid-lick and assumed a hangdog expression. 'But they have – I used to eat twice as much.'

He launched into a detailed account of his sessions with a psychotherapist called Carol who had a crisp British accent and wore tight sweaters and black stockings. Carlene interjected with the occasional helpful suggestion, (start a journal to express your emotions, exercise to get the endorphins going, a life coach to help define his goals) which Thommo duly acknowledged with a thoughtful nod before resuming his monologue. After what seemed an interminable period of time and two more glasses of wine, Carlene's eyes began to glaze.

'It's been lovely seeing you, Finn,' she said, stifling a yawn, 'but I hope you don't think it rude of me if I go to bed.'

'Not at all,' Thommo said. He jumped up and gave her another hearty hug. 'Have a great Christmas. And look after Rubie – make sure he doesn't get too drunk.'

'I've been telling you for the last twenty-five years not to call me Rubie,' Reuben said. 'You'd think you'd get it into your fat skull by now.'

'Sorry, it just slips out.'

Thommo waited a couple of minutes after Carlene left then peered down the corridor. 'I thought she'd never go, I was running out of stories.'

He sat down on the couch again, arms folded across his chest. 'It's your turn now; spill the beans. Think of me as your therapist, your Carol.'

'Too much of a stretch, you don't have the legs. Is she real?'

'Of course not. What do you think I am? Crazy?'

It was obvious Thommo wasn't going home until Reuben had told him what he wanted to know. And he supposed he owed Thommo an explanation. Reuben inclined his head in the direction of the patio – he wanted to make doubly sure Carlene wouldn't overhear them. They took their glasses and the second bottle of wine outside, and settled at the table.

The night was warm and sticky, the air filled with the pungent odour of over-ripe bush mangoes from the tree next door. A dog yapped and a car roared up the street. Shrill voices and bicycle bells pierced the night, children enjoying the freedom of the summer holidays under cover of darkness.

Reuben gave him the abridged version of his life so far. Thommo sat up in his chair and stared at him.

'Geez, I remember reading about you in the paper when you went to jail. They called you 'Blackheart' because you targeted all the people with black money.'

'Typical media hype.'

'But then you sucked in some poor guy who had a terminal illness.'

'My partner did that without my knowledge. I would never have condoned it. Anyway, Derek didn't know about his illness until it was too late.'

He could see Ivan Kominsky as clearly as yesterday – only fifty-four, sunken eyes in a face that was literally falling away, ravaged by his wife's recent death and his diagnosis of cancer. His money was legitimate, earned through shrewd property investment since he'd emigrated from Russia in the 1970s. Derek had been introduced to Ivan, and unable to resist the opportunity, signed him up for their Deluxe Investment Plan and persuaded him to hand over his life savings.

After Reuben and Derek were charged, the news broke that Ivan had been diagnosed with cancer and was forced to borrow money from his son for his cancer treatment. Reuben confronted Derek and they almost came to blows – it took every inch of willpower he possessed not to knock his block off.

He tried to push it out of his mind by telling himself it was Derek's fault, not his. But it still haunted him. Over the ensuing months of the court hearings, he often woke up in the middle of the night, sitting bolt upright, sweating, his heart pounding. Two months into his jail sentence he found out Ivan had died.

'Whatever,' Thommo said. 'Anyway, you can't change the past. So you're on the straight and narrow now?'

'Absolutely.'

'So that's why you paid me three hundred dollars to help you prevent a crime, and a carton of beer for my rent-a-friend, slash alibi service.'

Reuben craned his head around to look through the glass doors into the living room. No sign of Carlene. Hopefully she was in bed asleep.

He poured himself another glass of wine. 'Okay, maybe the straight and narrow has a bit of a bend in it.'

He may as well tell Thommo everything – someone else should know what was happening in case he, Reuben, didn't make it alive out of Operation Luce End. At least someone would know the truth, and Frank and Bomber would get their just desserts. Not that it would matter to Reuben if he were dead.

'It's like this,' he said. 'A crim called Frank Cornell has a plan to bump my parole officer off. He asked me to help him but I refused. Then he blackmailed me, threatening to kill Carlene if I didn't help him. And he also threatened to kill me if I told the cops; reckons he's got friends in the police force and he'd know if I told them. So I didn't have a lot of choice.'

Thommo gaped at him. 'Holy fuck! You're going to kill your parole officer?'

'Of course I'm not. I'll get the police involved before the bomb goes off.'

'Bomb?'

Thommo looked at him in horror. Reuben recounted the full story, up to and including the New Year's Eve plan. Thommo shook his head.

'Man, this sounds like something out of a movie. When exactly are you going to call the police?'

'Bomber will message me once the bomb's planted, and then I'll call them.'

The plan had been fermenting in the back of his mind and it wasn't until he said the words out loud that he realised he'd made the decision. It wasn't the brilliant idea he'd hoped would occur to him, but he was running out of time. It wasn't that his ingenuity had deserted him, he argued to himself, this was one of those rare situations to which there was no brilliant solution. Just a flimsy plan that relied on timing and circumstances being in alignment. Like the planets.

'But what if they think it's a hoax? Or they're too busy to respond? Don't forget on New Year's Eve they'll be out all over the countryside.'

'They should be able to respond pretty quickly then. The streets will be crawling with them.'

Thommo shook his head. 'There's a gaping hole in your plan. Wouldn't it be better to give the police some prior warning so they can stake out the car park and arrest Bomber in the act?'

'I can't take the chance that Frank won't find out I've told them - even if I do it the day before. It could be bullshit that he's got friends in the police force, but plenty of crims do and I don't want to call his bluff. And once he knows the police are onto him, he could do a runner and come after me as well. Whereas if I don't call the police until the last minute, hopefully they can catch Frank unawares and arrest him.'

'You're still leaving a hell of a lot to chance,' Thommo said. 'If it was me, I'd be calling the police now.'

'That's easy for you to say, you're not the one whose life is threatened. And it's not only my life, it's Carlene's as well.' He sighed. 'Sorry, I didn't mean to snap at you. Look, even if I told the police now, I couldn't trust them not to fuck it up. When they arrested me for this last stint, they went to my mother's old house. Not only was she dead but I hadn't lived there since I was eighteen. When they finally turned up on my doorstep, I was waiting for them with a glass of champagne and my bag packed.'

He looked hard at Thommo. 'Promise me you won't call the police. Let me do this my way.'

Thommo shrugged. 'Okay, I promise. It's your funeral.'

'Sorry,' he said hastily, 'I didn't mean that literally.'

'So that's the reason I had to invent Finn,' Reuben said. 'Not because I've been playing around with other women.'

'I'm glad,' Thommo said. 'I thought that was pretty low of you, to tell you the truth.' He looked thoughtful. 'If the worst happens and Frank kills you, am I still Finn?'

26

'Jingle Bell, Jingle Bell, Jingle Bell rock.'

Reuben stood in the corner in his dinner suit, listening to the six-piece band pumping out the irritatingly catchy tune. Pushing its way through the crowd towards him was a huge gift-wrapped box. Lucy's head and bare shoulders protruded above it and her bare legs poked out from underneath. She was carrying the present and as she came closer it appeared that behind it she was wearing nothing at all. She smiled and held the present out towards Reuben. Tingling with anticipation he reached out to take it, but it vanished before him.

He opened his eyes and sat up. He was clutching the sheet between his fingers as if it were the Holy Grail. The strains of 'Jingle Bell Rock' floated into the bedroom from the living room. He groaned and flopped back onto his pillow. Why did Carlene have to be so goddamn Christmassy at Christmas?

The aroma of bacon and eggs wafted around him. He looked at the bedside clock. Seven o'clock. No sleep-in today. He dragged himself out of bed, threw on some clothes and staggered into the kitchen. Carlene was standing by the frying pan in red shorts, a green t-shirt embroidered with a Christmas tree and a piece of tinsel sparkling in her hair.

'Merry Christmas, baby! Breakfast is just about ready, then we have a heap to do before the others get here.'

In the tradition of quaint family customs, Carlene's family took it in turns to host the Christmas festivities and this year, as luck would have it, it was their turn.

'I think we should have a casual, low-key affair,' she'd said initially, 'I want to relax and enjoy our first Christmas together.'

She then spent the next few weeks in a frenzy of preparation, with Reuben as her sidekick. She had a real

Christmas tree delivered ('for the kids') and decorated it till you could hardly see the greenery. The fridge groaned under the weight of food and drink crammed inside it, and the house sparkled like something out of a cleaning ad. And they still weren't ready.

'What happened to our relaxing first Christmas together?' he asked.

'It will be relaxing once we've finished these chores. Can you hose down the patio again and put the drinks in the tub with ice?'

At eleven o'clock on the dot, the rest of the family arrived, laden with more food, alcohol and presents. There was much hugging and kissing from the women and backslapping from Alec and Wayne. Even Nancy gave Reuben a peck on the cheek, albeit as if she were performing an unpleasant but necessary task. Jo, carried away by the Christmas spirit, gave him a one-armed hug, the other arm being full of Brayden. Indya offered her cheek to Reuben, saying, 'Have you got me a present, Uncle Reuben?'

'You'll have to wait and see,' he said. He presumed Carlene had done the Christmas shopping for her family – it had taken all of his ingenuity (and money) to buy her present. It occurred to him as he'd walked aimlessly around the shops on Christmas Eve in a last minute shopping panic, that despite being married to her for almost six months, he hadn't a clue what to buy her.

Reuben got drinks for everyone and they all settled in the living room to perform the present unwrapping ceremony. The children had already unwrapped their presents from Santa and brought their favourites with them – Indya's was a Barbie campervan complete with a travelling Barbie and Ken, and Brayden's was a huge dump truck with an assortment of levers and switches. As soon as he spotted the Christmas tree, he abandoned his truck, waddled towards it and began to taste test the baubles.

Alec volunteered to be Santa. With a Santa hat perched rakishly on his head, he dipped into the pile of presents under the tree and began handing them out. There was a strict protocol to the present unwrapping – each person took turns to unwrap a present while everyone else watched, followed by the requisite 'oohs' and 'aahs' once the gift was revealed. 'Deck the Halls' boomed from the stereo. Reuben felt a headache coming on.

A growing sense of irritation crept over him. As a child he'd looked forward to Christmas, but every year it proved to be a disappointment. He gave Mum something he'd made at school; and she gave him something he needed, like new shoes or a schoolbag. They ate roast chicken and home brand plum pudding in front of the TV watching *Miracle on 34th Street*. Mum insisted on watching it every Christmas, and every Christmas the tears ran down her cheeks when, at the end, the judge declared that yes, there really was a Santa Claus.

Afterwards they visited a musty old aunt or uncle she'd dragged out of the family closet, which was excruciatingly boring. When Reuben was old enough to be left at home on his own, she sometimes worked on Christmas Day. He preferred that option, to spend the day on his own with the freedom to do whatever he wanted.

Indya and Brayden refused to stick to the present-opening protocol and tore into their presents simultaneously. Indya was more taken with Carlene's present to Brayden, a school bus full of movable plastic children, than with her own present of a purple My Little Pony with its own grooming equipment. She raced the bus around the living room, over feet and under legs, while Brayden chewed on her pony's plastic hoof before ditching it to play with the box.

Then it was Carlene's turn to open her present from Reuben. It was a small, square box; jewellery was the obvious guess. Her fingers fumbled with the wrapping. She seemed nervous. Why? Was she afraid his present wasn't up to scratch? That she'd be embarrassed in front of her family?

She lifted the lid gingerly from the box, as if expecting a scorpion to leap out at her. She reached into the tissue paper and pulled out a necklace – single strand sterling silver with a diamond-edged heart. Of course they weren't really diamonds; he couldn't afford them. The shop assistant had assured him that cubic zirconia were the next best thing, and it was impossible to tell unless you were an expert.

'Oh, Rubie, that's lovely.' She held it up to show the others who responded with suitable exclamations. She leaned over and gave him a quick hug. 'Can you put it on for me?'

He breathed a sigh of relief as he fixed the clasp at the back of her neck. She seemed to like it. Although in this situation it was hard to tell, because she'd have to pretend in front of the others, even if she didn't like it. Maybe that was the real rationale behind the present-opening ritual.

'Can't go wrong with jewellery,' Alec said.

Nancy gave Reuben a look that said she suspected it had fallen off the back of a truck. Alec opened his present from Carlene and Reuben – a box of his favourite imported cigars and a bottle of Gentleman Jack bourbon. Reuben looked at the bottle enviously. Carlene had shown it to him after she bought it, and he'd hoped she'd buy one for him as well, to replace the bottle Wayne and Thommo had drunk.

'Your turn, Reuben,' Alec said. 'Lucky last.' He handed him a small, flat package. 'To Rubie, xxxxx,' read the gift tag in Carlene's large, sprawling handwriting. No bottle of Gentleman Jack.

Reuben opened the package. Inside was an envelope. He opened it. There was a hush, filled with a chorus of angelic voices. 'All I want for Christmas is you...hoo.'

Out of the envelope fell a card. 'Gift Certificate. Inner Radiance Life Coaching. Ten sessions, valued at six hundred dollars.'

He opened the card. 'Welcome to Inner Radiance. We help you to formulate your goals, chart the course of your life's journey, get rid of excess baggage and weed out unnecessary distractions. You will achieve the serenity and inner radiance of someone who feels good about themselves and is in charge of their life. This is our personal guarantee.'

Two faces shone out from the card, a male and a female, sparkling-eyed and glossy-haired, glowing with evangelical zeal. Their signatures were underneath. Molly Adams and Bradley Curtis.

'What is it?' Wayne asked.

'It must be good,' Alec said. 'He's lost for words.'

'It's a gift certificate for life coaching sessions,' Carlene said. She looked anxiously at Reuben. 'What do you think, honey?'

'He's thrilled, obviously,' Wayne said. 'About as much as I'd be if someone gave it to me.'

'Shut up Wayne,' Jo said. 'No one asked you.'

'Daddy, what's life coaching?' Indya asked. 'Is it like tennis coaching?'

'Sort of, sweetheart. Only without the racquet and balls. Or the net. Or the tennis court.'

Carlene gave him a dark look and Wayne got up, holding his hand out to Indya. 'Come on, sweetheart, let's see if we can find some more of those candy canes.'

Reuben met Carlene's gaze. He wouldn't spoil the day by saying anything now, but he wasn't going to pretend, either.

'We'll talk about it later,' he said and stuffed it in his pocket. 'Anyone for more drinks?'

***

Christmas Day was not a success. No brawls or even arguments, just a simmering tension that threatened every now and then to boil over until someone – usually Nancy with one of her looks – clamped a lid on it.

Carlene darted around all day like a dragonfly, two red blobs burning on her cheeks as she prepared food, served and cleaned up. She refused Reuben's attempts to help her with a curt, 'I'm fine, thanks.'

They all crowded around the small table on the patio and ate stuffed turkey breast with cranberry jus, glazed ham, goat's cheese quiche and salads containing a dozen varieties of lettuce. For dessert, there was the traditional Christmas pudding, citrus tart with double cream and brandy snap baskets with cognac-drenched strawberries and chocolate jus. The children sat in front of the TV and ate peanut butter sandwiches, with Brayden sampling a papier-mache angel from the Christmas tree for dessert.

The weather matched the mood of the day, sultry and heavy with the threat of rain. Even the crickets could only manage a desultory chorus. The day had a strange, breathless quality about it, as if this Christmas Day marked the end of the world. Reuben set up a pedestal fan outside to cool them down as they ate, but all it did was blow hot air around, with Jo complaining that it was making her food go cold.

After they'd finished dessert and were doing the obligatory groaning and patting of stomachs, Wayne said, 'How about a game of cards, euchre or five hundred?'

Nobody answered. Carlene had already begun clearing the table, assisted by Nancy, whose help she didn't refuse. Reuben went into the living room. Indya was still glued to the TV, Brayden asleep on the floor with his head in her lap, clutching a decapitated angel.

Indya jumped up. Brayden's head flopped onto the floor and he woke up with a wail. 'Uncle Reuben, can you take me for a ride on the Barbiemobile? You said you would! Please, please, please?'

It was hard to resist her when she did the big pleading eyes bit. And at least it would get him out of the house for a while.

'I'd love to, but I don't know if your mother will let you.'

'Yes, she will,' Indya said. She opened her mouth and screeched at the top of her voice, 'Mummy!'

Jo came running in with a tea towel over her shoulder. 'What's the matter darling?'

She bent down and picked up Brayden who was still howling. 'What's the matter with your brother?'

'Nothing, he's just being sooky,' she said. 'Mummy, can I go for a ride on the Barbiemobile with Uncle Reuben? Pretty please?'

Jo hesitated. 'I don't...'

'It's Christmas, you said I could have anything I wanted!'

Jo's shoulders sagged. 'All right.' She looked at Reuben. 'It's okay with you?'

'It's fine by me. I've got a spare helmet.'

'Yippee!' Indya scooped up her Barbie and Ken dolls. 'Can they come too?'

'Have they got helmets?' Reuben said.

She shook her head. 'They don't have to at Christmas because it's a special day.'

She had an answer for everything; she was destined for politics. Reuben fetched the extra helmet and slipped his mobile phone in his shorts pocket. On his way out, he darted into the bedroom and pocketed the mobile phone Frank had given him. It was well-hidden but he wasn't taking any chances. He wouldn't put it past Carlene to do some snooping if she got half a chance.

They rode up and down the surrounding suburban streets – Indya perched behind him, her little head swimming in her crash helmet and her arms gripping his waist. Her Ken and Barbie dolls were stuffed down the front of her dress, with their heads peeking out so they could enjoy the view. In reality, the only view they had was the back of Reuben's sweaty t-shirt against which their faces were rammed.

The streets were deserted, steeped in post-Christmas-lunch torpor. The lifelessness and the oppression of the heat weighed him down. This was life in suburbia, the life he'd chosen. Same city as he'd live in before, geographically, but so different to the one he'd known before, that he may as well be living on another planet. His life stretched before him like an endless desert. *If I get out of Operation Luce End alive, I should be thankful to be living anywhere, even in a desert.* But no matter how hard he tried, he couldn't conjure up any gratitude. He couldn't even conjure up a Lucy fantasy to cheer himself up.

A shrill ringing made him jump. It was from the mobile phone Frank had given him. It could only be him. Or Bomber.

Reuben pulled over to the side of the road. By the time he'd dismounted, helped Indya off and taken off his helmet, the ringing had stopped. He checked the number of the missed call. It wasn't familiar, but Frank had used a different number each time he called Reuben. The ringing started again.

'Just got to take this call,' he said.

He wandered up the footpath, away from Indya, but she followed him, unstrapping her helmet.

'Merry Christmas, Littledick,' Frank's voice boomed at him. He sounded as if he had been indulging in some Christmas cheer. Probably Gentleman Jack, the bastard.

'Merry Christmas,' Reuben said, frowning at Indya, who was right beside him, unashamedly listening.

'Just wanting to check in re our operation. All still on track?'

'Yes.' He felt around for the volume switch on the side of the phone. 'The ... er patient is still away as per the schedule. As far as I know, she still gets back on the 29th, so I can confirm then.'

'Excellent. Stuff this one up, mate, and you're up shit creek without a paddle.'

Frank's voice bellowed through his head. He'd turned the volume up instead of down. He jabbed at the switch again.

'Yes, you've already reminded me of that. Everything's on track. The only thing that will prevent it, will be if the patient changes her mind about going to ... the hospital.'

Silence. 'You're not alone,' Frank said, in more subdued tones.

'No.'

'Okay. Talk to you on the 29th.'

'Hang on. What are you drinking?'

'What?' His voice rose again. 'You sound like my fucking wife. What's it to you?'

'Nothing. I'm just interested.'

'Scotch on the rocks. Johnnie Walker, black label. Anything else you want to know?'

'That's all.'

Frank hung up. Reuben didn't like Scotch. But if he did, Johnnie Walker black label would be his favourite.

'Who was that, Uncle Reuben?'

Indya regarded him with solemn curiosity, hugging her dolls to her chest.

'Just a friend. Come on, let's get back on and finish our ride.'

'Are you playing doctors and nurses?'

'Yeah, something like that.'

'Why did he call you Littledick?'

'It's just a nickname.'

'Mummy doesn't let me say dick, but I say it at kindy. Me and Ethan whisper it so Miss Watson doesn't hear.'

'Just as well,' Reuben said. 'Miss Watson sounds far too young and innocent for such language.' Indya giggled and he fastened the helmet back on her head before she could elaborate any further.

As they started off, a huge clap of thunder struck. It echoed around them and seemed to shake the earth. Indya gave a muffled squeal. Then came the rain in fierce, driving sheets, and in a few seconds they were saturated. There wasn't much point trying to find shelter. Reuben turned around and mouthed 'you okay?' to Indya. She nodded. She'd pushed Ken and Barbie right down her front, but they were still getting soaked. It hadn't been much of a ride for them.

They were about two kilometres from home. Reuben bent his head against the onslaught and rode at a snail's pace. His breath was fogging up the visor and he could hardly see. After the initial shock, he enjoyed the sensation of the wet clothes against his skin – it was cool and refreshing, and strangely exhilarating.

He was a child again, playing out in the rain while Mum was at work, knowing how much she would scold him (no, worse, give him a beating) if she could see him. That was part of the fun of it. Once he was wet through to the skin, he couldn't get any wetter, so he stayed out in the rain while everyone else cowered inside – racing up and down the street, slipping and sliding in the mud, tilting his head up and closing his eyes as it pounded his face, mouth open to drink it in.

Then he rushed inside, peeled off his saturated clothes and had a shower. By the time Mum came home, he was in front of the TV in his pyjamas, the washing machine chugging away in the laundry. She hugged him and told him how wonderful he was to do the washing. If it occurred to her that the only time he did the washing was when it rained, she never let on.

The rain was easing as he rode through the front gate into the carport. Reuben dismounted and took off their helmets. Water dripped in puddles around them. Indya was a picture of pathos, her thin dress plastered to her body and her hair hanging like a rat's tail, but her eyes were bright.

'That was fun, Uncle Reuben.' She held up the soaked Barbie and Ken, their rosebud lips still parted in vacuous smiles. 'And they liked it too.'

As Reuben led her around to the back door, he realised it was the most fun he'd had with his clothes on for a long time.

Jo rushed over and scooped Indya up in her arms. 'Darling! I've been so worried about you! Look at you!'

'But Mummy, I was having fun!' Indya wriggled out of Jo's arms.

'You won't think it's so much fun tomorrow when you wake up with pneumonia.'

With a venomous glance at Reuben, she bustled Indya off to the bathroom. Nancy, tight-lipped, followed them in. Reuben went into the bedroom, stripped off his clothes and stood in the shower, the warm water streaming over him. As well as his other numerous faults, it looked as if he were also responsible for the weather.

By four o'clock Indya was dressed again, her clothes fresh and warm from the dryer. As they were all getting ready to leave, she said, 'Can we go for another ride in the rain soon, Uncle Reuben?'

'Don't be stupid, Indya,' Wayne said.

'Don't call her stupid,' Jo snapped. 'It's damaging to her self-esteem.'

Indya ignored the comments, her self-esteem appearing remarkably intact. She looked up at Reuben. 'Can I help you with your operation?'

'What operation?' Then he realised what she meant. 'I don't think...'

'I've got a nurse's hat. Can I be a nurse?'

'What on earth are you talking about?' Jo said.

'Uncle Reuben said it on the phone. He's going to play doctors and nurses and do an operation.'

Sudden silence, as if someone had pressed the mute button on the conversation. Nancy dropped something on the kitchen floor that made a clang. All eyes were on Reuben. Alex cleared his throat.

'That was just a private joke between friends, honey,' Reuben said. 'Does anyone want this left-over ham?'

After they'd all gathered up their presents and hugged and kissed their goodbyes, with Reuben deserving only of air kisses and suspicious glances, they stood out on the street by the cars and talked for another half an hour. *Why don't women know how to say goodbye?* When men say goodbye, they leave, without further ado. For women the word 'goodbye' triggers the memory of several important topics that must be discussed right at that moment. Indya became bored and pinched Brayden. He wailed. That was the signal for them to bundle themselves into their cars and drive off.

The rain had only briefly cleansed the air, and an oppressive mugginess settled in again. Carlene slumped onto the couch. Her hair was lank and stringy, her face flushed. She'd managed to sneak in a few sips of wine during her hosting duties. Reuben poured himself another glass of red. He had a feeling he'd need the fortification.

'So,' Carlene said, 'what's this about an operation and playing doctors and nurses?'

Reuben came and sat down beside her. 'Just me regressing back to my childhood again. Nothing to worry about.'

'I am worried. Who were you talking to on the phone?'

Why did Indya have to be such a know-it-all busybody? Sadly, there was only one person he could have been talking to on the phone on Christmas Day.

'Finn rang me to wish me Merry Christmas.'

'And you're going to play doctors and nurses with him?'

'Of course not. We were just reminiscing about our school days when we played doctors and nurses.'

'And performed operations.'

'Pretended to. It was all very innocent.'

'Of course.'

'I don't know what you're so shitty about – it's the truth. Anyway, I'm the one who should be shitty with you, and in fact, I am.'

'Oh, really?' Her voice held a dangerous note. 'And why is that?'

She knew why. She wanted to make him say it.

'You know very well why. The gift certificate. Besides the fact I don't need counselling, which you don't seem to understand, life coaching is a total wank. I don't need some buffed, puncy tosser telling me how to live my life.'

'It seems to me he might have a better idea than you do. Tell me, what are your goals? What do you want to achieve in life?'

Her questions were impossible to answer. He'd been living from day to day, ricocheting from one event to the next. Employment, yes, an unfortunate necessity of life. Over and above that, he hadn't the slightest idea. A family? A home of his own? Stability? Predictability? It was too depressing to think about. Yet it's what Carlene wanted.

'I don't know,' he muttered.

'See?' She sat up, eyes sharp with triumph. 'That's exactly what I mean. If you don't know what you want, how can you hope to get anywhere? If you don't have goals, next thing you know, ten years will have passed and you'll still be a kitchen hand in a crummy cafe.'

'It might be boring and dead-end, but at least it's honest. And what's wrong with not knowing what you want? I've only been out of jail for six months, it's going to take time for me to work all that out.'

'A very convenient excuse. How long are you going to use that one for?'

'As long as I need to.'

The ceiling fan whirred above them, going at full pelt but barely moving the air. He'd wanted to ask her this question, it had been on the tip of his tongue for a while; but he couldn't quite bring himself to do it. Now he had to.

'Why did you marry me?'

She met his gaze, twirling the ends of her hair around her fingers. 'What a question! Because I love you.'

There was no tenderness in her words, rather an air of accusation. Honesty came in so many shades and subtleties – he hadn't always been honest with Carlene, but he owed her this now. And himself. If he didn't say it now, it might never be said. He took a deep breath.

'I think you're mixing up love with rescuing. You see me the same way as the refugees and the orphans you're trying to save.'

'That's bullshit! And you accuse me of psychoanalysing!'

She swiped at the tears running down her cheeks. 'So why did you marry me?'

'I thought it was what I wanted; that marriage would help me to stay straight. But now I'm not so sure.'

She stared at him, glassy-eyed. When she spoke, her voice was just a whisper. 'What about love? You said you loved me.'

He couldn't bear to look at her any longer. He dropped his gaze to the floor. 'I thought I did. I talked myself into believing it. The joke's on me now, I conned myself instead of everyone else.'

He looked up at her. 'And you, too. I'm sorry.'

'Sorry doesn't cut it, I'm afraid.' She sprang up from the couch and stood in front of him. 'You've humiliated me in front of my family, you've lied to me, for all I know you're probably having an affair; and worst of all, you don't love me and never have! I've just wasted the last six months of my life!'

He watched her as she marched into the kitchen, grabbed a tissue from the box on the fridge and blew her nose with a fierce honk.

'I think I should leave,' he said.

She stopped mid-blow. 'What do you mean?'

'I need some space; to think things through. It'll do us both good to have some time apart.'

She narrowed her eyes. 'Don't you tell me what's good for me! And don't give me that "need some space" bullshit. Next thing you'll be saying, "it's not you, it's me."'

Reuben got up. 'I'll pack some things.'

'Wait a minute!' Tears welled up again in her eyes. 'You're not serious! Where are you going?'

He shrugged. 'I'll find somewhere.'

A look of panic flitted across her face. 'So you're going to *her* place.'

'I've told you, there's no *her*.'

What else could he say to convince her? He felt as if all the life had been drained out of him by a super-suction hose. Looking at her flushed, tear-stained face, he couldn't even summon up the energy to feel compassion.

He went into the bedroom and threw some clothes and a toothbrush into an overnight bag. His body moved as if on automatic pilot. He didn't have a clue where he was going, dimly aware that at five pm on Christmas Day, his options were limited.

When he came back out into the living room, the TV was on – some Christmas sitcom full of American twang, canned laughter and people in Santa hats. Carlene was on the couch staring at the TV screen, tissues curled into a tight ball in her hand.

'Well,' Reuben said. 'I'm going. I'll be in touch.'

Carlene kept her eyes on the TV. 'Don't expect me to be hanging around waiting for you to call.'

'Right, I won't.'

He stood there; bag in hand. The air was thick with emotions untapped, words unspoken. How had this happened? Last night they'd made love, Carlene tipsy after a couple of Christmas Eve drinks, giggling as she wrapped a piece of tinsel around his erect penis. *It's only for a few days. Breathing space. For both of us.*

As he turned to go, Carlene said, 'I hope you're not going to drive.'

Reuben looked at her blankly then down at the Barbiemobile keys in his hand. She was right. He'd probably be over the alcohol limit. The cops would be out in full force – the answer to his accommodation problem was not a hard bunk in a watchhouse cell.

'Of course not,' he said.

He left the living room before she had time to say anything else – there was no point in prolonging the moment. As he closed the front door behind him, a car horn in the distance shrilled the first line of 'We Wish You a Merry Christmas.'

27

'Where to, mate?'

'Twenty-four Hill Street New Farm, thanks.'

The taxi driver did a U-turn with a screech of tyres and headed in the direction of Gympie Road. Despite the cab being air-conditioned, there was a huge sweat stain across the back of his white shirt. He reeked of onions and cigarette smoke.

'Had a good Christmas, mate?'

'Yeah, fine.'

It's not over yet. Maybe the next few hours will be an improvement. Who was he kidding? Even Thommo hadn't been too pleased to hear from him. Reuben had been just about to hang up when Thommo snapped, 'Yes?'

He sounded out of breath.

'It's Reuben. I've got a favour to ask.'

'Bloody hell, mate can't it wait? This is not a good time.'

'Sorry, I hate to do this to you on Christmas Day ... Merry Christmas, by the way.'

'That's not what I meant. What do you want?'

'A place to stay. Just tonight. Carlene and I had a bit of a blue.'

He gave a loud sigh. 'Whatever. My day's ruined anyway, you may as well come over and finish it off.'

'Thanks, I really appreciate it. What's your address?'

Thankfully the cab had arrived within five minutes. Reuben stared out the window as they passed shops, warehouses and factories, still and blank-faced. There were few cars on the road and the odd sprinkling of pedestrians. Thankfully the cab driver didn't pursue further conversation but turned up the music – Frank Sinatra belting out 'My Way'. At least it was better than Christmas carols. Only just.

The cab turned into Fortitude Valley and down Brunswick Street. When Reuben had last lived in this city, The Valley, as it was known, was the 'Kings Cross of Brisbane', full of seedy strip clubs, drug dealers and streetwalkers. Now it was the home of 'cool', with its bold, shiny shopfronts, intimate pubs and glitzy nightclubs. The seediness was still there but it had gone underground.

If he had his old life back, this would be his stamping ground. Being seen at the right places with the right people was all part of the job, networking like any legitimate business. There was a lot to like about it if you discounted the possibility of being caught and going to jail. Good food and wine, lavish home, expensive toys and holidays – anyone who said they were only superficial trappings and not worth striving for, was talking out of malice or envy. Maybe they weren't everything you needed but they were a good place to start. And now not only he had lost them, but what little he had was slipping out of his grasp.

'Regrets, I've had a few,' Frank warbled. On second thoughts, 'Silent Night' would be preferable. Reuben slouched in his seat and tried not to think about Carlene. *I'm not leaving her for good; just having some time out.* I'll go insane if I don't. I know I haven't been the perfect husband, but I don't think I've been a bastard. And if I have, it hasn't been intentional. So why do I feel like one?

The cab turned down a side street then another, and they were in New Farm. It was divided into two sections – the exclusive area with its upmarket apartment blocks, restored terrace houses and trendy offices; and the original New Farm of workers, students and migrants, with its shabby bedsits, tiny workers cottages fronting right onto the footpath and old tumble-down Queenslanders.

Thommo lived in the latter part, as befitted a struggling actor. His apartment was one of four in a converted old Queenslander, two down and two up. Dirty-white with faded blue awnings, it sagged in the heat. A straggle of weeds poked their heads above the cracked pavers of the front path. In a row of carports to the right of the building, Thommo's battered Ford Escort was the sole occupant.

Reuben paid the driver, got out and walked up the front path. Thommo's apartment, number one, was on the bottom right. The door opened and a girl bowled out, flinging her handbag over her shoulder. She stopped when she saw Reuben, scowled, then swept past him down the front path. She was short and squat with a sheen of blue-black hair and make-up applied so heavily it resembled plaster of Paris.

Reuben knocked on the door.

'It's no good running back to me now,' said Thommo's muffled voice from inside. The door flung open and he stood there bare-chested, a sarong draped around his lower half, his pale, hairy stomach suspended over the top.

'Oh, it's you.' He inclined his head in the direction of the girl, who'd now disappeared from view. 'You owe me, mate. Big time.'

'Sorry ... were you two...?'

'No we weren't, thanks to you. Getting all hot and heavy until you rang, then she went right off the boil.'

'Why did you answer the phone then?'

'I'm an unemployed actor, for fuck's sake, I always answer the phone, even on Christmas Day. Of course she had to know who it was, so when I told her she said, "There's not much point going on with it if your friend's coming over." Then when I suggested we kind of ... you know ... speed things up a bit so we could be finished before you arrived, she said "Fuck you, I'm not that type of girl", got dressed and stalked out.'

'You should have told me; I could have gone to the pub till you'd finished.'

'Forget it.' He stood aside and gestured for Reuben to come in. 'Don't worry that I was about to break the Great Drought of the Twenty-First Century. I'll think of a way for you to make it up to me.'

His flat was cramped and dingy, a typical bachelor pad with its sparse furnishings and lack of interior decoration. Evidence of the attempted seduction was obvious – the couch cushions had been thrown on the floor and two empty wine glasses stood on an occasional table next to a smouldering incense holder, which didn't quite disguise the stale cooking odours.

Thommo picked up the cushions and threw them back on the couch. 'I've only got one bedroom; you'll have to sleep here. Let's go down to The Crown and you can shout me a drink for ruining my day.'

At The Crown, they perched at the public bar with their beers and stared at the large TV screen flickering in the corner. Apart from the board outside that said, 'Xmas Day lunch. Roast turkey, veg, plum pudding. $29.95', it was just another day. The bar was buzzing – many looked as if they'd been there for most of the day, raucous and rosy-cheeked, some past that stage and drooping slowly into their drinks like wilting flowers.

'So, what did you and your wife have a blue about?' Thommo asked.

'She gave me a gift certificate for ten sessions with a life coach for Christmas.'

'Ouch! Say no more!' He looked contemplative. 'Though in my darkest hours, I've seriously thought of being a life coach, just to earn a buck. It's always easier to tell someone else what to do with their lives than take your own advice.'

'Yeah. Anyway, what's with the girl? Don't you have a family to spend Christmas with?'

'My mother's overseas with her latest boyfriend and my father hasn't spoken to me for years – ever since he kicked me out of home when I told him I was going to be an actor.'

'Do you ever think that maybe you'll never make it? That you'll wake up one day an old man still waiting for your first break?'

'There're plenty of roles around for old men. Look at Michael Caine.'

'Seriously.'

'Seriously, all the time. But I've got two options – give up on the dream, find another career and end up an old man full of regrets or keep on trying and end up an old man full of frustration. A choice between two sorts of unhappiness. Which one do I pick?'

Reuben shrugged.

'It's a rhetorical question. I've already picked option b. But there's always the chance that I might make it. I want my epitaph to read, "He was an exceptional actor, even his death scene was brilliantly portrayed."'.

Thommo signalled the bartender, ordered two more beers and paid out of Reuben's change on the bar. Reuben glanced at the faces around him. Most of them here to anaesthetise themselves against the boredom and loneliness of their existence. You wouldn't be at a pub on Christmas Day if you had family or friends to share the day with. Or maybe you would, if you needed to get away from them. Which was just as depressing.

'Anyway,' Thommo said, 'how long are you staying?'

'I don't know.'

He'd have to go back before New Year's Eve; he was supposed to be taking Carlene to the ball. He'd been intending to surprise her with the tickets. She might not want to go now. In fact, it would be easier for him if she didn't, as he wouldn't have to explain why he'd be arriving late. Shit, that was only six days away. Six days until he had to put his final, no excuses, definitive plan for saving Lucy's life into action.

What was she doing at this very moment? It was only Christmas Eve in Scotland. He imagined her huddled in front of the fireplace in a cottage in a quaint Scottish village, drinking rum toddies with her in-laws as snow blanketed the hills outside, blissfully oblivious to the fact that her life was hanging perilously in the balance. While he, Reuben Littlejohn, the only person in the world who could save her, was sitting in a pub, putting away beer as if he had not a care in the world.

He signalled the bar attendant and ordered two more beers. 'Make them schooners.'

Thommo was saying something.

'Pardon?'

'I said, don't rush back. Give her time to realise how much she misses you. Can you cook?'

'Passably, just basic stuff.'

'Great. You can stay as long as you like.'

Thommo nudged him. 'Hey, look.'

On the TV screen, Reuben's face flashed larger than life as he grinned at the girl sitting at the bar in front of him. The camera panned over her cleavage to a close-up of his hands as he pulled two Beckers beers with the easy assurance of a professional bartender – not an inkling of the number of takes before he could pull the beer with just the right amount of panache.

'You're famous.'

Reuben looked around to see if anyone else was watching his six seconds of fame. No one was.

'What's it like seeing yourself on the big screen?'

'Weird,' he said. 'I never realised before how lopsided my smile is.'

'It's good to have a trademark, makes you stand out. When you're famous, the reporters will refer to your rakish grin.'

Thommo raised his glass. 'To fame and fortune.'

They clinked glasses.

'And failing that,' Thommo said, raising his glass again, 'regular work and women.'

'Don't be so defeatist,' Reuben said. 'It's fame and fortune or nothing.'

They drank another toast to fame and fortune, followed by toasts to Becker Beer, Brigitte Bardot (when she was younger), sex on tap, XJ Jaguars, intravenous bourbon, not being killed by a would-be underworld figure and The Boston Stranglers. Although Thommo had never heard of them, he graciously conceded that they were the most under-rated group of all time. Encompassing so many toasts required the downing of a number of drinks, resulting in the toasts becoming more bizarre as the night wore on.

The next time the Becker ad appeared on the big screen, Thommo pointed to it and called out,' 'That's him, that's my mate,' and gave Reuben a hearty clap on the back. A group of drinkers at a nearby table glanced at the screen and at Reuben with a bemused expression before resuming their conversations. No one else took any notice. A brassy-blonde woman appeared at the bar beside them and ordered a drink. She looked sideways at Reuben. 'That wasn't you on the telly,' she said. 'That guy was much better-looking.'

Thommo choked on his beer, causing a spasm of coughing and spluttering, beer streaming out of his nostrils. Reuben thumped him hard on the back. The woman rolled her eyes and shook her head.

'Men,' she observed to no one in particular.

***

He was lying bound and gagged on a cold concrete floor. Frank was swinging blows at his head with a hammer – the pain was excruciating. He was going to hammer Reuben into unconsciousness then throw him in the river. From a distance, an auburn- haired vision in a floating white dress glided towards him. As she drew nearer, she reached down into her cleavage, whipped out a pistol and pointed it at Frank. Thank God, Lucy was going to save him.

Hold on, that was all wrong, he was supposed to be saving her! Stop it this minute! Stop this dream!

He jerked his eyes open. A wooden table leg swam into his vision. He looked around him. He was sprawled on the threadbare carpet, not much more comfortable than concrete, though thankfully not bound and gagged. And the hammering was still inside his head, as if trying to split it in two.

A foot came into view, pale and elongated with a large knobbly toe, like a misshapen piece of dough. The couch creaked and sagged, and a loud bang reverberated in Reuben's head as something was placed on the table above him.

'Did you have a good sleep?' Thommo said.

'Not really. I must have fallen off the couch.'

His throat was dry and he rasped like a blues singer.

'You didn't make it to the couch. You tripped over as you came in the front door and you just went to sleep where you landed.'

'Oh, yeah.' Reuben had a vague recollection of tripping over, as if it had happened in a dream. He realised his knee was throbbing, as a background accompaniment to the beat in his head.

Thommo picked up his coffee mug from the table. 'Want a coffee?'

'Yes, please. And would you mind not shouting?'

'I'm not shouting. But if it hurts your poor wee head, I'll be as quiet as a mouse.'

He tiptoed out with exaggerated care. Reuben wrenched himself off the floor, sank into the couch and cradled his head in his hands. How could Thommo be so full of good humour after the amount they'd drunk last night? His stomach must be one miraculous organ.

He became aware of a vibration in his jeans. He reached into his pocket and pulled out his phone. Without looking at the caller ID, he knew who it was.

'Hi baby, how are you?'

'I'm okay.'

'You don't sound okay. Where are you?'

'At Thom – I mean, Finn's. In his hotel room.'

'I thought he'd gone back to Sydney.'

'He decided to stay over Christmas. He's got relatives here.'

Silence. 'I found those tickets for the New Year's Eve Ball.'

What were you doing snooping in my underwear drawer? Reuben wanted to ask, but he wasn't up to another argument.

'I was going to surprise you,' he said.

'I was so upset when I saw them.'

'Oh. Don't you want to go?'

'Of course I do. I thought it was really sweet of you and it made me cry.'

Her voice faltered. 'I want you to come home.'

Reuben hesitated. So much for time apart to think. But he couldn't stay at Thommo's forever and he had nowhere else to go. And now that Carlene had found the tickets to the ball, he couldn't back out of taking her.

'We can work things out, baby. I'm sorry about the life-coaching voucher. I'll take it back. I know they'll give me a refund; they're friends of one of the girls at church. And I promise not to bring up about you going to counselling again.'

She sniffled. 'I miss you, Rubie.' Then she burst into tears.

'Okay,' he said. 'I'll come home.'

'Which hotel are you at?' she asked between sobs. 'I'll come and pick you up.'

'No need for that – you just relax. I'm having a coffee then I'll get a cab.'

'Okay, honey, see you soon.'

He rang off. She'd sounded so relieved, but it only made him feel worse. He was going back for the wrong reasons and he knew that despite her assurances, nothing would change.

Thommo came in and put Reuben's mug of coffee on the table. 'Going home?'

'Yeah.'

'You don't sound too thrilled about it.'

'It's hard to feel thrilled about anything with a jackhammer drilling through my head.'

' Pity, I was looking forward to sampling some of your baked beans in tomato jus, garnished with slivers of cheddar cheese.' He flopped onto the faded armchair. 'I've come to a decision. Brisbane's giving me the shits. I'm moving to Sydney; that's where you have to be to get anywhere in this business. Want to come?'

For a few moments, Reuben indulged himself in the fantasy of upping stakes and going to Sydney with Thommo – new city, fresh start, the excitement of the unknown. It's what he'd always done before, when he got bored or when the police were beginning to take an interest in his activities – packed his bags and left town, usually to another state. He'd seen most of Australia by keeping one step ahead of the authorities. But sooner or later the novelty of the new town or city wore off, and it became just like any other, and in his mind they all merged into one big place called 'Somewhere Else'.

'It's tempting, but I can't. It's not easy to move interstate when you're on parole.'

'You could give it a go. I reckon we'd have a great time down there. You could do a hundred beer ads in Sydney. And you wouldn't have Frankie-boy breathing down your neck.'

'If I can stop Operation Luce End, Frank will be behind bars, and if not, I'll be at the bottom of the river in concrete shoes. Anyway, apart from all that, there's Carlene.'

'Women,' Thommo sighed, with the air of the jaded playboy. 'When you haven't got one, they're all you think about and when you have, you're wondering how to get rid of them.'

***

The house was eerily quiet as Reuben opened the front door. All evidence of the Christmas festivities had been cleared away, every surface sparkling, the cushions plumped. Only the Christmas tree remained – a gaudy, glittering sentinel standing guard over the living room.

In the kitchen, the only sign of recent habitation was a bowl and spoon draining on the dish rack. He went into the bedroom and dropped his overnight bag on the floor. The bed was neatly made as usual, with the frilled pillows perched on top and Carlene's battered childhood teddy propped against them.

He'd only been gone a night but it felt like a year. He felt a strange sense of disassociation, as if everything had changed in his absence and he was now a stranger in his own home. And where was Carlene? Was this her idea of a joke? To invite him back and then disappear?

He wandered back through the house. As he passed the study, he glanced in and saw the computer was on. Something caught his eye and he went in. At the top of the screen were the words 'Department of Communities, Child Safety Services' and underneath was the headline 'Intercountry Adoption.'

Reuben scrolled down the page until he came to 'Eligibility Criteria'. There were a number, but the first mentioned was that the couple was required to have been married or living together for a minimum of two years.

That gave him a reprieve for the next eighteen months. But what then? It made his head hurt even more to think about it. He went into the kitchen, poured himself a glass of water and drank it all in one gulp. From the corner of his eye he could see Kiet, Sahra and Ali staring at him from the fridge, vying for his attention. He wandered out into the back yard.

The sun attacked him with a fierce intensity. Carlene was around the side of the house hanging out the washing on the rotary clothes line. She didn't see him approach and he watched her for a few moments. She bent down, picked up a pair of socks from the basket and plucked two pegs from the pegbag hanging on the clothes line. With swift, practised movements, she pegged the socks on the line side by side.

Was she thinking what a bastard he was for not liking his Christmas present? For buying her a silver chain when Jolene was flashing her diamond bracelet, for not settling down to a steady job, not wanting to start a family? There were a myriad reasons he fell short of her expectations and still she wanted him back. Did she still hold out hope that he would change, that she could mould him into the man she thought he should be?

She bent down to the basket again, and as she straightened up, she spied him. Her mouth curved into a wide smile but her eyes were strained.

'Hi baby,' she said softly.

'Hi.'

'I'll just finish this and I'll make us some coffee.'

'It's okay, I'll make it.'

They sat on the patio with their coffee. A lawn mower droned nearby and a chorus of children's shouts swelled and faded into the distance. But the air between them was thick with a silence that pounded in Reuben's ears, as if they were trapped in a soundless bubble.

'This is not...'

'Honey, I just want to...'

They both laughed awkwardly.

'You go first,' Reuben said.

'I just want to say that I'm sorry about the gift voucher, but I was hoping you'd be more open-minded about it and at least give it a go. I was really annoyed at your reaction – and hurt too. And in front of the family, it was even more hurtful. Sometimes you frustrate me so much, and then you go and do something like buying the tickets to the New Year's Eve Ball, and then I realise how much I love you.'

You wouldn't love me quite so much if you knew the real reason I bought the tickets.

A single tear welled up and pooled on Carlene's lashes, then spilled over and slid down her cheek. She gave him a shaky smile. 'What were you going to say?'

He shifted in his chair. 'Nothing important.'

'Yes it was. You said, "This is not." Not what?'

'I was going to say this is not very good coffee. What brand is it?'

'Moccona Kenya, your favourite.'

'I've gone off it. We should try another brand.'

***

He'd almost said it – 'this is not working', almost told her it was over, but the words had stuck in his throat. There was something so cold and final about them; the chill of failure. He'd never been good at long-term relationships, had never wanted to be before but now that he did, he still couldn't make it happen.

Could you tell after six months if it wasn't going to work? How long did you hang in for, trying to keep it together and being miserable? The worst part of it was that Carlene loved him. But her love was all-consuming and possessive; maternal and erotic; and calculating and irrational. The more he tried to give himself some space, the more she closed in on him. Perhaps the only answer was to pack up and leave her a note. He'd done that before in past relationships – it was the coward's way out but he hadn't cared before. It was too hard to think about now – he'd put the decision on hold until after the ball.

28

The ball hurtled down the alley, as if its only mission was to smash the huddle of pins and send them all flying. Its pearly sheen glimmered under the strobe lighting. At the last minute it veered off to the right and into the gutter, nudging one of the pins on the end. The pin wobbled drunkenly and almost fell, then righted itself. A grand total of zero. Barry Gibb's falsetto tones in 'How Deep is My Love' reverberated around them.

Reuben shrugged his shoulders and ambled back to his seat.

'Bad luck,' Frank said, grinning. He picked up his ball, strode up to the marker and sent it down the alley with such power and precision that the ball didn't dare not hit the pins. His third strike in a row. A purple star pulsated on the scoring screen above them. 'Congratulations, you're a star!' sparkled the message. 'Go and claim your prize.'

'I'll go,' said Bomber. He jumped up, went over to the counter and came back with a giant Mars bar. He put it on the side table next to the Crunchie and the Cherry Ripe. With his long, loping style, he rolled his ball down the alley, knocked down six pins and with the second bowl scored a spare.

There were a million other more enjoyable ways of spending a Friday night than disco tenpin bowling – almost anything, in fact. Judging from the crowd, a lot of people didn't share Reuben's opinion. It was all very well to be invisible in a crowd but why couldn't Frank have picked something he was good at? Like Monopoly. Or Poker. Or Cheat. It was patently obvious Reuben hadn't been bowling since he was a kid. Thank God this was their last meeting.

Frank took it as a personal insult when he didn't score a strike, scowling and swearing as he waited for his ball to be returned through the chute. Bomber's style was more erratic, but when he scored a strike he punched the air as if he'd just won an Olympic medal. Towards the end of the game, he became distracted by a group of young women in skimpy shorts and halter neck tops arriving at the lane next to them; and Frank galloped away to a resounding victory.

Under the cover of returning the balls to the racks and taking off their bowling shoes, Frank passed them both a mobile phone, which they slipped into their pockets. He then inclined his head in the direction of the cafeteria. They ordered coffees at the counter and took a table in the corner. The light was dim where they sat and Donna Summer blared out around them.

It reminded Reuben of one of his first childhood memories, peeking around the doorway into the living room when he was supposed to be in bed, watching as his mother swayed and shimmied around the furniture to the strains of 'Hot Love'. Head thrown back and her gaze in a distant place, she was oblivious to everything except her own enjoyment. He never saw her dance in later years.

Grief struck him like a blow to the stomach, as it often did at the strangest moments. He didn't believe in heaven or an afterlife, but still he wondered if she could see him now. *Appearances are deceptive, Mum.* I might be hanging out with two of the most notorious crooks around, but I really am going straight.

Their coffees arrived. They looked and tasted like dishwater.

Bomber spluttered over his mouthful. 'Shit, this is worse than the camel pee they give you in the Big House!'

'Shut the fuck up,' Frank said through gritted teeth. 'Now, are you both clear about tomorrow night?'

'Yes, boss,' Bomber said. Reuben nodded.

'Littledick, you've checked her Facebook since she came back?'

'Checked it this afternoon.' He'd gone to the internet cafe after work. 'She got back yesterday at about three. She's still jetlagged because she didn't sleep at all on the plane so when she got home...'

'I don't need her fucking Dear Diary. Is she still going to the ball?'

'Yes. And they're definitely going by car – she said her husband offered to drive so she could drink, but she thinks she'll nod off on the dance floor if she has even one drink.'

'Then it's up to you to make sure she doesn't leave before you get Bomber's message. What time does it start?'

'Eight.'

'You'd better be at her place by six in case they decide to eat out first.'

Hanging around Lucy's street on New Year's Eve on a pink motor scooter was obviously out of the question. As was borrowing Carlene's car for a journey for which he had yet to think up a plausible reason. He could borrow Thommo's car if he hadn't already left for Sydney.

'Sydney on New Year's Eve,' he'd said, eyes sparkling, 'Goes off like a bomb.'

'Oops, sorry.' He looked contrite. 'You know, it's going to spoil my fun thinking of you flirting with death as you mix it with the Beautiful People. I still think you should give the cops the heads-up.'

'I've got it all under control,' Reuben said with much more assurance than he felt. 'Just enjoy yourself and forget about me. I'll phone you after midnight to prove I'm still alive.'

Thommo would be in Sydney right now, in a bar somewhere chatting up a girl. He'd left a large empty hole in Reuben's life.

'Are you listening, Littledick?'

Frank's voice snapped him back to the present.

'As soon as the bitch parks her car, send Bomber a message with the exact location. You'll have to follow her right in so you know which floor and aisle, and then you can get into your pumpkin coach with your fairy godmother and go to the ball. Bomber will message you when the job's done.'

'Who are you going to be this time?' Reuben asked Bomber. 'Lenny the Locksmith? Double call-out fee on New Years' Eve?'

Bomber grinned. 'You're a funny bloke. I'm sorry we won't be working together after tomorrow night.'

Sorry I can't return the compliment. Reuben hoped his face didn't belie his thoughts. Under Bomber's matey facade lurked something dark and chilling, like the bottom of a well.

'I'm just being myself,' Bomber said. 'Been out for a drink, going home early, having a bit of engine trouble, if anyone asks. Not that they will. I'll go in about ten – late enough for everyone to have arrived but too early for people to be going home. And then, Candy baby, here I come!'

'Is she your girlfriend?' Reuben asked.

'One of them.' Bomber winked. 'Sweet by name, sweet by nature.'

'Where's she live?'

Bomber clapped a hand on his shoulder. It was a friendly gesture but his grip was hard. 'Now don't you be worryin' about little things like that,' he said in a bad Irish accent. 'When the sun comes up on the New Year, I'll be on my way to a better place. Not heaven but just as good.'

He pushed his cup away, still half full. 'I gotta go. This coffee is making me sick.'

'One more thing, Littledick,' Frank said. 'I've got my mate in the police force on the lookout for any mysterious alerts about bombs. And in case you've got any funny ideas about calling the cops on the night, I'll have my spies in there watching your every move.'

Maybe he's bluffing – act as if you don't give a shit. Reuben shrugged. 'Suit yourself. I've already told you, I'm playing it straight.'

Frank gave him a friendly slap on the back. 'Just think of it as insurance, in case you have a sudden attack of principles on the night. And same deal with the phones. Dispose of them immediately. And no contact afterwards.'

'No matter what happens,' he added ominously.

They got up and Bomber scooped up the pile of chocolates Frank had won. Frank nodded at Reuben. 'Give them to him.'

Bomber held them out to Reuben. 'Happy New Year.'

'Thanks.'

Reuben took them and shoved them into his pocket. He didn't want them but it seemed pointless to refuse.

Bomber held out his hand to Frank and then to Reuben. 'Nice doing business with you.'

Frank grunted. Reuben said nothing. As they walked out into the clammy night air, the rhythm of crashing pins and pulsating lights behind them, Gloria Gaynor belted out the opening bars of 'I Will Survive'.

***

As soon as the Barbiemobile rounded the corner into his street, he saw the Corolla ahead of him in the carport. Fuck. It was only eight-thirty, Carlene wasn't supposed to be home this early. She'd gone to her parents' house for a pre-New Year's Eve cocktail party. Reuben had begged off going, pleading a severe headache. When she left, he was lying on the bed with a wet cloth on his forehead after taking three Panadol and drinking a cup of green tea at her insistence.

'I'll stay and help Mum clean up, so I won't be home till about nine,' she said. She stroked his forehead. 'Will you be okay?'

'I'll be fine; I just need to rest,' Reuben reassured her, with a hint of martyrdom. He waited fifteen minutes after she left in case she'd forgotten something, then sprang up from the bed, locked the house, raced out to the Barbiemobile and zoomed down to the tenpin bowling alley at Clayfield. He was relieved he could use a more creative alibi (if you could call a headache creative) for his meeting with Frank than the usual Finn crisis. He'd counted on being home and back in prone position before she returned.

As he walked in the front door, he put on a strained expression. Carlene came out in her bathrobe. She had a face cloth in her hand; one half of her face was made-up and the other scrubbed clean, giving her a peculiar two-faced appearance, like a Picasso painting.

'Where have you been?' she demanded. 'I've been worried about you. You're supposed to be sick!'

'I am sick,' Reuben said. 'I went to the day and night chemist to get some stronger tablets.'

'What did you get?'

'They were out of the gel capsules so I didn't get anything.'

'What's in your pocket?'

Reuben looked down at his bulging jeans pocket and pulled out one Mars bar, two Cherry Ripes, a Crunchie, a giant Freddo and a small Caramello Bear. He gave a sheepish grin.

'I bought them to share with you.'

Carlene sighed as she dabbed at her face with the cloth. 'It'll only make your headache worse. Anyway, I'm off chocolate. I put on two kilos over Christmas. I think it's all the stress.'

As Reuben sat up in bed munching on the Caramello Bear, Carlene said, 'You've made a remarkable recovery for someone who was on death's doorstep a few hours ago.'

She was beside him in her nightie, propped up with pillows reading *Angel Magic – a guide to discovering your angels and tapping into their powers.*

'Chocolate cures headaches – it's been scientifically proven.' He held up what was left of his bear, one small chocolate foot. 'Your head is so full of endorphins and serotonin, there's no room for the headache.'

It sounded quite plausible for something he'd made up on the spot.

'I think you just invented the headache so you wouldn't have to come to the cocktail party. And then I caught you out coming home from your little outing, probably to see your girlfriend.'

'You know I don't have a ... '

'You don't like my family, do you?'

'Hang on, what's this all about?'

'You know what it's about.'

Her voice was quivering.

'No, I don't.'

'Just answer the fucking question!'

'I don't not like your family – I mean, I like them!'

Even to himself, his words sounded unconvincing. 'Sometimes I find them a bit overwhelming. I don't mean in a bad way though.'

Whoops, the hole just got deeper. Was it possible to be overwhelming in a good way?

'I'm glad you like them,' Carlene said, 'because they're coming to the ball.'

She glared at him, defying him to object.

'When did they decide that?'

'Mum's good friends with one of the organisers. She offered her a couple of tickets for helping out, and then Mum managed to get hold of two more so Wayne and Jo could come.'

'Great, the more the merrier.'

Hopefully he'd be able to mingle with the crowd and not be stuck with his in-laws all night. He'd have to if he was keeping an eye on Lucy. And dodging Frank's spies.

He had to assume the worst-case scenario that Frank wasn't bluffing. It was all too likely that he was suspicious of Reuben and leaving nothing to chance this time. If his spies were watching Reuben closely enough to prevent him making a phone call, they'd be disguised as guests at the ball to blend in. Or maybe waiters. Or bouncers. Somehow he'd have to suss out who they were and give them the slip. Would they be armed? Don't even think about it...

He finished the Caramello Bear and started on the Mars Bar. Carlene put her book down and turned off her bedside lamp.

'I wish you wouldn't eat in bed, it's a disgusting habit.'

She turned her back to him and slid under the sheet. He looked at her hunched body, only inches away from him, but she may as well have been in the next suburb. Already they were like an old married couple who went through the motions out of habit and could no longer remember the pleasure they'd once enjoyed from each other's company. She was punishing him, but how much punishment could a man take? It was only three days since they'd last had sex – fervent, post-argument, homecoming sex; but it felt like a year.

His mind moved on to Lucy, as it usually did when he thought of sex. The only way he could think of, to follow her to the ball, was to wait for Carlene to arrive home from work at five-thirty, persuade her that he needed the car for a short but urgent mission he'd tell her about later; and ask her to get a lift in with Jo and Wayne or Nancy and Alec. She'd be annoyed, to put it mildly, but he'd keep his promise to tell her the full story when it was all over. If it all went to plan, he'd have nothing to lose.

It's a pretty big 'if'. His plan had so many loose ends, so many variables that could go wrong, that his mind was spinning like a disco ball thinking about them all. He threw his Mars Bar wrapper onto the bedside table, turned off his lamp and stretched out under the sheet, listening to the noises of the night outside his window. He'd never noticed before how noisy stillness was. Or perhaps it was his head. He realised he had the beginnings of a headache.

29

His mobile phone rang as he was unlocking the front door. By the time he got inside and fished it out of his pocket, it had gone to MessageBank. The message was from Carlene.

'I won't be home till about six-thirty – there's a Red Cross function on at the Bowls Club and I have to help out with a few last minute things. Sharon was supposed to do it but she's gone home sick and I can't leave Barry in the lurch. I'll be as quick as I can.'

Reuben sank onto the couch. Six-thirty was too late – he had to be at Lucy's by six. Why did Sharon have to go home sick, tonight of all nights? Who gets sick on New Year's Eve anyway?

It was three forty-five now. He had less than two hours to find another car. Could he steal one? In prison, Revhead had instructed him on how to break into a car and steal it in less than two minutes. But he wasn't confident he could do it without any practical experience. Think up an emergency and ask Nina to lend him her car? He didn't want to involve her in something that would undoubtedly lower her opinion of him if she found out the truth. Jump into a taxi and order the driver to follow that car? He'd always wanted to do that but it was too risky under these circumstances. Hire a car?

That wasn't so bizarre. He grabbed the Yellow Pages and flipped through to the Rental Cars. Cheap-as-Chips Car Rental. Sounded promising. And at Aspley, only a ten-minute drive away. He dialled the number.

'Cheap-as-Chips Car Rental has closed and will reopen for business at eight a.m. on January second. Please leave a message after the tone and we'll contact you as soon as possible.'

'As soon as possible is too fucking late.' He was just about to hang up when a female voice said, 'Hullo?'

'Oh ... hullo. I didn't realise anyone was there.'

'I was just about to go home. I wouldn't have answered the phone except you sounded pretty desperate.'

'I am. I need to hire a car for tonight.'

'I'm sorry, all our cars are out at the moment.'

'Shit. I mean are you sure? You haven't got one secreted out the back somewhere?'

'I'm sure. The only one I have left is an old MG that I'm driving home myself.'

An MG was not a car in which you could blend in with the rest of the traffic, but what choice did he have?

'That sounds perfect! Could you hire it out to me and I'll give you a lift home?'

'I don't think so.' Her tone was wary. Perhaps she thought it was a pick-up line.

'Look, I know we've never met, but I assure you I'm a fine upstanding character. It will be no trouble to drop you home.'

'No thanks. But I'll tell you what, I'll hire it out to you on two conditions – that you have it back here by ten tomorrow morning and that I add my taxi fare home and back to your fee.'

'Where do you live?'

Not at the Gold Coast, I hope.

'Mount Gravatt.'

Halfway to the Gold Coast, almost as bad. It would be.a good fifty-dollar cab fare each way. Operation Luce End was becoming an expensive exercise.

'Okay, it's a deal.'

'How soon can you get here?' she asked.

'I'll be there in fifteen minutes.'

It was twenty-five minutes before he pulled up at Cheap-as-Chips. He'd got stuck in peak hour traffic, with commuters leaving work early for the New Year celebrations, and had caught every red light as well. As he darted in between lines of traffic, he narrowly missed being crushed between two hulking four wheel drive vehicles.

Cheap-as-Chips lived up to its name appearance-wise, a tired, faded wooden building at the end of a small block of shops on Gympie Road. A sign on the front door announced it was closed. Surely she hadn't gone home? He was only ten minutes late.

He peered in through the glass. The office was deserted, although a fluorescent light beamed above the small reception desk. He banged frantically on the door.

A woman hurried out from the back. Close up, she looked barely eighteen. Petite, a sheen of blonde hair, exuding a dewy innocence. She unlocked the door.

'No need to break the door down.'

'Sorry, I thought you'd gone home. I got stuck in traffic.'

'I thought as much. Follow me.'

He followed her through the tiny, cramped office, out the back door to a row of carports. All were empty, except the one at the far end, in which was parked a red convertible MG with the hood down. It was quaint in a Noddy's Toyland way, but close up, with its scratched paintwork and faded leather seats, it resembled more a tired old relic at the bottom of the toybox.

'Looks great,' Reuben said. 'How much?'

'Two hundred and fifty dollars.'

'You've got to be kidding! For one night?'

Her eyes widened. 'Double time for New Year's Eve. And my return taxi fare.'

So much for youthful innocence! They went into the office where he filled out the paperwork and tried not to wince as he took the receipt from the EFTPOS transaction.

She thrust the keys at him. 'Don't forget, it has to be back here by ten tomorrow at the latest. I'm going away.'

'Just one thing ... would you mind if I parked my motor scooter in one of your carports? I don't want to leave it parked out the front all night.'

She shrugged. 'If you want. Fifty dollars for parking.'

He was about to protest then realised it was pointless. Where was she when he needed a sidekick, someone who could extort money without blinking an eye? He pulled out a fifty-dollar note from his wallet and slammed it on the desk.

She stood at the back door, hands on her hips and a sardonic smile on her face as he rode the Barbiemobile round and parked it in the carport next to the MG.

'Now I know why you were so desperate for the car.'

***

By the time he arrived home it was five-twenty. He wolfed down a sandwich, had a quick shower and dressed in the evening suit he'd hired. He surveyed himself in the mirror. Evening suits for men were surely invented by women, to stop men from turning up to formal occasions in their jeans or footy shorts. But what man really felt comfortable in this get-up? He looked like a waiter with his satin waistcoat and bow tie, as if he should glide around with a tray and a supercilious smile, filling up glasses and offering platters of steamed crab's claw with octopus jus.

He entertained himself with this vision as he pulled on his shoes and socks – Nancy and Wayne, his most disliked in-laws, tucking into the crab claws laced with arsenic and falling down in a heap on the floor, writhing and clutching their throats. But it didn't dislodge the cold lump of fear in the pit of his stomach.

He slipped the mobile phone Frank had given him into his jacket pocket, scrawled a note to Carlene and left it on the kitchen bench. 'Had to go on an unexpected errand. Can you go without me and I'll meet you there between eight and nine pm? Really sorry – will explain all when I see you.'

It was a relief to avoid confrontation by writing a note, but it was only delaying the inevitable. One positive point was that

Carlene wouldn't dare make a scene at the ball. Or would she? He pictured her, lips pursed and eyes glittering like a madwoman, throwing her drink in his face, wine dripping onto his spotless white shirt. Yes, she would, but she'd be discreet about it as well – inveigle him into a corner away from the public eye, to allow optimum satisfaction and minimum humiliation for herself. *Keep well away from corners.*

The MG rattled and clunked through the peak hour traffic on Gympie Road. On the tattered passenger's seat was an empty Coke can and on the floor, two empty crisp packets. She hadn't even bothered to clean out the car. How dare she take advantage of him because he was desperate!

It was five past six when he arrived at Lucy's street. He drove past it and parked outside the Henry Mitchell Park. From there he had a clear view of any car leaving the street and Lucy would have to pass him on her way to the city. Two boys of about ten kicked a ball desultorily around the brown-patched grass. Sweat trickled into all crevices of Reuben's body. He wrenched off his jacket and loosened his bow tie. The air was hushed and still with the expectancy of a thunderstorm. He searched the console until he found the button that said 'hood' in case he needed it, and hoped the rain would hold off for an hour or so.

Reuben slumped down in his seat, aware that a lone man loitering outside a park was bound to arouse suspicions. Especially a man in a dinner suit in a battered MG convertible. He would have been better off riding the Barbiemobile in drag.

He turned the radio up. The New Year's Eve party mix had started and 'Celebrate Good Times' boomed out. He had nothing to celebrate. He switched the station. Deep Purple's 'Highway Star'. That was better, a beat you could lose yourself in, meaningless words. Meaningless to him anyway.

After ten minutes, the boys dawdled out of the park, kicking the ball between them.

'Cool car, mister!' one of them yelled. The other pushed him and they raced down the road, chasing the ball and laughing boisterously.

Reuben rifled through the glove box – a packet of butter menthols, a mauve lipstick and a tattered paperback emblazoned with the title *His Regal Heiress* above a bosomy blonde in an evening gown.

He took out the book and skimmed through the first chapter, but at the end of it couldn't remember a thing he'd read. He put the book back in the glove box and drummed his fingers on the steering wheel. He glanced frequently in the rear-vision mirror, although he was sure that in the still air, he would hear any car approaching. If anyone asked, he was waiting for a friend, but apart from an old woman watering her garden a couple of houses down, there was no one around. What was the point of watering your garden when it was obviously going to rain?

Dusk gave way to darkness and the smell of rain filled the air. An engine purred behind him. In the rear-view mirror he saw a car stopped at the corner. In the darkness, he could see it was a Mazda 2, but not the numberplate. But he was sure it was Lucy's car.

He started the engine, swung around and headed off in the same direction. He kept well back, allowing another car in from a side street in front of him. Once on Gympie Road, he was three cars back but it was easy to keep sight of her, as the traffic was slow with revellers on their way into the city.

A clap of thunder boomed. Reuben jumped. A drop of water plopped onto his cheek, and the next moment the rain was attacking him in blistering sheets. He flicked on the wipers and pressed the hood button. Nothing. He tried again and again, pressing it frantically. No response. He was drenched, his clothes plastered against his skin, water dripping off his hair into his eyes, his coat saturated on the seat beside him. Wait till he saw that girl tomorrow, he'd give her an earful about charging him an exorbitant fee for a convertible that didn't convert. He'd demand his money back and insist she pay the dry -cleaning bill for his suit.

The rain eased and he peered ahead of him – as far as he could tell Lucy was still three cars in front. In his peripheral vision, he was dimly aware of faces staring at him from car windows on either side, but he looked straight ahead at the frenzied rhythm of the wipers on his windscreen.

The journey into the city seemed interminable. Reuben was on edge all the way – ready to change lanes the minute he saw Lucy's car pull out. Fortunately she took the most direct route to the city and soon the rain stopped completely, making it easier to keep her in sight. The two cars ahead turned off and as they crawled down Adelaide Street, he was only one car behind.

The wet road gleamed in the city lights and gutters sloshed with water, which sprayed up from the wheels of passing cars. Christmas decorations and coloured lights still festooned the buildings, banners waving from hotels and restaurants announcing their New Year's Eve specials. A group of youths wearing low-hanging jeans and baseball caps, and holding drink cans, swaggered along the pavement – periodically yelling 'Happy New Year!' By midnight they'd be either passed out or in a police car.

The car in front of him darted into another lane and suddenly he was right behind Lucy. The hulking person in the driver's seat was obviously her husband. What was his name? Damien? Donald? Duncan, that's right. Thank God – he wouldn't recognise Reuben and even if he had noticed an MG following him all the way from Aspley, so what? Everyone was going to the city tonight.

As they drew near to the King George Square car park, the Mazda's right indicator flickered on. He'd guessed they'd park there – it was the nearest public car park to the Grand Plaza Hotel. He followed them in, taking a ticket at the barrier gate. 'New Year's Eve special', the sign read. 'First three hours $20, $10 per hour every hour after.'

What kind of a special was that? If you wanted to take advantage of the special rate, you'd be home before the New Year had even begun. Which, under the circumstances, was an attractive proposition.

Reuben kept a respectable distance behind the Mazda as it wound its way through the concrete maze. His tyres squealed on the smooth floor and the motor's rough grumble echoed in the cavernous space. He prayed that Lucy wouldn't look behind her and spot him. They climbed up to level six before the Mazda was able to slide into a corner parking bay. It looked small and defenceless wedged in between a post and a Range Rover. Making a mental note of its exact position, Reuben drove up to the next level and slid into a parking spot.

He waited in the car for ten minutes to give Lucy and Duncan time to leave the parking station, then got out of the car, shrugged on his jacket and ran his hands through his hair. The wet jacket was heavy over his damp shirt and made him shiver. If he'd thought the suit was uncomfortable before, it was unbearable now and was starting to itch in the crotch as it dried. *For God's sake, don't scratch.*

He checked the time. Ten past eight. The ball only started at eight. Surely Carlene couldn't be too upset. He caught the lift down to the ground floor of the car park with a bunch of young, clean-cut couples in evening dress. Perhaps going to the same function. The women gave him curious looks and giggled as they stepped out of the lift.

Reuben adjusted his bow tie and waistcoat, and stepped out into the night. The rain had cooled the air to a refreshing crispness. The pavement, the buildings and even the other partygoers hurrying to their celebrations, all glistened with freshness and vibrancy, in sync with the coming new year. Reuben found a seat, still wet from the rain, in King George Square. He pulled his mobile phone out of his jacket pocket and punched in a message.

'King George square car park. Level 6, row e.'

His finger hovered over the send button. Once Bomber knew the location of Lucy's car, the plan was in action. Every cell in his body was resisting it, but he couldn't not do it. Hand shaking, he pressed the button. 'Sending.' He imagined the message whizzing through cyberspace, landing in Bomber's phone. 'Sent successfully'. He slipped the phone in his pocket and got up. His trousers clung to his backside from the seat as he crossed the square to the Grand Plaza Hotel.

30

Although it looked like every other hotel in the city, it was obvious from the moment you approached the front doors of the Grand Plaza Hotel that it considered itself a notch above all the others. A swarthy, uniformed doorman watched Reuben approach. His expression didn't change one iota, but Reuben sensed his disapproval. Surely he wasn't going to refuse him entry? He was conforming to the required dress code even if he did look as if he'd had a bath in his suit.

The doorman stepped in front of him. 'May I help you, sir?'

'I'm going to the charity ball.'

'Do you have a ticket?'

Shit, the tickets. In his haste to pick up the rental car, he'd forgotten to bring his ticket. In any case, Carlene would have it.

'My wife has it. She's already here.'

The doorman's heavy-lidded eyes flickered over him. 'The ballroom's on the third floor. But you won't be allowed in without a ticket.'

He stepped aside and waved him through. 'Have a good evening, sir.'

It was clear from his tone of voice that a good evening was highly improbable in a wet dinner suit without a ticket, supposedly in the possession of a wife who may or may not exist.

He shared the lift with two couples of sixty-odd, the men portly and ruddy-faced and the women, wide-arsed and aggressively bosomed. An aroma of aftershave mingled with heady floral perfume. Reuben kept his gaze fixed on the lift doors.

'The last time I wore this suit was to Muriel's Wedding,' one of the men boomed.

'The gallery opening wasn't what I expected,' his wife said to the other woman, ignoring him. 'Very under-catered, if you know what I mean.'

The other woman nodded, pursing her lips.

'That wasn't a bad movie,' the second man said. 'But that's going a bit over the top, isn't it, mate? Wearing a suit to the cinema?'

'I think Helen's losing her touch,' the first woman said. 'Ever since her husband was ... you know ... downsized.'

The first man inclined his head towards his wife. 'Muriel's her mother. Got married at eighty-five. In white, too.'

His wife frowned at him, as if he'd just revealed a dirty family secret. Reuben, visualising an elderly woman hobbling down the aisle on a zimmer frame, her long white dress flowing around her ungainly ankles, couldn't avoid catching the man's eye. He nodded to Reuben.

'Get caught in the rain, mate?'

Reuben gave a resigned grin. 'Hood wouldn't go up on the Porsche. Brand new, too.'

The two men looked anew at him and Reuben fancied he saw the glow of envy in their eyes. Not because he supposedly owned a Porsche – he was sure money was no object to either of them – but because he was young enough to drive one. There was an age after which a man in a Porsche looked like a poser, trying to compensate for his declining attractiveness and sexual prowess.

The first man shook his head. 'They don't make 'em like they used to.'

As the lift door opened, the strains of a saxophone floated in. The ballroom was an acreage of polished floor, bordered by giant carved pillars and lit by several ornate chandeliers. Balloons and decorations were strung across the walls along with the usual 'Happy New Year' banners. On the stage was a seven-piece band called The Groove Merchants, playing a torch song Reuben vaguely recognised. No one was on the dance floor – people weren't drunk enough yet. Waiters with trays of food and drink glided amongst the crowd like evening-suited storks.

At the reception desk, a Kojak look-alike in a three-piece suit was taking tickets. Reuben peered through the crowd, straining to find Carlene, or even one of the other family members.

'Yes? You have a ticket to pick up?'

Reuben stepped up to the desk. 'No, I mean yes. My wife has my ticket. She's here already.'

A thought dawned on him. 'Maybe she left it here for me. Littlejohn.'

The man flicked through his box of tickets. 'Nothing in that name.'

Of course not. That'd be too easy. She had to make him suffer.

'Can I go in and find her? I promise I'll come straight back and give you the ticket.'

The man shook his head. 'Sorry, mate.'

Reuben reached into his pocket for his phone to ring Carlene then remembered he'd left it at home. The only one he had was the one Frank gave him. The number would show up as unknown on Carlene's phone and she'd want to know whose phone he was using.

He moved away from the reception desk and peered through the glittering sea of suits and evening dresses. He felt Kojak's eyes upon him, as if suspicious that he might make a run for it into the crowd. What colour dress was Carlene wearing? He couldn't remember if she'd even told him – once upon a time, before a social occasion, she'd involve him in a detailed discussion about her choice of outfits and the pros and cons of each one. She was probably deliberately avoiding him. Maybe she was so mad she hadn't even brought his ticket. *Don't even think it.*

The room was packed and it wasn't surprising that he couldn't see the rest of the family either. A group of people in the middle of the room dispersed and suddenly there were Lucy and

Duncan talking to another couple. His heart jumped. Lucy wore a long, strapless silver and black evening dress and her hair was up, with soft tendrils falling onto her cheeks. A pendant hovered above her cleavage and her bare shoulders reminded him of a movie star from the forties – seductive, yet vulnerable. She shone from the crowd as if someone had highlighted her with a fluorescent marker.

For God's sake get a grip. She was facing him and she only had to avert her gaze for a moment to catch him staring. He looked away and caught the flinty eye of Kojak. He smiled and shrugged.

'Can't seem to find her.'

Then he did see Carlene, in the far left-hand corner, talking to another woman. She wore a long, cherry-red dress, if wore was the right word for something that looked as it had been poured onto her in liquid form and set on her body. It accentuated her curvaceous body but also made her look tarty. He couldn't help comparing her to Lucy, whose outfit didn't need to scream 'Look at me, I'm sexy!' because it was there, in the way she stood and moved, and smiled.

Reuben waved and gesticulated to catch Carlene's attention, but she was standing side on and engrossed in her conversation. He jumped up and down and waved some more, and finally a woman standing near Carlene noticed him and raised her eyebrows. Reuben pointed behind her and drew a curvy figure in the air. The woman looked behind her, spotted Carlene and tapped her on the shoulder. Carlene swung around and the woman pointed to Reuben. Her expression changed in an instant. She made her way through the crowd. The band was playing 'Strangers in the Night'.

She stood in front of him. 'I'm not even going to ask you where you've been because you'll probably give me some pathetic, totally unbelievable answer.'

She leaned forward and pinched his jacket. 'And you're all wet!'

Reuben opened his mouth to answer.

'Don't bother, I'm not in the mood.'

She reached into her evening bag, pulled out a ticket and thrust it at him. 'You're lucky I brought it. I was so tempted to leave it at home.'

'Thanks, honey. I appreciate it.'

She drew her shoulders back and gave him her Nancy look. 'Don't honey me. And I'll have a champagne, thanks.'

She swept back into the crowd. Her buttocks, jiggling against their tight confines, radiated so much anger they looked in danger of self-combusting. Reuben handed in his ticket. Kojak, who'd been watching Carlene's butt, swivelled his eyes back to Reuben.

'Looks like you've got a bit of making up to do.'

Reuben ignored him. Entering the ballroom, he grabbed two glasses of champagne from a passing waiter. As he wove his way through the crowd, he looked around to see if he could spot Frank's spies. Perhaps a couple of guys without female partners who didn't quite fit in with the crowd. If they were proper spies, they'd bring along partners for cover, but Reuben suspected they were probably just a couple of thugs Frank had hired for the night. People milled around in couples or groups, balancing drinks and paper napkins of hot savouries. No one stood out. Then he spotted Carlene. She was standing with the rest of the family, and they all watched him as he approached.

'Evening, everyone.'

He handed Carlene her champagne.

'Thanks,' she said, in a tone which said, 'I'm only being gracious for the family's benefit.'

'I trust you finished your business satisfactorily?' Nancy asked. She wore a long black skirt and cream chiffon blouse and was accessorised right down to her formal glasses, edged in a black and white geometrical design. In the nouveau poor style manual, the rule was the simpler the outfit, the more expensive it was. The idea was to look as if you'd bought it from Target, a look Nancy had managed to achieve with ease.

'Yes thanks,' Reuben said.

'Unfortunate having to do business on New Year's Eve,' Alex said. 'Is it something you can tell us about? Or is it all hush-hush?'

'It's still in the early stages, but all will be revealed soon.'

Carlene looked at him and rolled her eyes.

'Hey mate,' Wayne said, 'is that the new wet look, or are you too dumb to come in from the rain?'

Reuben didn't answer. Wayne's speech was slurred, his face blotchy. His suit strained against his bulk. It was obvious he'd begun his New Year celebrations well before he arrived.

'Rubie,' he said in falsetto, 'I asked you a question.'

Jo nudged Wayne. 'Honey, don't be so rude.'

Reuben looked levelly at Wayne. 'If you don't call me Rubie, I'll answer your question.'

Wayne shrugged. 'No matter. I think it's option "b" myself.'

Jo looked horrified. 'Wayne!'

'Oh Jesus. I'm going to find someone to have an intelligent conversation with.'

He wandered off, just stopping himself in time from upending his beer into a passing woman's cleavage.

'Oh shit,' Jo said.

'You'd better keep an eye on him,' Nancy commanded. 'The last thing we want is for him to disgrace us by getting thrown out.'

'Look' Alec said, relieved. 'Here's John and Edna.'

A grey-haired couple bustled up and greeted Alec and Nancy. Jo trotted off after Wayne. Carlene pulled Reuben aside.

'Now tell me the truth,' she hissed.

Reuben took a gulp of his champagne and grimaced. It tasted like vinegar. You'd think that for the price of the tickets they'd supply a decent drop. 'You said you didn't want to know.'

'Don't be so fucking stupid. Where were you? Or perhaps I should ask, who were you with?'

Reuben took another sip, playing for time. 'I wasn't with anybody and I'm sorry, I can't tell you what I was doing. As soon as I can, I promise you'll be the first to know.'

'I suppose you're going to tell me you're a Russian spy. Or a member of the CIA.'

'Nothing like that. Someone's life is at stake, that's why I can't say anything.'

'And that someone wouldn't happen to be a woman?'

He hesitated. 'It is. But I can assure you I'm not having an affair with her.'

Only in my mind. That doesn't count.

'So tonight you were out saving her life, but you weren't actually with her.'

'Yes.'

She stared hard at him. 'You're so full of shit. Being in that TV ad has gone to your head; you think you're James Bond.'

Reuben took her empty champagne glass. 'Let me get you another drink.'

'And don't think you can ply me with alcohol and get all romantic, because it won't work!' she called after him.

Where was a waiter when you wanted one? They were like cops, hung around like a bad smell then disappeared when you really needed them. He saw one in the distance, made a beeline for him and came face-to-face with Lucy.

'Reuben!'

His mind raced for a witty reply, something James Bondish.

'Hi,' he said.

'What a surprise!'

'Yes, isn't it?' Reuben said. He guessed the last place she'd expect to run into one of her clientele was at a a-hundred-and-twenty-a-head gala ball.

Her husband appeared at her shoulder. His evening suit barely contained his powerful build and he exuded the radiant good health of someone who spent a lot of time outdoors. James Bondish repartee was out of the question.

'Duncan, this is Reuben.'

They shook hands. Duncan regarded him with curiosity but was too polite to ask how they knew each other.

'Are you enjoying the night?' Lucy asked.

'Yes, I am. How was Scotland?'

He felt Duncan's eyes boring into him, probably wondering how Reuben knew about their trip. Reuben felt a brief moment of panic before remembering that Lucy had mentioned it in their last interview.

'It was great. We only arrived back two days ago and I'm still jetlagged.'

The only sign of it was the washed-out pallor of her skin, which even her make-up couldn't disguise. But to Reuben it made her look more vulnerable and desirable. How much more vulnerable would she look if she knew that at that very moment someone was preparing to plant a bomb in her car?

Reuben swallowed hard and looked down at the two empty champagne glasses in his hands. 'I'd better go. I'm supposed to be getting my wife another drink. She'll send out a search party soon.'

He nodded at Duncan. 'Nice to meet you.'

'See you ... er, later,' Reuben said to Lucy – he'd nearly said 'at my next appointment.'

He fetched a glass of champagne and a mineral water for himself from the bar. He'd had his quota of alcohol for the night – he had to keep a clear mind as well as drive the MG home. How was he going to explain that to Carlene? *Forget it, that's the least of your worries.* He felt in his coat pocket for the reassuring touch of his mobile phone and checked his watch. Eight-thirty. Ninety minutes to go before Bomber even arrived at the car park. It was going to be a long night.

When he returned to Carlene, she was tucking into a mini quiche from the selection of tidbits on her napkin. She offered it to him but he shook his head. The thought of food made him feel ill.

'Who was that woman you were talking to?' she said.

'That was Lucy, my parole officer.'

'Really?' Carlene looked disbelieving. It probably hadn't occurred to her that his parole officer would be young and attractive. It hadn't occurred to him, either, till he'd met Lucy. 'She looks a bit like that woman in your photos, the ones you were playing around with in the middle of the night.'

Reuben shrugged. 'Maybe. But it's not her.'

Carlene looked at him accusingly. 'Why didn't you call me over and introduce me?'

'I wanted to get back to you, honey.' He put his arm around her waist and gave her a squeeze. 'Maybe I'll get a chance to introduce you later.'

He'd have to make sure that Carlene and Lucy were on opposite sides of the room for the rest of the night. Once Carlene had Lucy's ear, she was sure to raise the topic of his supposed PTSD, thereby giving Lucy a reason to send him to a psychologist. But being on the opposite side of the room to Lucy would make it difficult for him to keep an eye on her. From a quick reconnaissance of the ballroom he'd ascertained that apart from the emergency exit stairwell, there was only one way to leave – the same way they'd come in. He had to make sure he had a clear view of it at all times.

'Let's get out of the crowd a bit,' he said, steering Carlene to the edge of the crowd. The band broke into the Blues Brothers' 'Shake Your Tailfeather'. The dance floor started to fill up.

'Come on, let's dance,' Carlene said. It was a command rather than a suggestion. Reluctantly, Reuben placed his drink on a nearby bar table and followed her onto the dance floor. He mooched his way around, scrutinising the crowd standing around it, for disguised thugs. He spotted Lucy leading Duncan onto the floor and immediately picked up his pace, jiggling and bouncing and swirling Carlene around, to show Lucy he wasn't one of those guys who just shuffled around on the dance floor looking embarrassed and trying to peek down his partner's cleavage.

Carlene jiggled and bounced back at him with grim, martyred enjoyment and Reuben had the absurd impression that they were duelling for the title of fastest bopper. Lucy and Duncan set a more sedate pace, and during 'Brown-eyed Girl', Duncan put his arm around Lucy's waist and held her close as they danced. Reuben looked away.

After a couple more dances, he'd had enough and nodded to Carlene in the direction of the bar. She followed him off the dance floor and immediately three women she knew from Orphans International appeared, engulfing them both in hugs and excited squeals. Standing in a pool of frenzied female chatter, Reuben had an idea.

'Just going to the Gents,' he told Carlene. He made his way through the crowd to the toilets at the back of the hall. Frank's spies were sure to follow him into the Gents, as that was the only sure way he could make a private phone call.

He opened the door of the Gents. The toilets were unoccupied and there was one man standing at the far end of the urinal. Reuben positioned himself at the middle, unzipped his fly and began to pee. The door opened and a man entered, stood a respectable distance away from Reuben and unzipped. From the corner of his eye Reuben could see he was dark-haired and of solid build. He glanced at him quickly. The guy looked Italian or Greek, with a large misshapen nose that had obviously seen a few fights.

He looked ill at ease in his suit – the top button of his shirt was undone and his bow tie was askew. Odds on, this was him. Or one of them.

The man caught his eye. Reuben smiled and nodded. 'Great evening.'

The man hesitated. 'Yeah.'

To the accompaniment of the steady gush of urine, Reuben said, 'How's our friend Frank?' He kept his gaze ahead at the tiled wall, but felt the man looking at him.

'Who's Frank?'

'Look, I know who you are. I don't know your name but I know you're working for Frank Cornell and I know why you're here. Where's your partner in crime?'

'Listen, mate, I don't know who the fuck Frank Cornell is and I don't care.'

Reuben looked at him. He shook his dick, put it away and yanked his zipper up. 'And quit gawping at me or I'll deck you.'

He washed his hands vigorously at the basin, punched the button on the hand drier and rubbed his hands under it for a few seconds. 'Bloody pervert,' he said over his shoulder as he pushed open the door. The other man hurriedly zipped up, washed his hands, and without bothering to dry them followed the first man out, darting suspicious glances at Reuben.

Fuck, I could have sworn it was him. Maybe it was and he'd just carried out a monumental bluff. As Reuben opened the door to leave, he heard a toilet flush. He stopped. There'd been no one in the toilets when he'd entered the Gents. Someone must have come in while he was at the urinal. Whoever it was had entered very quietly. Reuben closed the door and made a beeline for the closest bar. From there he had a clear view of the entrance to the Gents.

Seconds later, a man came out. Medium height, slim build, balding, with ears that stuck out like handles and a narrow, pinched face. Neat and spruce in his evening suit, right down to the shiny bow tie and knife-edge pleat in the trousers. He scanned the crowd as if looking for his wife. His eyes met Reuben's with not the slightest sign of recognition before he moved away into the crowd. He looked nothing like Reuben had imagined, but some instinct deep within him knew he was Frank's spy. Or one of them.

He looked at his watch. Nine-twenty. He reached into his trouser pocket for his mobile phone. He'd put it there, hoping he would feel it vibrate when Bomber messaged him. It was too early but he couldn't help looking anyway. No message. He slipped it back into his pocket. Better go and check out where Lucy was.

A man hurried towards him; so fast he didn't have time to escape. 'Reuben!' Pastor Bryan held out his hand and pumped Reuben's enthusiastically. 'Nice to see you again!'

His suit was obviously hired – the trouser cuffs bunched over his shoes and his hands disappeared back into his coat sleeves. His trousers, at least a size too large, looked as if they were held up by prayer. His cheeks shone with perspiration and cheerfulness.

'Pastor! I didn't expect to see you here.'

'Just because I'm a man of God doesn't mean I don't like to enjoy myself!' He pointed to his glass of champagne and gave a knowing wink. 'And please call me Bryan.'

'Right.' He had to escape before the Pastor tried to recruit him again. 'I'm looking for my wife, have you seen her anywhere?'

'I just said hullo to her. She's over there, talking to that young lady in the silver dress.'

He looked in the direction of the Pastor's nod. Carlene was in earnest conversation with Lucy, Duncan standing a little back, as if to give them room to have a confidential discussion. Carlene must have headed straight for her – he'd only been in the Gents for a couple of minutes.

It would look too obvious if he just walked over and dragged Carlene away. The Pastor's genial expression gave him an idea.

'You know, Pastor, I've been having second thoughts about getting involved in your project for disadvantaged youth. I think I can help you out.'

Pastor Bryan looked at Reuben as if he had just announced the second coming of Christ. 'That's wonderful, Reuben! You know, I had faith you'd come around eventually.'

You know more about me than I know myself, then.

'Let's go over and talk to Carlene about it right now,' Reuben said. 'I know she'll be as delighted as you are about it.'

He headed in the direction of Carlene and Lucy, and motioned for the Pastor to follow him. Carlene spied him and stopped talking, watching him as he approached.

'There you are honey,' Reuben said. 'Hullo again, Lucy. And Duncan.'

Lucy smiled and Duncan nodded. It was weird seeing your wife and your parole officer together. Almost as weird as seeing your wife and your mistress together.

'Sorry to interrupt, but I was just telling the Pastor that I'd changed my mind about getting involved in his youth projects and we decided that now is as good a time as any to discuss it. Didn't we, Pastor?'

'Yes, indeed. And please call me Bryan.'

'This is the first I've heard of it,' Carlene said.

'That sounds like something worthwhile,' Lucy said. 'We'll leave you all to discuss it. Have a Happy New Year!'

'You too,' Reuben said.

Lucy smiled again and looked up at Duncan. 'I'm not sure if I'll be up to seeing the New Year in. We might head off soon.'

'You can't!' They all looked at Reuben. 'I mean, you have to stay at least until midnight, otherwise what's the point of being at a New Year's Eve ball? They're drawing the lucky door prize at midnight.'

He'd made that bit up, out of desperation.

'Really?' Lucy said, 'I haven't heard anything about that. What's the prize?'

'Er...' Reuben said.

'We'll go and check it out,' Duncan said. They disappeared into the crowd. Reuben broke out in a sweat. Would they leave once they found out there was no lucky door prize? *Just hold out for another hour, Lucy.*

'So what's this about helping Pastor Bryan?' Carlene said. 'When did you decide that?'

'I've been thinking about it for a while. I thought I'd mentioned it to you.'

She gave him a steely look. 'I know nothing of what goes on in your mind. And I thought nothing you did would surprise me. Turns out I was wrong.'

Pastor Bryan cleared his throat. 'God works in mysterious ways, my dear. Often when we least expect it. Now, Reuben, we have our first meeting of the year next week...'

Where the hell had Lucy gone?

'Excuse me, Pastor.' Reuben interrupted. 'I really have to ... er ... visit the Gents.'

'You just went a few minutes ago,' Carlene said.

She was keeping track of his excretory habits now?

Reuben rubbed his stomach. 'I think it was the curry puffs; they didn't agree with me.'

'You didn't have any,' Carlene said.

'Just the smell made me feel sick,' he said and escaped in the direction of the toilets. On the way, he searched the crowd and spotted Lucy and Duncan talking to another two couples – maybe Lisa and Spike and the others from Facebook. Thank God. Hopefully they'd keep her talking for a while. He scanned the crowd again. Jug-ears was a few feet away talking to two men who had the well-fed, complacent air of successful businessmen. He didn't blink when Reuben looked his way and gave the appearance of being engrossed in conversation, but his body was tense, as if ready to spring into action at a moment's notice. Would he have a gun hidden inside his jacket?

'Reuben.' He felt a hand on his shoulder. It was Jo. Her face was drawn and her jaw set.

'Could you do me a favour and have a word with Wayne? He won't listen to me and if he drinks any more he's going to do something really embarrassing, I just know it.'

Reuben looked over her shoulder and saw Wayne holding court to a middle-aged couple. He was swaying and hugging a pot of beer to his chest. The expression on the man's face was amused, verging on embarrassed. His wife was plainly disapproving.

'He won't listen to me either. I don't think he likes me very much.'

'He does, honestly. He needs another man to take him aside and talk some sense into him. Please?'

A tear welled up and hovered on her lower lid.

'All right,' Reuben said, every instinct in his body screaming against it. 'Just give me a couple of minutes and I'll come over.'

'Thanks, I appreciate it.' She wiped away her tear and rejoined the group.

Reuben waited a couple of minutes then wandered over.

'And I'll tell you another reason the Poms won't win the Ashes this year,' Wayne was saying, 'it's because all their players are arse-licking fairies.' He jabbed the other man in the chest.

'Now, just a minute, mate,' the man said in a clipped British accent. He drew himself up, his face reddening.

'Reuben, this is Tony and Jan,' Jo butted in.

'Pleased to meet you,' Jan said. 'Come on, dear, I'm starving – let's see if we can find some food. Please excuse us.'

She grasped her husband by the arm and led him away.

'Bloody Poms,' Wayne said. 'Can't take a joke. Wouldn't know one if it bit them in the balls.'

He held up his empty glass in front of Reuben. 'Can you get us another drink, mate?'

'Don't you think you've had enough?' Reuben said.

He glared, cross-eyed, at Reuben. 'Who the fuck are you to tell me how much I should drink?'

'I'm simply saying maybe you should slow down. The security guard over there is bored out of his brain. I'm sure he'd love an excuse to escort you out the door.'

'Listen, mate.' Wayne poked Reuben in the chest. 'I don't need you of all people to tell me how to run my life.'

'Honey! That's unfair,' Jo said.

'You stay out of it,' Wayne snarled. 'It's about time someone told Mister Smartarse the truth and it looks like it'll have to be me.'

He turned to Reuben. 'You don't belong to this family. We've all tried to pretend you're one of us for Carlene's sake but you're not and never will be. A leopard never changes its spots and I reckon you've been back to your old tricks. You sure as hell haven't been doing anything else.'

'Wayne!' Jo was on the verge of tears again.

'I told you to shut up!'

Anger oozed from the shiny pores on Wayne's face. 'Unless you count dressing up in women's clothes and playing around on your wife. Carlene's right, you need help. Look at you!'

He gestured wildly at Reuben. 'You're ... you're...'

His gaze swivelled to the glass in Reuben's hand. 'You're drinking soda water, for fuck's sake. What kind of bloke drinks soda water on New Year's Eve?'

Reuben tensed. In his mind's eye he saw himself land a punch on Wayne's jaw. It gave a satisfying loud smack before Wayne swayed and fell in a bloated heap on the floor.

He drew in a deep breath. 'A bloke who's not going to waste his time with fuckwits like you.'

He turned around and almost bowled over Nancy, who was standing behind him. She gave Wayne a look that would have stopped a charging rhinoceros.

'Wayne, shut up!' she snapped.

Wayne put on a sulky expression and muttered under his breath. Reuben took the opportunity to escape.

Anger lingered in his chest like heartburn. He glanced over to Lucy's group. She'd disappeared, although Duncan and the others were still there. Why couldn't she just stay in the one spot?

He looked at his watch again. Nine-fifty. He pulled his mobile phone out and checked it again for messages. Maybe Bomber had done the job early. No such luck.

'Who are you ringing?' Carlene appeared, looking accusing.

'No one.' He slipped the phone back in his pocket and to divert her attention from further interrogation, he grabbed her hand. 'Come on, let's dance.'

The dance floor was packed by now and there was only room to bop up and down on the spot. 'Can't get no satisfaction!' the lead singer warbled plaintively. Reuben tried to scan the crowd unobtrusively to find Lucy, but Carlene caught him out. She frowned and he smiled and bopped harder. He began an elaborate sequence of movements that involved lots of twirling around, like a rock 'n' roll version of the flamenco, so he could do a quick reconnaissance of the room during his twirls. He executed a high jump, rather like a pirouette, and spotted Lucy coming out of the Ladies. He caught Carlene's eye. She gave him a look that said, 'Whatever you're up to, I'm onto you.'

As he was starting to get a bit dizzy from the twirls, he did a few slow circle shuffles, searching for Jug-ears, but to no avail. But undoubtedly he was close by, watching Reuben's dance floor antics.

After the Rolling Stones bracket, the band announced a break and the crowd straggled off the floor. Carlene stopped to talk to a friend from church. Reuben craned his neck and saw Lucy and Duncan still talking to their friends. Lucy yawned and Duncan smiled down at her and stroked her cheek. Reuben moved away a little from Carlene and her friend, and checked the time. Ten-fifteen. He took out his phone again. Still no message. What the hell was Bomber doing?

A hand reached out and swiped the phone from his grasp. Carlene was beside him, stuffing it into her evening bag.

'Whoever you're expecting to call, she can go and get stuffed.'

'It's not a "she". Please give it back.'

'No way. You're driving me mad, looking at your phone every few minutes – that's when you're not checking out the other women here. Is she here? Have you got an assignation? Hoping to find a dark corner somewhere?'

Strands of her hair had fallen from her French knot and her cheeks were flushed.

'I keep telling you, there's no other woman.'

'And I keep not believing you.'

Reuben tried to keep his voice calm. 'Look, I'm expecting an important call. It's to do with the business I mentioned earlier. I promise I'll tell you all about it tomorrow.'

She shook her head. 'Nothing's so urgent you can't spend a few uninterrupted hours with your wife. It's hardly a matter of life and death, is it?'

She put her mouth to his ear. 'You owe me for all the shit you've put me through,' she hissed. 'Just this once, forget about everything else and concentrate on having a fun night.'

If only you knew how much I'd love to forget everything and have a fun night... Reuben's stomach clenched. How could he get his phone back? As if reading his thoughts, Carlene wound the strap of her bag tightly around her arm and clasped it to her side. He'd have to crash-tackle her – hard to do without causing a stir.

He thought quickly. No point now in waiting for Bomber's message, as he wasn't going to receive it. Better call the police now – by the time they turned up at the car park the deed would surely be done. Or even better, they'd catch Bomber in the act. If he waited any longer, it was likely that Lucy, who was slowly wilting, would leave and he wasn't confident of his ability to stop her. He searched the crowd. Could he borrow someone's phone? Where was Jo? She was sure to have her phone with her.

He couldn't see her anywhere. This was all going to shit. And how was he going to convince the police they should come immediately and not in an hour's time? Then he spotted Pastor Bryan walking away from the bar holding two glasses of champagne. He stopped in front of two svelte young blondes and handed them a glass each with an ingratiating smile.

'Excuse me,' Reuben said to Carlene. He felt the daggers of venom in his back as he made a beeline for the Pastor.

'I'm sure you'd enjoy our social evenings,' Pastor Bryan was saying to the women, 'they're very informal and lots of fun.' He gave a wink. 'And there are lots of handsome young men as well.'

'Sorry to interrupt, Pastor,' Reuben said. The women looked relieved. 'I wonder if you have a mobile phone with you.'

'As a matter of fact, I do,' Pastor Bryan said.

'Could I borrow it? I left mine at home and I have to make an urgent call.'

Pastor Bryan hesitated. 'It's supposed to be only for church business.'

'This is really important! And it'll only take a minute.'

'Is someone ill? Do you need an ambulance?'

Reuben took a deep breath. 'No, nothing like that. It's just an important business call.'

Pastor Bryan looked at him dubiously as he reached into his jacket pocket. 'As long as you're not calling your stockbroker in New York.' He winked again at the women. He produced a mobile phone and handed it to Reuben. 'Just press star and the green button to unlock it.'

'Thanks, Pastor, I'll be back in a minute.'

Reuben slipped the phone into his pocket and headed towards the emergency exit. It was on the other side of the room, through a vast expanse of jostling bodies. He made his way through them as quickly as he could, not daring to look behind him. If he could make it out the exit and into the street, he had a much better chance of giving Jug-ears the slip and calling the police.

A hand grasped his right shoulder. 'You're not leaving already are you, mate?'

Jug-ears was beside him, grinning. He dug his fingers into Reuben's shoulder in a painful grip and slipped his hand inside Reuben's coat. Something hard jabbed Reuben in the small of his back. Like the butt of a pistol.

'Keep going,' Jug-ears said in a low voice. 'I'm keeping you company. And give me that phone.' He pressed the pistol harder into Reuben's back.

Reuben gulped. 'You wouldn't dare in here.'

'It's got a silencer. I can put a bullet in your back and be out of here before you can blink. Hand it over.'

Reuben dug the Pastor's phone out of his coat pocket and Jug-ears snatched it out of his hand. He jabbed the pistol again. 'Let's go. Out the emergency exit. And no funny business.'

Reuben started walking, Jug-ears beside him. He'd removed the pistol from Reuben's back. Surely he wouldn't shoot him in the middle of a crowded ballroom. Reuben glanced sideways at him. His hand was in his jacket pocket, obviously ready to whip the pistol out if needed. Swallowing the panic rising in his chest, Reuben quickly scanned the room, looking for an escape route. Could he make a run for it before Jug-ears had a chance to shoot him? Create a diversion, yell 'Fire!' and escape in the ensuing panic?

'Don't even think about it,' Jug-ears said. 'I have friends here.'

He might be bluffing. Might not be. Think of something for fuck's sake!

Above the buzz of chatter, he heard a voice.

'It's all a load of bullshit. The Pakis have been fixing their cricket games since the caveman days when they played with tree stumps...'

Wayne was ahead of him. Right in the path to the emergency exit. He was holding court to a group of men who all appeared similarly under the weather. Ties were askew and shirts untucked. A couple sniggered at his remarks while the others looked on with good humour. And suddenly it was perfectly, brilliantly clear.

As Reuben and Jug-ears approached Wayne's group, he was guffawing at a joke he'd made. He didn't see Reuben until he was beside him. He turned his head and Reuben's arm shot out. His fist caught Wayne square on the jaw with a resounding smack. Wayne reeled back and Reuben hit him again. Wayne teetered, tried to regain his balance but toppled onto the floor, his beer flying out of his hand. Glass smashed on the polished floor. A woman screamed.

Arms surrounded Reuben, restraining him. 'There's a man with a gun!' he yelled.

'Steady on, mate, steady on,' a voice said.

'It's not a joke! He was beside me, he's got a gun!'

A woman screamed again. Was it the same one? He looked around for Jug-ears then someone put him in a headlock. His trousers felt damp. Surely he hadn't peed himself? He looked down at the pool of beer lapping at his feet. Wayne's beer had splashed him on the way down.

The buzz of conversation heightened to fever pitch. Two pairs of uniformed legs appeared in front of him. His 'headlocker' released him and the security guards yanked his arms behind his back.

'Did you get the guy with the gun?' Reuben shouted at them.

'Calm down, mate,' one of the guards said.

'What did he look like?' the other said.

'He was in an evening suit!'

'Listen, wise guy...'

The guard wrenched his arms even harder.

'He was bald, with sticking-out ears!'

'All right, mate, we're onto it,' the first guard said. They exchanged *'we've got a crazy one here'* looks. 'Let's get you out of here.'

They marched him out of the room, the crowd moving aside to give them a wide berth.

'Disgusting behaviour,' rang out an older female voice. 'And in this hotel!'

Reuben kept his eyes to the front. Kojak at the reception desk shook his head as if to say 'I knew he'd be trouble'.

'Have the police been called?' Reuben asked the first guard who seemed slightly less brutish than the other.

'They're on their way.'

'Thank God.'

31

'Wallet. Keys. Watch.'

The prison officer handed him the plastic bag. Reuben signed the forms to acknowledge he'd received them.

'See you next time.'

'There won't be a next time,' Reuben said.

The officer gave a sardonic grin. 'Isn't that what you said last time?'

How would you know, you prick, you weren't even here last time. The officer saw them come in and go out through the revolving door of so-called rehabilitation. They were all the same to him.

Outside the entrance Reuben kept walking and didn't look back. It was a good five kilometres to the railway station, but it was a bright, clear-skied February day and he had until four-thirty to present himself, back at the parole office.

He thought about the last time he'd been released from prison, sitting beside Carlene in her car, his hand on her thigh, feeling as if he'd burst out of his skin with joy. The world was magic, the future exciting – he saw it in the trees and sky and buildings, heard it in voices and laughter and music, inhaled it with every breath of sweet, clean air and felt it in every pore of his skin.

Only seven months ago. Another lifetime. Now he was trying to find some equilibrium between self-pity and despair. He was homeless, wifeless and jobless with thirty dollars in his wallet. He didn't know for sure about the 'jobless,' but not turning up to work for a month without explanation was usually sufficient reason to be fired. Every day, he'd told himself it was worth being arrested and charged with assault, and spending twenty-eight days in prison for beaching his parole, to have saved Lucy's life. But for once, he couldn't convince himself.

In the end it had all worked out pretty much to plan. As the two grim-faced cops escorted him handcuffed into the lift and out of the Grand Plaza Hotel into the crowd-filled night, he'd blurted out a garbled account of Operation Luce End.

'Get over there right away, she could be there any minute! King George Square car park. Level 6 row E.'

The cops bundled him into the back seat of a waiting police car. 'Good onya, mate! Happy New Year!' someone yelled. The older cop got in beside him.

'That's a good story. Ten out of ten for originality.'

'I'm not making it up!' Reuben's voice squeaked with desperation. 'My wife took my phone, so I borrowed one then Jug-ears took it and had a gun at my back, so I had no alternative but to hit Wayne, so you guys would come and I could report it.'

The cop looked at him, the cynicism of too many years in the job etched on his face.

'Look, charge me with assault, I don't care. Just get someone out to that car park, or you'll have a murder on your hands.'

'We'll be charging you with assault all right,' the driver said. His mate took out a mobile phone. 'Sir, it's Sergeant Bolen here. Got a joker by the name of Reuben Littlejohn; we're bringing him in for assault. He says there's been a bomb planted in a car at King George Square car park. Belongs to his parole officer Lucy Prentice.'

He listened for a few moments. 'Okay, sir, will do.'

He rang off and gave Reuben a hard stare. 'If this is a hoax, you'll be charged with more than assault.'

'It's real, all right.'

A thought occurred to Reuben. What if Frank or Bomber, for some reason, had decided at the last minute not to go through with it? And the bomb squad, especially mobilised for this task, found nothing? Hoax calls incurred thousands of dollars in fines, maybe a jail sentence. He broke out in a sweat. *Please, please, let*

Bomber have planted the bomb. Just make sure the cops get there on time.

At the city police station, Reuben was processed and taken to a cell in the watchhouse. He'd been sitting on his bunk for a few minutes when a police officer unlocked his cell door. Sergeant Bolen and his offsider entered and stood in front of him.

'Who are you in cahoots with, Littlejohn?' Sergeant Bolen said.

'I told you I'm not in cahoots with anybody. Frank blackmailed me into helping him, but there was no way I was really going to kill her. If I were, I would hardly have warned you about it. And I'm not answering any more questions until I see my solicitor.'

There was no point calling his solicitor at this time on New Year's Eve, but hopefully he could persuade Andrew to spare him some time the next day.

'You're sure no one else knew about it apart from you and Frank Cornell, and Bomber?'

'No comment.'

'We received a call a few minutes ago,' the other police officer said. 'Warning us about a bomb planted in a car park.'

Thommo. He was the only other person who knew.

'We were hoping you could shed some light on it,' Sergeant Bolen said. 'He wanted to remain anonymous. Said you would know all the details.'

They were watching him closely. He shook his head. 'No comment.'

He didn't want to implicate Thommo if he could help it – he'd wait for legal advice. He realised with a sick feeling that the police didn't believe his assertion that Frank had blackmailed him – he could have had a grudge against Lucy as well and wanted her dead. It was only one criminal's word against another. But why would he tell the police? Perhaps they thought he had a last minute attack of conscience, or that he'd had a falling out with Frank and

Bomber and ratted on them to cover his own backside. If he was found guilty of conspiracy to murder, he could say goodbye to the next twenty years. *Fuck. Fuck. Fuck.*

'Have they found the bomb?' He couldn't help asking even though he knew they wouldn't tell him.

The other officer looked at him impassively. 'Can't tell you, mate.'

They left, the cell door clanging behind them. So Thommo who had reneged on his promise not to call the police had probably called from a pub somewhere in Sydney, pissed and not making much sense. But he'd done it to save Reuben's life – and Lucy's. Reuben felt a deep longing to be there with him – drinking, telling nonsensical jokes and exchanging bravado about women. He tossed and turned on his unyielding bunk, trying not to think about the possibility that the bomb squad hadn't got to the car park before Lucy. But visions of exploding metal and flying body parts filled his mind. Amongst the stink of mildew and stale urine, and the yells and raucous laughter echoing from the other cells, the New Year crawled in.

Reuben's solicitor, Andrew McLeod, turned up the next day. He'd acted for Reuben in his previous court case and his youthful appearance and guileless air fooled criminals and magistrates alike, until he stood up in court and opened his mouth. He looked a little less youthful and guileless at ten o'clock on New Year's Day, presumably due to the excesses of the previous night.

With Andrew present, Reuben was formally charged with assault and gave his account of Operation Luce End to the detectives from the CIB. They tried in a dozen different ways to force him to admit he'd taken part in the operation voluntarily, and even suggested that he'd masterminded it. They were stonewalled each time by Andrew's objections. But Reuben had one small victory – although the detectives refused to divulge if Bomber and Frank had been arrested, they did admit that Ms Prentice was perfectly well and in one piece. He was so light-headed with relief he almost floated off his plastic chair.

***

An engine roared up behind him then slowed down. 'Want a lift, mate?' a voice yelled above the chugging of the motor.

A bronzed, rough-hewn face grinned at him from the window of a battered ute, a tattooed arm resting on the window. Reuben hesitated, touched by the offer, but wasn't in the mood for company.

'Thanks but I'll keep walking.'

'No worries. Have a good life.'

He sped away in a cloud of dust. Have a good life? It wasn't until Reuben boarded the train at Wacol that he realised they were kind words from a stranger, to a man trudging along a lonely road two kilometres away from a prison.

As factories, warehouses and drab shacks in weed-choked yards slid past him, his mind churned over the events of the past month. One of the few good outcomes was that although he hadn't yet been sentenced for the assault charge, Andrew was confident he wouldn't get another jail sentence. 'Because this is your first offence of this nature, I'm tipping a large fine,' he said cheerfully, 'or if you get a hardline magistrate, a suspended sentence at the worst.'

There'd been one other positive result. Frank Cornell had been arrested – eventually. Two weeks after Reuben's arrest, Andrew visited him in prison.

'Thought you might like to know our friend has been charged with trafficking, quite a nice little haul of cocaine. The police went to his house to interview him about the car bomb, got hold of his mobile phone, or one of them, and found all the coded messages. A couple of prominent property developers involved as well.' He shook his head. 'Some people just don't learn.'

'Did they charge him with planning the bombing? Conspiracy to murder, or whatever it's called?'

'He denied all knowledge of course, and the police haven't found any evidence to link him to it. Apart from your statement, of course, which in itself is not enough to charge him. By the time they got to the car park, the bomb was already planted and your mate Bomber, aka Stuart Rickman, had flown the coop. I suspect he's sunning himself on a beach at Rio as we speak, up to his eyeballs in fancy drinks and bare breasts.'

So Bomber's retirement plan had evolved as planned. If only one of his exotic floozies would get sick of him and poison his Tequila Sunrise. Or a renegade cop track him down and put a bullet through his head. Fat chance. That only happened in movies.

Jug-ears had escaped as well. The security guards did a token search of the premises but by then he had well and truly flown the coop. He'd probably slipped quietly out the emergency exit during the commotion of Reuben's attack on Wayne. And he'd scored the Pastor's phone. Reuben hoped he'd feel the full force of God's wrath for such an uncharitable act.

'So where's Frank now?' he asked.

'In prison.'

Andrew grinned at Reuben's expression. 'Not here; in remand. He's also breached his parole, so he won't be granted bail. In fact, he won't be going anywhere for a very long time, so you can sleep easy when you get out.'

And of course there was the fact that Lucy hadn't been blown up. But in the process of saving her life, his life had gone to shit. A life for a life. Maybe he could have made it as a medieval knight after all.

He got off the train at Central Station, bought a hotdog and Coke and fronted up to Centrelink, where he filled out the necessary paperwork and received his release from prison payment. It was two o'clock. His parole appointment was the next priority then finding a place to stay. Carlene had given up the lease on their house and moved in with Nancy and Alec.

He got off the bus a few doors up from the parole office. Not wanting to pass Joe's cafe, and risk Nina or Joe seeing him, he crossed the road, walked along the street for half a block then crossed the road again, approaching the building from the opposite direction.

Life went on around him as if he'd never been away, but somehow it was different. Then it struck him – the world wasn't different, it was him. He wasn't a part of it, he was in the audience watching himself play the starring role in a movie – one of those bleak modern movies that didn't have much of a plot, where the main character stumbled from one disaster to another and when it ended, left you wanting to kill yourself. Or him.

He trudged up the stairs to the parole office. 'Back again.' He handed the receptionist his discharge papers.

She looked at him with an expression that said she had no idea he'd been away and it had nothing to do with her. He took a seat in the waiting room, occupied only by a girl with a buzz cut and three nose piercings. She jiggled her foot and scratched at the sores on her arms.

Reuben thought back to the last time he'd seen Lucy. Three weeks ago today, in fact. When the prison officer poked his head into Reuben's cell and said, 'You've got a visitor, Littlejohn, your parole officer,' he almost fell off his bunk.

As the officer escorted him to the visiting room, a niggle of apprehension suppressed his initial flutter of anticipation. It wasn't standard practice for parole officers to visit offenders in jail, so it obviously wasn't a social visit. He hoped it wasn't to reprimand him for breaching his parole, or worse, to tell him his parole had been cancelled and he would have to serve the remaining four years of it in prison. A deep chill numbed him and he was aware only of the brisk, rhythmic clip of the officer's shoes on the concrete.

The officer led him into an interview room, a tiny concrete cell with a bench in front of a barred window. Lucy was already seated on the other side of the window. She wore minimal make-up. Her hair was tied back in a ponytail and her blouse buttoned up to the neck, in keeping with prison protocol that female visitors – or professionals at least – not expose too much skin. Being locked up sharpened male instincts and they could smell a woman's presence a mile away. Reuben sat down on the bench and faced her.

'Press the button when you're finished,' the officer said to Lucy and left the room, locking the door.

'Hullo,' Lucy said. She gave a tentative smile, no doubt unsure of his reaction, given that it was her responsibility to suspend his parole and send him back to prison.

'Hullo,' he said.

'How are you?'

'As well as can be expected under the circumstances.' He grinned to show there were no hard feelings.

'I had no choice but to suspend your parole.'

'I know. But there was a reason I punched my brother-in-law. It's complicated to explain.'

'The police told me about Frank Cornell's scheme and how he forced you to help him. I don't think they're entirely convinced by your story. But I believe it – you're no angel, but I don't think you're a murderer.'

'Thanks.' It had a sarcastic ring to it though he didn't mean it to, so he grinned again to soften the effect. He hesitated. 'It must have been a shock when you found out Frank was planning to kill you.'

She stared down at her hands folded in front of her then looked up. Her face was as white as her crisply ironed blouse. Reuben felt a jolt of shock. The goddess who made you want to leap mountains with just a smile had vanished. In her place was a young woman with a drawn face and weary eyes who was trying hard not to expose her vulnerability.

'Yes, it was. But you should have called the police as soon as you found out about it. Then none of this would have happened.'

'He threatened to kill my wife if I told the police – and me, too.'

'That's a pretty good reason for reporting it.'

'What could they do? Hire us a bodyguard? I couldn't take the risk. Much as I didn't want you killed, I didn't want Carlene to be bumped off either.'

'You really think he would have killed her?'

'Why not? He nearly succeeded in killing you.' She blanched again and he was instantly contrite.

'Sorry. But I wouldn't underestimate Frank. He's an idiot, but he's a foolhardy one and they're the most dangerous kind.'

She drew in a deep breath. 'I suppose I have you to thank that I'm sitting here right now.'

He shrugged. 'All in a day's work. Perhaps I'll set up as a private detective when I get out.'

She returned his smile and in her expression, for a fraction of a second, he saw the acknowledgement of him as a man and not just another offender, someone she might chat to over a coffee. Then she pressed the button on the wall in front of her. Two officers arrived – one escorted her out and the other unlocked his door and led him away. He felt cheated that he couldn't watch her leave.

***

'Reuben, come in.'

The door to the far interview room opened and a middle-aged, bespectacled woman stood in the doorway. As he sat down, she slid in behind the desk, tapped away on the keyboard, then looked up and said, 'Hullo, I'm Beth.'

'Where's Lucy?'

She looked surprised and at the same time reproving. She had one of those mouths that turn down easily and become permanently disapproving in old age.

'Lucy's been seconded to another department,' she said crisply. 'I'm taking over your supervision. I need to ask you a few questions.'

As Reuben left the interview room – his appointment slip for a fortnight in his jeans pocket – he pondered Lucy's secondment. Why hadn't she mentioned it when she visited him in prison? Then again, why should she? Maybe she hadn't known about it then. Had she sought it? Perhaps she'd had enough of being a parole officer and learning of Frank's plan had tipped her over the edge. He couldn't blame her for that.

He trudged down the stairs and opened the front door. As a shaft of afternoon sun dazzled him, the realisation hit him. It was okay that he wouldn't see Lucy again. He hoped she'd be happy in her new job and if their paths never crossed, he could live with it. The goddess who'd vanished upon her visit to him in prison had gone, maybe forever. Lucy was a flesh and blood woman with cellulite, morning breath and infallible shoe-sale radar who could drive you crazy just like any other. He'd always known it, deep down. The ache inside him was not because he was going to miss her – well, maybe a bit – but sadness for a part of his life and himself that he would never get back.

He was so absorbed in his thoughts that he forgot to cross the road to bypass Joe's Cafe and almost bowled over a woman coming out of the entrance.

'Reuben!'

Nina stood in front of him in her waitressing uniform. Some of her hair had escaped from its plait and curled around her face in frizzy tendrils. It seemed as if she were someone he'd met in a dream. A long time ago.

'Oh ... hullo.'

'It's good to see you again too.'

Her mocking smile was familiar. She was definitely real.

'Sorry, I didn't mean to be rude.' He hesitated. 'I'm sorry I just up and left. It's a long story.'

'I know.'

'You do?'

They were in the middle of the pavement, pedestrians swarming around them. 'We can't stand here,' Nina said. 'Come inside and have a coffee. I was on my way to the bank but I can go anytime.'

Reuben peered inside. 'Is Joe in?'

'Don't be a wimp. He's not, as it so happens.'

They went in and sat at a corner table. It was three o'clock, an hour till closing, and only two of the tables were occupied. A young waitress was behind the counter stacking coffee cups.

'Sally, could you could make us a latte and a short black please?' Nina said.

Sally gave Reuben an appraising look. 'No problems.'

A boy appeared from the kitchen, wiping his hands on his apron. He was thickset with blotchy skin and the beginnings of a moustache. Seventeen, at the most. He scooped up a tray of cups and saucers from the counter, and disappeared.

'Your replacement,' Nina said. 'His name's Victor. I don't know where Uncle Joe found him; he hardly speaks any English but that's a good thing. Uncle Joe says the most insulting things to him and he just smiles and nods his head.'

'So that's where I went wrong,' Reuben said. 'Not enough smiling and nodding.'

'He's a whizz at chopping onions too.'

Sally appeared with the coffees, forestalling any further elucidation of Victor's virtues. When she left, Reuben said, 'So what exactly do you know?'

'That you punched your brother-in-law at a ball on New Year's Eve and were charged with assault.'

'There's a story behind that.'

'I figured there had to be.'

'How did you find out?'

She raised her eyebrow. He'd never taken a good look at her eyebrows before – not as a separate part of her. They were dark and thick, but well shaped. He wasn't a fan of thick eyebrows in women but they suited her. Somehow, her features, which were not attractive on their own, were appealing when combined with each other – the whole, different from, and better than its parts. Was that a mathematical equation?

'You were in the newspaper for a couple of days. On TV as well. Didn't you know?'

'I'm afraid they haven't progressed to newspapers and TV in the watchhouse. I was there for three days before they took me to Wacol.'

Why hadn't Andrew mentioned anything to him? Maybe he'd thought it would upset him.

'Anyway, I can't understand why. It wasn't news – people assault each other every day.'

'Not usually at a society ball, and not claiming to be threatened by a man with a gun, who then mysteriously disappears.'

'No one believes me, but there *was* a man with a gun ... by the time they searched the place he'd escaped. They didn't expect him to be hanging around, twirling his pistol and waiting to be caught, did they?'

Nina smiled. 'If it's any consolation, I believe you. I suppose there's a story behind that as well?'

'You guessed it. I suppose the papers made me out to be a nutcase.'

'Not really. Apparently a journo from *The Courier-Mail* was at the ball and he recognised you from the Becker ad, so he did the story from that angle – Mr Nice-Guy bartender has a bad boy side to him – not evil-bad, like Lex Luthor, more naughty-bad, like Captain Jack Sparrow.'

'That's all I need.' Reuben drained his cup and slammed it into the saucer. 'Now that the world knows I've got an assault charge against me, I can kiss goodbye to any job prospects.'

Nina looked at him appraisingly. 'Do you want me to tell you the rest?'

'There's more?'

'They obviously did some digging around because they also mentioned your history of fraud convictions and your prison sentence.'

Reuben let out a long sigh. 'It's not as if it's fresh news – it was reported in the paper at the time. But I suppose it's too much to hope it could have stayed in the past.'

Nina touched his hand briefly. It was cool but surprisingly comforting. 'It's not so bad. Any publicity is good publicity in showbiz. You never know, it could land you a job.'

'Yeah.' He pushed his chair back. 'I guess I should be going. I've got to collect my things from Carlene's parents and find a place to stay tonight. Thanks for the coffee.'

She stared at him. 'What's happened to you and Carlene?'

'She's moved back in with her parents. She considers knocking her brother-in-law out for no good reason, apart from the fact he's a complete fuckwit, being carted away by police in front of the cream of Brisbane's society, and causing the complete humiliation of her and her family as good enough reasons to end the marriage. I guess she has a point.'

'I'm really sorry,' Nina said. She sounded as if she meant it.

Just then, Joe bowled in through the front door. He stopped dead when he saw Reuben.

'Hi Joe, good to see you.' Reuben got up and held out his hand. Joe looked at it as if it were a lump of maggot-ridden meat.

'Listen, here, boy, don't think you can just dance in here as if you're my best mate, which you never were and never will be, after walking out on me.'

'I didn't deliberately walk out on you. If there was any way I could have called you, I would have. I'm sorry.'

'Pah! You're sorry! What good is that? Anyhow, what do I care if you get yourself in a fight and go back to jail? It's no skin off my face.'

'It was a nice break from you. Some of the screws actually talk to you without yelling.'

Joe snorted. 'See? Jails are soft these days. What happened to hard labour?'

'Uncle Joe.' Nina got up from the table and touched his arm. 'Reuben doesn't have anywhere to stay tonight. Can he stay with us?'

'Hold on,' Reuben said. 'It's okay, I'll find somewhere.'

Joe glared at him. 'Where is your good lady wife?'

'We've separated. Look, I appreciate your offer but I'd rather be on my own for the moment.'

'What offer? I offered you nothing.' Joe waved his hand in dismissal. 'If he changes his mind, Nina, you can make up the spare room.'

He strode off to the kitchen.

'I won't change my mind,' Reuben said, 'but thanks. That was a generous offer, coming from him.'

'I told you he likes you. But not enough to give you your job back.'

'Probably just as well. I think I can strike kitchen hand off my list of potential careers.'

He looked at his watch. 'Anyway, I'd better go.'

Nina looked down at her feet and then at a customer entering the shop.

'You'll have to tell me your story sometime.'

'What? Oh, yeah, that story. I'll give you a call when I'm settled and we can have coffee.' He grinned. 'Somewhere where the proprietor doesn't insult you.'

Nina gave a shy smile as she moved off to serve the customer. 'I'll look forward to it.'

***

Out on the street, he flagged down a passing taxi. 'Hamilton, please. Ibis Street.'

He slumped down in the back seat and stared out the window. Could things get any worse now that not only his latest misdemeanour but the full litany of his crimes had made headlines? At this rate he'd have to migrate to Uzbekistan to live a normal life and get a job.

And he'd done it all to save Carlene from being shot and thrown in a dark alley, or some equally horrific end. Not that she'd ever know. She probably wouldn't even give him the chance to explain it. He hadn't seen her since the night of the ball, since his last glimpse of her wide-eyed shock as the police carted him away. Going to Nancy and Alec's house was like walking into the lion's den. He'd phoned from prison that morning to ask if he could call around that day to pick up his gear.

'The sooner the better,' Nancy snapped before hanging up on him.

In his mind's eye he saw the letter he'd received from Carlene ten days into his prison sentence. Two typewritten pages, her round, flourishing signature at the bottom.

'Dear Reuben (she hardly ever called him by his full name, so he knew instantly it was serious)

I'm sorry to do this by letter but I simply can't come and visit you. To be there in the visiting room with you in your prison browns would bring back too many memories of happier times. So I'll make this short and to the point.

'I'm sure I don't have to tell you how furious I was at the whole New Year's Eve fiasco, not to mention humiliated – not only me but the whole family. What on earth could have possessed you to punch Wayne, I'll never know. The police told me you said it was all part of a plan to save your parole officer from being blown up, which of course was news to me, but then you never told me anything that was going on with you.

'And frankly, I don't want to know. How could Wayne possibly have anything to do with blowing up your parole officer? He doesn't even know her. It's obvious you've become quite delusional and I can only hope you're getting some psychiatric help in jail. It's also obvious our marriage isn't going to work – not at least until you deal with your problems and by then it may be too late. I can't hang around forever waiting for you to get yourself sorted.

'To add insult to injury, I got a phone call at ten o'clock on New Year's Day from some mad woman from a car rental agency, ranting and raving about how you hadn't returned her MG, and she and her boyfriend were supposed to be going away and their plans were ruined. Of course I had no idea what she was talking about and she said she'd have to report it to the police as a stolen car. I said, 'Go right ahead, he's already in jail.' Then she swore at me and hung up. After everything that had happened, that was the last thing I needed.

'Then your solicitor called around the next day and gave me the keys to the MG and your suit. I rang the car rental woman back and said I had the car keys and she said the car had been returned to her, along with a bill for parking overnight in the car park and another from the towing company – a total of five hundred dollars – and she was passing them both on to you. Then she said she had possession of your scooter and would sell it to recoup some of her losses. I told her that was illegal and she swore at me again, and said if I wanted it I'd have to come around right then and there and pick it up.

'I've put up with a lot for you, Reuben, but being sworn at by a woman I've never even met, about a car I had no idea you'd hired, is more than any wife should have to put up with. I'm not going to ask why you hired it – I can see that it's perfectly logical

351

that driving around in a beat-up MG when you have a perfectly good scooter and a car at your disposal is all part of the plan to save your parole officer from being blown up. I went round there and picked up the Barbiemobile – not for you, but because I knew how much Jo and Indya wanted it, so that's where it is at the moment. You'll have to use all of your charm and more if you want it back.

'I've given up the lease on the house and moved back in with Mum and Dad. I need to be somewhere I can get some support. You can come around when you get out and pick up your things.

'That's all I wanted to say. I'm so disappointed in you. You have so much potential but you're just throwing it all away. I've given this a lot of thought, it's a big decision to end a marriage after only six months, but it seems we are travelling along different paths. I still love you, but it's obviously not enough for you.

Carlene.

'P.S. AND you stole Pastor Bryan's mobile phone! Being the generous, saintly person that he is, he's forgiven you – not that you'd care.'

Her letter had evoked mixed emotions – sadness, but also relief. Because they'd both known it wasn't working and neither wanted to be the first to say it. Reuben wondered why he'd ever thought it would. What had he been thinking – marrying someone he'd known for only two months and only from within the confines of prison? It was a huge, foolhardy leap into the unknown – like taking a plunge into a rock pool that looked cool and inviting from the top of the cliff, not being able to see what lay beneath the water, but just shutting your eyes and hoping for the best. A triumph of optimism over realism. But then no one had ever accused him of being a realist.

He realised the cab driver had said something. 'Pardon?'

'What number, mate?'

Reuben looked around. They were on Ibis Street already. Time flew when you were contemplating your failures.

'Thirty-three, thanks.'

Jo and Wayne's Range Rover was parked in front of the house. Jesus, the whole family was here to welcome him home. The cab pulled up behind it.

'Would you mind waiting?' Reuben said. 'I just have to collect some things.'

The driver nodded and turned the engine and the meter off. 'Take your time, mate, I'll have a smoke break.'

Reuben opened the front gate and walked up the zigzag pebble path. Late afternoon was slowly fading around the spotless lawn and immaculate flowerbeds. There was something artificial and staged about the front garden, its stillness and neatness. You could put a frame around it and hang it on the wall.

Children's voices and splashes floated around from the rear of the house. They were out at the pool. He wondered whether Wayne and Jo were here because they knew he was coming. If anything, he thought they would have gone out of their way to avoid him, but perhaps Wayne wanted to exact revenge. Good luck to him, he could beat Reuben to a pulp but he wouldn't lay a finger on him. There was no way he was going to cop another assault charge and parole suspension.

He pressed the doorbell, heart hammering. He had a vision of the family lurking behind the front door and as soon as he stepped inside, falling upon him and tearing him to pieces, like a pack of wild dogs. The door opened and Nancy stood there. Just one mean-eyed bull terrier.

She stood aside to let him in. 'Stay here,' she barked, as if he were liable to run riot through the house and make off with the silver.

She went to the bottom of the internal staircase and called out, 'Carlene!'

As she turned to go back into the house, Reuben said, 'Just a minute, Nancy.'

She stopped.

'I remember what you said about making Carlene unhappy and I'm really sorry it didn't work out. I gave it my best shot. We weren't a good match in the first place.'

'You won't get any argument from me there,' Nancy said.

'And whatever Carlene's told you, I wasn't having an affair. There was stuff going on I couldn't tell her about but it was nothing to do with other women.'

She pursed her lips. 'I've got work to do. Is that all?'

'Yes. Oh, and I'm sorry about Wayne and ... all that,' he ended lamely.

Her bosom heaved as she gave a sigh of resignation. 'Out of everything you've done, that's the only thing I don't blame you for.'

She swept out of the room. Was that a smile he'd seen? For all of two seconds?

Carlene appeared at the top of the stairs holding two suitcases, and with a backpack slung over her shoulder. She was barefoot but still in her work clothes.

'Hi,' Reuben said. He bounded up the stairs to relieve her of the suitcases, glad of the opportunity to do something rather than have to think of something to say. He carried them down the stairs and placed them on the floor beside the front door.

Carlene followed him down and handed him the backpack and a large envelope.

'What's this?'

'Bills. Like I said in my letter – car park, towing and there's a late fee for your suit because it was three days late by the time I got a chance to return it. I was very tempted to not to return it at all so you'd have pay the full replacement cost, but lucky for you I'm not a vindictive person.'

'No, well ... thanks.'

'Plenty of women would have, though.'

'Yes. Thank you for not succumbing to the temptation.'

She looked thinner and more fragile. Her hair was cut to shoulder-length with auburn highlights, giving her face a warmer look. Women often changed their hairstyles after a relationship break-up, a literal washing of the man out of their hair. She could have at least waited until he'd collected his gear.

'I like your hair,' he said.

She put her hand to her hair and smoothed it self-consciously behind her ears. 'Thanks.'

'Honey, I'm really...'

'Don't call me honey.' Her voice trembled. 'And please don't say you're sorry – it's meaningless and totally inadequate for the situation.'

'I'm sorry – I mean, I'm sorry I was going to say sorry. I'll go, I've got a cab waiting outside.'

'Indya wants to see you. I told her she couldn't, but...' She shrugged. 'You know what she's like.'

'Oh ... okay.' Reuben put the backpack down next to the suitcases. Carlene nodded in the direction of the back deck. 'She's in the pool.'

He trod hesitantly through the house, half expecting Nancy to appear from nowhere and order him to freeze with his hands in the air.

Alec and Wayne sat at the outdoor table, drinks beside them and a large array of snacks laid out on the table. Jo was bobbing up and down in the pool with the children, to the accompaniment of their shrieks of excitement.

Alec and Wayne looked up as Reuben stepped outside. Wayne was in a pair of board shorts and nothing else, his stubby of beer perched on the distended, matted-curl shelf of his belly. His lip curled.

'Well, look who's here, Anthony Mundine himself.'

'Hullo,' Reuben said.

Alec nodded. 'Hullo.' His eyes were wary. He looked to beyond the pool, where Nancy was in the garden clipping away at the mayflower bush with a large pair of garden clippers. The ferocity of her attack on the hapless bush suggested she may well have been imagining Reuben's balls adorning its branches.

'I hope you're not here to apologise,' Wayne said.

'I'm here to say hullo to Indya,' Reuben said. 'At her request.'

'Just as well,' Wayne said, 'because no apology could make up for what you've done.'

Reuben said nothing. He glanced at Wayne. There was not the slightest mark on his face to signify what had happened. After all, it was over a month ago.

'So you're not going to talk to me at all now?' Wayne said.

Reuben was saved from replying, or *not* replying, by the children spying him from the pool.

Indya waved frantically. 'Hullo, Uncle Reuben!' She swam to the edge and climbed out. 'Mum, can I go and say hullo to Uncle Reuben?'

Jo hauled herself and Brayden out of the pool, and opened the gate.

'Don't run, Indya!'

Indya dashed across the tiled area to the deck. She had on a pink polka dot swimsuit and looked taller and longer-limbed than when he'd last seen her. She flung herself at him and wrapped her arms around his waist, dripping water all over his jeans and sandshoes. A lump rose in his throat. It was the first time she'd shown him any physical affection. So this was what it took for his niece to like him – a month in prison.

Indya looked up at him. 'Are you back from jail, Uncle Reuben?'

'That's a stupid question,' her father said.

'Wayne!' Jo was approaching the deck with Brayden squirming in her arms.

'I didn't say she was stupid; I said the question was stupid.'

Brayden wriggled out of Jo's arms. The drawstring in his swimmers had come loose, and they hovered perilously close to full exposure. Following his sister's lead, he raced over to Reuben and wrapped his chubby arms around his legs, bringing a fresh round of dripping water to his damp jeans.

Indya shoved at him. 'I got here first!'

Brayden let forth a piercing howl.

'Steady on,' Reuben said, 'you can share me. There's plenty to go round.'

Their enthusiasm, while touching, also made him feel awkward – it accentuated the fact he was there only under the sufferance of the rest of the family.

'And yes,' he said to Indya. 'I am out of jail.'

'Did the jailer have a big key hanging on his belt? And lock you in a cell?'

'Something like that.'

'Indya honey, I'm sure Uncle Reuben would rather not talk about it,' Jo said.

'By all means, tell us all about it,' Wayne said. 'True confessions of a reformed criminal. You could be in the next *Underbelly* series.'

'Wayne, mate, I think you've said enough,' Alec said.

'No, I bloody well haven't.' Wayne looked at Reuben, his eyes narrowed to slits in his pouchy face. 'You're lucky I'm not the vindictive type, otherwise you'd be out cold on the floor right now instead of standing there with that smug look on your face.'

He nodded to Alec. 'Could you pass me another one, please?'

Alec reached down into the esky at his feet and passed another bottle to Wayne. It was then that Reuben noticed it was ginger beer.

'Uncle Reuben, are you taking the Barbiemobile home?' Indya asked, her eyes imploring.

Reuben smiled down at her. 'No, Indya, you can keep it, I think it will be much happier at your place.'

'Yippee!' Indya yelled.

'Ippee!' Brayden echoed.

Reuben looked across at Jo. A flicker of gratitude sparked in her eyes before she looked quickly away.

'Anyway, I have to go,' Reuben said. There was an awkward pause. 'Goodbye, and thanks ... for everything.'

Wayne opened his mouth, looked at Alec then closed it.

'Bye, Uncle Reuben!' Indya said. She gave him a wave and raced back towards the pool.

'Bye!' Brayden echoed, toddling after her. His swimmers lost their battle to stay up, exposing his pudgy white buttocks, but he kept on regardless. Undoubtedly neither of them was aware it was probably the last time they'd see him.

Reuben went inside, heaviness in the pit of his stomach. He picked up his suitcases at the front door. Carlene appeared from the kitchen, holding a mug of coffee. What did you say at the end of a marriage? Words were too simple – and too complicated.

'Bye,' he said.

'Bye,' Carlene said. She nodded at the suitcases. 'If I've missed anything, let me know.'

She turned away quickly and walked out.

As Reuben walked down the front path with his luggage, Jo came running around from the side of the house.

'Reuben!'

He stopped. She had a towel wrapped around her over her swimmers. Her damp hair hung over her face, partially obscuring it. Her cheeks reddened as she met his eyes.

'I'm sorry about Wayne being so rude. He's really angry at you.'

Reuben shrugged. 'I can't blame him for that.'

'Yes and no. What you did was wrong, but he was behaving so horribly that night that I realised how much of a problem he's got. So I told him that if he didn't give up drinking, I'd leave him. And take the kids. Of course he didn't want to but he had no choice. We're going to counselling too, which he doesn't like. And he thinks it's all your fault.'

The counselling hadn't made Wayne any less obnoxious. But maybe it was a matter of time. Reuben felt a pang of sympathy for her.

'It's okay. I really hope you two can sort things out.'

She gave a tentative smile. 'Thanks.' She looked down at her feet. 'And I'm sorry about the whole ... you know ... paedophile thing. It's just that being a mother, I'd kill anyone who laid a finger on...'

'It's all right, no hard feelings.'

The cab driver beeped his horn. 'Gotta go.'

She darted forward and gave him a peck on the cheek. 'Goodbye. I hope things work out for you too.'

32

After consulting the accommodation list the clerk at Centrelink had given him and making a few phone calls, Reuben found a room in a boarding house at New Farm, not far from where Thommo had lived. It was an old Queenslander that had been converted into half a dozen bedrooms with a communal kitchen and bathroom. It smelt of stale cooking oil, sweaty socks and old men; but at $150 a week, it would do until he found something else.

His room reminded him of his childhood bedroom. Faded floral wallpaper, single bed with chenille bedspread and an old wooden cupboard with the door ajar because there was no key to lock it. It was musty but clean.

Hey Mum, I've blown it again. He saw her face before him, disappointment etched in the lines. The same look he'd seen countless times before. *I really gave it a go – it'll be different next time.* She looked unconvinced. 'Remember your number one rule,' he told himself, 'convince yourself before you try to convince someone else.'

He dragged his luggage inside, closed the door and sank down onto the bed. Was there anything sadder and more pathetic than a single bed when your marriage had broken up? The only thing worse was a bunk in a prison cell. He opened the first suitcase and rummaged through his things. No Mandrake comics. Surely Carlene wouldn't have thrown them out – she knew how valuable they were to him. Which was a good reason to do just that. She'd said she wasn't vindictive, but most people were capable of spitefulness if pushed too far. He opened the other suitcase and scrabbled through the contents. Not there either. Fuck.

He opened his backpack and pulled out a plastic bag. The comics were bundled neatly inside it. He slumped with relief. He opened the bag and rifled through them – they were all there. He slipped out the oldest comic – *The Earthshaker*, from 1943. It was his favourite comic as a child, a story full of giants and monsters, all of whom Mandrake subdued with his magic powers. The drawings were so detailed and lifelike they both fascinated and terrified him. One in particular, of a giant face staring through the window of a house, with Mandrake's girlfriend Narda cowering inside, gave him nightmares for weeks. Every night when he went to bed he saw the giant's eyes, huge and menacing, staring through his own bedroom window. It was strange to look at the face now and remember so vividly the terror he'd felt. When you were an adult, your giants just took a different form.

The pages were soft, the images still as crisp as if they'd been drawn yesterday. The comic was almost as immaculate as when Albert had given it to him twenty-five years ago. Reuben had looked after it, had looked after them all like precious jewels. They were possibly quite valuable to a collector, but he hadn't bothered to have them valued as he'd never once considered selling them, even when he was down to his last dollar.

He slipped the comic back into the plastic bag and dug out his mobile phone from his backpack. As the battery had run flat while he was in prison, he plugged the phone into the power point beside his bed. Checking that he had his wallet, he left his room, locking the door behind him.

Halfway down the narrow, dank hallway of the boarding-house, was a small coffee table. On it sat a phone, padlocked to the table, and two battered phone books; a White Pages and a Yellow Pages. They were for the use of the residents, with an honesty box for depositing the payment for your call. Strange that management had faith the residents would pay for their calls, but not that they wouldn't steal the phone.

Reuben picked up the White Pages. Pages here and there had been ripped out, but fortunately not the K's. Reuben searched until he came to Kominsky. There was only one – V. Kominsky. Viktor, Ivan's son, still at the same address at West End. Had Ivan gone to his death consumed with hatred for Reuben and Derek? He'd never know, had to live with not knowing. It was a fair bet that Viktor hadn't forgiven him – he'd sat in the courtroom all through the hearing, his dark eyes fixed on Reuben, the loathing so intense Reuben could feel its heat from the dock.

As he walked to the takeaway shop on the corner to buy dinner, he mulled things over in his mind. He knew what he had to do. Every inch of him was resisting it, but there was a force bigger than himself at work. The evening was darkening as he headed home with his hamburger and chips, and the sultriness of the night air clung to him. Two old codgers in shorts, t-shirts and thongs sat on the front step smoking roll-your-own cigarettes, their stick-thin legs stretched out in front of them.

'Evening,' they nodded. Reuben nodded back.

'That smells pretty darn good,' one said.

'Dinner at your place, mate?' the other said, and they both chuckled. As Reuben came through the front door of the boarding house a wave of mustiness swamped him.

He went again to the table in the hallway and picked up the Yellow Pages. He looked up comics in the index and was directed to Books – Secondhand and Antiquarian. There was a comic shop on Adelaide Street in the city – 'Comics Incorporated. We buy and sell new and old comics.' They'd do for starters.

His room was stuffy – there was no ventilation apart from a small window. He opened it as wide as it would go and sat on his bed to eat his dinner. The food didn't live up to the promise of the aroma – the hamburger roll was stale and the chips were soggy. But it was better than jail food. Afterwards he checked his phone. There were three messages in his voicemail box. 'Message received at eleven-twenty pm on thirty-first December,' intoned the MessageBank voice.

Thommo's voice boomed in his ear.

'G'day mate. Look, I'm sorry, but I've rung the cops in Brisbane and told them about' – he'd lowered his voice to a dramatic whisper – 'you know what. I had to, it was spoiling my New Year's Eve sitting in the yacht club surrounded by all these hot Sydney chicks – networking, of course, they're all in the movies – and all I could think about was whatshername getting blown up or you at the bottom of the river with cement shoes – do they do that in real life? Anyhow, as my father used to say, I hope one day you'll thank me.'

The next message was on January first at eleven twenty-five a.m. Thommo again.

'G'day again. I guess wishing you a Happy New Year isn't in order. I just rang your home number and spoke to your wife and she told me what happened. I couldn't believe it at first – I picked you as a lover, not a fighter. Still, Wayne is a bit of a wanker. Anyway, at least you're alive. Give me a ring when you get out. Hey, this might be just the thing your career needs. Didn't do Russell Crowe any harm.'

He'd phone Thommo tomorrow and thank him for trying to save his life, if he could be bothered picking up the phone in between drinking and networking.

The third message was a familiar woman's voice.

'Reuben, it's Posie.' She gave a theatrical sigh. 'You're a naughty boy, getting yourself into trouble. Really, I don't know what you were thinking of.' She sighed again. 'Anyhow, when you get out, give me a ring. Jonathan Huntley from Brightstar Films wants to talk to you about auditioning for a feature film. He saw you in the Becker ad and was impressed. Anyhow, hope you're okay,' she finished chirpily.

Was that for real? Reuben pressed the button and replayed the message several times. A feature film. A giant step up from a TV ad. What did 'a part' mean? Could be another non-speaking part, maybe a promotion from bartender to waiter or cab driver. *Don't get too excited. It's only an audition; you mightn't get the part.*

But later as he sank into bed, heavy with weariness, the excited flutter in his chest kept him awake into the early hours.

33

He called Posie as he strode down Adelaide Street, weaving his way through the morning peak hour crowds.

'She's in a meeting at the moment,' the receptionist said aloofly, 'I'll give her your message.'

For some reason he'd been expecting Comics Incorporated to be a small, dingy shop, overflowing with dusty piles of comics and manned by a just-as-dusty proprietor. But it was a large, airy, cheerful store, with floor-to-ceiling bookshelves stacked with neat piles of plastic-covered comics. In the middle was a table on which stood boxes of loose, unwrapped comics. A couple of teenage boys were flicking through them.

'Can I help you?' the attendant asked. He wore a name badge that said 'Tim' and was shortish and podgy, with dark hair falling over his forehead and chipmunk cheeks. He had one of those eternally youthful faces that made him look anywhere from twenty to forty. Much more appropriate for a comic shop than a dusty old man.

Reuben took off his backpack, opened it and placed his plastic Myer bag of comics on the counter. 'I want to sell these. How much will you give me?'

Tim slid out the comics and studied them carefully, one by one. He whistled as he held up *The Earthshaker*.

'This one is worth quite a bit – it's not in mint condition but it's still pretty good. The others aren't worth as much but you'd still get a few dollars for them.'

'How much all up?'

'If you're asking me how much I'd pay, I'd say fifty dollars.'

He grinned when he saw the expression on Reuben's face. 'That's if I was an unscrupulous dealer taking advantage of you. And I'm guessing you'd go elsewhere and find out their true value.'

He leaned forward on the counter. The Mickey Mouse face on his watch winked at Reuben. 'You look like an honest, genuine sort of guy so I'll help you out. There's a collector I know in Melbourne who's a bit of a Mandrake fan, and I reckon he'd jump at these. If you can wait, I'll go out the back and give him a tinkle.'

'Thanks, I'd appreciate it,' Reuben said.

'Josh, counter please!' Tim called. A sullen, pimply-faced youth slunk out from a door at the back of the shop. Tim picked up the comics. 'I'll take these with me so I can give him a detailed description.'

He disappeared through the back door. Josh stood at the counter with an expression that said, 'I'm only here because I have to be and I'll be really pissed off if anyone wants to buy anything.'

Reuben browsed through the comics in the boxes on the table. They were an eclectic mix of superheroes, Walt Disney and even some romance comics, obviously well-loved and not valuable enough to be kept in plastic. He should buy a few as a thank-you to Tim for going the extra mile for him. He picked up a *Phantom* comic. Two dollars was the original price, the store sticker said six dollars. Two comics would be enough.

After what seemed an eternity, during which Josh had been forced to ring up two sales on the cash register and had retired to the back of the shop in a fit of pique, Tim emerged from the back room with the comics.

He beamed. 'Good news. Ron is prepared to give you three and a half. He was stuck on three for a while, but I talked him into the extra half.'

Three hundred and fifty dollars. Hardly worth selling them.

'That's three-and-a-half thousand,' Tim said.

'Thousand?' Reuben said. 'Really?'

'Yep. If you give me your bank details, he'll put the money in today, and I'll take care of packing and posting them. Just one small detail,' he added, 'I charge ten per cent commission. So Ron will put three thousand, one hundred and fifty into your bank account and three hundred and fifty into mine. I've got a contract here to make it all legal.' He waved a sheet of paper in the air.

Three thousand and a bit sounded pretty damn good, more then he'd dared hope for. But should he try elsewhere for a better price? Not that he was in the mood – the wrench of parting with Mandrake was hard enough without prolonging it.

'It's okay if you want time to think about it,' Tim said. 'Or if you want to see if you can get a better price. But I'll tell you, Scout's honour,' he held up three fingers, 'you'll go a long way to find someone who'll pay you more than that.'

'And he's prepared to buy them sight unseen?' Reuben said.

'I've been in this business for twenty years, from way back when every kid had a pile of comics under his pillow, and I've known Ron for almost that long. He trusts my judgement.'

'Okay, it's a deal,' Reuben said. He filled in his bank account details on the contract and signed it.

'And I'll buy these,' he said, placing the two *Phantom* comics he'd chosen on the counter.

'Do you like the Phantom?'

'Not really, he's not a patch on Mandrake.'

'I agree. I like the fact that he's not a superhero, just a regular guy with a girlfriend. Except for his hypnotic powers.' Tim came out from behind the counter, rifled around in one of the boxes on the table and pulled out a handful of comics. He handed them to Reuben. 'On the house.'

There were four Mandrake comics, later editions from the 1990s, battered and dog-eared. Reuben scanned their covers; he hadn't read any of them.

'Thanks, that's really good of you.'

'No worries, I can see it's hard for you parting with yours. Do they have sentimental value?'

'Not really,' Reuben said, 'the old man next door gave them to me when I was a kid. But they've been everywhere with me and I've read them so many times, they've sort of become part of my life.'

'So, sentimental value.' Tim grinned. 'Well, I guess you must really need the money, otherwise you wouldn't be selling them.'

'Yeah,' Reuben said.

***

Posie returned his call as he was walking back down Adelaide Street towards the bus stop.

'Reuben! I'm so glad you're back!' she trilled so loudly that a woman passing by looked back at him. Reuben turned his phone volume down. Posie lowered her voice. 'Are you all right?'

'I'm fine.'

'I couldn't believe it when I read about you in the paper. What on earth were you thinking of? I would never have picked you as the brawling type.'

'I'm not. It's a long story.'

'I'm sure it is. Never mind, you're here now. But you didn't tell me you'd been in jail before.' Her tone was gently reproachful, like a kindergarten teacher chastising one of her charges for not putting his crayons away.

'I'm sorry, I thought you wouldn't hire me if you knew that.'

'You'd be surprised the people we have on our books. Anyway, it doesn't seem to worry Jonathan Huntley. He's making a feature film on the Gold Coast, and the exciting thing is he wants you to audition for the lead role. This could be your big break!'

Lead role. Reuben stopped dead in his tracks. Someone slammed into his back and gave an exasperated grunt. He moved out of the way to a shop window.

'What's the role?'

'He didn't say, it was only a brief call – he was about to board a plane. He's at a conference in L.A. but he'll call you when he gets back.'

On the bus home, Reuben stared unseeing out the window. Lead role. Hopefully not a remake of *King Kong*. And it was only an audition, there was no guarantee he'd get the part. But he couldn't stop the bubble of excitement from floating up inside him.

34

The Brisbane River gleamed in the late afternoon sun like a giant brown slug. Was it ever any other colour but brown? If so, Reuben had never seen it. In earlier times it was one of the many reasons he'd thought Brisbane a depressing place to live; now he was willing to see it as part of its elusive charm. He couldn't quite pin down what it was, but he was getting used to it; it was seeping into his bones.

In the week since he'd found the run-down flat on a little dead-end street at West End, he'd walked down to the park every afternoon to sit in the coolness of the Moreton Bay figs and watch the day fade into dusk. It transported him back to his uni days. He'd shared student digs at another run-down flat not far away, as well as dope, booze and cheese sandwiches, and swapped highly exaggerated anecdotes of women and sex. Trying to make a life for himself that didn't fit. If he closed his eyes, he could pretend he was back there, raw and green and unformed, without the burden of knowledge and experience holding him back.

He felt his head drooping and he jerked it up. Doing nothing all day was tiring. He'd gone to Employment Initiatives a few days ago for the usual post-prison interview. He was looking forward to telling Droopy Dave, in the nicest possible way, that he could stuff his positive outcomes right where it hurt.

'I've been head-hunted by one of the biggest film production companies in Australia,' he imagined himself saying, 'and I've scored the starring role in a movie destined to become a box office success.'

Not completely true, of course. In fact, none of it was true. At that stage, he'd been for the audition, and although told by Jonathan Huntley that he was a 'shoo-in,' he hadn't officially been given the part.

But the satisfaction was denied him. Droopy Dave wasn't there.

'He's left,' his new case manager Greg said. Had his fantasy about Dave being downsized out of the company become reality? Grumpy Greg wasn't forthcoming.

'He's gone to another job,' he said tersely. He took out some forms from his desk drawer. 'There's a forklift and warehousing course starting soon. It's subsidised, so it won't cost you anything.'

'That won't be necessary,' Reuben said. 'I've been given the lead role in a feature movie.'

If Greg was impressed, he hid it well.

'On the Gold Coast,' Reuben added.

Greg looked at him impassively then shoved the forms in front of Reuben. 'Read these and sign at the bottom.'

Reuben looked at the forms and back at Greg. He had a thin moustache over a pencil-line mouth. Never trust anyone with thin lips, his mother had said. No baby is born with thin lips. They become thin through meanness.

Reuben shoved the forms back at Greg, got up and walked out.

***

Then yesterday he got the call. 'Congratulations, you've got the part,' Jonathan Huntley said. 'I'll email you the contract and you can have your agent look at it.'

Reuben pressed the 'off' button on his phone. He looked around his flat, at the patchy, baby-poo yellow walls and the worn carpet. His furniture consisted of two beanbags and a cumbersome TV out of last century on a laminex coffee table. He wanted to shout, laugh, dance, sing, do cartwheels. Maybe not cartwheels – but everything else. He didn't know which to do first. So he did none of them. He wiped a tear from his cheek. 'Well, Mum,' he said.

He looked up at where he imagined she'd be if there were such a thing as heaven, and she was looking down at him. She'd be looking through the doorway into the kitchen where last night's dishes were still piled on the sink, shaking her head, a mixture of exasperation and affection on her face.

'I think I'll make it. You'd be proud of me.'

Usually exasperation won out. 'Come on, stop pretending. You know you will.'

Wait till Thommo heard the news. Reuben picked up the phone to call him then put it down again. He'd be seeing him in a couple of days. Thommo was flying up for the weekend to celebrate his own good fortune – he'd won a part in a series of tourism ads for Sydney as the stressed businessman who chills out on the beaches, and in the bars and restaurants. 'It's a non-speaking part, but who cares? I'm surrounded by hot chicks playing volleyball on the beach or smiling suggestively at me over my oysters Kilpatrick. I may never speak again!'

Let Thommo have his moment of glory then he would break the news, and they could have a double celebration. And matching double hangovers.

***

He looked at his watch. Five-thirty. He got up, walked through the park, past amblers, joggers and dog-walkers, joined Boundary Street and headed towards the heart of West End. A man in a suit came towards him – slim and dark-haired with a businesslike stride. Reuben's heart quickened. As the man came closer, he looked up, met Reuben's eyes and looked away.

Reuben breathed a sigh of relief. For a minute he'd thought the man was Viktor Kominsky. Although he lived on the other side of West End, the trendier part, the chances of running into him sooner or later were pretty high. Reuben had sent a bank cheque for three thousand, one hundred and fifty dollars to Viktor, enclosed with a note. 'I hope you will accept this in the spirit in which it is intended. In no way can it be reparation for what your father lost, but it's all I can give you at present. Reuben Littlejohn.'

He deliberately omitted his address from the back of the envelope so it couldn't be returned.

The pubs and sidewalk cafes were abuzz with the after-work crowds. The Cat's Whiskers was a cafe/bar sandwiched between a Greek restaurant called Bouzouki Bob's and the Mystic Angel bookstore offering tarot card readings by appointment. He could see why Nina had chosen it when he'd rung to invite her for coffee – it was full of pale, skinny, arty-looking types in earnest conversation over their green tea.

There were no spare tables at first but when a couple got up from a sidewalk table, he grabbed it and pushed their glasses to one side. He pondered on what to order. An alcoholic drink would make it seem as if he were settled in for the night, whereas a coffee was more something you had in between other activities. When the waitress with the kohl-lined, raccoon eyes appeared, he ordered a long black for himself and a latte for Nina. He didn't want to give the wrong impression.

He wiped his sweaty palms on his jeans. Why was he feeling jittery? It wasn't as if this was a first date or anything, but it was different from working with her at Joe's Cafe. And even if it was a first date, since when had he felt nervous about that? Not since his literal first date at fifteen – taking Laura Mikkelsen to the movies to make out in the back row when her parents thought she was going to the Pentecost Tabernacle youth group.

'Hi.'

He jumped. Nina slid into the seat opposite. She wore jeans and t-shirt, and bits of her hair had escaped from her ponytail and were hanging around her face.

'Sorry I'm late. Thanks for the coffee.' She took a large gulp.

'You're looking harassed,' Reuben said.

'I am. The short film I told you about, the one I'm doing for the course, is turning out to be a total disaster.'

'Why?'

She sighed. 'I don't want to talk about it.'

'Come on, you'll feel better if you do. Trust me, I'm a fellow thespian.'

'Oh, all right.' She took another gulp of coffee. 'I have the worst two people in my class in my group. Josh is a pothead and can't even talk straight, let alone do anything else; and Yvette is having boyfriend problems and doesn't even turn up for our meetings half the time. Even when they're at her place! So that leaves me to write the script, shoot it and edit it pretty much by myself. And to top it all off, our lead actor decided this afternoon he didn't want to do it any more and just walked out.'

'I see what you mean. Maybe I should have bought you a drink instead.'

'It's okay. I told Uncle Joe I'd be home by seven. And I've got to do some ringing around to find another actor.'

'I could do it if you want.'

'Do what?'

'Be your lead actor.'

She looked at him sceptically. 'It's a non-paying role.'

'No probs. It's all experience; something to put on my resume.'

'Can you do existential angst?'

'As it so happens, that's one of my strengths.' He slumped down in his chair and stared broodingly at his empty cup. 'Why did I drink that coffee? Such a small and insignificant act in the history of the universe! What was the meaning of it? Oh, woe is me!'

'Everything all right, sir?'

Reuben looked up at the waitress hovering in front of him, her dark eyes wary.

'Yes, fine. Perhaps two more coffees?'

He looked at Nina who was trying to suppress a smile. She nodded. After the waitress had left, she said, 'I'm sure she thought your angst was a reflection of the quality of the coffee. Still, you showed some promise. I'll talk to the others about it. And as their input has been minimal so far, you'll probably get the part by default.'

'Great!' Reuben said. 'My second piece of good news.'

'Oh sorry. What's the news you wanted to tell me?'

He told her the story from the start, when he received the message from Posie, to spin out the suspense as long as possible. 'Jonathan Huntley is a friend of Bruce Berkley, who hired me for the Becker ad. He owns a film production company called Brightstar Films – as he described it, "small but dynamic with some fabulous young talent". He saw me in the Becker ad and thought I'd be ideal for the lead in a feature film they're shooting on the Gold Coast. So I went for the audition last weekend.'

'So what happened?' Nina asked. 'I take it you didn't ask me for coffee to tell me you didn't get the part.'

'How did you guess? He called me yesterday to tell me I'd got the part.'

'That's fantastic! That's how it happens a lot of the time – good luck meets good timing.'

'Actually, I did play a small but active part in the process – he read about my recent brush with the law and thought the bad boy reputation would add to my appeal.'

Nina smiled. 'Didn't I tell you? A publicist couldn't have planned it better. What's the movie about?'

'It's called *High Jinks*, it's an action-comedy about an ordinary man with a family and a respectable job who moonlights as a small-time thief, and what happens when he gets a chance to do a job with the big-time criminals.'

'Let me guess,' Nina said. 'You play the part of the small-time thief.'

'You've got it.'

She looked at Reuben and he looked back at her. They burst out laughing simultaneously. Their neighbours shot them curious glances. Nina wiped her eyes with her napkin. They'd lost their strained look and her shoulders had relaxed.

'That's the first time I've heard you laugh,' Reuben said. 'As in a real belly laugh.'

'It's probably the first time I've laughed in a while.'

'I'm glad I could oblige, even if it was at the irony of my life.' He hesitated. 'Do you mind if I ask you something personal?'

She looked down at her coffee, stirring it vigorously. 'Depends what it is.'

'Joe mentioned a while ago that you'd had a hard life. What did he mean?'

She shook her head. 'Uncle Joe exaggerates – my life has been no tougher than a lot of other people's.'

'He must have said it for a reason – I had visions of you as a kid being kicked out of bed at the crack of dawn, put to work in the coal mines for twelve hours a day and sent to bed after a bowl of gruel.'

She laughed. 'Nothing like that. He's talking about my parents. They were killed in a light plane crash when I was fourteen.'

Her matter-of-fact tone was belied by just the slightest tremor in her voice.

'God, that must have been horrible for you,' Reuben said.

'Yeah.' She looked away, eyes following the waitress as she wove her way through the tables with a tray of drinks. 'They went to Malta for a holiday to visit my mother's family – she was Maltese, Joe's sister. I didn't go. I had exams so I stayed with Uncle Joe and Aunt Ettie. They took a plane to one of the islands and it crashed. No survivors.'

She repositioned her coffee cup in its saucer. 'For a while I wished I'd gone with them because I'd have been killed as well. But I got through it, somehow. It's all a bit of a blur now. A couple of years later, Auntie Ettie died of cancer so now there's only Uncle Joe and me.'

'That explains it,' Reuben said, 'why he's so protective of you.'

She smiled again, her eyes moist. 'He thinks I'm still fourteen, that I've somehow been frozen in time. But it doesn't worry me. I know it's only out of concern for me.'

'So you're an only child?'

'Yes.'

'Then we've got two things in common.'

'We have?'

'We're both only children and we're both orphans. If that's not a case for existential angst, I don't know what is.'

He screwed up his face in exaggerated torment. The waitress paused at their table with her empty tray, but when she noticed Reuben's expression, she kept walking.

They both burst out laughing.

***

I made her laugh. She looks so beautiful when she laughs. The evening was muggy as he headed home along Boundary Street after walking Nina to her car and giving her a chaste kiss on the cheek. But his footsteps were light, as if he were hardly making any imprint on the ground. The lights and chatter spilling out from the pubs and restaurants were just a dim background to his churning thoughts.

He tried to imagine himself shooting a movie. Would he have his own trailer? And make-up lady? 'Small but dynamic' was probably a euphemism for low budget start-up. He'd probably be lucky to have a patch of dirt under a tarpaulin and have to do his own make-up. There'd be an awful lot of lines – would he have to learn them all at once? And would it be like making the ad, with the director running around yelling 'Cut!' every time Reuben looked at the camera?

There was one good thing – it wouldn't be such a stretch playing a small-time thief. But hopefully he wouldn't be typecast in that role, unless of course there was a lot of money in playing criminals. That would really make Nina laugh.

And maybe in a cinema somewhere, Lucy would be watching *High Jinks* and would nudge her husband and say proudly, 'I used to be his parole officer.'

THE END

ACKNOWLEDGMENTS

There are many people who have contributed to the writing and publishing of this book and if I have forgotten anyone, I apologise, and can only offer a writer's natural absent-mindedness as an excuse.

Sarah Endacott of manuscript critique agency Edit or Die suggested the title and gave me invaluable feedback and encouragement on all aspects of the novel, which helped me to re-write and polish it. Inga Simpson and Nike Bourke from Olvar Wood, an organisation for emerging writers, also offered excellent advice in the early stages. Christine Cranney, my copyeditor, did a wonderfully thorough job and also offered some editorial input.

My heartfelt thanks to Pam Mariko, my critique buddy, who has appraised this book, chapter by chapter, and given me constructive feedback over countless cups of coffee and the occasional champagne. Fellow writer Ian Walkley has also provided me with lots of useful information and tips on publishing as well as support and encouragement.

Thanks also to all my family for their advice and support – especially Jenny Busch for her idea for the cover design. And finally, my eternal gratitude to my partner Aaron Parker, who's also my brainstorming buddy, reviewer, technical advisor, marketer, PR agent and cheerleader.

Watch for PERFECT SEX, also by Robin Storey, available on Amazon from August 2013. Here's a teaser:

What happens when a middle-aged woman leaves a long, unfulfilling marriage and discovers she has the sex drive of a teenage boy?

Freelance writer Susie Hamilton joins an internet dating agency, attracts a long list of admirers and begins an exhausting dating schedule – all under the guise of professional research.

When she writes a novel based on her experiences and it becomes a best seller, her dream of being a successful author is realised. But after dozens of dates and some disastrous encounters, she's still relying on Fred, her vibrator, for sexual fulfilment.

Is perfect sex an oxymoron? Will Susie meet Mr Right on the internet, or will she have to make do with Mr-As-Good-As-It-Gets?

Robin Storey is a freelance writer and creative writer from the Sunshine Coast in Queensland, Australia. She's published a number of short stories and plans to write many more novels. Read more of her work and join her on her blog at **www.storey-lines.com**.

Robin would also love to connect with you on:

Facebook http://www.facebook.com/RobinStoreywriter

Twitter https://twitter.com/RobinStorey1

Google + https://plus.google.com/u/0/112965761114777383158/

Printed in Great Britain
by Amazon.co.uk, Ltd.,
Marston Gate.

13959494R00225